OUT OF THE
FAR NORTH

AMIR TSARFATI
AND STEVE YOHN

TEN PEAKS PRESS®
EUGENE, OR

Cover design by Faceout Studio, Jeff Miller

Cover images © Evgeniy Kurt, gabriel12, Lillian Tveit / Shutterstock

Interior design by KUHN Design Group

This is a work of fiction. Names, characters, places, and incidents are products of the authors' imagination or are used fictionally. Any resemblance to actual persons, living or dead, is entirely coincidental.

For bulk or special sales, please call 1-800-547-8979. Email: Customerservice@hhpbooks.com

 TEN PEAKS PRESS is a federally registered trademark of The Hawkins Children's LLC. Harvest House Publishers, Inc., is the exclusive licensee of this trademark.

Out of the Far North
Copyright © 2023 by Amir Tsarfati and Steve Yohn
Published by Ten Peaks Press, an imprint of Harvest House Publishers
Eugene, Oregon 97408

ISBN 978-0-7369-8644-1 (pbk)
ISBN 978-0-7369-8645-8 (eBook)

Library of Congress Control Number: 2023934164

Printed in the United States of America

23 24 25 26 27 28 29 30 31 / BP / 10 9 8 7 6 5 4 3 2 1

AMIR DEDICATES THIS BOOK TO...

God, the true giver and sustainer of life.

All those who are still searching for the truth in the midst of a frighteningly volatile world. Also, to everyone who knows that there is more than just what we can see and touch, but is afraid to make a step of faith and trust that Someone higher is in full control. Hope, peace, and an end to fear are waiting for you in the arms of your Savior and Lord, Jesus the Messiah.

STEVE DEDICATES THIS BOOK TO...

The God who is always there. There is so much peace in knowing that no matter the journey, we are never traveling it alone.

Nick, my brother. While I write about the dark side of Russia, you've lived it. I have so much respect for you as a thinker, a writer, and an adventurer. Somewhere, there's a dirt farm calling our names.

ACKNOWLEDGMENTS

God, You continue to show us that You are faithful. It is only through Your gifts and creativity that this series of books has been written, and we give You all the glory for what You have done.

Amir thanks his wife, Miriam, his four children, and his daughter-in-law. Steve thanks his wife, Nancy, and his daughter. You bless us beyond measure and our joy and pride in you knows no bounds.

Thank you so much to the Behold Israel Team—Mike, H.T. and Tara, Gale and Florene, Donalee, Joanne, Nick and Tina, Jason, Abigail, and Kayo. God has brought us together from all over the world and created a family. We are so grateful for you.

Thanks once again to Ryan Miller for your military and weapons expertise. Finally, we are so grateful to Bob Hawkins Jr., Kim Moore, Steve and Becky Miller, and the whole Harvest House team. You have become part of our family, and we are so thankful to be partnered with you.

"In Russia, the government is
autocracy tempered by strangulation."

MADAME DE STAËL
(1766–1817)

"Russia is a country with a certain future;
it is only its past that is unpredictable."

SOVIET PROVERB

"Therefore, son of man, prophesy and say to Gog, 'Thus says
the Lord GOD: "On that day when My people Israel dwell
safely, will you not know it? Then you will come from your
place out of the far north, you and many peoples with you,
all of them riding on horses, a great company and a mighty
army. You will come up against My people Israel like a cloud,
to cover the land. It will be in the latter days that I will bring
you against My land, so that the nations may know Me,
when I am hallowed in you, O Gog, before their eyes." ' "

EZEKIEL 38:14-16

"The burden against Damascus.

'Behold, Damascus will cease from *being* a city,
and it will be a ruinous heap.'"

ISAIAH 17:1

GLOSSARY

ARABIC

Allah yerhamha – "may God have mercy on her"

almughafil – "mutt, idiot"

as salaam alaikum – "peace be upon you"; typical Arabic greeting

habibi – "my love, my friend"

habibti – female "my love, my friend"

inshallah – "if Allah wills, God willing"

ma'assalama – "peace be upon you, goodbye"

shukran – "thanks"

ya amar – "my moon, my most beautiful"

yalla – "let's go"

HEBREW

a dank – "thank you" (Yiddish)

achi – "my brother, my friend"

ahabal – "moron, idiot"

aliyah – lit.: "ascent, rise"; refers to a Jew's immigration to Israel

balagan – slang: "chaos, a mess"

be'shu'shu – slang: "doing something secretively or behind the scenes"

bobkes – "nothing, nonsense" (Yiddish)

bul – lit.: "stamp"; slang: "exactly, bingo"

boker tov – "good morning"

boker tov Eliyahu – lit.: "good morning, Eliyahu"; slang: "nice of you to finally show up"

chai b'seret – lit.: "living in a movie"; slang: "totally unrealistic, impossible"

eizeh seret – lit.: "what a movie"; slang: "what a series of bad events"

elef ahuz – lit.: "1,000 percent"; slang: "without a doubt"

gilita et America – lit.: "you discovered America"; slang: "obviously, duh"

ha'mefaked – military: "sir, commander"

idyotim – "idiots"

ma pitom – lit.: "what suddenly"; slang: "no way, unbelievable"

mashu mashu – lit.: "something something"; slang: "awesome, fantastic" *maslul* – military, lit.: "way, path"; refers to countersurveillance activities

motek – "sweetheart, darling"

nafal lee ha'asimon – lit.: "my token dropped"; slang: "I get it, aha"

otzma enoshit – "human strength"

oy vavoy – slang variant of *oy vey*

oy vey – lit.: "oh, woe"; slang: expresses frustration, exasperation, sorrow (Yiddish)

ramsad – head of the Mossad

root – "yes, sir"

sababa – "great, perfect, wonderful"

savta – "grandmother"

shtuyot bamitz – lit.: "nonsense in juice"; slang: "total nonsense, ridiculous"

walla – slang: "wow, oh really?"

yalla – "let's go"

yeshiva – school for learning the Torah and rabbinic writings

yoffi – lit.: "beauty"; slang: "well done, great"

yutz – "jerk, fool" (Yiddish)

RUSSIAN

boyar – member of the old Russian aristocracy

da – "yes"

devushka – "young woman"

dobroye utro – "good morning"

dorogaya – lit.: "expensive"; slang: "my dear, sweetheart"

drug – "friend"

Masha – diminutive of "Maria"

Nika – diminutive of "Nicole"

nyet – "no"

Seryozha – diminutive of "Sergei"

spasibo – "thank you"

Tatia – diminutive of "Tatiana"

tsar-batiushka – "dear tsar, father tsar"

voenkory – "military correspondents"

za zdorovie – "to your health"

zatknis – "shut up"

CHARACTER LIST

SYRIAN OPS TEAM

Unit 504 – Alif (leader), Ba (Syrian), Gim (Syrian), Ra (Syrian)

Kidon – Lead (Nir), Hamza (Dafna), Nun (Imri), Qaf (Dima), Sin (Doron), Waw (Lahav), Zay (Yaron)

ISRAELIS

Zakai Abelman – Kidon team leader

Dima "Drago" Aronov – Kidon agent

Lavie Bensoussan – Kidon team leader

Malka Bieler – ramsad's executive assistant

Efraim Cohen – assistant deputy director of Caesarea

Ravid Efrat – Kidon team leader

Irin Ehrlich – Kidon team leader

Yaron Eisenbach – Kidon agent

Karin Friedman – assistant deputy director of Mossad

Yossi Hirschfield – Mossad analyst

Ira Katz – ramsad (head of Mossad)

Doron Mizrahi – Kidon agent

Asher Porush – deputy director of Mossad

Daniel Ramon – prime minister

Liora Regev – Mossad analyst

Dafna Ronen – Mossad analyst

Idan Snir – prime minister-elect

Lahav Tabib – Mossad analyst

Nir Tavor – Kidon team leader

Imri Zaid – Kidon agent

SOUTH AFRICAN

Nicole le Roux – Mossad agent

BELARUSIAN

Myechyslau Aleksandrovich Sharetsky – oligarch in potash industry

BELGIAN

Mila Wooters – executive assistant at Yael Diamonds

HUNGARIANS

István – Hungarian Mossad agent

Mónika – Hungarian Mossad agent

LEBANESE

Baqil – Hezbollah camp guard

RUSSIANS

Major General Sergei Sergeyevich Bogdanov – military liaison in Syria

Anatoly Mikhailovich Kvashnin – oligarch in fertilizer industry

Polina Viktorovna Kvashnin – wife of Anatoly

Dmitry Leonidovich Livanov – Wagner Group Mercenary

Colonel General Leonid Anatolyevich Moshev – deputy in the Ministry of Defense

SYRIANS

Abdul – Derifa's uncle

Derifa – little girl

Muhammad – Derifa's uncle

Wael – Derifa's father

Yusuf – Derifa's grandfather

CHAPTER 1

DER SALMAN, NORTH OF DAMASCUS, SYRIA—OCTOBER 4, 2022—02:05 (2:05 AM) EEST

A carton of cigarettes is the passkey that will open the gates to a great many checkpoints around the world. The man sitting in the passenger seat hoped that this was one of them. The Russian-made GAZ-3308 Sadko army truck bounced and rumbled to a stop in front of one of the hastily constructed, but now seemingly permanent, roadblocks that littered the thoroughfares outside the city of Damascus, Syria. Two rows of concrete barriers reached into the road, leaving a gap just wide enough for a truck to pass through, but only if the driver was watching his mirrors. Across the tops of the barriers, razor wire stretched in wide, lazy coils.

A uniformed soldier stepped forward, looking young and bored. Two more remained in the guard shack, not looking up. Their eyes were locked on a point in front of them, and a blue glow filled the small building.

Must be a game on, thought the man. *For a country at battle with itself, these guards seem less than zealous about their stations. Seems the rumors of war fatigue are true.*

"*As salaam alaikum.* Cool night," said the driver in Arabic.

"What business do you have at this time of night?" the guard replied.

His terseness seemed to indicate that he was upset at being pulled away from whatever was on their television.

The driver seemed a little affronted that his traditional greeting was not returned. "What business? Lieutenant colonel business," he said with a nod toward the passenger, who continued to stare out the front windshield.

After standing up on his toes so he could clearly see the man in the other seat, the soldier said, "That still doesn't answer my question. What business do you have out here at this time of night?"

"The none-of-your-business kind of business," the driver replied. His smile remained, but his voice had hardened.

The lieutenant colonel noticed that one of the guards in the shack had looked up and was now watching the action outside. His hand moved slowly to the grip of his pistol.

"Give me your papers."

As the driver reached next to him on the seat, he said, "Of course." When his hand came around, he was holding a few sheets of paper and a carton of Alhamraa cigarettes. "For the chilly nights," he said with a wink.

The guard stared hard at him before taking the stack. He ducked briefly, presumably to put the cigarettes on the truck's step, then began scanning the papers.

"Is everything okay?" called out the second guard as he leaned out the doorway.

An almost imperceptible tension passed through the truck, both front and back. All knew that this was the moment when the whole operation could take an ugly turn. The likely result of that eventuality was that not everyone at this roadblock would still be breathing five minutes from now.

But the guard at the truck waved the other man off, and the adrenaline spike began to subside. The passenger let his hand slide back toward his armrest.

"Let me call this in," said the soldier, stepping away from the truck.

"Are you sure you want to do that?" called the driver. When the guard paused, he continued, "Think about it. When you call, the person who answers will have to ring someone above him, who will have to ring someone above him. And when that one rings the person above him, do you know whose phone is going to buzz?" He pointed at the passenger. "That guy's. And what do you think he will say?"

The soldier, looking a bit nervous now, answered, "Let them through?"

"Good, yes! But you're only half right. The lieutenant colonel will say, 'Let them through. And send that idiot kid who made me wait so long off to the Kurdish front.'"

The young guard's eyes widened at the prospect.

The driver waved the man back toward the truck. "Come now. You have seen that our papers are in order. So, lift the gate, let us through, and go share those smokes with your friends."

After one more glance at the officer who remained focused out the windshield, the guard nodded. He stepped back and signaled toward the guards in the shack to lift the gate.

The diesel rattled back into action and the truck lurched forward. "*Ma'assalama*. And don't forget your cigarettes," the driver called out, putting his hand outside the window and pointing down.

Out of his peripheral vision, the passenger could see into the guard shack. The third guard had still not looked up from what he could now see was a small television that indeed was showing a football match.

It wasn't until the truck was clear of the roadblock and back up to speed that the lieutenant colonel allowed himself a tense sigh. Catching the driver's eyes, he gave him a wink and a grin. Then he turned forward again to watch the road ahead.

CHAPTER 2

OUTSIDE DAMASCUS, SYRIA—
OCTOBER 4, 2022—02:10 (2:10 AM) EEST

"CARL, Lead. We're through the checkpoint," Nir Tavor informed his ops center. "How's the road look to target?"

"Traffic stop fifteen kilometers ahead," replied Liora Regev, one of CARL's analysts. CARL was Nir's team of odd specialists back at Mossad headquarters. The acronym itself stood for absolutely nothing, an inside joke amongst the small group of millennials. "Appears routine. Otherwise, clear."

Turning toward the driver, Nir said, "Nice work with the guard."

"He was just a clueless kid. Easily controlled," *Alif* chuckled. "I could have had him doing pushups on the street if we had the time."

Nir laughed, figuring he probably could. *Alif* was a member of the HUMINT-gathering Unit 504, who were masters of human intelligence collection, interrogation, and PSYOP. When Nir was a kid, he and his friends used to talk about the shadowy unit, but always with hushed voices. Formed soon after the creation of the State of Israel in 1948, it is one of three divisions of the Israeli Defense Forces' Military Intelligence Directorate—and, by far, its most secretive. Recently, he read an article in which one of the unit's officers said that if you want to understand the activities of Unit 504, you should go to a theater and watch a thriller double feature. Only then will you scratch the surface of the work they do.

Reading those words had sent a little twinge through Nir. As he had approached the end of his mandatory military service and begun weighing the options for his future, he had considered applying for Unit 504. He wanted action in his life. He wanted to make a difference. But living a secret life for years at a time in an enemy country had seemed exhausting to him. Many of the undercover agents that 504 had deployed around the world, and particularly in the Middle East, reminded Nir of Cold War moles deeply hidden by their governments on the opposite side of the Iron Curtain. There is the loud war that Israel fights with rockets and fighter jets, then there is the larger quiet war. It is this silent war that Unit 504 fights.

Except for nights like tonight.

When his "What-am-I-going-to-do-with-my-life?" moment had come, Nir decided that Unit 504 might end up being a little too much action for his taste. So, he had joined the State Security System in the Ministry of Foreign Affairs instead. Calm and easy, with excitement coming in the form of international travel to exotic lands. But action had a way of finding him. His courage and skill in a shootout in South Africa had caught the attention of the Mossad, which quickly recruited him. Not long after, he was brought into the intelligence agency's Kidon unit. Kidon was the tip of the Mossad's spear—a finely honed point that always seemed to be dripping blood.

For a guy who was not looking for too much action, he had done a very poor job of avoiding it. In recent years, he had been stabbed, shot, kidnapped, and tortured. And now here he was in Syria, in a stolen truck, wearing a counterfeit officer's uniform and leading a combined team of five Kidon operatives, four Unit 504 agents, and two analysts. And then there's the secret weapon in the back of the truck—can't forget about that.

Maybe living undercover in a hostile nation under constant threat of death would have been a safer career choice, he thought with a shake of his head.

He had been introduced to the Unit 504 guys after the Israeli Air Force's Yanshuf helicopter had set them down in the hill country near the village of Talfita, north of Damascus. The flight in had been necessarily low to keep them below radar detection. But low altitude meant a turbulent trip. So, during the introductions, his brain was still bouncing.

Thankfully, Unit 504 wasn't big on names, even with people on their side. The team lead, an Israeli, had introduced himself only as *Alif*, and with him were three Syrian subordinate agents also with Arabic letters as names. Nir had figured that when in Damascus, he might as well do as the Syrians do, so he had followed suit, assigning the operators on his Kidon team Arabic letters for their operational names.

The flashing blue lights of the traffic stop passed on Nir's right. The officer was talking to a man in a vehicle and didn't seem to take notice of them.

"CARL, Lead. We've cleared the traffic stop," said Nir into his coms unit.

"We see you," Liora answered. "You're clear to target."

Operation Boom began a little over two weeks ago. Nir had just flown into Tel Aviv, having been summoned by text while he was at Yael Diamonds, his precious gems company located in Brussels, Belgium. When he arrived at Mossad headquarters, he went straight to CARL. His text on the way in made sure the team was already sitting around the conference table waiting for him. Before joining them, Nir walked over to Lahav Tabib's desk and placed a green ball cap on the head of the analyst's life-sized Chewbacca mannequin. On the hat was a large shamrock embroidered with the words *Kiss Me I'm Irish*.

Applause broke out around the table.

"Well played," said Yossi Hirschfield.

"I never knew," added Dafna Ronen.

"You can hear a little lilt when he does his…" And here, Nir tried to do a Chewbacca roar, which turned out as poorly as did all his attempts at impersonation.

"That was such a *balagan*! Don't ever do that again," chided Liora.

Nir laughed as he sat at the head of the table surrounded by his little band of brilliant analytical misfits. To his left was Liora, a cute, tiny brunette with a gift for sarcasm that punched far above her weight class. To her left was Dafna, tall and thin with more tattoos and piercings than an entire all-girl punk band. On Nir's right sat Yossi, whose hipster beard and man bun perfectly fit his laid-back surfer vibe. And, finally, next to him was Nir's problem child—Lahav. Bespectacled and pocket-protected, he was relationally inept, wickedly smart, and ambivalent when it came to the law and authority. Lahav was the perfect guy to have around when you needed him, and like fingernails on a chalkboard when you didn't.

The only member of the team who was not there was the one Nir wanted to see the most. Nicole le Roux's face filled Nir's mind. Ice-blue eyes, dark brows, full lips, all surrounded by curly brown hair that was perfectly made for someone, preferably him, to run their fingers through. He would have loved for her to be in the ops center with them, but instead, she was on assignment for her other job, doing a photo shoot in New York City for some makeup company.

"He's thinking of her again," said Dafna. "You can tell by the wistful look in his eyes."

Liora leaned toward him. "I'm not so sure. How do you tell the difference between wistful and vacant?"

Nir glared at her. In the center of the table sat a bowl filled with little green bags of Klik chocolate-covered corn flakes. He snatched one and pulled it open. "We're still waiting for Efraim."

As if on cue, the door opened and in walked Efraim Cohen, assistant deputy director of Caesarea. Caesarea, pronounced with a hard *c*, is the ops branch of the Mossad and the parent division of Kidon.

"*Boker tov Eliyahu*," Nir chided his friend.

Pointing toward Chewbacca's hat, Efraim laughed and said, "I never knew."

Everybody booed.

"Already been said," Yossi said with an eye roll. "Maybe if you got here on time."

Efraim laughed as he sat, and said to Nir, "Try controlling your people."

"Yeah, right," replied Nir through a mouthful of candy. "Okay, you've got us here. What's up?"

"*Sababa*. Straight to business. We've tracked a shipment of arms from Iran to Damascus," began Efraim.

"Is that all?" asked Lahav. "Just send some F-16s from Ramat David and blast a new crater. Done and done." He brushed his hands together as he said the last three words.

"That's very helpful, Lahav. You know, we hadn't thought of that," an excited Efraim replied, pretending to punch a number into his phone.

Lahav beamed, then his smile disappeared. "Wait, you're mocking me, aren't you?"

With a glance at Nir and a shake of his head, Efraim continued. "The cargo plane was unloaded rapidly, and the contents were immediately trucked to a new storage location in Harran al-'Awamid, less than two kilometers from the airport. Because of the speed of the transfer, we couldn't get a clear look at what Tehran sent to them."

"Any thoughts?" asked Dafna.

"Might be drones. We're concerned that Iran might be upping the quality of the UAVs available to the militias in Syria and to Hezbollah in Lebanon. Since, thanks to you all, our airstrike cratered their nuke program last year, they've been pouring money and technology into building the effectiveness of their proxies."

"I've picked up pieces of that chatter," said Yossi, who was among the Mossad's best at intercepting and analyzing COMINT, or communications intelligence.

"I know. Your work is one of the reasons we're concerned."

The team cheered Yossi, and Liora tossed him a bag of Klik that he caught one-handed and pulled open.

Efraim continued, "There's also the possibility of it being a better series of missiles than the next-to-worthless Katyusha rockets the dirties are usually sending our way. *Be'shu'shu*, Russia has been promising to upgrade Iran's precision missiles ever since the two became bed buddies over Iran's high-quality drones. Whatever it is in that shipment, it's created a big stir amongst the bad guys, so it's also creating a big stir amongst us."

Nir said, "There has to be a reason we don't just send a couple Delilah missiles their way. I'm guessing it's the storage location."

"*Bul*. That's it exactly. Toss me four of those Klik bags."

Liora complied.

"Hospital," said Efraim, placing one bag on the table. He set a second one next to the first. "Maternity hospital." Then he placed a third just a short distance away. "Across the street, a newly built orphanage." Then, setting the fourth one next to the "orphanage" pack, he said, "And guess what that is."

Dafna let slip a non-synagogue word, and said, "They're terrible people."

"*Ma pitom!* Who uses their own children as human shields?" added Yossi.

"Exactly," said Efraim. "The location was perfectly chosen to create an international incident. One rocket or missile just a few meters off target from their brand-new weapons storage warehouse and we've got the UN passing another resolution against us. Oh, and, by the way, just up the road from the hospitals are two schools," Efraim said, pointing to the appropriate place on the table. "Wouldn't be in session when we attacked, but would still make a nice headline."

Efraim let the gravity of the situation sink in, then said, "Now, guess what your job is."

The discussion went well into the evening. Plan after plan was suggested and developed until a flaw was found that caused it to crash like a house of cards. It was Lahav who finally offered up the winning idea, which led to Nir and his team riding in a stolen Syrian army truck with a squad of Unit 504 guys and very expensive cargo in the back.

Yossi had come up with the name of the operation quite accidentally. As they were working through the details of the plan, a song he had heard the previous day on his classic rock playlist kept rustling around in his mind and out of his mouth. Soon, every time the words "Boom, boom" slipped from between his lips, everyone else around the table called out, "Out go the lights." Nir refused to present Operation Boom Boom to the shadowy spooks in Unit 504, so the name was shortened to Operation Boom. This was despite no actual "boom" being necessary to complete the mission if everything went according to plan. In fact, Nir was hoping for no explosions at all.

The name is still a bit embarrassing, Nir thought as he glanced sideways at *Alif* in the driver's seat. *But I suppose you've got to keep the kids happy if you want them to play nice.*

CHAPTER 3

HARRAN AL-'AWAMID, SYRIA—OCTOBER 4, 2022— 02:40 (2:40 AM) EEST

The truck continued its southeasterly journey into the town of Harran al-'Awamid. Nir had read up on the community earlier in the day while he was waiting for the team's insertion into the country. There wasn't much to learn—12,000 people, with its one claim to fame being the ruins of a third-century Roman temple likely built during the reign of Emperor Philip the Arab. Now, as they entered the city limits, his original impression of "not much to see here" seemed to be justifying itself.

"Lead, you're approaching a five-way roundabout," said Liora. "Take the fourth exit, which is just after the gas station. At the back of the station on the right is a large berm. Pull in there."

"Got it," answered Nir. Houses and small compounds passed by in the headlights. Well-maintained trees lined either side of the street and the center divider. *Alif* slowed the truck as it approached the roundabout, then began turning. Nir counted, "*Wahid, itnan, talata, 'arba'a.*"

Alif banked to the right. Nir pointed out the berm, and *Alif* turned the truck in just beyond it.

"CARL, Lead. We've arrived at prep site. Shut down their communications."

"*Root,*" came Nicole's voice. She had flown in for the operation, and Nir was relieved to have her available.

"Communications down," she said.

In case they were spotted during their preparations, Nir didn't want the word spreading around. So, Nicole had spent a few hours working her way into the town's phone system, as well as the two cell towers closest to the warehouse. This area was now effectively isolated.

The troop carrier swayed on the dusty, uneven ground as *Alif* eased it forward, then turned a wide circle.

"Not made for maneuverability," said the Unit 504 man as he brought the vehicle to a halt.

Nir winked at him, then said through his coms, "Go. You've got ten minutes."

Immediately, Nir heard activity in the back of the truck. His ops team, Yaron Eisenbach (*Zay*), Doron Mizrahi (*Sin*), Dima Aronov (*Qaf*), and Imri Zaid (*Nun*) began to assist in the assembly of the weapon. The lead roles, however, when it came to using the weapon, belonged to Lahav and Dafna.

During their brainstorming session, the team of analysts had come to the realization that, because of the sophistication of the weapon, two of them would have to come along. Lahav was an obvious choice since he best knew the technology. He also had a history of deploying with the ops team. Liora deferred, reminding Nir that she was "a lover, not a fighter." Besides, she and Imri had a thing going, and Nir didn't trust them to not let protecting each other become a distraction. Nicole would be needed at CARL for some border radar-hacking work at the end of the mission. That left Yossi and Dafna. While Yossi's physical strength would be beneficial in assembly, it was Dafna who had experience firing a gun at a real person. During her mandatory military service, she had been involved in two incidents while guarding the Erez Crossing from Gaza to Israel.

Thus, Lahav had been designated *Waw* and Dafna became *Hamza*, which rounded out the team at eleven. Nir's innate desire to be overprotective of women caused him to second-guess his decision several times, but a phone call to Nicole, during which she had affirmed his decision and absolved him of any wrongdoing on behalf of woman-kind, had finally put his mind at ease.

That first trigger pull in anger is a tough one, Nir had thought. *And this op will demand there be no hesitation. Dafna's been there; Yossi hasn't. Besides, Dafna is a good shot and, judging by her Mossad disciplinary record, she's not afraid to use her fists.*

Opening his door, Nir stepped to the ground and adjusted his gear. Everyone on the ops and Unit 504 teams was equipped identically. They wore standard-issue Syrian army olive camouflage uniforms—Nir's adorned with shoulder boards bearing a lieutenant colonel's one star and the Hawk of Quraish. Attached to their belts were two F-1 hand grenades, a holstered Russian-made Makarov PM handgun, and spare magazines for the pistols filled with Makarov 9x18mm rounds instead of the NATO standard 9x19mm. Strapped across their chests were AKMS assault rifles, looking very much like their better-known AK-47 ancestor but with a folding stock. Also on their chests were six magazines for the Kalashnikovs, holding 30 rounds each for a total of 210 rounds for each person, including the mag in the rifle.

If we need more than that, then this op will have really gone to sham-bles and we probably won't be getting home alive anyway.

One more item each operative had was a Feldjaeger Russian mili-tary knife strapped to their thigh. The knives bore a Kraton/Polyamide handle and a six-inch blade. If all went according to plan, this would be their primary weapon, if needed, inside the warehouse.

The only equipment that they didn't have, which was causing Nir great concern, was body armor. They didn't even have helmets. It was a very difficult decision, and advisers from the IDF had been brought in. The consensus amongst the Israeli Defense Forces was that one sure way to give away that you weren't really members of the Syrian army was to be well-equipped enough to have body armor for each soldier. They could even talk away their cargo in the back, saying it was a new weapon that they were transporting for Iran's Islamic Revolutionary Guard Corps. But if you have full gear in the woefully supplied Syrian army, then you most definitely are not legit. Ultimately, Nir agreed with the advisers, and since then, had been praying he wouldn't regret his decision.

Looking around in the light of the three-quarter moon, Nir spotted the 504 men taking point. *Ba* and *Gim* were on one knee set up at opposite corners of the passenger side of the truck. Their rifles were ready, and they were scanning the surroundings, looking for movement. He knew that on the opposite side of the vehicle, *Alif* and *Ra* would be doing the same.

From inside the truck, Nir heard Lahav say, "Tarp."

Nir walked around to the back to check progress. As he did, Imri and Yaron jumped out of the back and began untying the tarp that covered the cargo bed.

"How's it coming?" Nir asked as he looked in.

"Shut up, we're working," growled Lahav, connecting one mysterious-looking piece to another mysterious-looking piece.

Dima smacked him in the back of the head.

"Ow! Knock it off, you hypothyroidish Cossack."

Nir smiled. When he had first been forced to take Lahav on a mission, he had been concerned that it would turn into a race as to who would kill him first—the enemy or the ops team. But Lahav had acquitted himself well and had earned a certain amount of respect from the Kidon guys.

Dafna didn't have to earn their respect. Her cred was gained while in the IDF, and her plethora of piercings and tattoos could be intimidating, especially for guys, for some reason. However, right now she was anything but intimidating. All the jewelry was out of her ears and off her face, and her hair was temporarily dyed brown and tucked up under her hat.

She looked toward Nir and caught the grin on his face. "Shut up," she said.

Even with all the jewelry gone, there was no way that Dafna's face would pass as male. So, the fine folks at the Mossad had crafted her a beard. They had done a fantastic job, and all would have been fine if Imri hadn't said, "Hey, you kinda look like Castro."

That was it. The nickname stuck.

"How come Fidel didn't get hit for saying, 'Shut up'?" Lahav asked Dima.

In reply, the oversized Russian émigré smacked him again.

Yaron came around the corner. "Ready to tear down."

Carefully, as the analysts continued the weapon assembly, the four members of the ops team folded back the dark green tarp they had untied from over the truck bed. Once that was down, they removed the four rear crossbars, laying them on the ground next to where they had placed the roof tarp.

While they were doing that, Nir dropped to the ground and slid himself under the truck. Above him was a green metal box that Unit 504 had bolted to the underside of the vehicle. He unfastened four clasps, and the box separated from its lid. Nir slid back out, pushing the box next to him.

Liora's voice broke in. "Four minutes."

"You heard her," Nir said into the truck.

"*Zay, Qaf,* help us lift this," said Dafna.

Doron and Dima quickly answered her call.

Now that the overhead tarp was gone, there was room to lift the weapon to vertical. With audible grunts, the two ops men tilted up what could best be described as a flat, squarish satellite dish. While they kept it propped up, Lahav and Dafna quickly secured its locking mechanism.

This weapon is crazy, thought Nir. *I hope it works. But, even more, I really hope we get it back in one piece.*

As he lifted the metal box to the step on the truck's passenger side and began unwrapping its contents, he thought back to before they had left Mossad headquarters. Efraim Cohen had opened the door to his office.

"You know how expensive this weapon is, don't you?" he had asked, leaning against the doorjamb.

"Very?"

"Exactly. And, unfortunately for you, you have a reputation for breaking expensive things that belong to the state."

Nir shrugged. "Can I help it if sometimes things get messy?"

Efraim didn't smile. Instead, he stepped in, closed the door, dropped into a chair, and stared at Nir for a moment. Then, leaning forward, he said, "Where are the keys to your Mercedes?"

"My what?"

"Your keys. To your precious little Mercedes AMG GT coupe."

Nir didn't move.

"What? Do you need me to say it slower?" Emphasizing each word, Efraim reached out his hand and said, "Give me the keys to your car, Agent Nir Tavor."

Still, Nir didn't move.

"*Yalla*, come on. Do you have so many cars that you've forgotten the one I'm talking about? I can show you the picture of it you sent to me six days ago with the caption 'My Baby.' It's the one that is currently parked in some bougie private parking lot at the Brussels airport, waiting for you to come home."

"Wait, did you just say 'bougie'?" Nir asked.

"Give me the keys. Now!"

This is balagan. *They can't just take my car.* "There's no way you're getting my keys."

"*Sababa*. You're right, *achi*. The keys are not for me. They're for the *ramsad*. He said that if you don't bring the weapon back in one piece so that he can return it to the air force, then your pretty little coupe is going to make a great new addition to the Mossad's vehicle fleet." He paused as if he was considering something. "You know, the first time I requisition it, I think I'm going to eat me some Cheetos while I'm driving."

Now, as Nir watched the weapon coming together in the middle of a suburb of Damascus, he wondered if he would ever again smell the soft leather of his Mercedes' interior or hear its beautiful low rumble as he pressed the ignition and brought it to life.

CHAPTER 4

02:55 (2:55 AM) EEST

E verybody gather in," Nir ordered. "*Zay, Nun*, take up your positions."
"*Root*," Yaron and Imri replied. Each removed an Orsis T-5000 bolt-action sniper rifle from the bed of the truck and began to low-run behind the gas station in the direction of the warehouse.

When all were gathered, Nir passed out the contents of the box he had removed from under the truck. Each member of the team except for *Ba* and the analysts received a TNV/MOD-3 Bravo unit to slip onto their heads before entering the target. These high-quality, commercial-grade night vision goggles weren't at the same level as those used by the IDF. But if one were accidentally left behind and discovered, they had the advantage of pointing toward usage by American mercenaries rather than Israeli intelligence. In the cab of the truck, Nir placed the two remaining night vision devices for Yaron and Imri, along with two microdrones, in case they were needed. A third microdrone was currently overhead, being remotely operated by Liora through a signal satellite-routed back to CARL.

Turning back to the team, Nir said, "*Gim, Ra*, go prepare for traffic control."

"*Root*," they acknowledged. They trotted to the street, turning left toward the roundabout.

"Done," called out Lahav. The analyst moved to the truck's gate. He scanned the faces until he spotted *Alif*. Pointing at him, he said, "You're driving. This weapon is solid, but it's top-heavy. We can't afford any bumps along the way. Understood?"

"No problem," answered *Alif*. "I'll just put the truck on float mode."

"I'm not joking! This is a sensitive piece of weaponry. One serious jolt could..."

Nir interrupted Lahav with a wave of his hand. "*Waw*, stand down. We get it. But look around. There is no way we are getting there bump-free."

Dafna took Lahav's arm and pulled him back toward the weapon. "Calm down. We don't want anyone shooting you—at least, not yet."

Alif looked at his 504 teammate and shook his head. "That's the problem with bringing a pencil-pusher on an operation. Can't handle the stress."

Nir took a deep breath and let the comment pass. *Alif* had a great reputation as an operator, and he knew Syria better than Nir knew Jerusalem. But the man carried with him a condescending attitude toward anyone on his home turf. Nir got the feeling that in *Alif*'s mind, Nir might be the operational leader, but he was the one who knew what was best.

Let him do what he does, and you do what you do. You can deal with him if he really becomes a problem.

"It's time," said Liora.

"Let's mount up," Nir said.

Ba joined the analysts and Doron and Dima up in the bed. Each of them took a position from which they could help steady the weapon. As Nir climbed into the cab of the truck, he said, "*Zay*, *Nun*, engage."

Just before the truck rumbled to life, Nir heard two cracks from the suppressed sniper rifles wielded by Yaron and Imri.

"Confirm two guards down," said Liora through the coms. "No other signs of life. Traffic at the roundabout is clear."

"*Yalla*. Let's do this," Nir said to *Alif*.

The truck lurched forward, and Nir heard swearing from the bed of the truck. If he didn't have such high regard for the professionalism of Unit 504, he would have thought the driver might have done it on purpose. A muttered curse from *Alif* confirmed that it was likely just the nature of old Russian-made trucks.

Turning left, *Alif* steered the truck toward the roundabout. Up ahead, they could see *Gim* standing in the street ready to hold up any traffic that might approach. The truck entered the roundabout the opposite way, passed one exit, then halted.

Now came the part when Nir was glad he wasn't driving the truck. Putting the Sadko into reverse, *Alif* backed the transport truck onto the exit he had bypassed. Behind the truck, *Ra* walked, directing *Alif* up the street. They passed the gas station, then came to where the warehouse stood on the truck's right. Just beyond it was the orphanage, and to the left stood the hospital and the maternity center. *Ra* directed *Alif* in a reverse turn until the truck was perpendicular across the street with its nose toward the hospital and its bed toward the warehouse.

Nir slid out of the truck and looked around. Being part of Kidon, he was used to operating behind the scenes and in the shadows. This was as opposite of "in the shadows" as one could get. The only advantage they had was the time of night and the delayed reaction any onlooker might have as they tried to figure out what in the world was going on.

On the ground in front of the warehouse, Nir spotted one of the guards who had fallen to a sniper's bullet. There would be a second at the back of the building.

"Time until ready?" he asked.

"Four minutes," replied Dafna.

Nir prayed that this would work.

Back at that brainstorming meeting, when Lahav had first suggested using an electromagnetic pulse weapon, the whole team had looked at him skeptically. All Nir knew of EMPs was what he had read in a few briefs. The theory was that a nuclear weapon could be exploded up in one of the "spheres"—atmosphere, stratosphere—he couldn't remember which—with devastating results. If done the right way, the electromagnetic effect of the blast could kill everything electronic for thousands of miles around. This meant no phones, no cars, no electrical grid, no running water. Essentially, it could knock a country back into the early nineteenth century. What that had to do with the precise destruction of a shipment of weapons, Nir couldn't fathom.

"Okay, stay with me," Lahav had said. Then, looking directly at Nir, he had added, "This is going to be difficult for some of you to understand."

"Keep going," Nir had answered.

"Okay, the US has found practical use for the EM technology in their ADS crowd-control weapons."

"ADS?" asked Efraim.

"Active Denial System. It shoots a short-wavelength microwave burst. Those on the receiving end feel like they're on fire for a few moments. Theory is that they'll scatter because they don't want to feel it again."

"Does it work?" said Yossi.

"*Meh.* Once people realize it is just a very uncomfortable inconvenience, they tend to keep pushing forward."

Nir shook his head. "I still don't get what this has to do with a warehouse in Syria."

"So, that's the short-wavelength application. Raytheon in Arizona, under contract by the US Missile Defense Agency, started focusing its time on high-powered microwave technology that could be used to fry the internal electronics and guidance systems of missiles and hypersonic weapons." Lahav paused here, then gave a furtive look around the room for dramatic effect. "Rumor has it that military intelligence from a certain eastern Mediterranean country might have availed itself of the details of this secret technology from their American friends."

Everyone looked at Efraim.

"I can neither confirm nor deny such a shocking accusation," he said, tipping the remnants from a Klik bag into his mouth.

Lahav continued. "Well, maybe you can confirm that by using this possibly borrowed technology, the IDF has developed a weapon that acts like a mini EMP device, sending a pulse that will fry any electronics that are in its path."

Efraim was silent, looking like he was fighting some internal battle.

"How about if you blink once for yes and twice for no?" suggested Liora.

After a few more moments, Efraim said, "How do you know this?"

Then with a sigh, he held up his hand, jumped up from the table, and headed for the door. "I don't want to know. I've got to go talk to the *ramsad*."

"Wait," Nir called out. Efraim stopped. "Listen, I don't want to waste time, *achi*. Just tell me, should we keep pursuing this line?"

"You're going to get me fired," he replied, looking down at his shoes. "Okay, keep running with it. It will be up to the *ramsad*, and probably the IDF, whether your efforts end up being a waste."

Liora's voice shook Nir from his recollecting. "Lead, you have visitors coming. It's a police car. Maybe the one from up the road."

"*Alif*, *Ba*, prepare to intercept. *Waw*, how long until ready?"

"30 seconds," Lahav answered.

"Okay. Finish prep, then hold. *Alif*, I want the police detained, but not harmed."

"Sure, whatever," said *Alif* with a sarcastic tone. As he trotted past Nir toward the roundabout, Nir grabbed his arm.

"They are not enemy combatants."

Alif shook himself free of Nir's grasp. "Maybe not to you, but you're just visitors in this country. You don't know these guys. Every one of them is a criminal. Extorting money, kidnapping people's family members, beating anyone who doesn't do what they say. You don't know them; I do."

"That may be so, but that isn't why we're here. You can do what you want on your own op, but this is my mission, and I will not have us killing noncombatants. Flex-cuff them and put them in the back of their car." Nir turned from him. "*Hamza*, can you hear me?"

"*Root*," Dafna replied.

"When the truck relocates, I want you to follow it in the police car. Everyone clear?"

"*Root*," echoed through Nir's com.

When Nir turned back around, *Alif* was nearing his teammate, who was already in the roundabout waving his arms as the vehicle was making its way through. Nir watched as it slowed.

Nicole's voice came through the coms. "Lead, understand that you are now on a tighter time clock." The police car had stopped, and the officers were getting out while the 504 men approached. He couldn't make out the words, but it all looked friendly enough.

"Go on," he said to Nicole.

"We shut down cell and landlines, but we did nothing about police radios. They've likely called it in. Backup will eventually come. Recommend you deploy a second drone to cover the police station."

Nir cursed under his breath as he reached back into the truck. "Good call. What's the distance to the station?"

"Five-minute fast drive," answered Yossi. "You may have a little more cushion if they're waiting on further communication from the car."

"Is there anything—" Nir's question was stopped short when he saw *Alif* slam his fist into the midsection of one of the policemen, doubling the man over. Meanwhile, *Ba* unholstered his Makarov and pointed it at the other officer's face. *Alif* punched the first policeman two more times to the side of his head, dropping him to the ground. As the other officer kept his wide eyes locked on *Ba*, the 504 man drove his pistol into his temple. He, too, dropped.

Nir took quick steps toward them as *Alif* pulled flex-cuffs from a pocket in his uniform pants. Looking toward Nir, he dangled them a couple times with a grin, then proceeded to tightly bind the policeman's hands behind his back. Nir pulled up. When the second officer was also secured, the 504 men roughly tossed them into the back of the car, closed the doors, then jogged back to their positions by the truck. Neither looked at Nir.

Stuffing his anger, Nir placed the drone on the ground.

"Drone is ready," he said. Immediately, the tiny blades began whirring, and it shot up into the sky. "Status on the weapon?"

"We're ready to go," reported Dafna.

"CARL?" asked Nir.

"Roads are now clear. No sign of external movement," said Liora.

"Okay. *Waw*, *Hamza*, fire it up."

The theory was that with the weapon angled this way, everything in front of it, including the warehouse and all its contents, would have its electronics fried. Meanwhile, everything behind it, particularly the hospital and maternity ward, wouldn't have any of its lifesaving equipment harmed.

That's the theory, thought Nir. *Let's hope it's right.*

CHAPTER 5

E veryone to the front of the truck," Lahav ordered.

Nir stood by the hood, out of range of the weapon. As he waited for it to fire, he realized he had no idea what to expect.

I'm pretty sure it won't sound like a gunshot or an explosion. Will I even know when it goes off?

A *whump* sounded from the truck's bed, and Nir felt the hair on his arms and neck stand up.

That's it!

"*Yalla*, let's go," he called out.

Yossi had discovered the schematics for the warehouse attached to an email sent six months ago to an Islamic Revolutionary Guard Corps general as the building was being erected. According to those plans, the IRGC designed the warehouse with three entrances—one northwest, one northeast, and the main one, facing southeast. *Alif*, *Gim*, and *Ra* fast-walked toward the northeast, rifles at the ready. Nir knew that Yaron and Imri would have already left their sniper positions on their way to the northwest. He and Doron made their way to the front entrance, while Dima ran around to the back, taking night vision goggles and fresh coms units for Yaron and Imri to replace the ones that would have been fried by the EMP.

Behind him, Nir heard the truck start up. *Ba* would drive it back around to the staging station behind the berm, where he, Lahav, and Dafna would try to make quick work of dismantling the weapon. Unfortunately, this would now be complicated by the need for Dafna to follow behind in the police car.

As they arrived at the entrance, Nir and Doron flattened against the wall. "Lead in position," he said.

"Side team in position," said the 504 man. Nir wasn't concerned about *Alif* now that the action had started. No matter what personal issues there might be, for now, they were all part of one team and would all die for one another.

"Rear in position," announced Dima.

"Make entrance," Nir said.

Once inside, the goal was to determine what was in the shipment, then confirm that it was destroyed. Nir's hope was that they could do this with minimal bloodshed and even less noise.

Doron was the best lockpick on their team, and he had the deadbolt and the handle lock tripped in under a minute. Nir fired up his night vision goggles, turned on the attached infrared, or IR, light, pulled open the metal door, and peeked in. Not surprisingly, it was completely dark, and, because there was no ambient light for the NVG to pick up, without the IR light he wouldn't have been able to see anything. Picturing the schematic in his mind, he knew that on his right was a wall, beyond which was a barracks that would hold ten men. Immediately to his left was the southwest wall of the warehouse. In front of him on the right was the floor of the warehouse, and ahead on the left was the wall of the kitchen, which led to a bathroom and a break room.

The plan was for the 504 guys to watch the barracks, while Yaron's team guarded the rooms along the southwest wall. That would allow Nir and Doron to examine the boxes.

Nir paused. There was no sound and no movement. Letting his rifle rest against his chest, he slid his knife from its sheath and walked in.

Across the warehouse floor stood a stash of large crates. The IR light gave his night vision googles a flashlight beam's worth of sight, allowing him to count the stacks at eight high and eight wide. From his vantage point and limited light, he couldn't tell how deep the stacks went. There had to be at least three to four hundred boxes. Nir and Doron began to move across the floor, but a sound to their left brought them up short.

It was a toilet flush.

Dima began moving. He was amazingly silent for his size. As the bathroom door opened, Nir could hear the man grumbling in Arabic about the lights going out. Dima clamped his hand over the man's mouth, lifted him up by his belt, and carried him out the back door. A few moments later, he walked back in and gave Nir a thumbs up. Looking to his right, Nir saw the 504 men in position by the barracks.

Nir and Doron crossed the floor to the boxes. The writing on their sides was in Farsi. But as Nir scanned the writing, there was a word and number combination he could decipher—Shahed 136. He pointed to it, and Doron nodded in recognition. These crates were filled with parts that would be assembled into weaponized drones.

Is this part of Iran's new offensive against Israel in place of their nuclear aspirations? Are they going to start sending suicide drones over the Syrian border? It didn't make any sense to Nir. As far as he knew, the Iron Dome antimissile technology that kept Israel safe from the thousands of rockets that had been fired over the borders would make short shrift of any drones being sent their way.

Doron hit Nir's arm and motioned with his hands. Nir nodded. They needed to get inside a box and confirm that the EMP had dealt with the electronics inside. They moved down the line to the furthest corner from the barracks. Doron pulled a small electric sawblade from his pocket and turned it on.

There is no way to make metal cutting wood a silent process, but the tinkerers at the Mossad had done a good job of muting the mechanical noise emitted by the saw itself. Still, Nir noticed that each member of the 504 team turned their way when Doron put the blade to the first box. That was not a good sign.

Two minutes later, Nir and Doron were removing the end cap from the box and placing it on the ground. They pulled out packing material and let it fall to the floor. Soon they could make out a wide, flat wing.

They kept pulling out the insides but couldn't find the circuitry they were looking for. Doron moved on to the next crate and began cutting.

Something caught Nir's eye. "*Qaf*," he whispered into his coms. A few seconds later, Dima stood next to him. "I think the letters on the wing are Cyrillic. Can you read it?"

Dima ducked down so that he could see inside. He pulled out a little more of the packing material before saying, "It says 'Geran-2.' That's Moscow's designation for the Shahed-136. These drones are bound for Russia."

"Holy Mother of Lenin, we've fried a couple hundred of Putin's new drones."

"He's not going to be happy about that," said Dima. His wide smile looked eerie through Nir's goggles.

Efraim's voice broke through on the coms. "What did I just hear you say?"

"Get off the mic," Nir whispered. "This channel is operational. *Qaf*, help *Sin* get that endcap off."

Efraim wasn't easily deterred. "Right, and it's my operation! Did you say you just fried a couple hundred Russian drones?"

"It became my operation the moment our boots touched Syrian soil. And I meant possibly fried."

"Oh, they're fried alright," said Doron. "They're as fried as Colonel Sanders's thighs."

Nir turned to him. He had both hands deep in a box. Wires trailed out to a multimeter that Dima was holding for him. Doron's head was halfway in the box as he looked at the gauge.

Gunfire erupted by the barracks.

"Flash-bang," called out a voice.

Must be the 504 guys, Nir thought as he closed his eyes, covered his ears, and opened his mouth against the shock wave. *But I didn't authorize any flash-bangs!*

Nir's reaction wasn't fast enough, and he was momentarily disoriented by the blast. He shook his head. "*Sin, Qaf,* go to the barracks," he said.

In front of him, the door to the kitchen flew open. Nir lifted his rifle and had just enough time to see a cot set up in the room before he pulled the trigger.

If they were housing someone in the kitchen, then the break room...

"*Zay, Nun,* clear the break room!"

"*Root!*"

After taking a moment to let his eyes settle down, Nir moved forward to the kitchen, rifle raised. The gunfire at the barracks was slowing down.

Nir eyed the body at the door and saw that the lower half of the man's face was gone. Stepping over the man, he swept into the room. It was empty. Going back to the body in the doorway, he squatted down to confirm what he thought he had seen on the man's uniform.

There it is, he thought, eyeing the patch on the dead officer's arm. Over the background of a globe, an arm thrust up an assault rifle. Below the rifle was the image of the Qur'an, and the verse, "Make ready against them whatever you can of power."

"CARL, Lead. Confirm we have one IRGC KIA," he said, reporting the dead Iranian back to Efraim.

"Lead, CARL. Confirmed," answered Liora.

"Team, sitrep," he said.

"Barracks cleared. Eight dirties down," reported *Alif.*

Eight down, Nir thought angrily. But he held back any response until he could hear *Alif*'s account. He couldn't quickly judge a situation he wasn't a part of.

"Bathroom and break room clear. One down. One wounded. But you better come here and see this," said Yaron.

Nir stepped out of the kitchen and turned left. Kneeling between Yaron and Imri was a man with his hands on his head. Nir ran over and recognized the problem right away.

"*Qaf,* get over here," Nir ordered. Turning to Imri, he said, "Tell me about his wound."

"Through and through under the collarbone. Going to hurt like a mother, but he'll be okay."

Nir could hear the big man's boots trotting across the warehouse floor. Using his chin, he motioned Dima toward the prisoner. "Look at his insignia."

On the man's uniform was a fierce-looking skull in the red cross-hairs of a rifle scope.

"Wagner Group," Dima said.

"You got it. Putin's own band of hired mercenaries."

"They're wreaking hell in Ukraine," said Imri. "Last I heard, eighty percent of them were hired straight from the Russian penitentiaries."

"I say we shoot him," said *Alif*.

Nir turned and saw *Alif* walking up. "Of course you do. What happened down there?"

The man shrugged. "They woke up."

"Last time they make that mistake," laughed *Gim*, who came up behind *Alif*.

Nir glared at the Syrian before turning back to *Alif*. "You and I are going to talk about this later."

"A Kidon man afraid of a little blood," said *Alif* with a laugh. "That's like a rabbi who is afraid of the Torah."

"Jews, huh?" said the Russian in Arabic. He coughed, spit, then added, "I should have known."

Alif raised his rifle. Nir's right hand shot forward so that his palm struck the 504 man in the chest. The spook stumbled back four or five paces. "Stand down, soldier!"

Turning to Dima, he said, "Find out who he is and what he's doing here."

"Lead, this is CARL." This time it was Nicole on the coms.

"Go ahead."

"We have four police cars leaving the station."

"Copy. *Qaf*, save that interrogation for later. Let's get—"

"Wait, that's not all. Coming out of a vehicle shed next to the station we've got three BRDM-2 armored scout cars trailing the police cars."

Eizeh seret, Nir thought, picturing in his mind what the heavy machine guns mounted on the scout cars could do to their truck. *This is turning into a nightmare.*

"Everybody, let's move," Nir ordered. "*Qaf*, explain to the prisoner that he is coming with us. But that if he gives us any trouble, I'm going to shoot him in the gut and let him bleed out on the side of the road."

"*Root*," Dima said, lifting the Wagner Group man by his collar and dragging him along.

Nir burst out the rear door of the warehouse into the open night air. As he ran, he said, "*Waw*, how's the breakdown?"

"I need two minutes," answered Lahav.

"You have one. *Hamza*, get under the truck and retrieve our emergency box."

"*Root*," said Dafna.

If someone is going to give chase, we've got a few surprises for them.

The team sprinted across the rocky field to where the truck hid behind the berm. When they arrived, Dafna was still under the truck and Lahav and *Ba* were struggling to put the tarp's framework back onto the truck. The other team members jumped in and, within a minute, the tarp roof was being tied down.

Nir took a quick look into the back of the police car. The two officers were attempting to yell at him through gagged mouths. He turned and ran to the passenger door of the truck. *Alif* already had the engine going.

"Do we have a nine count back there?" he asked.

"Ten, with our new friend," answered Yaron.

"*Yalla*, let's get out of here."

Alif dropped the parking brake with a *thunk*, and the truck pulled onto the street.

CHAPTER 6

The dirties are arriving at the warehouse." Liora was giving a blow-by-blow of the Syrians' progress as seen from the microdrone she was controlling.

"Do you mind?" *Alif* asked Nir. He nodded to the knife in Nir's hand, the handle of which Nir was using to tap out his nervous energy on the dashboard.

"Sorry," Nir answered, sliding it back into its sheath. Dread continued to build in him as Liora narrated the Syrians' entrance into the warehouse, their frantic exit, the detection of a series of footprints leading behind the berm, and the discovery of dusty tire marks heading northeast.

"CARL, Lead. How much time do you think we have?" Nir asked.

Yossi answered, "Assuming everyone is going full speed, I'd give you ten minutes. Max of fifteen."

"And how far are we from the exfil LZ?" asked Nir, thinking how thankful he was that they weren't facing any roadblocks on the way to their exit landing zone.

"LZ is twenty minutes. Yanshuf's ETA to pick you up is twenty-seven."

"I'm not a fan of that math," *Alif* said.

"Me neither. Let's even it up just a bit."

Alif nodded and began slowing.

"CARL, how does the road look?" Nir asked.

"Clear both ways," answered Nicole.

"Okay, guys, as soon as we've stopped, deploy emergency measures."

"*Root*," sounded from his Kidon team.

When the truck halted, Nir slid out and moved to the back. His guys were already jogging away from the vehicle. Doron and Dima each began unfolding one of two spike strips ten meters separate from one another. Running farther down the road were Yaron and Imri. They each were carrying a mine that could be detonated remotely.

That should slow them down quite a bit, if it doesn't completely stop them, Nir thought.

Then he saw Yaron and Imri running back, each still carrying his mine.

"You were supposed to leave those back there," Nir joked to cover his anxiety.

"They won't arm," said Imri. "I think they're fried."

"That's impossible! We purposely put them well forward of the EMP. Let me see it," Nir said, reaching for Yaron's explosive.

The Kidon agent pulled back. "Not a chance. I'm your explosives guy. I'm not going to have you fiddling with the arming switch next to our truck!"

It suddenly hit Nir what he had almost done. "Stupid! You're right. Load up. We'll have to improvise."

The other two Kidon operatives returned and climbed into the back while Nir pulled himself up into the front seat.

"Go," he said to *Alif*, who put the truck in gear and accelerated.

"So, *Waw*, what happened? Why don't our mines work?"

There was silence.

"*Waw*, you still back there? Why did our explosives fry?"

After a few more moments of silence, there was a sharp sound followed by an "Ow!"

"He's talking to you, idiot," said Dima.

"Oh, sorry. Forgot my name," said Lahav. "I have no idea why they didn't arm. The EMP must have a little bit of a blowback effect or some sort of electromagnetic curl. It shouldn't have happened."

"But it did," said Nir.

"*Gilita et America.*"

Nir heard another *thwack* and an "Ow!" He was certain it was Dima hitting Lahav once again, this time for speaking Hebrew over the coms.

"The dirties are making good time. Should be on your spike strips in five minutes," announced Liora. "You're coming to Otaybah. Just before you hit the town, you'll go left for one-and-a-half kilometers, then turn right again, and you'll be on open road to the LZ."

"Hacker, you have any ideas?" Nicole hated when Nir called her that, but he didn't want to use her name over the coms.

"Unfortunately, you're in the middle of nowhere between Harran al-'Awamid and your LZ. Those vehicles behind you all have computers in them, but I have no way of getting to them."

"Wait, that's it," Nir said, his mind racing. "*Waw*, how long would it take to prep the weapon again?"

After a moment, there was another smack.

"Ow! I know he was talking to me. I was thinking." After another brief pause, Lahav said, "If we pull over here, I could have it ready to fire in twelve minutes."

"You don't have twelve minutes," said Yossi.

"We don't have twelve minutes," repeated Nir. "And we can't just pull over. We've got to reach our LZ in time. You've got seven minutes to put it together, and you're going to have to do it on the fly."

"What? Put it up while we're moving? *Chai b'seret!* You ever heard of physics? Have you ever heard of velocity pressure? Wait, what am I saying? Of course, you haven't. What do you think is going to happen when we raise a large, flat surface into a one-hundred-kilometers-per-hour wind?"

"*Waw!* Shut up and get it done. Hold off lifting the dish until you absolutely must. When you're ready, let me know. We'll slow it down to forty kilometers per hour, but that's all I can give you. *Hamza*, you've got nine warm bodies back there, and you've got rope that's holding the roof tarp on the frame. Improvise something."

"*Root*," said Dafna.

"*Waw*, get this done and I'll give you the entire day of Comic-Con off. Screw it up and you'll get a chance to explain electromagnetism to your guard in a Syrian prison."

Lahav sighed. "Understood. Everyone, switch to the alternate channel so I can give you your assignments."

"He's a weird one," said *Alif*. He had just made the second turn, and they were on their way into open country.

"You don't know the half of it. He once shut down the electrical grid in Eilat because the government folk wouldn't take his warnings seriously."

Alif laughed. "That was him? I thought he was in prison."

"Long story. Suffice it to say, he's my problem now."

"Dirties are coming up on the spikes," said Liora.

Nir waited quietly, hoping the armored scout cars were in the lead. They could deal with the police cars if needed. The scout cars would chew them up.

Cheering erupted in the coms from CARL. Liora announced, "Success with the strips. The police cruisers hit them square. The lead tried to swerve and cartwheeled off the shoulder. The next two cars hit directly but took the strips with them. Their tires should be airing out soon enough. That leaves one police car and all three scout cars still closing on you."

"Time?"

"Six minutes," said Yossi.

Suddenly, a loud *thwap* hit the roof of the truck's cab. Nir looked in the side mirror in time to see the truck's roof tarp drifting toward the ground. Soon after, he heard a clang, followed a few seconds later by a second clang as the two rear tarp frames were tossed onto the road.

So far, traffic had been incredibly light. Only four cars had passed them going the opposite way, and they had encountered none going their direction. *Hopefully it stays that way. Don't want anyone getting in the crossfire.*

"Four minutes," announced Yossi.

"The last police car is out," said an excited Liora. "Hit some big dark something in the road and spun into a tree."

The tarp, thought Nir. *Maybe the frames will get a couple more.*

"Ready," called Lahav. "Slow down, slow down!"

Alif let off the accelerator. Nir turned around in his seat and looked out the back window. The three-quarter moon gave just enough light for him to see the large, flat dish being hoisted to perpendicular by ropes that were looped around the remaining tarp frames. All nine were working to lift and stabilize it. Nir looked for the Russian prisoner and saw him on his side, hog-tied and pushed into a corner.

"Two minutes," called out Lahav.

Still looking out the back, Nir saw a series of flashes go by. Then more followed.

Tracers, Nir thought. *They're getting a bead on us.*

"They're on you," said Yossi. "Your speed reduction brought them right to your bumper."

"504, lay cover fire," Nir ordered. Moments later, the blast of their AKs echoed in the night.

"*Waw*, we need it now," he said.

Two metallic *thuds* shook the truck.

"*Hamza's* down," said Yaron.

"No!" called Liora.

"CARL, keep it together," commanded Nir. "Time!"

"One minute," said Lahav.

"Anyone not needed on the EMP, engage. *Waw*, we don't have a minute! Do it now!"

More hits on the truck.

"*Gim* is down," called out one of the 504 men.

Nir heard Doron say, "Give him to me." That was good. Doron was their best-trained medic. However, he also knew that him going to *Gim* meant that either Dafna was going to be okay, or she was already gone.

"They're just about on us," yelled Imri. "Fire the weapon!"

God, protect my people. Get us out of this. If you're there, answer me!

Nir heard a *whump* and felt the hairs on his arms and the back of his neck stand up.

Four more bullets slammed into the truck. Then Yaron said, "They're falling back!"

"CARL, sitrep!

"I can't tell you anything," Liora said. "You just fried my drone."

"Yes!" Nir cried out, knowing that a fried drone meant fried scout cars. Somehow, Lahav had gotten the EMP to fire again. "*Waw*, Comic-Con here you come! Tear the weapon down. *Alif*, floor it. Hacker, can you take your drone for a look-see on the scout cars? *Nun*, think of something creative you can do with those mines to vaporize this truck when we're out of here. *Sin*, update me."

Doron answered, "*Hamza* took shrapnel to her neck and a sharp blow to her head when she dropped. Keeping an eye for a concussion, but she should be okay. *Gim* took a round to the arm and one to the leg. He's going to need to evac with us if we want to save that leg."

Nir looked to *Alif*, who said, "Please, take him. Take him."

Two minutes later, the truck turned off the road. After another three minutes, they were at the landing zone.

Nir stepped out of the truck and hurried to the back. Dima was helping a very woozy Dafna to the end of the bed.

"Step down. I've got you," Nir said.

Dafna took a step, then her legs gave way. Nir caught her and began carrying her away from the activity in the truck.

"Put me down. I can walk," she said.

"Not happening, Fidel," Nir said. Up close, Nir could see her more clearly in the moonlight. She was a mess. There was a bandage affixed to the shaved side of her head, and another on the left side of her neck just under her chin. Unfortunately, to clean and sterilize the wound, Yaron had to pull away half of her fake beard. So, now she had half her head and half her face shaved.

"You look like you walked too close to a giant razor," Nir said as he set her down where she could lean back against a tree.

"Shut up, you're not helping," she replied, but there was a grin on her face. "Oh, listen."

Nir heard it too. The *thump* of a rotor. "Let us get this loaded up, then I'll come back and get you."

"Don't forget about me," she called. "And make sure your prisoner stays inside the helicopter."

He stopped and turned around. Dafna had a wide grin on her face as she shot a finger gun at him.

There had been a minor incident in his past when Nir had accidentally let a prisoner jump through the open door of an airborne helicopter. It was a simple mistake that could have happened to anyone, but now it seemed that no one was about to let it go.

As Nir got back to the truck, his team was lifting the weapon down to carry it to the helicopter.

"Bad news and worse news," said Lahav. "Bad news is that I was in front of the EMP when it went off. I'm not sure if this means I won't be able to have kids."

Nir wasn't sure that was actually bad news, but he held back from telling that to Lahav. "And the worse news?"

Lahav motioned to the guys carrying the weapon and said, "Hang on a second." He then pointed. On the satellite dish were two large, gaping bullet holes.

Nir's heart sank. "I'm never going to get to drive my car again."

Lahav took hold of his arm. "Sorry, boss. Probably time you go electric anyway."

Yaron walked by, leading the prisoner, whose legs were now untied. He said, "I'll watch him, boss—you know, make sure he stays inside."

"Everyone's a comedian now, is that it?" Nir asked. He spotted a pair of legs sticking out from under the truck, and walked toward them. "You get it figured out?"

Imri slid out on his back and looked up at Nir. "I did. Got the mines and some of our grenades under the gas tank."

"How are you going to trigger them with the electronics fried?"

"Got an idea. Ever make a deadfall trap?"

"Of course. My buddies and I used to set them up to kill mice on the kibbutz," said Nir, looking under the truck. "But I don't think dropping a rock on the mines is going to set them off."

Imri smiled. "Watch and learn, *Ha'mefaked*."

"Lead," Nir heard someone call out. He turned to see *Alif* walking up to him. "Take care of my man."

"Like he's my own."

"Listen, we may not see eye to eye on everything, but I respect how you lead your men. I doubted your reputation, but you've lived up to it."

"I appreciate that," Nir answered, surprised that he apparently had a reputation.

They shook hands, then *Alif* and the remaining two men of his team walked toward an SUV they had parked here earlier in the day. Nir squatted again to look under the truck.

"Hey, Lead," the Unit 504 man called out.

Nir stood and looked back at him.

"One more thing. Make sure the Russian stays strapped into his seat." He winked and turned away.

"You too?" Nir called after him.

Once everything was loaded up, Nir carried Dafna over and lifted her into the helicopter. Then he called into his coms. "CARL, Lead. Deploy the ghosts."

"Deploying ghosts," responded Nicole.

Even while flying low, there was a good possibility of the helicopter being spotted by radar or from the ground. So, Nir had asked Nicole to create a diversion for the Syrian military. Their radars were about to light up with what would appear to them to be a large-scale attack of many fighter jets across four different border zones. While they were scrambling to meet this threat coming into their country, Nir's Yanshuf helicopter would quietly slip across the border going the other way.

Once Nir saw that everyone was on board, he climbed in. Immediately, the chopper lifted off. When it was 30 meters up and 75 meters away from the truck, it began hovering. Because of the excess weight of having two extra people on board, all the team's weapons had been left in the back of the truck—except for one of the sniper rifles. Imri hurriedly dropped the rifle's bipods to the chopper floor, then stretched out behind it at an awkward angle because the EMP was taking up most of the cargo space.

Nir watched as the man sighted his target, exhaled, then pulled the trigger. The rifle coughed out a round, and Imri cursed. He ran the bolt, chambering another round. Reacquiring his target, he exhaled and pulled the trigger. Another curse.

Yaron stepped forward and kicked Imri's boots. "Get out of there. Let an old man at it."

Reluctantly, Imri moved aside, and Yaron laid down.

"We've got to get moving," said the pilot through the coms.

Looking up, Nir saw a head peering back from the cockpit. He signaled "one minute" to the man, and the pilot turned back around.

From behind Nir, he heard Dima say, "Hundred shekels he hits it first time."

"You're on," answered Imri.

Yaron breathed out. The rifle cracked. The .338 Lapua Magnum bullet flew at over 900 meters per second, striking the metal box that had previously contained the night vision goggles. This box, which had been standing on its end, flew backward, allowing the "emergency box," which was now filled with rocks and had been leaning up against the first box, to deadfall to the ground. As it dropped, it pulled tight three wires that ran from its top to the pins of three grenades taped to the mines under the truck.

As Nir watched, there was an explosion under the truck, followed by a second massive explosion as the mines and the gas tank split the huge vehicle in half, with the front flying one way and the back flying the other.

The shock wave rocked the Yanshuf, and the pilot quickly lifted and banked toward the border.

Nir helped Yaron to his feet. As the agent, who was turning 50 in just two months, lifted the sniper rifle and began folding its bipods, he said, "Never send a boy to do a man's job."

Ooooohs sounded through the chopper's intercom system.

"Good shot, old man," admitted Imri, taking the rifle from his friend's hand.

When Nir had first boarded, he recognized the pilot as Naor Shapira, a guy he had known from his mandatory military service. He leaned through the cockpit opening to greet him. After a few words, Nir turned back to the cargo area.

"Oh, Lead," Shapira called out.

Nir stopped and leaned back in.

"I counted nine back there. Try to make sure there are still nine when we get to our destination."

Everybody on headsets broke into laughter. Nir shook his head, wondering if he was the one who should take a nosedive through the open door.

CHAPTER 7

Although the low flight was bumpy, Nir wasn't ready to sit down. There was too much adrenaline coursing through his body from another near miss. He took hold of a hand tether and looked around the cargo area.

Standing four feet high in the center of the bay was the EMP weapon. Lahav had covered it with a canvas tarp before it was secured to the floor. Not being able to see the damage on the weapon was a relief to Nir.

Maybe when we lift the canvas after we land, voilà, it will be back in one piece, and I'll be given the keys to my Mercedes. Yeah, and maybe when I walk into my apartment, I'll discover a golden unicorn that poops rainbows and sneezes baklava.

"It's not so bad, *Hamefaked.*" Nir spotted Lahav looking at him from the other side of the tarp. His Nintendo Switch was resting on his lap. The handheld gaming device was against all protocols on an operation like this. But Nir knew his team, and he knew Lahav. A distracted Lahav was a quiet and calm Lahav, and that meant a much more peaceful environment for everyone. The analyst continued, "I gave it a quick once-over. The only place it got hit was in the dish. I doubt the repairs will even reach three million shekels."

Nir quickly did the math and realized that it would take at least seven of his beautiful little Mercedes coupes to pay for the damage. "Thanks, Lahav. I feel much better now."

"Thought you might," said Lahav, returning to his game console. To Lahav's left sat Dafna, then Imri. The rest of Dafna's beard had been removed, and she had her head on the operative's shoulder with her eyes closed. Imri caught Nir's eye. He gave a quick glance at Dafna and flashed Nir a thumbs up. Nir nodded.

On the other side of Lahav sat Yaron. He was unstrapped and was unloading and reloading all the 9mm magazines that were stored in an ammunition can. They were for the small arsenal of Jericho 941 pistols that were stashed under the seats in case something happened to the chopper and they went down. Before the operation, Yaron had loaded all the magazines himself. But because they had been out of his sight for a time, he felt it necessary to recheck all the loads.

On Nir's side of the bay to his right sat Dima, silently staring out the open door. To his left, Doron was rebandaging the Russian's wound. As Nir turned toward them, he saw the prisoner watching him. Nir looked away. A few moments later, he glanced back over and saw that the Russian was still staring at him, this time wincing at something that Doron was doing to him.

Nir turned away again and squatted down to better see out the door, taking hold of the seat next to him for balance.

"*Habibi.*" At the faint sound of the word, Nir turned and saw the Russian nodding toward him. He wasn't wearing a headset, so his voice was barely discernable. Nir looked back out the door. "*Habibi,* I speak you." The man's Arabic was atrocious.

Staying focused out the door, Nir swatted Dima on the knee and asked, "Did you get a name for your fellow countryman?"

"Dmitry Leonidovich Livanov."

"Is he as shady as he looks?"

"I wouldn't trust him with my worst enemy's *savta.*"

It took Nir a moment of mental gymnastics to realize that Dima's grandmother comment was a negative. "Could you go figure out what your friend wants?"

Out of his peripheral vision, Nir saw the operative's straps drop as he rose to his feet. He walked past, and a couple minutes later, Nir felt Dima's hand on his shoulder.

"He says he wants to talk to you. Says he has information and wants to make a deal."

Nir shook his head. "Is the universe just determined to get me fired today? First, the warehouse turns into a massacre, then the weapon gets shot up. Now I'm supposed to interrogate a prisoner in a helicopter of all places?"

"It's like you're drowning in a cauldron of irony," said Liora from CARL. Nir had forgotten they were still connected in.

"It's like you're drifting in a sea of paradox and the tsunami of fate is racing your way," added Yossi.

"Captain Shapira, please cut the feed to Mossad headquarters," Nir said.

"Disconnecting feed," said the pilot. Nir heard a brief protest from CARL before they went silent.

Sometimes you've got to put the kids in time out, he thought as he stood. *Nicole would want to hear this, but she'll understand.*

Nir walked to where the Russian was sitting and took hold of the helicopter's frame.

Turning to Dima, he said, "Tell him that I'm going to have you interpret because his Arabic sucks."

Dima did so. The Russian smiled, shrugged, and replied through Dima. "It is a gutter language for gutter people. My effort was minimal."

What a very Russian statement. "Ask him: Why is he in Syria?"

The mercenary rubbed his fingers together. "The money. Why else would I be in this dung pit?"

Nir shook his head. "Not you personally. I don't care about you. Why were Russians at that warehouse?"

The smile on the Russian's face widened. "That's the big question, isn't it? Maybe nothing, maybe something big. Or maybe something very, very big. Maybe it's something that you Jews are going to regret you didn't know about sooner."

When Dima finished interpreting, he added, "He's toying with you.

Trying to get a rise out of you. I can't get enough of a read on him to see whether he really knows something or if he's just being an *ahabal*."

"Understood. It's also possible that he does know something and is still being an idiot." Nir thought for a moment. "Okay, stay with me here. I'm going to try something. And if you need to remind him to be polite, feel free."

Nir took a quick look around. All eyes, including those of Doron, who was still sitting next to the Russian, were on him. Lahav had even put his Nintendo down. "Relax everyone. He's not going anywhere."

Looking at his captive, Nir asked, "So, what prison were you in?"

When Dima interpreted, the man looked surprised. "I am not a prisoner. I am a member of the Wagner Group. I am an elite soldier."

Nir laughed. "Elite soldier? Come on now. I know you Wagner scum. Most of you are murderers and thieves and rapists. Which were you?"

"I am none of them."

Nir leaned casually with his shoulder against the copter's frame. He eyed the man up and down. "The fact that you are the only one left alive tells me that you are not brave enough to be a murderer. You look too stupid to be a thief. I'm guessing rapist. You're some deviant predator, aren't you? Yeah, that's exactly what you are. That's why you jumped at the chance to join Wagner, because I know what they do to degenerates like you in Russian prisons."

The man let out a string of words that Nir didn't understand, but that earned him an open-handed cuff by Dima to the left side of his face.

Nir leaned in close to the man. "I'm betting that's why you came to Syria. So you could carry out your sick, twisted deviancies on a helpless population. At night, you go skulking around the villages because no real woman would give you a second look."

Again, the man swore at Nir, and once again, he received a slap from Dima. The side of his face was bright red now, and there was blood trickling from his nose.

Nir turned from him. "I've got no time for perverts like you." He walked back over to his previous position and squatted down.

"*Habibi! Habibi!*" Nir could barely hear the man yelling out his name. He let the man wait.

After a minute, Dima said, "He says he's ready to talk."

"Tell him I've got no time for sick freaks like him."

Nir let another minute pass, then two, as the captive continued calling out, "*Habibi!*"

Finally, he stood and walked back over. Looking down at the man, he began asking rapid-fire questions. "What is your full name?"

"Dmitry Leonidovich Livanov."

"What prison were you in?"

"I was at Vladimir Central, about halfway between Moscow and Nizhny Novgorod."

"What did you do?"

"I was convicted of homicide in the commission of a robbery."

"I didn't ask what you were convicted of. I asked what you did."

Livanov sighed. "Me and another guy robbed a gas station. The attendant reached for something under the counter. I thought it was a gun, so I shot him."

"What was your sentence?"

"Twenty years."

"Who is in charge here?"

"You are, *habibi.*"

"Call me *habibi* again, and I'll have this guy break your arm," Nir said, tilting his head toward Dima.

"Yes, sir."

"Better." Nir let the moment hold, then said in a calmer tone, "Now, what is this big thing that is about to happen?"

"I don't know."

Nir stepped back and walked away.

"Wait, wait!"

Nir stopped. "You're wasting my time, Livanov."

"I don't know anything, but I know who does." When Nir took a step closer, the Russian said, "Please. They are planning something big. It is directed at your country. I know this from stories and rumors. But I also know from what I've seen."

"Go on," Nir said.

"Most of the UAVs that you saw are going to Russia to use against Ukraine. However, a few are staying behind for the Syrians and for our people to train on. That's why I was there with the other Wagner soldier, the one that you guys killed. For a time, I was in engineering school before…well, before life went badly. The man who was with me had run an electronics store that he burned down for the insurance money. Wagner sent us to the warehouse for the UAVs. But there were boxes in the back of the stack that we weren't allowed to know about. The rumor was that they contained a special kind of rocket, the high precision kind, and that they were going to use it against Israel."

"And you have no idea what it was?"

"I don't. But I know that very soon, a contingent was due to arrive from the Russian forces. They were coming because of what was in those other boxes."

"Who was coming? I need names."

"I have only one name. But he is the leader of the group. He is the one who will know what is in those boxes."

"Give me his name," Nir demanded.

The smile crept back onto Livanov's face. "*Habibi*, now is the time for us to talk about a bargain."

Dima pulled his arm back as soon as the Arabic word for *friend* exited the man's mouth, but Nir held him back. Livanov was right. He had information that Nir wanted, and he was anxious to make a deal. Rather than beat the name out of him, it was time for negotiation.

"What do you want?"

Livanov laughed. "What do we all want? Freedom."

"Yeah, and I want a date with Gal Gadot," Nir replied, hoping that the coms with CARL were still disconnected. "What's second on your list?"

"There is no second. I can give you this name and you can give me my freedom. I have done nothing against your country. If you send me back to Russia, Wagner will put me on the front lines in Ukraine, where I won't survive the winter. Please, sir. Can we strike a bargain?"

Nir stepped away and thought for a moment. Then, looking around at the team, he said, "Okay, everyone, you heard him. I'm inclined to make the deal."

"What do you have to lose?" said Dafna. "Keep him in custody while we run out the lead."

Imri added, "Agreed. If the tip pays off, it'll be well worth it. If it doesn't, we let Lahav introduce him to some of his old friends in Maasiyahu Prison."

"I could do that," said Lahav.

"I don't trust him as far as I can throw him," said Yaron, turning back down to his ammunition can. "But I agree. It's worth the gamble."

Returning to Livanov, Nir said, "Okay, you have a deal. Give me the name."

The Russian shook his head. "Wait. How do I know you are going to live up to your side of the bargain? Maybe I give you the name, then you just throw me out of the helicopter?"

Livanov looked at Dima with curiosity when the big man had a hard time interpreting his words. He appeared even more surprised when everyone else in the chopper suddenly burst into laughter—all except for the team's leader, who just rolled his eyes.

When all calmed down, Nir said, "You're just going to have to trust me. I have given you my word. Take it or leave it."

Livanov stared at Nir for a long moment, then said, "Major General Sergei Sergeyevich Bogdanov."

CHAPTER 8

Nir stood outside the office. He didn't want to go in. He had just faced gunfire and a low-altitude helicopter flight through enemy territory, but somehow this was the first time in the last 24 hours that he was legitimately nervous. For his team's operation, the *ramsad* had gone out on a limb with the IDF and gotten him the EMP weapon. Nir had committed to the man that he would bring it back in one piece.

Which, truth be told, I did. It's just that the one piece happens to have two large bullet holes in its main component. Crud, I'm toast.

Mustering up his courage, Nir walked through the door and up to the desk. Malka Bieler, the *ramsad*'s executive assistant and chief pit bull, glared at him.

"*Boker tov*, Mrs. Bieler," he said, forcing a smile. The only person who intimidated him more than the *ramsad* was the woman to whom he was now speaking. "The *ramsad* sent for me."

The ops team had all arrived back at Mossad headquarters a little over two hours ago after an hour-and-a-half shuttle drive from Ramat David Airbase in the Jezreel Valley. They all went straight to the locker rooms, where they showered off the remains of the previous night's mission, before heading over to CARL to get to work.

Nir had just put the shampoo on his hair when a voice called into the showers, "Tavor, the *ramsad* is waiting for you." Quickly rinsing off and getting dressed, he had rushed across the campus to the office of the head of the Mossad to learn his fate.

"Yes, Mr. Tavor. He did. It's nice to see you here with an actual appointment for a change. You may enter."

Nir fought the urge to bow and walked to the door. Upon entering, he found the *ramsad* sitting behind his desk. Also seated around the room were Deputy Director Asher Porush, Assistant Deputy Director Karin Friedman, Efraim Cohen, and two of Nir's fellow Kidon team leaders, Ravid Efrat and Lavie Bensoussan.

"You shot my weapon," said the *ramsad*, as soon as Nir sat down.

"Technically, *Ha'mefaked*, I wasn't the one who shot it," Nir answered, immediately wishing he could hit rewind on his answer. Out of his peripheral vision, he saw Bensoussan grin as he stared down at the ground. "I mean, I'm sorry, *Ha'mefaked*," he quickly corrected.

The *ramsad* picked up several papers from his desk and perused them. Then, holding them out toward Nir, he asked, "Am I to understand that after you gave me your assurance that you would protect this multimillion-shekel weapon, you chose to reassemble it in the back of a speeding transport truck in the middle of a firefight?"

Nir wasn't sure if he was supposed to take the papers. He leaned forward, but the *ramsad* let the papers fall to his desk. Reversing course, Nir settled back into his chair. "Well, the firefight didn't start until partway through the assembly. But, yes, *Ha'mefaked*, that is essentially it." He could feel his face turning red. *This is not good. Not only am I about to get reamed out; it's about to happen in front of Efrat and Bensoussan.*

"Quite honestly, I didn't even know it was hit until afterward," he added, quickly realizing how irrelevant his statement was.

"Well, you can't imagine how relieved I am to hear that," Ira Katz said, shaking his head and sighing. "So, you thought this was the only option you had that would keep your team alive and the weapon out of enemy hands?"

"It may not have been the only option, but it was the best," Nir answered with a little bit of an edge. Katz hadn't been there. None of these people had been there. *I would have dumped 20 of the ramsad's precious weapons into a big pile and lit them on fire if it meant getting my team home safely*, he thought. "Seriously, I don't know what other choice we had. The enemy was approaching quickly, and we didn't—"

Nir was interrupted by the *ramsad's* raised hand, which he then used to point at him. "We always have choices, Tavor. But I agree with the one you made. That was quick thinking. I'm amazed that it worked. I think the generals at the IDF may have had their eyes opened to a few more strategic methods for utilizing their EMP weapon."

"Thank you, *ramsad*," said Nir, relief filling him as he realized he wasn't about to get fired or arrested. "I was just protecting—"

Again, Nir was interrupted by Katz's hand. "But I'm still keeping your car." He reached toward Efraim, who deposited Nir's key fob in his outstretched hand.

"What? But you just said…"

"I know what I said, Tavor. But a deal is a deal."

Nir looked around for support and found none. Friedman had never liked Nir, and the rumor was that Porush hadn't smiled since Golda Meir's government. The two other Kidon leaders wouldn't make eye contact, but their bodies were shaking with laughter. And Efraim was licking from his fingers what Nir could only assume was imaginary Cheeto dust.

Could Katz legally do this? Technically, the answer was probably no. But this was the Mossad, and legality wasn't always the number one consideration. Besides, it was Katz's predecessor who had set Nir up in his Antwerp diamond business. Without that initial cash infusion, he never would have been able to create his European cover or make the kind of money that allowed him to buy his precious Mercedes. Even though he had repaid the Mossad every euro, he still owed them a big debt.

Defeated, Nir leaned back in his chair. "It's due for an alignment, *Hamefaked*."

"I'll let them know," the *ramsad* said, depositing the key fob into a desk drawer. "Now, tell me about Dmitry Leonidovich Livanov."

Livanov had remained at the air base in the hands of the military police. Nir wasn't sure whether the Mossad would send people to him or if they would bring the mercenary to Tel Aviv. Either way, the man wasn't his problem anymore. He had gotten what he wanted from him. He had a name—Bogdanov.

Nir spent the next hour debriefing the operation and justifying the taking of the prisoner. While it seemed that everyone took a shot at second-guessing Nir's decisions, the toughest questions came from the other Kidon leaders. He answered them the best he could, understanding that they weren't attacking him. This was the necessary rough evaluation that allowed them to learn from what had been done and determine what could be done better next time.

When the grilling was finally completed, Nir was excused so they could continue their discussion in private.

"Have a nice day, Mrs. Bieler," he said as he hurried past the executive assistant. She didn't respond.

Once Nir was free from the office, he slowed his pace as he made his way across the campus to CARL. He was exhausted and wanted a few moments so he could just be alone and breathe. There were many hours of work ahead of him, but at least there was a very bright light at the end of the tunnel. Nicole had already accepted his invitation to a late breakfast at Benedict restaurant after they finished this next meeting. They hadn't been able to carve out any alone time since her arrival in Israel. This would be their first chance to pull away and catch up.

She was the first one he spotted as he walked into the team headquarters. She looked as if she also had taken the shower time to freshen up. Her hair shined as it hung in loose, wet curls. She caught his eye and blew him a small kiss that he felt through his knees. Next to her, the tandem desks of Liora and Dafna were dark and quiet, a rarity for those two hardworking analysts.

After the Yanshuf had landed at Ramat David, Dafna and the injured Unit 504 man had been taken into the medical center. While he had gone straight into surgery, Dafna had a doctor clean up and rebandage her head and check her for signs of concussion. Not seeing anything too concerning, the doctor had cleared Dafna to make the trip back to Tel Aviv with the rest of the team. Nir had called ahead to

Liora, who took Dafna home with her so she could watch her friend for the rest of the day.

To the right of their empty work area, Yossi was busy typing at his station, while Lahav had pulled two chairs together and was sound asleep. Next to Lahav's desk, Chewbacca wore a maroon Syrian special forces beret. Nir figured the analyst must have pilfered it when they were checking back in their borrowed Syrian uniforms.

At the conference table sat his ops team. Imri and Doron were each messing with their phones. Yaron had placed his head on his arms and his eyes were closed. Dima was in the process of peeling an orange. Normally, Nir would have sent them home following an operation. But this time he had asked them to stick around. Whatever next steps were decided at this meeting, they were going to be involved, and he wanted their input.

"Okay, everyone, bring it in. Sooner we get going, the sooner we'll be done."

Had to have been Liora who left the fruit, thought Nir, choosing a pear out of a large bowl in the middle of the table. *I'd love to have her here for this meeting, but what she's doing is more important.*

He sat down, rubbed the pear on his sleeve, and took a bite.

CHAPTER 9

CARL, MOSSAD HEADQUARTERS, TEL AVIV— OCTOBER 4, 2022—10:30 (10:30 AM) IDT

Someone wake up Lahav," Nir said before taking another bite of his pear.

Dima rocketed the orange he had been peeling, pegging the sleeping analyst between his shoulder blades. The fruit burst apart in segments and juice.

"Ow! Idiots," Lahav yelled, sitting up and turning toward the table.

"I meant go over and wake him up," Nir said, suppressing a smile.

"That's not what you said," responded Dima, lifting a replacement orange from the fruit bowl. "You should be more precise in your use of language."

As the ops guys laughed and high-fived Dima, Nicole pulled some paper towels and walked toward the mess.

Nir pointed and said, "*Achi*, if she cleans up your crap, you and I are going to have words."

"Nicole," Dima called out. He jumped up and moved her way. "Here, I've got that." Imri followed him.

Nicole handed him the towels and took her seat, smiling at Nir.

Nir winked at her as he bit off more pear.

Lahav grumbled as he sat down. Yossi sniffed toward him. "Dude, you smell good. Kinda citrusy."

"Shut up, man. That hurt."

"Dude, it was fruit," called Dima from his kneeling position by Lahav's workstation. "Seriously. Fruit, man."

"Okay, everyone, enough stupidity. We all good?" There were nods all around as Dima and Imri rejoined the table. "*Sababa*. Tell me what we know about Major General Bogdanov, then we can figure out why we care."

Nicole tilted up an iPad and began reading. "Bogdanov, Sergei Sergeyevich. Born November 20, 1964, in Yaroslavl, which is about 250 kilometers northeast of Moscow. Parents are Sergei Vladimirovich Bogdanov and Natalia Nikolaevna Bogdanov née Vavilov. Both deceased. Father was military. Died when Sergei was four."

"1968?" asked Yaron, his eyes tilted toward the ceiling. "Not too much going on with the Soviet military then. That was the Prague Spring, right?"

"Exactly, Mr. Military Historian," Nicole said, giving him an air clap. "Bogdanov's father died the same way as did most of the invasion's casualties—in a car accident en route to Czechoslovakia."

"Not quite the warrior's blaze of glory," said Doron.

Nicole continued, "Joined the military at seventeen and went straight to Afghanistan. From that point on, he moved from conflict to conflict. South Ossetia, Abkhazia, Transnistria, both Chechnyas. Then, in 2015, he came to Syria as a major. He learned Arabic and got to know all the right people in the Assad government and amongst the militias. He made a name for himself, and in seven years he was promoted to general and earned his first star."

"Okay, good history. Now, what kind of guy is he?" Nir asked, shooting the core of his pear in a practiced arc and landing it in the center of the trash can. "Nothing but net."

"Bogdanov's what you'd expect," answered Yossi. "He previously served under General Sergei Surovikin, and he is currently serving General Alexander Chaiko. Both have reputations as being butchers—Surovikin in Syria and Chaiko in Ukraine—and Bogdanov fits right in."

"Any incidents in particular?"

"In Chechnya, two of his soldiers were ambushed and killed. Bogdanov lined up all the men in the village, including all the teens, and had his men move down the row shooting two out of every three. Just *boom, boom,* skip, *boom, boom,* skip. He's developed the same kind of ruthless reputation in Syria."

"Harsh. What about family? He married? Kids?"

Nicole jumped back in. "Yes, and yes. Married for thirty-five years to Maria. Three grown children—two sons and one daughter. Seven grandchildren. The daughter lost her husband in Ukraine, and she and her three kids are living back with Bogdanov and his wife."

"Any vices?" asked Nir.

"Vodka!" all four ops guys cried out.

"*Za zdorovie,*" toasted Dima in Russian. He pretended to throw back a shot, then slam his imaginary glass onto the table.

Nicole smiled and rolled her eyes. "Yes, the general does like to drink. He also doesn't seem to have a strong commitment to fidelity in his marriage."

"Scandalous," said Nir. "So, we've got a cruel Russian general who partakes too much in vodka and sleeps around. It kind of feels like we pulled this guy from central casting."

"There is a reason that stereotypes become stereotypes," said Dima. "Being surprised that a Russian general is a drunk womanizer is like picking up a fish and being surprised it is wet."

Nir laughed. "Spoken like a true Cossack. So, do we know what his role is in Syria?"

"He is the liaison between Moscow, Tehran, and Damascus," said Yossi. "He also deals with some of the militias through the IRGC and Hezbollah. His reputation is cruel. He is hated. He is feared. And, because of that, he is respected."

Leaning forward, Nir plucked up an orange. When he settled back, he saw Nicole looking at him with eyebrows raised.

That's right. We've got breakfast when this is done. So, instead of peeling it, he called out "Yaron!" then tossed the fruit to the agent. The old agent caught it with one hand. "*Achi,* you've got the floor. Give me one reason why Russia would want to hit Israel."

Without hesitation, the man said, "Iran. Moscow and Tehran are becoming fast buddies through the supply of military drones. And because the enemy of my friend is my enemy, that relationship is affecting Russia's attitude toward us. Besides, they're not happy that we keep air-striking a lot of the drones that the ayatollahs are smuggling to them through Syria."

"Toss it to me. I need a turn," called out Lahav. Yaron did, but the analyst bungled the catch and the orange rolled across the floor and settled at Chewbacca's feet. Boos met the analyst's failure. Lahav reached into the bowl and pulled out a replacement. "What you said is true for now, but it's not going to matter much longer. Yes, we're blowing up some of the Moscow-bound stuff. And whenever that happens, Moscow gets their panties in a wad. But now, more and more drone wreckage is being found in Ukraine with Persian writing on it, so it's hard for the IRGC to say, 'Drones? We aren't sending any UAVs to Moscow through Syria.' So, very soon they are just going to skip the middleman and send it direct. Expect to see Iranian cargo planes landing in Russia very soon."

"Good. Now, over here," said Nicole. Lahav tossed the orange high, but she still managed to snatch it out of the air to a series of appreciative comments. "I hear what you're saying about war materiel, Lahav. But I think the bigger deal is the friendship. Russia doesn't have many friends right now. They've got Belarus, which is mostly a kiss-up relationship. Then there's kind of China, kind of Hungary, and there's Iran. Putin has been warning Israel about carrying out airstrikes in Syria. But I don't think he's doing it simply because he's worried we're going to hit Russian bases or even militia stuff. He's trying to protect Iran's weapons and military. He's watching his friend's back."

Nir snapped his fingers and held up his hand. Winding up, Nicole threw a strike across the length of the conference table. Nir shook out his hand in pretend pain. "Nicole's right. Think about it. What's Russia doing in Syria right now? Very little. They aren't bringing people in. They're pulling them out. They're abandoning bases all across the country because they need as many warm bodies in Ukraine as is possible. And who is moving into those vacated bases? Our Iranian friends and their little proxy minions."

It was Imri's turn now. Nir lobbed him the orange, and as the young operative talked, he tossed the fruit up and down in his hand. "Listen, I agree that there is some sort of friendship element. But I think alliance is a better word. Russia and Iran hold nothing but disdain for one another. But since they need each other, they put on a happy face and pretend to be pals. But let's back it up a step. When we're looking for the root motivation of most questionable deeds done in the world, what do we do?"

"Follow the money," everyone said in unison.

"Exactly." Imri pulled the fruit bowl in front of himself. "So, let's say that I am the only one at this table with a fruit bowl. I've got tons of fruit—orchards of the stuff—but you all have none. Still, you love fruit. You've got to get you some. If you want your pears and your oranges and your dates and your bananas, what do you have to do, Yossi?"

"Come to you."

"Right," said Imri, tossing a banana to the analyst. As he continued to speak, he rolled a piece of fruit to each person at the table. "As long as you keep coming to me, you'll get your fruit." When he came to Lahav, however, he stopped. "But what if I decide I don't want to give my fruit to Lahav anymore?"

"Hey, come on, man," Lahav protested.

"Not only that, but I also decide that I'm going to start pounding on Lahav because he needs a good beating." Setting down the orange, he took the analyst's arm and started lightly hitting it.

"That doesn't hurt." Imri gave him a harder hit. "Okay, point made. I get it," said Lahav.

"If you guys try to stop me from hitting him, I'm going to stop giving you fruit. So, what do you do now?"

Dima stood to his full height and leaned over the table. "We take the fruit from you."

"But what if I'm the only person with one of these?" Imri drew the pistol from his hip holster. He pulled the mag and locked back the slide to ensure it was unloaded, then set it on the table. Dima quickly sat back down.

"Whoa, that escalated," said Yossi.

"Doron, what would you do, *achi*?" asked Imri.

"If I need the fruit, I let you pound on Lahav. However, it's likely I would let you pound on Lahav even if I didn't need the fruit."

Imri laughed. "Okay, maybe a bad example. But now, one more step." He slid the fruit bowl over to Nicole. "Let's say that Nicole suddenly discovers that she, too, has a fruit bowl and orchards full of fruit, and she is more than happy to give you all you want. What would you do?"

"Go to Nicole," said Doron.

"Heck yeah," said Yossi.

"And how will that make me, your former fruit provider, feel?"

"Not so happy," said Nir. "All your power would be gone. No more leverage. I'm guessing you'd either want to take Nicole's fruit bowl for yourself or you'd blow it to pieces."

Imri pointed to himself and said, "Russia." Sweeping his finger across the rest of them, he said, "Europe." Pointing to Nicole, he said, "Israel." Then, holding up the fruit bowl, he said, "Natural gas." Pushing back his chair, he stood, spread his arms, put one foot in front of the other, and bowed deeply.

Applause echoed through the room. Orange peels and pear cores showered him as they all cheered.

"Once a theater kid, always a theater kid," said Yaron with a roll of his eyes.

Nir calmed everyone down. "Well done, Imri. And I think we can all agree that with the sabotage of the Nord Stream pipelines in the Baltic, Europe has their eyes on us more than ever."

"That wasn't us, was it?" asked Nicole.

"I don't think so. It would be too obvious for us. You've got two fruit stands. One mysteriously blows up. Who is suspect number one? Besides, our market is developing extremely well naturally. We don't need to resort to sabotage."

"Then who did it?" asked Imri.

"Maybe Ukraine. Maybe the US. Maybe Russia did it themselves as some sort of false flag op. Just don't know yet. But, if I know Ira Katz, I'm guessing we will know in not too long."

"Want me to look into it?" asked Yossi.

"No, we've got enough on our plate. We've got a whole intelligence agency and four other Kidon teams around us. Let them get off their butts and figure something out for a change."

Cheers of affirmation sounded around the table.

"So, back to our situation. I think we've figured our possible motivation for a Russian attack on Israel. And I'm guessing it's a both/and, rather than an either/or. Putin wants to show his loyalty to Khamenei, but he's also incredibly ticked that Europe is turning to us for natural gas. Even if it is technically through Egypt, he knows where the gas originates—right off our shoreline in the Mediterranean. As long as we're in the picture, his power over Europe is diminished. And now with Nord Stream leaking like a sieve, the cost of getting gas to the Euros might soon become prohibitive. That's why he's forced to develop new markets in China and Iran."

Lahav spoke up. "Big deal that we know why Russia might hit us. We still have no idea how they're going to do it. Isn't that what's important?"

"Motivation is typically a good clue to the type of action. But you're right. What they are going to do is more important than why they are going to do it. Whatever was in those other boxes in the warehouse was destroyed by the EMP, so it's going to have to be replaced. That should buy us a little time, but I'm guessing that our window should be measured in weeks rather than months. So, let's turn back to our friend General Bogdanov, since it seems he might have some of the answers we need. Anyone have any idea where the good general might be in the near future?"

Nicole fluttered her hand.

"Yes, Miss le Roux?"

"Maybe we should take a look at the general's personal calendar that he keeps on his computer, encrypted and locked behind a fifteen-digit passcode."

"Now she's just showing off," said Yossi to Lahav.

"I'll own that," she answered with a smile. "The general is in Moscow until October eleventh, when he'll fly to Hungary. He'll be in

Budapest from October twelfth until the fifteenth, after which he will jet off to the beautiful vacation hotspot of Tehran, where he will remain until the twentieth. Then it's back home for a week before he flies to Dubai, where he'll stay from October twenty-seventh until November first."

"Wow, he gets around," said Lahav.

Yossi nodded his head. "Liaisons got to liaise."

"We're not going to Moscow," said Nir. "That's a logistical nightmare. Tehran is obviously out of the question. Dubai would be ideal, but I don't want to wait that long. Anyone up for a trip to Budapest?"

"That gives us only a week," said Nicole.

"Then we better get started."

CHAPTER 10

Nir slid the metal chair forward as Nicole sat down. After taking the opposite chair, the two accepted menus from the server. Nir ordered water for each of them and a cappuccino for himself.

Opening the trifold menu, Nicole flipped it front and back. "Okay, that's a lot of choices. You said you've wanted to take me here for years, so what do you recommend?"

"Breakfast."

Nicole folded up the menu and swatted Nir's arm with it. "Thanks for the help. You bring me to the restaurant that's known all over Israel for its breakfast, and what do you recommend?"

"Well, their lunches are good too," Nir said with a grin.

"Sometimes, mister…" She held up the menu like she was going to swat him again, but instead, she opened it and started reading.

"They've got a rabbit food section down on the left," he said.

"I see that." As she continued to scan, she said, "Remind me what shakshuka is."

"Breakfast casserole with tomatoes, onions, garlic, poached eggs. It's great stuff. Some people call Tel Aviv the shakshuka capital of the world."

"Everyone's got to be known for something. If it's so popular, you'd think I would have tried it by now. I guess it's because when I'm in Israel, I spend so little time outside of CARL. If I do get out, it's usually just for coffee with you. But it's the same when I'm out on shoots. The meals are typically catered. Then when I get back to my hotel it's just room service salads, or rabbit food, as you like to call it."

"Looking forward to the day when you can be done with modeling and just let yourself go? Eat what you want, wear sweatpants all the time, let your mustache grow out?"

Nir was saved from Nicole's response by the server coming back with their waters and Nir's cappuccino, but her eyes still flashed at him from across the table. When the young lady took out her pad, Nicole asked for the Caesar Breakfast, and Nir ordered the Philly Benedict.

Once the server walked away, Nicole grabbed Nir's hand in a tight grip and said, with mock seriousness, "Never talk about a woman's mustache."

"So, I'm just supposed to ignore it?"

Nicole leaned back. "First of all, I do not have a mustache. Second of all, yes!"

Nir put up his hands in surrender. "Fair enough. Off limits." He looked around before he continued. Even though they were careful to never "talk shop" in detail when they were out, he was still always careful of his surroundings. With them being in a crowded outdoor café patio, they would have to be extra diligent in their subject matter and word choices. "What did you think of Imri's performance today?"

"Great illustration. One of the best I've heard. But it wasn't anything I didn't already know."

"Yeah, you and everyone else in there. Except for maybe Yaron and Dima. They're more 'Me break things' than they are analytical thinkers. But Putin gunning for Israeli gas is something that most people in this café likely understand."

"Then why did you let him go on?"

"Imri's still the new guy on the totem pole. He needed the *W*. This gave him the chance to show his understanding and feel like he was educating the team. It also let the others affirm him and let him know that they recognize that he is more than just the young pretty face on the ops team."

Nicole bowed her head in reverence. "You are the Jedi master. The analyst team likes to give you a hard time about not always understanding their technical talk. But you have got wisdom those kids can't even touch."

Nir took a sip of his coffee. "I know they're just messing around, and I let them do it because I know it's how they express their respect—"

"And love…"

Nir shrugged. "Yeah, maybe. But we've got a good team. Even the ribbing with Lahav. He's able to take it well, and he knows that he's earned the respect of the ops team."

"Speaking of…Do you know where they all are right now?"

"I don't. I got that call from Efraim, and everyone but you was gone by the time I came out." Nir took another long draw from his porcelain cup.

"Dima felt badly about hitting Lahav a little too hard with that orange," said Nicole. "So, he's taking Lahav and Yossi, along with the rest of the ops team, out to some place called Taqueria for fish tacos and margaritas."

"Good to hear," Nir said. Putting down his cup, he pulled out his phone. "Give me a second."

He thumbed in a text and hit send. Five seconds later, his phone pinged a response. Nir slipped his phone back into his pocket.

"What was that?" asked Nicole.

"It's a hot afternoon after a tough mission last night. I texted Yaron to tell him that I'm paying for everyone to Uber home. The last thing I want is to be bailing anyone out of jail today. Especially Lahav. I'm sure it would be some kind of parole violation for him."

They spent the next minutes catching up on each other's lives. Nicole had gone back home to South Africa to attend her twin brother's wedding. It was a great celebration, she said, of the grace of God and the redeeming love of Jesus Christ. Nir was just happy that Christiaan had finally turned himself around, gotten himself clean, and found a great woman to settle down with. After their trainwreck of an upbringing, Christiaan and Nicole were all each other had left for family. Now that tiny sibling twosome had expanded for Nicole by a sister-in-law and a niece and nephew, all of whom she loved like she had known them her whole life.

They talked Milan and Antwerp, photo shoots and diamonds, *CSI* and *Fauda* until the food came out.

After the server walked away, Nicole pointed to his plate and said, "That is not breakfast."

"What are you talking about? It's the Philly Benedict, as in eggs Benedict. What could be more breakfasty than eggs Benedict?"

"It is quite literally a cheesesteak sandwich with two fried eggs on it. That is lunch."

"No, the eggs qualify it as a breakfast food. Look at the rule book."

"Nir, it comes with a side of French fries."

He examined his plate. "Okay, you got me there. But you're not really one to talk. Your Caesar breakfast is nothing but a Caesar salad with a hardboiled egg."

"Busted," laughed Nicole. "So, we came to the best breakfast place in Israel, and we both ended up ordering lunch. By the way, I didn't even know you could get a cheesesteak in Israel. Isn't that against some kosher law?"

"This is Tel Aviv. You're about as far away from the Talmud here as you are from the moon. As for me, I haven't been kosher since I left the kibbutz." Taking his knife and fork, Nir sliced his eggs into ribbons, letting the yolks run down into his sandwich. Then he cut off a piece and put it into his mouth.

"Oh, that is so good," he said as he chewed. "Want a taste?"

"I'll pass. I like my arteries to be totally free from obstruction."

Nir laughed as he took another bite. Then, putting down his utensils, he lowered his voice and, mindful of their public setting, said, "Okay, change of subject. I need to know before we move any farther forward with our little trip to Central Europe—are you sure you're good with this? I mean, no one wants you to do anything, you know, like sexual or anything. But you are being asked to use your, um, you know, your assets to get our friend's attention."

"That was quite likely the most awkward sentence you've ever spoken to me," Nicole said with a chuckle. "You're asking if I'm comfortable being a honeypot."

"No. I mean, yes…kind of. But no, not in the traditional 'sleep with the guy' meaning. Of course, not that at all."

"But you still want me to use my assets, as you call them."

Nir focused on his plate as he cut another piece of his sandwich. "Well, I mean, yes. But not in any bad way. It's just…" Nir dropped his knife and fork again without taking the bite. "*Oy vavoy*, Nicole. Could you make this any more difficult?"

She was laughing now. "I'm sorry, *motek*. I'm just having fun. It's not often I get to see you squirm."

"*Motek*? Oh, *mon cheri*. You know how I love it when you speak Hebrew to me," he said, reaching his hand toward hers and bouncing his eyebrows.

"Stop." Still laughing, she slapped his hand. "Now you're making me squirm. I appreciate your concern, Nir. Really, I do. But honestly, I don't know how I feel about our trip. I think I'm okay, but I'll know better when it's all over. It's quite possible I'll get to the end and say, 'Nope, never doing that again.'"

Picking up her fork, she rolled a crouton to the side of her plate as she thought, then followed with a second. Nir watched, wondering whether the little seasoned chunks of dried bread were up for grabs or if he needed to ask first. Nicole continued, "As for 'using my assets,' I guess it's no different than modeling. I hope this doesn't sound obnoxious, but I didn't make myself this way. God did. He gave it to me, and He could take it away at any moment. So, I figure that as long as I still have it, I have a responsibility to use it to serve Him. Whether it's in situations like we're about to go into, or it's for modeling that helps, you know…" she mouthed the words *keep my cover*, "I figure that as long as I'm using it to help Israel, I'm doing the right thing." Following his eyes, she said, "Take them."

"Your thinking makes sense," he said as he took her plate and dumped the dressing-drenched croutons onto his own.

Taking the plate back from him, she said, "I may be a Gentile, but

I love Israel. Not just because it's become a second home, but because of my faith. I know God loves Israel, so I love Israel and I'll keep doing what I can to protect the nation. Then, once I get too old to model or do fieldwork, I'll just hang out with the gang in CARL, talk about old times, and grow out my moustache."

Nir grinned. "I love a woman with a plan."

CHAPTER 11

Nicole's finger slowly traced circles on the rim of her cocktail glass. A man with a French accent wearing an undoubtedly ridiculously expensive Ferragamo suit was walking away from her to a table where his two laughing friends were waiting for him. He was the fourth gentleman who had slid into the open seat next to her at the bar. This one had wanted to know what a beautiful woman like her was doing all alone on such an enchanted night. Politely, she had told him that she was waiting for somebody. Thankfully, at posh places such as the Múzsa bar in Budapest's five-star Four Seasons hotel, it seemed the men usually accepted defeat with grace and moved on.

As planned, a couple vacated two seats at the bar when she had first arrived, and, as she sat down, she had adjusted her short dress. She was wearing a black Dolce & Gabbana heavy lace cocktail dress with a three-quarter sleeve. Christian Louboutin was on her feet and her Bottega Veneta Knot clutch went onto the bar next to her. Nicole's hair was down, and her low-hanging earrings held large sapphires surrounded by several carats worth of diamonds. She had no idea how much they were worth, but Nir had insisted that she wear them and had asked Mila Wooters, his executive assistant at Yael Diamonds, to have them shipped in from his office in Antwerp.

When the bartender had asked her what she would like, she told him to give her something that he thought fit her. A few minutes later, he placed a shallow cocktail glass in front of her filled with an iridescent orange liquid.

"We call it the Sunglow," he said.

"It's beautiful. What makes it shine?"

"Passion fruit and saffron give it the amazing color. The shimmer comes from lemongrass bubble."

Slowly, Nicole turned the glass's stem between her fingers, trying to figure out what in the world a lemongrass bubble was. "It's perfect. Thank you."

Now, she took another small sip, enough to prove to anyone watching that she truly had a reason to be there, and recommenced tracing circles. While the Gresham Palace was at least a century old, Nicole guessed that Múzsa was part of a recent remodel project that had eventually taken over the hotel's lobby. The check-in desk had been pushed back into a corner, along with the concierge. In its place, the mosaic floor was covered with various Art Nouveau seating areas specially designed for intimacy. This closeness was somehow accomplished despite being covered by a high iron and glass vaulted ceiling, surrounded by stained glass, and lit by an immense Preciosa chandelier.

Nicole clapped politely as, on a stage to her right, a jazz pianist finished a tune and moved on to the next. The man at the keyboard smiled and nodded at Nicole. She smiled back, then returned to her glass. As she did, she saw the man she had been waiting for. Clean-shaven, with tight white hair, fleshy lips, and pale blue eyes that could be beautiful if they were in a different face, General Sergei Sergeyevich Bogdanov with his two bodyguards approached the hostess. All three had left their uniforms behind and were wearing dark suits.

One of the bodyguards said something to the hostess, who smiled and led them to a table surrounded by three plush chairs. Removing a

"Reserved" sign, she said something to the men, then retreated to her post. Soon, a server stopped at the table and took their order.

Nicole observed all of this by looking at the mirror that was positioned behind the top-shelf liquor bottles. Her seat had been specifically chosen by a small team of analysts back at Mossad headquarters once they had found out which table had been reserved for the general. These three female agents, who called themselves the honey gals, knew everything there was to know about how to bait, hook, and reel intended targets into their little honey traps. This included the perfect bar seat that would show off Nicole's best view as she slowly traced circles on her cocktail glass.

There were a lot more tricks those women wanted to tell me about. Way more information than I wanted, Nicole thought as she fought to hold back a grin. *Okay, Lord, I've prayed this through. This is for the saving of lives. You know how I love your people, and I think I'm doing the right thing for them. If I'm not, then please forgive me. I'm certainly not meaning to do anything against You.*

The minutes passed. Once, as she was looking around, she allowed her eyes to pass by Bogdanov's table. He was watching her. He nodded, and Nicole gave a small smile then turned back to her drink.

Bait is out. Time to set the hook.

With her left hand, she let her fingernails roll three times on the bar top. Then she waited. Two minutes later, a man approached her and slid into the chair next to her.

"Are you a working girl or are you just lonely?" he said. His breath reeked of alcohol, and he had a slight slur to his speech.

Nicole ignored him.

"Whatever you are is fine by me. I'm rich, so I can guarantee that you'll get paid either way," he said with a laugh.

She turned to him and said, "Leave now." There was anger and a little fear in her voice.

"Come on, sweetheart. I'm in one of the river-view suites. Why don't you come up and check out the scenery?" His hand grasped her bare thigh, and Nicole gasped.

"Hey, knock it off," said a bartender striding in their direction.

In a flash, the man became irate and pointed at the bartender. "Don't take another step, buddy. Do you know who I am? I could buy a serving boy like you three times over."

A hand suddenly came down on the man's shoulder. The drunk flinched under its grip. Nicole followed the arm back and saw the profile of Sergei Bogdanov. The general leaned close to the man and began whispering to him. Nicole couldn't hear what was being said, but at one point, Bogdanov nodded toward his bodyguards, who were still sitting at their table, and the man's eyes got very wide. Finally, the general straightened back up.

"I am very sorry, ma'am," said Nicole's unwanted suitor as he stood. "I become a fool sometimes when I drink. I didn't mean to offend. I'm so very sorry." Then the Hungarian man, who at their preoperational meeting had introduced himself to her as Péter, slunk out the door.

Bogdanov turned to Nicole. "I am very sorry for that, madam," he said in heavily accented English. "Is there anything I can do to make up for this incident?"

In a flustered voice, Nicole said, "No. Thank you. For your help, thank you."

"I am at your service," he said with his head inclined.

But when he turned to walk back to his table, Nicole said, "Wait."

CHAPTER 12

21:45 (9:45 PM) CEST

Sergei Bogdanov stopped and turned back to Nicole.

"I'm sorry, I'm not thinking clearly. I'm just a little shaken. Maybe you could join me for a drink, just so I could say thank you," she said, indicating the open seat next to her. "It would be my treat."

Smiling, the general slid onto the stool next to her. "If I ever let a distressed woman pay for my drink, my father would disown me, and my mother would turn her pictures of me toward the wall. I am Sergei," he said, holding out his hand.

Nicole took it. "I'm Nicole, and I certainly wouldn't want to deprive your mother from looking at your face."

"Would you like another?" he asked, nodding to her drink.

Nicole gave a small grimace. "No, thank you. It's beautiful to look at, but it's too sweet for my tastes. What would you recommend?"

"Hmmm…have you ever tried pálinka?"

Nicole laughed. "I've never even heard of it."

"Ah, I think you'll like it. It's a traditional Hungarian fruit brandy. They have an exceptional taster flight here with plum, apricot, and sour cherry."

Not good. Nir said to be careful with the alcohol consumption. But Bogdanov seems like he wants the role of teacher, which the honey gals said is a good thing. Gives them a sense of authority and strokes their pride.

"Sounds perfect."

Bogdanov signaled the bartender over and ordered. Then he said to Nicole, "I'm detecting an accent. South Africa?"

"Guilty. Cape Town, born and raised. And with a name like Sergei, I'm guessing you're Russian. I must admit, I haven't met too many Russians before."

Bogdanov stretched his arms out. "And what do you think?"

"You don't seem quite as scary as some people make you out to be. At least not to me. That drunk idiot sure seemed scared of you. What did you say to him?"

"I told him that it is not proper to be impolite to beautiful women," he said with a wink.

Nicole laughed. "So, it's okay to be impolite to ugly women?"

"Good question. I guess it depends on how ugly they are."

Several minutes passed as Bogdanov educated her about the hotel. He was well versed in its history, architecture, and interior design. When the bartender returned with the pálinka, Nicole said, "I feel bad for your two friends. Should we invite them over?"

"No, it's okay. They work for me."

"Interesting. Are you some sort of businessman? No, wait. Are you one of those mega-rich Russian oligarchs everyone talks about?"

Bogdanov laughed. "No. No oligarch. I have money, but heaven save me from that kind of money. You have heard the saying 'More money, more problems'? Never is that truer than with the oligarchs. No, I am just a businessman. In town for a few days before I go back home to Moscow. And you, why are you here in beautiful Budapest?"

Interesting that he's lying about who he is, Nicole thought. *Maybe he was testing me, seeing if I gave any indicator that I knew he was lying. I hope I didn't. Come on, Nicole, stay sharp!*

"I'm just in town from Milan for a couple days for a photo shoot," she said.

"Why am I not surprised to hear that you are a model?"

Nicole looked down demurely. "Anyway, my agent, Fabiola, received a panicked call from a client. The girl they had booked came down with some sort of flu and they needed a last-second replacement.

Somehow, Fabi talked them into doubling my usual fee and putting me up in a suite at this amazing hotel."

"Wow. Well, here's to good agents," Bogdanov said, lifting the first of the three small glasses on his flight. Nicole lifted the same from hers, clinked his glass, and sipped the brandy. It tasted like she had lit a piece of dried apricot on fire, then swallowed it.

"It's good," she said with a gasp.

The general laughed. "Try one of the chocolates they gave you. It will clear your palate."

The next two hours passed as they talked. Nicole had to admit that the man was charming and could be quite funny. *If he wasn't a womanizing murderer who liked to torture people, I could get to like him*, Nicole thought bitterly. *Play the role, but never forget who he is. You can't feel guilty or have any hesitation about what's in store for this criminal.*

As Bogdanov continued to drink, he became increasingly handsy and suggestive in his comments. Thankfully, his touches only went to her shoulders and her arms, but that was still enough to give her the creeps. Even though Nicole had spent the last 90 minutes nursing the glass of wine that had replaced the fruit brandy, her demeanor was becoming progressively more tipsy and more ditzy. When he began talking about how amazing the view was from his suite, she decided that he was ready for the next step in the plan.

Oh Lord, I'm scared. Protect me. And help me to do what needs to be done.

"*Seryozha*—that's how you say it, right? *Seryozha*, do you know the best thing about modeling?"

"Tell me, *Nika*."

"The money," she said, then burst out laughing. "The crazy tons of money. I'm serious. They actually pay me to sit around and look pretty. I remember when I was younger and I had the sudden thought, 'You know, I'm going to sit around and look pretty anyway. I might as well get paid for it.'"

Bogdanov joined in her laughter.

"And they pay me so much money, it's stupid. Look at my earrings. Do you see them, *Seryozha*?" She pulled her hair back with her right hand, and as she did, she swiped her index finger behind her ear. Then, letting her hair drop, she leaned forward and grabbed both his hands. "Those are sapphires and real diamonds. All from sitting around and looking pretty."

The general pulled his hands back. On his right hand was a bright red scratch. "My little pussycat, I think you got me with one of your claws."

"Oh my gosh," she cried out, looking at her left hand. "Sergei, I'm so sorry. I have a crack in my nail. That's so embarrassing."

"Nonsense, *Nika*. It's just a tiny scratch."

Nicole stood and lifted her clutch from the bar. "Give me one minute. I'm going to go take care of it. Will you wait for me? Then when I'm back, maybe we can talk about relocation plans," she said with a smile.

"I'll be here, *dorogaya*."

Hurrying into the bathroom, Nicole went to the third stall and locked the door behind her. Using her left hand, she reached behind the commode and removed a small bag that had been affixed to it. Keeping her right hand as far away from her body as possible, she brought her left hand to her mouth, grasped the top of the ziplock with her teeth, and slid it open, trying not to cringe over her lips touching something that had just been attached to a toilet.

The first item she pulled from the bag was a pair of tweezers. With her left hand, she used the small tool to pull from the pad of her right index finger a very thin, transparent piece of silicone that she laid on the porcelain. Then, removing a small bottle, she squeezed a high-powered cleanser into her hands and rubbed vigorously.

Next, she put on a pair of protective gloves and removed her right earring. In place of the typical back was one that had a thin 25-millimeter by 25-millimeter box with a magnetic flip cap. Nicole set the small box aside, then proceeded to sterilize the back of her earring and then the back of her right ear and any skin around it. She then put the silicon finger pad, the tweezers, and the back of the earring into a fresh bag. Removing her gloves, she added them also, then zipped it closed. The new bag went into the original, and after she had scrubbed her hands one more time, the cleanser went in.

There were still a few items left on her checklist. Using her clippers, she snipped off the tiny metal spike attached to the nail on her left index finger. She replaced her earring into her ear using a new back. Then she squeezed some Ahava lotion onto her hands to cover over the smell of disinfectant. Once everything was back in the bag, she reaffixed it to the back of the toilet for one of the Hungary-stationed Mossad agents to pick up later.

Nicole flushed the toilet, then walked to the sink. The bathroom was empty, so she took a moment to look in the mirror and collect herself.

I can't believe I pulled that off. Even though I pushed back against Nir for having me practice that behind-the-ear move a full 150 times, I'm so glad he did. He said that it would all be different when my adrenaline was pumping, and he was right. I needed the muscle memory.

There was another reason Nicole took a couple extra minutes. Right now, the fast-moving scopolamine-based concoction that the Mossad chemists had whipped up was passing through the skin of Bogdanov's left hand and into his bloodstream. Using the spike to scratch his right hand had been Liora's idea, and it worked perfectly. All his attention went to that hand, so any possible feeling of moisture from the chemical transfer to his left wouldn't be noticed. It also gave Nicole a good excuse to quickly go to the bathroom to give herself a good cleansing.

Soon, the chemical would have Bogdanov feeling loopy, confused, and very open to suggestion. It was this mixed-up state of mind that would open him to the idea that her suite was a much better option than his. The fact that scopolamine has also been used at times as a truth serum would come in handy once they got to her room.

Checking herself one more time, Nicole took a deep breath and slowly let it out.

We're almost there, Lord. Thank you for protecting me this far. Please take me the rest of the way.

CHAPTER 13

00:20 (12:20 AM) CEST

Ah, *Nika*, my little pussycat," Bogdanov slurred as she approached him. He was standing next to the bar with his arms open wide. "Have you tamed your claws?"

"Stop," Nicole said with a laugh, hitting his chest with her clutch so that she could avoid the hug. "I'm already so embarrassed." Then, lowering her voice, she purred, "I just wish there was some way I could make it up to you."

"Hmmm, it's hard to say. It was a grievous wound you gave to me. Maybe we could discuss your penance up in my suite."

Oh Lord, this is starting to feel dirty, she thought, pretending to consider his offer. *But I'm in so deep. Nir and the others are depending on me. Besides, this could help to save so many lives. I have to go through with this.*

Forcing a seductive smile on her face, Nicole said, "I would love to talk over this matter with you further." The general stepped closer to her. "But on one condition, *Seryozha*. We do it in my suite, not yours."

He stopped and blinked once, and then a second time. It looked like he was trying to process what Nicole had just said, but his drug-affected mind wasn't quite getting the gist.

"But *Nika*, I have beautiful rooms with an amazing view of the chain bridge."

Nicole sat back on her bar stool. "I'm sorry, darling, but I don't go to the rooms of men I've just met. Let's just say it's a lesson I learned the hard way. Besides," she said, raising her eyebrows, "I can promise you much better views inside the hotel room."

Bogdanov managed a lecherous look, even with his glassy eyes and wobbly stance. Then a frown crossed his face. "But my men not allow it. So overprotective of me."

"Really? Your men won't let you? I thought you were the boss." Nicole began to pout. "Maybe I should be inviting one of them up to my room instead of you."

"No," the general said angrily, causing some heads to turn. Then, beckoning with his hand, he called, "Oleg."

One of his men stood and walked toward him. A heated conversation began in Russian. It was obvious that Oleg was not happy about their change in plans.

Bogdanov turned to Nicole. "Please key to your room give him, so check first."

"And let the little pervert install his microphones and cameras? Not on your life. Why is this suddenly getting so complicated, *Seryozha*? I just want to spend time with you. I don't know, maybe it's not worth it." Again, she let her brow furrow and her lower lip extend.

Turning back to Oleg, the general spoke. When the bodyguard protested, Bogdanov shut him down with a few harsh words.

Returning his attention to Nicole, he extended his arm, stumbled a step, then righted himself and said, "You said view in your room. Show me."

"It's a view you'll never forget," Nicole tittered, resting her hand in the crook of his arm. As they walked toward the elevator, the two bodyguards fell in step behind them.

"Must they come?"

Bogdanov moved his other hand to rest on hers. "Only for safety, Tatia. Not inside will come."

Nicole wasn't sure who Tatia was, but she did know that if this had been a real date, she would have been out the door the moment he called her by another girl's name. She did her best to keep Bogdanov on a somewhat straight path to the elevators, and when they arrived at the lift, she used her key to choose the right floor.

Although she couldn't see Oleg and his partner as they stood behind her inside the elevator, she could feel their strength and violence.

I can't let these guys get anywhere near my room. If they hear anything, there's no telling what they'll do.

The doors opened. Nicole stepped forward, but Bogdanov remained standing where he was, staring straight ahead. Taking his hand, she said, "We're here, *Seryozha*."

He shook his head like he was just waking up. "Oh, of course." She led him off the elevator to the hall.

When the bodyguards followed, Nicole stopped. "I am not going to have these two perverts standing outside my room with their ears pressed to the doors. There are two very comfortable chairs right here by the elevator. Tell them to wait here, so that we can have some privacy."

Obediently, Bogdanov said something to the two men in Russian. When Oleg protested once again, the general shouted an order loud enough to echo down the halls. The two bodyguards nodded and retreated to the chairs.

Nicole took Bogdanov's arm. "Thank you, my darling."

The general mumbled something in reply. She led him down the hall to her room, pressed the key to the lock, and opened the door. As soon as she had taken three steps inside, she heard rustling behind her. She turned and saw Yaron closing the door as István, one of the two Hungarian Mossad agents stationed in the room, inserted a syringe into Bogdanov's neck.

Dima was standing with them, and, once the syringe was removed, he and Yaron carried the general to the couch along the far wall by an immense picturesque window. A hand took Nicole's shoulder, and she spun around and into Nir's arms.

He held her tight as he whispered to her, "You did so well, Nicole. We were watching the whole time. You were amazing. You okay?"

"I'm okay," she said, with her cheek pressed against his chest. She was so relieved that she felt like crying, but she didn't want her tears to flow in front of the Hungarians. "I'm just so glad that it's over."

After a moment, she stepped back. Looking over toward the couch, she could see that Bogdanov was out cold. Yaron and Dima were busy removing his suit while Doron and Imri were in conversation with Ist-ván and the other Hungarian, Mónika.

"Why don't you go get changed?"

Nicole turned back to Nir. "What? Oh, yeah. I'll be out in a few minutes."

Leaning forward, Nir kissed her forehead. "I'm so proud of you. You did a wonderful job."

Putting her hand on his chest, she looked up into his eyes. Then she walked past him into the bedroom.

CHAPTER 14

00:40 (12:40 AM) CEST

Ten minutes had passed while the team prepared Bogdanov for his interrogation. He was now stripped down to his boxers and zip-tied to a wooden chair. István plunged another needle into his neck and emptied the syringe. Almost immediately, the Russian's head started to slowly bob.

Nir heard a sound behind him and saw Nicole stepping out of the bedroom. She was wearing a thick, white hotel robe. Her earrings were off, and her hair was disheveled.

How can she still be so beautiful even when she's trying to look like a mess? Nir wondered. He raised his eyebrows and put up his thumb. She nodded and raised her thumb. Then she moved into the kitchen, out of Bogdanov's line of sight. The man was going to be confused enough due to the chemicals in his system without having to process seeing her.

"Nir, he's ready." This was Mónika. She was going to act as interpreter. Dima was good at interpreting Russian, but this woman was a professional and would be able to keep the conversation going real time.

Nir moved in front of the man and sat down. "What's your name?" he asked, using his practiced estuary British accent. Even though the man would likely not remember a thing about this whole evening, Nir had thought that it was best to stay as undercover as possible.

When Mónika finished interpreting, Bogdanov turned to her and answered in slurred Russian.

"My name is Sergei. But you can call me *Seryozha*, my pretty little *Tatia*," Mónika said.

Nir leaned forward and gave the man a light slap to his cheek. "Hey, you're speaking to me."

The general turned and squinted. "Who are you?"

"I'm the one asking questions, not you."

"Well, that doesn't sound very fair."

"Those are the rules, *drug*. Now, tell me your full name."

Sitting straight up, he replied, "I am Sergei Sergeyevich Bogdanov, major general of the Armed Forces of the Russian Federation."

"Good, Sergei Sergeyevich. You may call me Thomas."

"Why?"

"Because that's my name."

"Oh. Very well. Thomas, do you have any vodka? I would love some vodka."

"I'll tell you what, Sergei Sergeyevich. We talk first, then vodka."

"But talk is always better after vodka."

Nir smiled reassuringly. "Don't worry, our talk will not be long. But first, I must tell you a secret."

The general leaned forward. "Secrets are good. Secrets have power."

"Yes, they do. My secret is that I am the one who destroyed all your drones in Syria, along with that other little surprise you had stored there."

"What other little surprise?" asked the general, looking genuinely confused.

"The one in the other boxes. The one for Israel."

Bogdanov smiled widely. "Oh, the missiles." Just as quickly, the smile went away. "Vladimir Vladimirovich is very mad at you."

"Yes, I suppose Putin is."

"It is President Putin. And I mean he's really, really mad at you. He said he's going to find you and—oh, I just remembered. This is wonderful. He said he would reward anyone who found out who you are. And now I've found you. You are under arrest." He tried to lift his right hand, then seemed to realize for the first time that he was restrained. "Thomas, would you mind uncuffing my hand so that I can call the president?"

"What a gift fate has given to you, Sergei Sergeyevich. You are certainly destined for glory when you turn me in. The only problem is that your phone was dead. We are charging it for you now. When it's ready, you can call Putin."

"President Putin," Bogdanov corrected once again. "And thank you. That's very kind."

"Don't mention it. In the meantime, may we get back to the missiles in Syria? Would you mind telling me what they were for?"

"To attack those sewer-dwelling Jews."

Nir saw Dima stiffen behind the general. "I think we've established that. But what is so special about those missiles? Why are they going to be used against the Jews?"

Bogdanov looked up to the ceiling, then down to the ground. Finally, he turned back to Nir. Confusion showed on his face. "I don't know."

"You don't know? You're a major general and you say you don't know? I think you're lying to me, Sergei Sergeyevich."

"Oh, I can't blame you for thinking that. I lie to a lot of people. I lie all the time."

"Are you lying now, General?"

"No, I don't think so. I'm pretty sure I'm not."

Nir took a moment to consider his next steps. "Okay, if you don't know, then who does?"

"Vladimir Vladimirovich does. But he has to because he's the president."

"Agreed. Who else knows?"

"I'm afraid I can't tell you that, Thomas." His voice lowered to a whisper, and he said, "It's a secret."

"But you do know the names?"

Sitting up straight, he replied, "I am Sergei Sergeyevich Bogdanov, major general of the Armed Forces of the Russian Federation. Of course I do."

"If you do know the names, Sergei Sergeyevich, then you must tell me."

"No. That I cannot do. I'm sorry. Now, is it time for the vodka?"

Nir snapped his fingers and motioned with his hand. Imri passed him an iPad. Nir turned it toward Bogdanov and asked, "Do you recognize what is on the screen?"

The general leaned forward to look closely. "It is dark, but that looks like my house." He began to tear up. "Oh, I miss my *Masha*. She deserves so much better than me. I'm sorry, *Masha*." Then he stopped and looked up at Nir. "Why is there a video of my house on your iPad, Thomas?"

"It is there because if you choose not to tell me the names of those who know the details about the plot against the Jews, then I am going to have my men go in and kill your family. Your wife, your poor widowed daughter, and your three cute little grandchildren."

Bogdanov's eyes grew big. "No! Thomas, what are you saying? You mustn't hurt them. They've done nothing. Oh, *Masha*." The general began to weep. Abruptly, he stopped again, then looked defiantly at Nir. "How do I know that this isn't a trick that you and your MI6 people concocted? That could be old video. I bet there's no one even near my house right now."

"Give me a number between one and five."

"What?"

"A number. Between one and five. Tell me."

"Four."

Nir nodded to Doron, who said something into a phone. A hand appeared on the screen, lit by a red light. One finger went up, then another, then another, then another.

"Oh, *Masha*," cried Bogdanov. "I'm so sorry."

"Are you ready to give me names?"

"Yes, Thomas. You are not a nice man. Instead of arresting you, I think maybe I should kill you. What do you think?"

"Let's discuss that after. I need you to understand, Sergei Sergeyevich, that if you lie to me, your family will die. You now know that I can get to them at any time, right? They will bear the punishment for your deceit, and I will let you live to bear the guilt."

"I know. I will not lie." He paused a moment and took a deep breath. "There may be others, but the ones I am certain of who know of the plan to strike the Jews are Chief of the General Staff Konstantin Belousov, Director of the FSB Anatoly Baluyevsky, First Deputy Director of the FSB General Gennady Pochinok, Deputy in the Ministry of Defense General Leonid Moshev, and Chief of Armaments of the Ministry of Defense Yegor Oreshkin."

"That's it?"

Bogdanov nodded.

"What about Surovikin? What about your boss Chaiko?"

"They probably know. I am only telling you ones that I am sure of."

"And the minister of defense? Would the deputy know without his boss knowing?"

"Again, he probably knows. But I have no certainty. Besides, chain of command in the Russian forces is not as linear as one would expect."

Nir looked to Mónika, his Hungarian interpreter. "Are you giving me exactly what he is saying, or are you cleaning it up? That sounds like a pretty-well-put-together sentence for someone on scopolamine."

The interpreter flushed. "My apologies. His words are a little jumbled at times. I'm trying to make him make sense."

"Understood. Straight interpretation from here on, okay?"

The woman nodded.

"Is there anything else I need to know?"

"Please don't hurt my family."

"Is there anything else I need to know?"

"No. That is all I know."

Nir sat back. "Thank you, Sergei Sergeyevich. You have been most helpful. Would you like that vodka now?"

"Thank you. I would."

Nir nodded to István, who stepped forward and put another needle into Bogdanov's neck. Immediately, he slumped over.

"I want this room set in four minutes. Let's go."

There was a flurry of activity in the suite. Bogdanov was cut free of the chair and stretched across the couch. Two glasses of champagne were set on the coffee table, then one was tipped over. The rest of the bottle was poured down the sink before being returned to a champagne bucket filled with a mix of ice and water.

Once every trace of the team was erased from the living space, all piled into the bedroom except for Nir and Nicole. Nir put his hands on Nicole's shoulders. "Last performance. You ready?"

"Are they sure he won't remember anything about tonight? If he decided to come after an international model named Nicole, it wouldn't take him too long before he found me."

"The guys at the lab in Tel Aviv said that the stuff István gave him erases memories better than a *Men in Black* neuralyzer. And the bodyguards don't even know your first name."

Nicole chuckled. "A neuralyzer. You're such a geek. Okay, let's do this."

"Be careful, and remember, we're right behind the door."

Nir retreated to the bedroom. He heard Nicole open the front door and begin yelling outside in the hall. She sounded somewhat drunk and extremely angry.

"Hey, Chip and Dale, come get your boss! The useless piece of trash is passed out on my couch. Hurry! Chop, chop! Get him out of here!" When she spoke again, it was obvious that she was back in the room. Her volume hadn't decreased, though. "People pay me a lot of money just to take my picture. But when your boss gets to see the real thing, he can't even stay awake. Idiot! No, you better lift him all the way. A Russian who can't handle his liquor. Hah!"

The bedroom door opened, and Nicole stepped halfway in before turning around again. "Either of you commies speak English? Yeah? Okay, then listen closely. If you Russians think of coming back and doing anything to me like sending me to Siberia or poisoning me with polonium, just know that I took a picture of dear old *Seryozha* in all his glory and uploaded it to my agent. If I disappear, the picture will hit every news source from Moscow to L.A." She slammed the door again.

The ops team remained quiet while Nicole threw a few things around the bedroom. Then Doron, who was watching a camera feed of the living room, said, "We're clear. They're gone."

Quiet cheers sounded as everyone filed out of the bathroom.

Congratulations were given to all, but especially to Nicole. Nir watched with pride as she received her accolades.

I'm glad she's gotten this success under her belt. She's going to need the confidence, because what I'm going to ask her to do next is going to make this op look like a walk in the park.

CHAPTER 15

01:05 (1:05 AM) CEST

The spotters reported that Bogdanov and his bodyguards just entered his suite on the next floor," said Mónika, holding her phone. "Time for evac."

"Thank you," Nir said, reaching out to shake her hand. He did the same with István. "You and your team are true professionals. Next time you're in Tel Aviv, Goldstars are on me."

Everyone else said their goodbyes, and the Hungarian agents left the room. As Nir's team moved toward the door, he said, "Okay, you know what to do. We go in pairs three minutes apart. Yaron and Imri first, then Doron and Dima. Nicole and I will bring up the rear. Go straight to your vehicles, then on to the safe house using the predetermined *maslul* to ensure you're not being followed. We meet there by three at the latest. Questions?"

Imri half-raised his hand. "Yeah, how come you started by saying, 'You know what to do,' then you followed it up by telling us again what we're supposed to do?"

When the others voiced their agreement with Imri's question, Nir rolled his eyes and turned to Nicole. But rather than finding support, she said, "It's a fair question."

Feigning shock, Nir said, "*Et tu*, le Roux? Okay, old man, you and junior get out of here."

"See you soon," Yaron said as he and Imri exited the room.

While Nicole went into the other room for a quick change, Nir zoned in on his watch.

"Okay, guys, your turn," he said. The two men opened the door and stepped out.

"That was fast," Nir said as Nicole walked out of the bedroom.

"You've got to be able to undress and dress very quickly in my line of work."

"You mean being a honeypot?"

Nicole stopped and pointed at him. "That's not even funny, mister."

"You good?"

She answered as she walked the rest of the way to him. "I'm tired, but good. My adrenaline has been racing nonstop for the past four hours. I think my tank is finally running out."

"Understandable. Hopefully, you can find enough reserves for the next couple hours. Then you'll have most of the morning to crash at the safe house before you need to head to the airport."

"I'm good, boss," she said with a wink. "I'll stay sharp."

Nir raised an eyebrow. "Boss? Really? That's what I am to you now? Isn't boss-zoning one step below friend-zoning?"

Nicole laughed. "We've got our boss times. We've got our friend times. And we have our, well, our little-more-than-friend times. This is a boss time. It helps me to remember that I need to respect you, even in those times when you might be totally in the wrong."

"Wait, what times? Are you talking tonight? When was I in the wrong tonight?"

"Seems to me it's pretty obvious. I'd explain it to you, but this is boss time. It would be insubordinate, and possibly disrespectful."

Now Nir was curious and a little miffed. "Listen, Nicole, if I screwed up something tonight, I need to…" He trailed off when he noticed her grin.

"Sometimes you're so easy."

Nir shook his head. "I'll show you boss time." He pulled her close and wrapped her in a hug. "You really were great tonight. A true professional."

A minute passed with him holding her before he raised his wrist, then said, "Let's go."

The elevator took them to the lobby level. They walked out the back to the parking garage. István had given him a set of keys and a space number. Nir and Nicole were easily able to find their black late-model Opel Astra hatchback. The car was a tight fit for Nir, but when he slid the driver's seat all the way back, he was comfortable enough. Exiting the garage, he turned the car right onto a narrow brick street. Up ahead, all lit up, stood the century-plus old neoclassical Saint Stephen's Basilica with its great dome and two large bell towers. The top-of-the-hour chiming of one of the church's bells had helped Nir to mark the passing of time until Nicole was through with her operation. Unfortunately, at 10:00, the ringing had stopped.

After a couple more rights and a left, the two found themselves on the Széchenyi Chain Bridge crossing the Danube, leaving Pest for Buda. Once across, Nir turned north, skirting the thirteenth-century Buda Castle. This began a scripted 90-minute series of turns and backtracks that had them all over the city. Conversation remained minimal for most of the journey while Nir drove and Nicole navigated. They travelled back and forth from Buda to Pest no less than seven times before they finally came alongside a large park in the Óhegy neighborhood in the eastern suburbs.

"I thought we'd never get here," Nicole said, unplugging her phone from the car.

"I'm betting it's a beautiful city in the daytime."

"It is. The view from Buda Castle to the Danube and across to Pest is amazing."

"I should have figured you'd been here before."

"Budapest Central European Fashion Week. Only missed one since its inaugural 2018 show."

Nir shook his head. "That's right. I knew that. Been a very long day."

"Here it is," Nicole said, pointing to a series of five-story cement apartment buildings.

Nir angled the car to the curb. "Not much to look at. They've got to be holdovers from the 'function is everything' Soviet days."

Without bothering to turn off the car, the two stepped out. Immediately, a man appeared from behind a tree. He walked to the car, slipped into the driver's seat, closed the door, and drove off.

"What they lack in friendliness, they make up for in efficiency," Nir said.

Nicole laughed. Then, setting off, she said, "It's the third building right up ahead."

The others had already made themselves comfortable by the time the two arrived. They were spread out over two couches, and each had a bottle of Dreher Bak in their hands.

"More in the fridge," Yaron said, holding up his bottle.

"No, got a call to make," Nir said. "Wouldn't mind having you guys at least listening in."

Imri got up and lifted a laptop from the kitchen table. Handing it to Nicole, he said, "The guy who was here when I arrived said that this is connected to a secure WiFi, but I'm thinking you'll still want to do whatever wizardy encryption you normally do."

"Thanks," said Nicole, taking the laptop. Dima and Doron made room for her to sit in the center of their couch. Setting the computer down on a coffee table, she opened it, typed for about a minute, then sat back.

Nir walked over, then made as if he was going to sit on top of Doron until the Kidon agent moved. As soon as he settled in, the screen came to life.

CHAPTER 16

ÓHEGY, BUDAPEST, HUNGARY— OCTOBER 15, 2022—02:55 (2:55 AM) CEST

Nicole!" All four members of the analyst team were sitting at the conference table in CARL, smiling and waving. Open laptops sat in front of each.

"Hey guys," said Nicole, waving back.

Nir leaned in toward the laptop's camera. "Just Nicole? What am I?"

"Starving for attention?" offered Liora.

"In desperate need of affirmation?" suggested Dafna.

"Good to see you too," laughed Nir. "Okay, I forwarded you guys a list of names. Let me hear what you've got. And, Yossi, while Liora and Dafna are doing that, I want you to cross-reference each of them with a guy named Anatoly Kvashnin."

"Yeah, that's the oligarch dude with the yacht, right?" said Yossi.

"That's him. I've got the beginnings of an idea, but I need to know if Kvashnin has a connection with any of these *idyotim*."

"You got it, boss."

"What's with everyone calling me boss all of a sudden?"

"If the crown fits…" said Liora. "Okay, first guy, Konstantin Konstantinovich Belousov. He's a four star. Hero of the Russian Federation. Chechnya, Syria—he led the Battle of Izium in Ukraine in March. He's chief of the general staff and very close with Putin."

Dafna jumped in. "Born in Kazan, in what's now Tatarstan. Sixty-seven years old. Married with a son."

"Sounds untouchable," Nir said. He looked at the ops team. "What do you guys think?"

"Might as well go after Putin himself," said Dima.

Liora spoke up. "Okay, if you guys are eliminating untouchables, you should drop Anatoly Baluyevsky too. He's the director of the FSB. Might as well try to steal the Mona Lisa while you're at it."

Nir waved to Imri. "Water, please?"

"Two?" added Nicole.

"Sorry, make that two. Okay, scratch Belousov and Baluyevsky. Wasn't there another FSB guy?"

"Gennady Borisovich Pochinok," said Liora. "First deputy director. Another four star. Actually, all these guys are four stars. Saw action in all the major wars since the second Chechnya."

Nir caught a bottle of water tossed by Imri. He set it down at his side so he could catch the second one. He cracked its seal and passed it to Nicole. "Thanks, *achi*. So, Dafna, family?"

"Again, wife and son. He's sixty. Well known to have mafia ties."

"The mafia in Russia? Shocking," said Yaron.

"*Sababa*," laughed Dafna. "But here's something to keep in mind. He's the godfather to a guy named Medoev who was awarded the Order of Saint George medal for being a special forces sniper with a crazy number of kills."

Dima shook his head. "Medoev. I've heard of that guy from a cousin of mine who does counter-piracy operations for the Russian special forces. You take out Medoev's godfather, you'll be looking over your shoulder the rest of your life."

"No one is talking about taking anybody out," said Nir. "This isn't that kind of operation. Let's keep him on the list, but way down at the bottom. Next, Liora."

"Next is Leonid Anatolyevich Moshev. Deputy in the Ministry of Defense. This guy is interesting. Even though he's a four star, he's more of a desk general. He's spent much of his time with EMERCOM, which is the Russian Ministry of Emergency Situations. If there's a

plane crash, he's there. He's also overseen a bunch of post-disaster res-
torations, like cleaning up the massive oil spill in the Kuril Islands after
the 1994 earthquake. That kind of stuff."

Dafna added, "Married with three daughters. Born in Krasnoyarsk.
Sixty-six years old. Moshev's fun fact of the day—he was one of the six
Russians sanctioned by the EU for the cholinesterase inhibitor poison-
ing of outspoken Putin opponent Alexei Navalny."

"Choni-terri-who?" asked Nir.

With a heavy sigh, Lahav said, "Cholinesterase inhibitor. It prevents
the breakdown of certain neurotransmitters. If given in high dosages,
it can cause nausea, vomiting, hypotension, coma, and death. Duh."

"There are a lot of 'duh' things in this world. That is not one of them,"
Nir said defensively.

"Navalny recovered, didn't he?" asked Imri.

Dima answered, "He did, but Putin's arrested him again and has
him back in Penal Colony Number Two in solitary confinement. I
hope Navalny has his life insurance paid up, because I don't think he's
going to be around much longer."

"And what was our friend Moshev's role in this whole thing?" Nir
asked.

"Don't know," said Dafna. "But if he was one of only six to be sanctioned, then the EU had to have something connecting him."

"Okay, dig some more into him. He's interesting. Last guy, Liora?"

"Yegor Aleksandrovich Oreshkin. Like the rest, he's a four star. Chief
of armaments of the ministry of defense. Another desk general. He's
mostly involved in military procurement."

"Like missiles?" asked Nir hopefully.

"Missiles. Really, any type of weapon. He's probably right in the
middle of Russia's drone acquisitions from Iran."

"So, he's probably not too thrilled with what you guys did in Syria,"
said Nicole. "Seems like he's a good possibility."

"He does," said Nir. "Dafna?"

"Fifty-seven years old. Born in Dushanbe in the Tajik SSR. Wid-
ower with a son and a daughter."

"Fun facts?"

"His deceased wife has family in Petah Tikva."

Nir sat up. "Really? Is he Jewish?"

"Doesn't look like it. I don't believe the wife was either. Looks like her uncle married a Jewish woman whose parents later made *aliyah*."

"Interesting." Nir took a long swig from his water bottle. "Yossi, how are you coming with the Kvashnin connections? Does this Oreshkin guy know him?"

"Not that I can see," answered Yoshi. "But again, I've had about fifteen minutes to look. There are three who know him for sure. Belousov—"

"The untouchable," said Doron.

"Pochinok—"

"The mafioso," said Lahav.

"With the sniper godson," added Nicole.

"And Moshev, the failed assassin."

"The fact that he's a failed assassin makes him a little more appealing," said Dafna.

Nir pointed at the screen with his bottle. "I also like the fact that he's a desk jockey. That might make him a bit softer of a target than some battle-hardened Chechen War veteran."

"Agreed," said Imri. "But, still, how do you plan on going against someone like this? When you hit four-star status in Russia, you essentially live with immunity and you can act with impunity. Am I right, Dima?"

The Russian Jew acknowledged Imri with a tilt of his beer bottle.

Nir leaned back into the couch. "Guys like Moshev may not be afraid of opposition or prosecution, but I guarantee you there is one thing he and all the other generals are afraid of. Dima?"

"Vladimir Vladimirovich Putin."

"*Yoffi*, you got it. Putin is the new tsar of Russia. It doesn't matter who you are or what position you're in, he can take you down. It may not be immediate, it may not be public, but he can and will do it."

"Exactly," said Dima. "But unlike his predecessors, who just took their opponents to Lefortovo Prison and shot them, Putin's biggest weapon is the courts. It's like when I told you Navalny is back in prison.

It's on some trumped-up fraud and extortion charge that will keep him there for years. Often, though, Putin will just charge people with crimes that everyone else in the country is doing too. Like, in Russia, there is a social distinction between bribery and extortion. Bribery is expected. It costs money to make money. But extortion is frowned upon. So, bribery is everywhere, and extortion is rare. If Putin wants to get someone, he'll change the rules and suddenly bribery will become a crime again. Any of you ever hear of Nikita Belykh?"

"Governor in one of the Volga District oblasts, right?" said Lahav.

"Exactly. Score one for Tabib," said Dima. "Belykh was governor in Kirov Oblast, appointed by Putin's errand boy, Dmitry Medvedev. But before he had become governor, he headed the Union of Right Forces party that was in opposition to Putin's government, a party that had been started by Boris Nemtsov."

"Nemtsov was an opponent that Putin took care of the old-fashioned way. He had him assassinated on a bridge near the Kremlin," added Lahav.

"Now, Putin has a long memory, and the time finally came when he wanted to get Belykh out of the way. So, six or seven years ago, he had him charged with accepting a four-hundred-thousand-euro bribe at a restaurant in Moscow. Again, this is something that happens every day in every level of the Russian government. But when Putin wanted someone gone, suddenly bribery became illegal again, temporarily. The governor was convicted and sentenced to eight years in prison. Another opponent bites the dust."

"What a turd," said Lahav.

"Elegantly put, Lahav," said Liora. "So, Moshev, like everyone else, is afraid of Putin. I'm not sure how that helps us. The president doesn't have any reason to be angry at him."

"But what if he does? What if we were to discover that Moshev actually is betraying his bare-chested, horse-riding friend?" asked Nir.

Dafna grimaced. "Thanks for the visual. Finding out that Moshev is betraying Putin is *chai b'seret*; it's a huge long shot. I mean, the guy tried assassinating one of Putin's opponents."

"But is it really a long shot? I think that it is very likely that Moshev is secretly working against Putin. In fact, his betrayal is so secret that I doubt even Moshev knows about it. At least not yet," Nir said with a mischievous grin.

The grins spread around the safe house and across more than a thousand miles to CARL.

Dima drained the last of his beer, then said, "I don't know exactly what idea is in that evil little head of yours, *achi*, but I do know that I already like it."

CHAPTER 17

Nir, who was now seated at the kitchen table, closed the lid to the laptop and pushed himself back. Balling his hands into the small of his back, he stretched until he was looking up at the ceiling. He held the pose for a count of ten before straightening up and walking to the refrigerator. He scanned the contents and saw one more beer.

After drawing it out, he pried off the cap using an opener affixed to the wall, then caught the cap before it fell into a small aluminum collection bin that looked like it hadn't been cleared out for a decade. Although the chances were slim that the sound of a cap falling on caps would wake one of the four men sleeping just a few meters away, it just felt like the courteous thing to do.

Nir returned to his chair and sat. While everyone else had crashed out more than an hour ago, he had spent the time talking to Deputy Director Asher Porush and Assistant Deputy Director Efraim Cohen. Nir was glad to have gotten them both on the line right away despite the hour so that he didn't end up wasting half of today trying to get permission for his plan. Neither of his superiors were thrilled with the direction he wanted to go, but they understood that sometimes the only way to get to a wolf is through other wolves.

Porush had greenlighted the operation, then Nir had spent the rest of the call time letting Efraim poke holes in his plan. Efraim had a great gift for "What if…?" Loose ends, possible twists, unexpected turns, Efraim could sniff most of them out ahead of time. This enabled Nir to go into an operation not only with Plan *Alef*, but also Plan *Bet*, Plan *Gimel*, Plan *Dalet*, all the way down to Plan *Tav*.

Nir put the bottle to his lips and took a deep draw. The dark, bitter bock felt thick going down, and it settled uncomfortably in his stomach. He scanned the kitchen for something to eat, some pretzels or bread, but there was nothing.

A noise caught his attention. The door to the single bedroom opened, and Nicole peeked out. She smiled when she saw Nir, and he waved her over. She walked quietly across the room in the dim light, almost stepping on Imri, who had stretched out on the floor.

When she arrived next to Nir, she nodded toward the bottle. "When they say, 'It's five o'clock somewhere,' they usually mean p.m."

He slid the bottle away. "It was a force-of-habit choice."

Nicole opened the fridge. "We've got water, juice, and Gatorade."

"I'll take a Gatorade. Don't care what color. Is there anything in there to eat?"

Nicole looked around. "No, but I think we've got some stale, packaged pastry thing in one of the cupboards."

"Sounds appealing. Would you mind cutting me a piece?"

Nicole tossed him a plastic bottle filled with a pale blue liquid. "What did the deputy director say?"

"He gave it a thumbs up. Then Efraim and I fine-tuned it for a bit."

"And they were good with you doing it alone?"

Nir took a long sip. "Not really. But there isn't any other option. If Kvashnin gets any sense that I've brought a team with me, he'll shut down, and I might end up buried in one of his big piles of fertilizer."

Nicole set a paper plate holding a large piece of cherry torte in front of Nir. She followed with a napkin, plastic fork, and plastic knife. "How confident are you that that's not going to happen anyway?"

Ignoring the utensils, he lifted the pastry and took a bite. "Wow, that is the polar opposite of good."

Nicole sat. "Couldn't find an expiration date. It looked a little dry."

He took another bite, then set the pastry down. "It's like the Sahara and the Gobi had a baby."

"Sorry, it's all we have. Now, back to my question that you so deftly deflected. How confident are you that the fertilizer magnate isn't going to take one look at you and have his little mini-garchs bury you in a mound of ammonium nitrate?"

Nir laughed. "Mini-garchs. I'll have to remember that one. Of course, there's a risk. Kvashnin is an oligarch, so he has a little touch of psycho to him. But more than anything else, he's a businessman in a very competitive business. He'll know that I represent an opportunity for him to lessen the impact of one of his competitors."

"So, he'll ask you to kill someone."

"He might. I'll refuse that. I'm not a hired assassin. But there are other ways to cause a shake-up in a company."

"Like…?"

Nir took another bite of the torte, then pushed it away. "I don't know. I'm not a businessman. I'll leave that to Kvashnin."

A sour waft from the beer reached Nir. He snatched up the bottle, walked to the sink, and tipped it over. A voice behind him called softly, "Are you pouring out a perfectly good beer?"

Imri was walking to the table.

"It wasn't a perfectly good beer. It was a Dreher Bak," said Nir, draining it out.

"Still, that's just wrong. Anyone mind?" Imri retrieved the torte from the middle of the table and took a bite. "Good night! That's drier than Ezekiel's bones."

Nir retrieved a Gatorade from the fridge and tossed it to Imri. "You're going to need that."

When Nir sat back down, Imri suddenly looked at the other two with wide eyes. "I'm sorry. Am I interrupting anything?"

Nicole reached over and put her hand on his arm. "No, you're fine. Which reminds me—how is it going with you and Liora?"

"Okay, I suppose. Her parents hate me. My mom thinks she's 'cute as a button,'" Imri said, imitating his mom's voice at the end.

"Understandable on both counts," said Nir.

"Ignore him," said Nicole, giving Nir a dismissive wave. "I think you and Liora seem great together. You should hear her go on about you."

"She does, huh?" Imri grinned. Then he asked, "So, what were you two talking about?"

"We were just discussing Nir being buried in a giant mound of ammonium nitrate," she answered.

"Interesting. You two really are a renaissance couple."

Nir rolled his eyes. "I'm not going to be buried in fertilizer. Kvashnin is going to see me as a chance to stick it to someone he hates, and all it will cost him is an introduction to General Moshev."

"And once we get to Moshev, you think that we will be able to convince him to tell us about the attack on Israel? I guess I still don't fully understand why he would," said Nicole.

"It's all about self-preservation. Russia operates on paranoia from the top down. Putin is paranoid that the political and business elites and the generals are plotting against him. And all those people are paranoid that Putin will think that they're plotting against him."

"Are there people plotting against him?"

"There are," said Nir. "Now more than ever. Last week, Efraim arranged for me and him to have coffee with a guy name Yaakov Kedmi."

"You met with Kedmi? Wow," said Imri.

To Nicole, Nir said, "Kedmi was born and raised in Moscow, then made *aliyah* in 1967 when he was twenty. For a while in the nineties, he headed Nativ, which helps Jews immigrate to Israel from Eastern Bloc countries. He knows Putin personally and is one of the few people that the president trusts because Kedmi's able to look at Putin with an unbiased eye."

Imri jumped in. "He's a regular panelist on Russian news shows, and sometimes he shows up on Israeli television too."

"And Kedmi says that people are plotting against Putin?" asked Nicole.

"He does," said Nir, getting up. "Hang on."

CHAPTER 18

05:00 (5:00 AM) CEST

Nir walked to where Dima was stretched out on a couch. Giving him a little shake on the shoulder, he whispered something. The big man nodded, then followed Nir into the kitchen, where they both sat down.

"We were just talking about factions in Russia," said Nir. "Thought it would be worth adding you into the discussion."

As he spoke, Nicole got up and retrieved a Gatorade from the fridge for the Russian. "*Spasibo*," Dima said, taking the bottle from her. "Anyone eating this?"

"It's all yours," Imri said, sliding the paper plate holding the remaining pastry. He winked at Nir.

Dima took a large bite. "Mmmm, not bad. You told them what Kedmi said to you?" In two more quick bites, he stuffed the rest of the torte into his mouth.

"Just about to. Right now, Putin is in a tough place because of the war. The elites—these are the billionaire businessmen, the high-level politicians, and the generals—are divided into two camps. On one side you have the hawks. They want to keep unleashing holy hell on Ukraine until Zelenskyy finally gives up."

Still chewing, Dima said, "The new big leader of this group is

Yevgeny Prigozhin. He's the guy who started the mercenary Wagner Group."

"Like that Livanov guy you picked up in Syria," said Nicole.

"Exactly," said Dima, cracking open the bottle of Gatorade. "Prigozhin's outside the government, so he has no oversight. A lot of those in the governmental system are nervous of him because he's got such a strong grip on Putin's ear. But the president needs to keep his eye on Prigozhin and his Wagner lunatics. They are constantly complaining about being undersupplied and disrespected by Putin and the military. I wouldn't be surprised to see that mad dog rise up one day and bite the hand that feeds it."

"Very true. You've also got a lot of politicians on the hawk side," said Nir. "Then there are Putin's other close advisors, like the Kovalchuk brothers. One's a billionaire and the other is some kind of physicist. But he trusts them. Then you also have the crazies like Ramzan Kadyrov, the Chechen leader."

"That dude is flat-out nuts," said Imri.

"And these are the people that Putin trusts?" asked Nicole.

"To an extent," answered Dima. "Even in this group, he has to be wary. Some of the hawks are hoping that victory in Ukraine will lead to a whole restructuring of Russia's economy and political system. They'll keep supporting Putin as long as Putin supports the war."

"Got it. So, what about the other side?"

Nir answered, "The other side are the pragmatists. These are mostly technocrats, businessmen, and lower-level military and police. They see the economic and human cost of the war, and they're wanting Putin to pause the action and reevaluate. Most of them don't see a path to a Russian victory, and they want to find a way for the country to cut its losses and pull out with dignity."

"And what does the ordinary citizen want?" asked Nicole. "Or does that still not matter in Russia?"

"Putin has two things going for him when it comes to popular opinion," said Nir. "First, he has the media. The Kremlin makes sure that all the war news is favorable so the people don't hear the truth."

Dima interrupted. "That's true for the mainstream news. But just like in the West, the news culture is changing. A lot of people have begun to look for their information on social media. Hundreds of Telegram channels critical of the war have been started over the past months by military officers and *voenkory*."

"*Voenkory*. I don't know that word," said Nir.

"It's a holdover from Soviet times. The *voenkory* are war correspondents. A lot of them have embedded themselves into military units. Some have upward of a million subscribers. They're opening a lot of Russian eyes to what is really going on in Ukraine."

"You're going to have to set me up on some of those channels," said Nir. "But, even if there are dissenting media voices, that brings me to the second huge advantage for Putin. That is the citizenry's tsar mentality."

Dima laughed. "Truth! 'The tsar is good; it is his *boyars* who are bad.'"

"*Boyar*?" asked Nicole.

Nir answered, "A *boyar* was a high-up member of the nobility under the feudal system. They were like the level of leadership just under the tsar. The Russian default setting is autocracy. Remember, 'tsar' is just the Slavic way of saying 'Caesar.' That is the attitude that permeates the soul of the everyday citizen. They want their freedom, but they want it in the context of their *tsar-batiushka*. Did I say that right?"

Dima nodded. "*Tsar-batiushka*. Their 'dear father.' The one in the government that they can be sure of to uphold their rights and to understand their needs. 'We may have a good republic, but we must have a good tsar at its head.' That is why the West will never understand the Russian mind. They think only with their Western mindset. 'Why would the Russians not want freedom? Why would they not want citizen rule? What about the rights of the individual?' They forget that Russia is not just Europe. It is Europe and Asia. It is West and East. 'We will accept democracy, as long as it fits into our autocracy.'"

Nicole waved her hand in front of her. "Okay, I think I'm getting it. Some of the elites may be turning against Putin, but he still has the hearts of 150 million people on his side. And even when they may hear that the war is going poorly, he's not held responsible, because..." She pointed to Dima.

"Because 'The tsar is good; it is his *boyars* who are bad.'"

"Got it. But Putin has eyes. He sees that the war is not going well. He sees the Russian casualties building. Is it possible that Putin will see the light and pull out of Ukraine?"

"Dima?" Nir asked. When the Russian shrugged and shook his head, Nir said, "First thing to remember is that the Russian military is not built on quality. It is built on quantity. That's always been true. Just look at the military death toll in World War II. The rising number of dead in Ukraine doesn't weigh as heavily on the minds of the Russian generals as it does in the West. But will he pull out? Anything is possible. Here's what I know about Putin. He believes in Kievan Rus. This is the original kingdom from which Russia, Ukraine, and Belarus were all born in the ninth century. One people, one history. It wasn't until about seven hundred years later, when there was some treaty between Ukrainian Cossacks and the Poles with the tsardom somehow fitting into the mix, that anything resembling a separate entity of Ukrainian people can trace its roots."

"The Cossack Hetmanate," said Dima.

"Yeah, what he said."

The Russian continued, "But despite the Hetmanate and a few hundred years of history, Putin and many Russians will still say that we all have the same roots and the same ethnic identity. We are Big Russia; Ukraine and Belarus are Little Russia. By the way, don't be surprised if you see a willing annexation of Belarus to Russia soon. President Lukashenko is such a Putin worshipper that he'll probably just hand the country over."

Nicole was shaking her head. "I don't get it. How can Putin and his cronies look at the last four hundred years of Ukraine's history and say it doesn't exist?"

Nir answered. "First of all, the actual name *Ukraine* as a recognized political entity is only about one hundred years old, and seventy-some-odd of those years was as a Soviet Socialist Republic. But secondly, it doesn't matter what history says. In Russia, history says what you want it to say."

"An old Soviet joke goes, 'Russia is a country where the future is certain; it's only the past that is unpredictable,'" said Dima.

Nicole laughed. "So, you're saying that despite history and what's on modern maps, Putin doesn't see that he is invading another country. He is simply reclaiming that which already belongs to Russia. To him, this is not so much political or economic. It is moral. Reunification is the right thing to do."

"Exactly," said Nir. "Now, full circle around, because Putin still believes in the war, there are those elites who want to oust him. And even amongst those who support the war, there are some who see it as the beginning of a bigger revolution that will overhaul the Russian political system. So, our friend Vladimir is paranoid as heck, which we will exploit by informing Moshev that we have discovered his disloyalty to Putin. If he talks, we'll lose the evidence. If he doesn't talk, his treachery will be revealed and it's Lefortovo Prison for him, or maybe the president will serve him a polonium cocktail instead."

"Okay, she gets it already." The voice came from the living room. Yaron was sitting up on a couch rubbing his eyes. "I have never heard in my life so many words spoken for so long at such an ungodly hour. Don't you people ever sleep?"

"Sorry, old man," said Nir. "I forgot it takes the elderly longer to replenish their tanks."

"There you go. More words. Just stop."

Nicole laughed as she stood. "I'll go get myself ready. Then you guys can hit the shower." Looking to Nir, she said, "And, for you, there's an empty couch over there with your name on it. Try to get a little sleep. Sounds like you're going to need it."

CHAPTER 19

The Greek islands. What a nightmare, Nir thought as he looked over the beautiful sands of the Santa Marina resort's private beach. It was a little cool for sunbathing, reaching only 20 degrees Celsius this afternoon, but there were still a handful of diehards who were determined to get their daily ration of sun. *I can't fault the islands' beauty or their luxury. This is the kind of place I'd love to bring Nicole for a vacation someday. But these tiny rocks surrounded by water are an operational nightmare.*

He had spent much of the roundabout series of flights from Budapest to Mykonos attempting to plot good routes of escape in case everything went south and he had to evade law enforcement or an angry herd of Russian bodyguards. But there were no good methods. Essentially, if the airport closed to him, the only way off this 85-square-kilometer boulder was to steal a boat and try to navigate the rocky waters that surrounded it. With his miniscule amount of navigational sea training, the chances were great that he would end up at the bottom of the Aegean Sea.

But hopefully there will be no need for an escape plan. Just be polite and respectful. Kvashnin is a businessman. He'll recognize a good deal when he sees it. But just as Nir was beginning to feel a little hopeful, another thought came to his mind. *It's possible, though, that he could still be mad about the time you pointed a gun at his face. Ocean bottom, here I come.*

Several years back, the Azerbaijani government had asked for a little help dealing with an oligarch who was funding a Chechen militia. The Muslim militants were crossing the border and raiding Azeri villages. The Mossad was tasked by Israel's prime minister with convincing the oligarch that supporting violent, radical nut cases was not the best use of his finances. The oligarch was Anatoly Kvashnin, and the agent tasked with passing on the message was Nir.

One night, as Kvashnin slept on his superyacht off the shores of Cyprus, Nir showed up with Yaron. The first vision the Russian had when he was rousted from his slumber was the barrel of a gun just centimeters from his face. Nir promised the man that he would not pull the trigger if the oligarch would cut his funding of the Chechens and if he would promise to fulfill a favor to be named sometime in the future. Kvashnin had readily agreed to the deal, and the two Israelis had slipped back off the yacht as quietly as they had arrived.

Now that he was here on this island, Nir wished that, stashed away in a cove somewhere, he had one of the underwater scooters that he and Yaron had used to get to and from the yacht. But there was no scooter on Mykonos, nor did he still possess that favor promised by Kvashnin. Nir had called it in last year during an operation to get explosive-laden artwork distributed to a select group of bad guys. As he walked up the stone steps to the entrance of the Buddha-Bar Beach, he knew he was doing it empty-handed and unarmed, relying only on his charm and the oligarch's sense of reason to walk back out in one piece.

I'm doomed.

When he reached the top of the short flight of steps, he looked to his right and took in the view one more time from the secluded peninsula. Not far offshore, several small boats floated on the pale blue water. There was a time when this meeting would have taken place out in the bay in the oligarch's superyacht. But Kvashnin didn't have his superyacht anymore. Earlier in the year, the French government had seized his ship while it was moored in Marseilles. They cited EU sanctions that were placed on Kvashnin and other Russian oligarchs following the invasion of Ukraine.

Do not mention the yacht, Nir chided himself. *You will not mention the yacht.*

Turning back to the patio bar, he began scanning faces. Dafna had tracked Kvashnin's phone to this location 30 minutes ago. He spotted him halfway across the wood plank floor, lounging in a white wicker chair. Next to him sat a giggling girl who looked to be about a third of his age. His arm was around her and they were clinking champagne glasses. No one sat across the table from them, but at the next table over were two muscular men wearing tight black T-shirts and matching pants. Their eyes were locked on Nir.

It takes an operator to spot an operator.

In his mind, he nicknamed them Bentz and Arik, after two characters in an educational show he used to watch as a kid. Bentz was the big guy on the right, and Arik was the bigger guy next to him. Nir quickly thumbed a text to CARL.

Going in.

Nir was operating coms dark. Wearing a wire or an earpiece to a meeting with a shady oligarch was one good way to visit the rocky Aegean Sea bottom. If 30 minutes passed without him checking in with CARL, the analysts would raise the alarm bells. Not that it would do any good. By the time any assets could get to the island, whatever was going to happen to him would likely have already happened.

Nir's eyes met Bentz's, and he nodded toward the oligarch. Bentz said something to Arik, and they both stood. They were taller than he had thought. If he ended up in a physical altercation with these guys, he would likely be crushed like a grape. Bentz leaned down and said something to his charge. Kvashnin looked up, and Nir met his gaze. The older man lowered his sunglasses and squinted. His eyes suddenly widened, followed rapidly by his brow furling. Putting his sunglasses back on, he said something to Bentz, who began walking toward Nir. Arik followed.

As they came toward him, Kvashnin said something to the girl.

When she protested, he grabbed the back of her neck, causing her to tense up. A few more words were said by him, and she quickly stood up and exited out the other side of the long patio.

"Open shirt," Bentz said.

Nir, who was wearing a dark, untucked linen shirt and jeans, began to unbutton. This was the time of year when the Grecian air began to cool, so the bar was not nearly as full as it was during peak season. Still, there were at least six other tables that were occupied. But as he looked around, no one seemed to be paying attention to the man opening his shirt at the bar's entrance. Nir supposed that was because one of the reasons many people came to Mykonos was its reputation for being a place where anything goes. A man being asked by two other men to unbutton his shirt was likely one of the more mundane sights most visitors would see during their day.

After undoing the last button, Nir opened his shirt wide.

"Turn," said Bentz.

Nir obliged. When he was facing away, he felt hands tuck down into his waistband. He stopped his turn. The hands ran down each leg, then tucked up into his crotch.

"Turn," said Bentz. Once Nir was facing forward again, the man said, "Follow."

As the group neared the table, Kvashnin said, "My night visitor. Imagine my surprise. Please, have a seat."

A fist drove into Nir's liver, buckling his legs and sending intense pain up his right side. One of the bodyguards pulled a chair out and Nir dropped into it. Leaning forward, he tried to catch his breath.

"That was for pointing a gun at my face."

Nir inhaled three times in quick succession, then squeaked out, "Fair enough."

That settled, the billionaire businessman reached back and lifted a bottle from a stylized black ice bucket emblazoned with *Dom Perignon* in gold letters. Reaching across the table, he filled Nir's glass. Then he topped off his own before returning the bottle to its home.

"To settling old debts," said Kvashnin, holding his glass toward Nir.

"It's the Russian way." Nir clinked the man's glass. Stretching his arm sent a fresh stab of pain. He winced, but managed to get the glass to his mouth.

"Now, before you tell me why I shouldn't have you killed, will you answer a question for me? Did the fulfilling of the favor I owed you in any way make me an unwitting accomplice in a targeted killing off the shores of India?"

Still hoarse, Nir replied, "I can neither confirm nor deny."

Kvashnin clapped his hands. "Hah! I hated that guy. Always posting pictures of his indoor and outdoor pools and his stupid little mini submarine."

Yacht envy. Apparently it's a real thing, thought Nir, wisely keeping that comment as part of his inner monologue.

A smug look still on his face, the oligarch asked, "So, what brings you here, my sneaky Mossad spook? The Chechens are no longer receiving anything from me, and I can't think of any other clients from my supplementary business that would have your prime minister sending you my way."

"I need another favor."

Kvashnin stared at him, then burst out laughing. "You're serious! You point a gun at me, then you come back with your hat in your hand wanting my help? What do you think I am? Make-A-Wish? We're not friends. I'm not your godfather. I still haven't decided whether I'm going to let you leave this island or sink you in the azure waters of the Mediterranean. What makes you think I would ever do another favor for you?"

"I'd make it worth your while."

There was a new round of laughter. "How? Are you going to give me money? I already have more money than I can spend in twenty lifetimes. Then, after I die, whatever is left will end up in the hands of my two worthless sons, who will squander it all on cocaine and whores."

"I'm not offering you money. I have skills that I can offer you."

Kvashnin stopped. "Interesting. Like what?"

"You're a businessman in a very competitive market. You tell me."

Nir saw the twinkle in the old man's eyes, and he knew he had him. The Russian reached again for the champagne. When he saw that Nir's glass was still almost full, he refilled his own before returning the bottle.

He sipped from his glass, then said, "I do have several competitors whom I wouldn't mind seeing removed from the table."

"Removed?"

"Removed." Kvashnin drew his thumb across his throat.

Nir threw up his hands. "Why does everyone think I'm just some assassin? Think more creatively, Anatoly. Give me the name of one competitor you would like to be dissuaded from pursuing his business with his usual vigor. Who is someone who needs an accident to happen to his factory? Now that you've evened the score with me, who's the person that's moved to the top of your liver punch list?"

The oligarch thought and sipped. "Just one?"

"Just one."

A smile began to spread across Kvashnin's face. "Yes. Yes, I have one." Then his smile dropped. "But this is a business transaction. You have done well selling me on your product. Now, what is its price?"

"I need you to hold a party at your dacha and provide me with an introduction."

"An introduction? To whom?"

Nir shook his head. "First we agree, then you get the name."

"Actually, it doesn't matter the name," Kvashnin said, waving his hands. "It can't be done. There is a war going on. This is not a time for parties in Russia."

"Do you mean that people just stay in their houses all the time so they can think good thoughts about the soldiers at the front? People never visit each other anymore? I don't care what you call it. It doesn't have to be a party. Say it's a gathering or a discussion or a vodka tasting. Just get the person I need to your dacha, and I'll take care of the rest."

Kvashnin raised his substantial eyebrows. "You'll take care of the rest? I thought you weren't an assassin."

Again, Nir threw up his hands. "Did I say I was going to kill him? I will not make you party to a murder, Anatoly."

"You mean, you will not make me party to another murder."

Nir sighed. "I just need to talk to the man."

"And you'll do whatever I want to one of my enemies."

"Short of murder and within reason."

Now it was Kvashnin's turn to be exasperated. "Within reason? Whose reason? Mine or yours?"

"I don't know. Within basic reason. I'm not going to cut someone's arm off, Anatoly. I'm not going to put the head of their favorite race-horse in their bed. Like I said, think creatively. You'd be surprised at just how far my reason goes."

The old man lifted his champagne glass and looked out over the water, almost as if he was hoping for a glimpse of his superyacht moored out in the Aegean.

Finally, he turned back to Nir. He held out his glass. "One favor. It's a deal."

Nir smiled as he clinked the Russian's glass, then sipped the costly wine.

"Now give me the name of the man you need to meet."

"General Leonid Anatolyevich Moshev."

Once again, the Russian exploded in his deep, throaty laughter. "*Lyonya*? He's the man? Yes, I can bring him to you. But you need to know, my sneaky young friend, that in *Lyonya* you may have bitten off more than you can chew."

CHAPTER 20

THREE DAYS LATER
RAUBICY, MINSK, BELARUS—
OCTOBER 19, 2022—02:15 (2:15 AM) MSK

Nir's mask broke the surface of the water. The house was directly in front of him, while the two outbuildings were off to the west side of the property. There was movement to his left as Yaron's head rose from the murky dark. He was followed by Imri, Doron, and Dima.

The five black bumps floated just above the surface of the Raubick-aje Reservoir in Raubicy, a high-priced suburb to the east of Minsk. Six minutes passed without movement in the water or at the house. Then, around the west corner of the 1,250-square-meter house came two security guards. Each carried an AK-12 infantry rifle strapped across his chest, and both were smoking. Five sets of eyes followed them as they walked and talked and took long drags off their cigarettes. One hundred and sixty seconds later, they turned south toward the front of the mansion.

Nir and Dima triggered into action. They both exited the water, running up the slope from the reservoir to the house in the low light of the half moon. They had removed their flippers while they were waiting, and now the cold dew on the grass caused Nir's bare feet to slip several times. Reaching the house, Nir pressed his back against the rear wall. Dima flattened next to him.

A quick look at his watch told him they had seven minutes to wait before the hired security made another round. A surveillance drone employed the previous night by a Belarusian Mossad asset had clocked the guards' rounds at a consistent ten minutes and twenty seconds.

Nothing kills you faster than routine, thought Nir, shaking his head. *Only this time, there better not be any killing.*

As he waited, his mind went back to Mykonos. Kvashnin had tried to up the ante, offering Nir cash and multiple favors if he would only be willing to "remove" a few competing pieces from the chessboard. Nir had refused, causing the old man to grumble. But then his eyes had lit up with a new idea.

"There is a man, Myechyslau Sharetsky, a Belarusian," he had said with contempt in his voice. "He is one of the primary suppliers of potash for my fertilizer factories. Because of the sanctions, he is trying to gouge me on my latest contracts. He needs to be convinced that raising my costs in an economic time such as this is not a good choice on his part."

"That I can do."

"Yes, I know. And I will tell you how you can do it. Sharetsky is a vain man who is in love with himself and with his wealth. Necessity has led me to attend functions at his house outside of Minsk several times. He shows me this and he shows me that. 'Oh, this was so expensive. Anatoly, do you know how much I paid for that?'"

"Sounds like a charming man," said Nir, wondering just how different Sharetsky was from the man sitting across the table from him.

Probably not much.

"But the worst is that each time I am there, I am forced to go with him to his specially built climate-controlled garage, where he keeps his car collection on display. Something like thirty vehicles, all lined up. It is a mini museum. Classic cars, muscle cars, rarities, they are all there. He loves those cars almost as much as he loves himself. And get this, my friend. Sharetsky is also a big fan of American action movies, and he has named each of his cars after a movie hero. This is a grown man! He even printed up little signs introducing each one and telling all about it. 'This is my Skywalker. This is my Ironman. Do you know how much I paid for it?' It is ridiculous."

"Sounds like it." Nir knew jealousy when he heard it, but he played along. It was better than having to fend off Kvashnin's 'I need you to whack this guy' fixation.

"If part of his convincing included him losing his precious car collection, oh, that would be glorious." Then the old man giggled. Nir couldn't believe it. The nearly 70-year-old billionaire businessman actually giggled in front of him.

Now, from the back of the house, Nir looked over to Sharetsky's long, state-of-the-art garage with its many high windows and multiple doors. At CARL, Liora would be using this time to shut down the building's alarm system, as well as that of the house. Kvashnin had thought it would be a great idea to blow the garage sky high, but there was no way to do that without taking out the house, too, and possibly causing debris damage to several other estates in the area.

No, there would be no explosives used tonight. Nir had a better idea, and the thought of it brought a smile to his face the same way it had when he had come up with it on his commuter flight from Mykonos to Athens.

Nir's watch told him that there were 15 seconds left before the guards would make their turn to the back of the house.

Right on time, the guards rounded the corner. Nir took the close one, clamping one hand over his mouth as he wrapped his foot behind the guard's feet and took him to the ground. He slid his combat knife from its sheath on his belt and pressed it to the man's neck with just enough force to draw a trickle of blood.

"*Zatknis! Zatknis,*" he hissed, telling the man to shut up. To his left, Dima was sprawled across the back of the second guard. To his right, the rest of the team was racing up the lawn. Imri arrived alongside him, and Nir let up from the man's body enough for the agent to flex-cuff the guard's wrists. Together, they flipped the man over and Imri slapped a piece of tape across his mouth. After lifting him up to his feet, they led him over to where Dima and Yaron were standing up the other guard.

Nir put his hand on Dima's shoulder. "Tell them that if they don't do something stupid, then it is likely they will get out of this alive." The big Russian did so. Both Belarusian guards emphatically nodded.

"Okay, sit them down on the grass over there," Nir said, indicating a place with a nod of his head. Turning to Doron, he asked, "You close?"

Doron had opened a waterproof bag and was pulling out a full set of clothes for each of them, including socks and boots. Pairing up, the men helped each other out of their wet suits, then got themselves dressed in black T-shirts and black cargo pants with loaded utility belts. Once everyone was suited up, Doron gave each man a handgun.

They all dropped the mags from their guns and checked to see that they had a full load before sliding the mags back in. Each one racked a round into the chamber, then holstered their weapons. Leaving the wet suits in a pile on the grass, they lifted the guards from the grass and crossed the yard to the garage.

Reaching the front door, the guard that Imri was leading began grunting. With one hand, Nir pressed a finger to his lips, and with the other he slipped his knife back out of its sheath and held it to the guard's throat.

"Dima, ask him what he wants."

The agent pulled the tape off halfway. There was a brief discussion, then Dima said, "He wanted to tell you that there is an alarm and only Mr. Sharetsky knows the code."

"Thank him for his concern, then ask him if he has the key to the door."

A moment later, Dima said, "The key is on his belt."

"He gives him a key, but no code," Nir said as he reached around the man's waist, then pulled loose a ring of keys. "That is completely devoid of logic."

Nir held up one key, but the guard shook his head. He held up a second and received the same reaction. The third key received an emphatic nod.

"*Spasibo*," Nir said, clapping the guard on the shoulder. Nir slid the key in, turned the knob, and opened the door. Silence greeted them, thanks to Liora's work back at CARL. The five Israeli agents and two Belarusian security guards walked in.

When Doron flipped on the light switches, a low whistle escaped Nir's lips. Although there weren't quite the 30 cars that Kvashnin had estimated, it was still a breathtaking display. There were two rows of a dozen vehicles each, all perfectly polished and with overhead lights and spotlights positioned to make them gleam and sparkle.

"Have him show you where the keys are," Nir said over his shoulder to Dima as he began walking down the aisle between the two rows. Like Kvashnin had said, each car had a little stand with a sign attached written in Cyrillic and English. The first vehicle Nir came to was a huge green Hummer H1. The sign indicated that its name was "The Hulk" and it carried the tagline, "You Wouldn't Like Me When I'm Angry." According to the bio, the H1 had been stripped down and rebuilt by a custom automotive production company. The interior was tricked out with Nappa leather and a Momo Prototipo steering wheel, while under the hood, the engine had been upgraded from a 300- to a 500-horsepower turbo-diesel.

Next in line was a 1969 Pontiac GTO convertible with a 400 4-barrel engine. The car's interior matched its verdugo green paint job, and on the floor between the seats was a factory Hurst T-Handle shifter for controlling its four-speed transmission. The name given to this classic muscle car was "The McClane" and its tagline read, "Yippee-Ki-Yay!" When the temptation to turn the car over just to hear it rumble became too much, he moved on to the next vehicle.

Looking back, Nir saw his four men in the process of taping the security guards to office chairs.

Looks like they've got that under control. I've got time for one or two more.

The next car brought him up short. It was a 1954 Iso Isetta, a tiny Italian car that had the distinction of being the only vehicle Nir knew of that you entered from the front. Known as the "bubble car" because of its shape, the blue-and-white Isetta may have been extremely compact and not much to look at, but it was certainly practical given the narrow streets of Italy. The sign called this frumpy car "The Westley," giving it the tagline, "As You Wish."

A hand dropped on his shoulder. He turned to see Imri. "You done gawking?" the young agent asked him.

"Of all the terrible things I've done in my life, this may be the worst."

"No kidding. Farther up, the dude has a '67 black-and-white rally stripe Camaro and a '68 Shelby Cobra GT350. You sure we can't just take one?"

Nir laughed. "If we could get it out of this pit of a country in one piece, I'd do it. But, sadly, it's like a clearance sale. Everything has got to go."

Up to their left, the first car began moving. With Yaron behind the wheel, Dima and Doron were pushing a bright red early '70s Plymouth 'Cuda. Yaron cranked hard on the wheel and the car began quietly rolling down the aisle. Only the door at the far end of the garage would be opened to minimize noise.

"Should we start easy?" Nir asked, pointing to the Isetta.

"Jump in. I think I can handle it."

Nir opened the front of the car and sat on the bench seat. As Imri closed the door after him, the steering wheel tilted back into his lap. After making sure the vehicle was in neutral, Nir knocked on the window next to him, and Imri leaned his weight into the rear of the car. Soon, they were rolling at a decent clip through the aisle to the door. When they reached the grass outside, the pushing was more difficult. But once Dima joined in, the two were able to get momentum going again. They crossed the yard, and Nir parked the Isetta next to the 'Cuda.

One by one, they pushed the cars out. It was nearing 3:30 a.m. by the time they rolled the last one out. It was the Hummer, and it took four of them pushing that beast while Doron sat up behind the wheel.

Despite the cold air, they were all out of breath and drenched with sweat. Imri passed out water bottles while Nir admired their work. Twenty-four cars, the pride and joy of a Belarusian potash billionaire and part-time smuggler, were all lined up in a long row stretching almost the full width of the property.

"Ready for a wake-up call?" Nir asked the group.

"Let's do it," said Yaron.

CHAPTER 21

While Imri and Doron went back to the garage to check on the security guards, Nir, Dima, and Yaron jogged up toward the house.

"CARL, confirming that the house alarm is off."

"The alarm is off," answered Liora. "Still no sign of movement anywhere on the street."

"Copy," said Nir.

"You guys sound like you're having fun out there."

"Maybe a little too much," answered Imri.

When they reached the back door, Dima inserted a house key he had lifted from the guards. The lock turned, and the three men stepped in. Small Maglites helped them to get their bearings. Just past the entryway was a wide-open room comfortably decorated with leather chairs and couches. Off to their left was a large kitchen. Nir turned them that direction. On the house schematic that Dafna had downloaded for him, he had seen a set of stairs that would take them up to the master bedroom much faster than the two grand staircases that ran along the perimeter of the house's foyer.

As he ascended the stairs, Nir glanced at his watch and did a quick calculation.

Still have almost 90 minutes before the house's staff arrives. We're making good time.

They arrived outside the entrance to the master suite. The double doors were gilded, and the handles were ornate.

"Showtime," Nir said as he turned the handle. The bedroom was divided into three sections. There was a sitting room to the right, a bathroom to the left, and a very large bed directly in between. Two forms were covered on opposite sides of the bed. Nir and Dima moved to the left, while Yaron went right.

Once they were in position, Nir said, "Now."

Dima and Yaron each clamped a hand down over the mouth of the person in front of them. The sleeping couple thrashed awake. The two agents used their body weight to keep their charges pinned to the bed. Nir leaned down and pressed the muzzle of his MP-443 Grach 9mm to the forehead of the man Dima was controlling, then lit up his handgun with his flashlight.

"*Dobroye utro*, Myechyslau Aleksandrovich," said Nir, wishing the man a good morning. He stopped moving, and his eyes crossed as he locked in on the barrel of the gun. To Dima, Nir said, "Ask him to tell his wife to stop moving."

Dima did so, then cautiously lifted his hand from Sharetsky's mouth. The man spoke some harsh words to his wife, and she stilled. Using Dima once again as his interpreter, Nir said, "I want the two of you to get up and walk to the end of the bed. If you yell or try to escape, I will shoot you. Do you understand?"

"I understand," Sharetsky said in heavily accented English.

He speaks English. The kids back at CARL dropped the ball on that piece of intel. Although I suppose the signs in the garage should have been a giveaway.

As the couple slipped out of the bed, Nir twisted a nob on a lamp and the room lit up. Sharetsky was wearing maroon silk pajamas. A wild thatch of gray hair reached up over the top button in front. His wife, who couldn't have been more than 30, was wearing a very revealing negligee.

"Dima, tell her to put a robe on." Yaron walked her over to a closet, where she slipped on a covering.

"Who are you?" demanded Sharetsky.

"Just a friend of a friend. We'll get to that in a moment. First, I have something to show to you. But before I can do that, I'm afraid I must secure you."

Dima pulled the man's arms behind his back and flex-cuffed them, while Yaron loosely cuffed the wife's hands in front.

"I must also warn you that if you make noise, I will gag you. And, if you continue to give me trouble even after being gagged, I will hurt you. Do we have an understanding?"

"Yes, I understand. Please don't hurt me."

"That will be completely up to you," Nir said, noticing that the man didn't say anything about not hurting his wife. "Wait here."

Nir crossed over to the sitting room, where he lifted a large, upholstered chair and carried it to a floor-to-ceiling window that had its curtains drawn. He followed that with a second.

"Please, come sit." Dima and Yaron escorted their charges to the chairs.

Once they were seated, Nir pulled a cord and opened the curtains. It was dark out back, with just enough moonlight to make out the reservoir and a line of black shadows in the yard.

"What is that?" asked Sharetsky, peering down.

"Lights, please," said Nir. Connected into the alarm system were emergency floodlights. Liora triggered them now, and the backyard lit up with brilliant white light.

Sharetsky gasped audibly. "My cars. Why are my cars in the yard? What are you doing?"

"You've been playing some dangerous games, Myechyslau Aleksandrovich. In a time of war when all should be sacrificing, you are renegotiating contracts and seeking to profit off the tragedy. I've been asked by certain manufacturers whom you supply to remind you of your patriotism, and to encourage you to aid in the effort by lowering your prices by one third."

"One third? I cannot do one third," argued Sharetsky. "Tell your friends that this is impossible. I will not be extorted into destroying my own business."

Nir looked down at the Belarusian for a moment, then shrugged. "That's too bad. How about we start with The Ironman?"

Down below, Imri walked to a bright red 2022 Ferrari 296 GTB 2-door coupe. He slid behind the wheel for a moment, then stepped back out as the car began to slowly roll in neutral down the decline.

Sharetsky yelled "*Nyet!*" as the car picked up speed, then hit the reservoir. Water quickly poured in through the open windows, and the car descended into the shallow depths.

The old man shouted a string of Russian words. Nir looked to Dima for the interpretation, but the Kidon man said, "You don't want to know."

Nir said in his coms, "Let's do The Toretto."

Again, Sharetsky yelled curses as the black 1970 Dodge Charger R/T rolled down the slope and into the water.

"That one hurt," said Doron with a laugh through the coms.

"Yeah, no kidding," said Nir. "You know, while you're at it, send The Batman. I hate DC."

A replica of the Adam West-era Batmobile rolled down to meet its fate.

Nir looked down at the man and saw tears in his eyes. A moment of remorse panged in his conscience. But then he remembered that this man's smuggling was helping finance Putin's war effort.

No. No tears for this guy. Part of what paid for those cars was the blood of Ukrainian soldiers and civilians. Besides, this bad guy is just another step toward figuring out what Putin has planned for Israel.

"Tell you what, guys. Just send them all."

Sharetsky cried out. He pleaded for Nir to stop as one by one the cars rolled down the hill into the water. The Skywalker, The Westley, The Hulk, The Logan—all drowned in their watery graves. Nir felt a moment of temptation as he watched Doron walk to the convertible GTO. But, like he had told Imri, there was no way to get one of these cars out of the country and down to Israel. Besides, he wasn't a thief. Tonight, he was feeling much more of a vandal vibe.

Nir leaned down to the Belarusian as they watched the Pontiac roll down the hill and whispered, "Yippee-ki-yay."

A quiet shock had overtaken Sharetsky as he watched the show. Nir straightened back up. "If you renege on dropping your price by a third,

I will come back. And if I have to come back, I'll bury you in the waters next to your precious friends down there. Do you understand me?"

Without turning his head, the man nodded slowly.

Taking hold of the man's face, Nir turned him so that they were eye to eye. "I said, do you understand me?"

"*Da.*"

"Good."

An unexpected sound caught Nir's ear. Laughter. He looked up and saw Sharetsky's wife. Her cuffed hands were covering her mouth as she watched the cars roll into the water. It seemed as if she had been trying to control herself but was finally losing the battle. Then the dam burst with a loud snort. Rolls of laughter shook her body. Sharetsky leaned toward her chair and growled something to her that earned him a thwack across his head by Dima. Whatever threat the man had spoken to his wife was ineffective. Her joy at witnessing the drowning of her husband's metallic mistresses continued unabated.

By the time the team was picked up outside the front of the Sharetsky mansion by a Mossad asset driving a van, Mr. and Mrs. Sharetsky had been flex-cuffed to chairs out in the garage next to the two security guards, who Nir figured would be looking for work very soon. They had a 45-minute head start on the staff arriving at the house, which was 15 minutes more than they needed to reach their rendezvous point in Minsk.

In a parking lot in an industrial area outside the city, they exited the van and tucked themselves away in a semi-comfortable compartment in the trailer of a big rig specially designed for smuggling. No one spoke much during the three-hour trip across the border to Vilnius, Lithuania. At the start of the drive, Nir had done a quick debrief with the guys. While nobody felt bad about the op they had just completed, nobody felt good about it either. This excursion to Belarus was missing its post-operational joy, like "Hey, we just saved Israel," or "Awesome, we just saved the world." This was more like "Hey, we just lowered the bottom line on raw materials for a Russian oligarch." Nir reminded them of the big picture, but he understood the letdown. He was feeling it too.

Once in Vilnius, they separated. Each of the Kidon agents would take their own circuitous route back to Tel Aviv. Nir, though, was heading west, back home to Antwerp. He desperately had to put some hours in on his business. He also needed to take this time to rest up, because it wouldn't be long before he was going to be back on an airplane. This time, his destination would be Putin's Russia, and his traveling companion would be a glamorous international model of whom he'd found himself becoming quite fond.

CHAPTER 22

So, you actually said, 'Yippee-ki-yay' to him when you rolled the GTO?" Efraim Cohen appeared to be enjoying Nir's retelling of the Minsk operation, using his cloth napkin to dab tears from his eyes.

"It seemed appropriate," Nir said, transferring a forkful of Victoria perch into his mouth.

"That's just cruel," said Nicole. "Hilarious, but cruel." Nir had picked her up from the airport this morning via Uber but had said she had to wait until lunch to hear the details.

Efraim took another bite of his veal schnitzel. "This is amazingly good. But I still can't believe I traveled all the way from Tel Aviv to Belgium for you to bring me to a kosher Israeli restaurant."

"Don't let the Hoffman brothers hear you call their food Israeli. It's pure Yiddish—Central European, not Mediterranean."

"I know the difference," Efraim said defensively.

Nir had been anticipating this meal ever since Efraim had told him he was coming. These were two of his favorite people in the world, and he was enjoying every minute with them. "We're here, my whining friend, because it's right next to the Antwerp Diamond Bourse and within walking distance of my office. Besides, the Hoffmans told me

I can use this back room whenever I need some privacy. So, quit your bellyaching."

"Do they know who you are? I mean, that you are more than just a diamond guy?"

"Diaspora Israelis think everyone is Mossad until they get proof they aren't. You know that."

Efraim laughed again. "Truth. Anyway, all I'm saying is you could have at least taken me to some place where I could get some Antwerpian food."

"It's Antwerpenaar, and you can get a Belgian waffle at the airport before your flight out."

Nicole pointed at both with her knife before slicing off a piece of her sole. "Are you sure you two aren't related? You fight like you're brothers, and it's usually about the stupidest things."

Efraim reached over and clasped Nir's shoulder. "Yeah, he's my kid brother. I got all the brains and all the looks. He just got the muscles."

"I have to admit, they're pretty nice muscles," said Nicole with a wink to Nir.

"Ha! Take that, bro. You're smart and pretty, but I still get all the chicks," Nir said, flexing his biceps.

"All the chicks?" Nicole asked, raising an eyebrow.

"*Achi*, you should have quit while you were ahead," laughed Efraim.

They talked and joked as they finished their meals. Then, once the plates were cleared away, Efraim changed the subject. "So, you two, explain to me how Kvashnin—or, better yet, how you guys—are going to get General Moshev to the oligarch's little soiree."

"We're going to appeal to his compassionate side," said Nir.

"Well, that's *shtuyot bamitz*! He's a Russian general. I think their compassion is surgically removed when they get their first star."

"I know, I know," said Nicole. "But think about it. As a general, what is the one thing that he cares about?"

"Money? Power? Vodka?"

Nicole waved her hands. "Let me rephrase. As a general, what is the one thing that he should care about?"

"His troops."

"Exactly," said Nir. "And whether he truly does care about them or not, as a deputy minister of defense, that is the persona he'll want to portray. Even in Russia, appearances matter."

"I would say especially in Russia appearances matter," said Efraim.

Nicole nodded. "That is why we are going to give him an opportunity to show his patriotism and support of the troops by attending a charity event."

Nir could sense Efraim's excitement growing. Getting his friend on board, who was also an assistant deputy director in the Mossad, was key to eventually getting a green light from the *ramsad*.

"Okay, I'm tracking," said Efraim. "So, what kind of fundraising event is Kvashnin going to put on? Is he going to do a 'Shoot the Serf' outing or something?"

Nir rolled his eyes. "*Achi*, your humor is so antiquated. Now they call the serfs comrades."

Nicole shook her head. "Says the guy who is apparently still fighting the Cold War. There are no more serfs or peasants or comrades. Now they just call them all cannon fodder."

Both men burst out in laughter and clapped.

Efraim leaned over to high-five Nicole. "That is the darkest, most cynical thing I've heard you say for a long time. You are truly becoming an Israeli!"

A knock sounded. "Come in," said Nir.

A server brought three dessert plates to the table, placing them in the center with an assortment of forks. "From the owners with their compliments," she said in Hebrew.

"*A dank*," Nir answered, thanking her in Yiddish. Then, switching to Hebrew, he added, "And please thank my friends for their kindness and generosity."

The server nodded, then left the room.

Nir said to Nicole, "I was just thanking her, and asking her to thank the Hoffmans."

"I actually got most of that," Nicole answered proudly. Picking up a fork, she pointed to each of the plates and said, "Okay, that's strudel and that's just fruit. But what in the world is that?"

Efraim answered, "Oh, my dear Nicole, that is sweet lokshen kugel. It's heaven on a plate."

Nicole grimaced. "Okay, but what is it?"

"It's a Yiddish dessert noodle casserole," he said with a smile, sliding it toward her. "It's got noodles, cottage cheese, sour cream, cream cheese, sugar, and cinnamon."

Nicole hesitated. "I have to admit, I had never imagined that the words *dessert* and *noodle casserole* could be put together in the same sentence."

"Come on. Just one bite to say you've tried it," Nir encouraged.

Taking a moment to strengthen her resolve, Nicole cut off a small corner with her fork and lifted it into her mouth. After chewing a few times, she said, "Nope. No thank you. It's all yours because that's not happening again."

"Your loss," said Efraim as both men cut large pieces off the dessert.

"No, it's really not," said Nicole as she slid the fruit plate toward her.

Through a full mouth, Efraim asked, "So, you're appealing to the general by asking him to help raise money for the troops?"

Nicole answered, "Close. It's for the families of troops who were killed or wounded in battle."

"And what kind of event will it be?"

Nir took over. "Kvashnin's wife—her name is Polina—she fancies herself a bit of a fashionista."

"You saw her on Mykonos, right?"

Nir chuckled. "The one I saw wasn't his wife. Polina rarely leaves Russia. Doesn't like to fly. Anyway, Kvashnin says that she likes to do a bit of designing, and she always keeps up on the latest trends."

Nir could see the understanding cross his friend's face. "Ah, *nafal lee ha'asimon*! Now I get it! You guys are putting on a charity fashion show."

"*Sababa, achi*. And we're bringing to Polina a highly sought-after international supermodel who will headline the show and actually wear her designs."

"Wow, you guys got Kendall Jenner?" Efraim exclaimed, cutting into the strudel.

Nicole threw a grape at him. "Brat."

Nir continued, "General Moshev will be the guest of honor and will make a brief speech thanking the people for being there. Afterward, Kvashnin will invite him to his study. The two have known each other for a couple decades. While Moshev was heading up Russia's disaster relief, Kvashnin would donate fertilizer for rebuilding damaged agricultural areas. Once Kvashnin has Moshev in the study, we'll show up and confront the general with the evidence of his treachery."

Efraim's face clouded up, and Nir knew that he had seen a problem. He was pretty sure what it was because it really was a potential flaw in the whole plan. Sure enough, Efraim asked, "And Kvashnin is good with this? Isn't this setting him up for the kill?"

"Obviously, that's Kvashnin's biggest concern," Nir admitted. "I'm still working on how to deflect suspicion from him. Barring some foolproof lie, I'll just add his safety to the threat against Moshev. 'If anything happens to Kvashnin, I'll release our evidence, and you'll have to face the wrath of Putin.'"

Nir wasn't sure whether his answer mollified his friend. He watched as the assistant deputy director silently finished off the strudel. It was obvious he was processing his answer and mulling over the whole plan, trying to find more holes. Nir turned to Nicole and raised his eyebrows. She shrugged in reply.

"And you," Efraim suddenly said, pointing at Nicole with his fork. "You're okay with this? You're good with the risk?"

"You know my beliefs, Efraim. As a Gentile Christian, I believe it is incumbent upon me to do all I can to protect God's chosen people. Whatever the Russians are planning against Israel, the death toll sounds like it could be terrible. To me, it's worth the risk to stop that from happening."

Now turning to Nir, he asked, "And you, are you okay with her taking this chance?"

Nicole answered, "Listen, Efraim, I can make—"

"Quiet," he snapped at her. Nicole retreated.

Again, to Nir he asked, "Nir, *achi*, as Nicole said, you and I are like brothers. I know you. I need to know if you are okay with Nicole taking this kind of risk. Will you be able to treat her like any other agent, or will your protectiveness of her be a distraction to you accomplishing your mission?"

Silence filled the room. Nir could feel Nicole's eyes on him. This was the primary question he had been wrestling with, even more than Kvashnin's safety. This plan had made so much sense when he had first come up with it. But when he began thinking through the possibilities of what could happen to Nicole, he started to have his doubts. She was perfect for the job, but was she the perfect person for his team?

"It's true. You do know me too well, my friend. But Nicole is exactly right. This is bigger than me. This is bigger than her. There are so many lives at stake. That's what's most important. I know that there are risks to both of us, and I've come to terms with that."

"You're certain?"

"*Elef ahuz,*" Nir said.

"You got me on that one," said Nicole.

Efraim answered. "*Elef ahuz.* It means 'one thousand percent.' We Jews don't just stop at one hundred percent, because in Israel, everything is ten times bigger. Like Nir's muscles."

"And Efraim's gut."

"Nir," Nicole scolded. "That's not nice."

Efraim mimicked Nicole. "Yeah, Nir, that's not nice. By the way, little brother, how are you getting around these days without the Mercedes? You using Uber? Lyft? You taking the bus?"

Nicole leaned toward Efraim and loudly whispered, "Why do you think he picked a restaurant that we could walk to from his office?"

Efraim laughed and clapped his hands. Then he stood, and the others joined him. "Been a great time, but I've got to run. I have a fifty-minute train ride to Brussels, then a 21:10 flight to Tel Aviv, and I've got a boatload of calls I have to make before I get on that plane."

Nir gave his friend a hug, then stayed behind to pay the bill while Nicole walked Efraim out. After settling with a generous tip, he stuck his head into the restaurant's office and thanked the one Hoffman brother who was there. Then he met up with Nicole on the sidewalk outside in time to see Efraim rounding the corner a block and a half away.

CHAPTER 23

ANTWERP, BELGIUM—
OCTOBER 25, 2022—15:00 (3:00 PM) CEST

Efraim had turned right for his seven-minute walk past the Diamond Bourse to the stately century-plus old Art Nouveau Antwerpen-Centraal railway station. Nir and Nicole, however, went left. Both were silent for the first block.

This was not the most attractive part of Antwerp, with many of the businesses on the narrow street shuttered behind roll-up doors or metal grilles. Often, this area of the city reminded him of the older sections of Jerusalem. Both locales had thriving businesses sitting right next to empty storefronts. And in both, Orthodox Jews could be seen on the street talking in groups or hurrying from one place to another.

Taking his hand, Nicole asked, "So, will you be able to put your chivalry to the side and let me do my job while you do yours?"

Nir had been pretty sure of his answer. But then their hands met, and he wondered whether he really could turn off his natural protectiveness. It was one thing to risk his own life. But to let Nicole step into harm's way without feeling the overwhelming compulsion to rescue her was a big leap. He loved this woman and would sacrifice absolutely anything for her.

And that's when the truth hit him.

Maybe what I have to sacrifice is my need to be in control. Maybe wanting to make sure that she is safe is more about me than it is about her.

A strong odor of the sea drew him from his thoughts. He hadn't realized that they had already reached the fish market. In a four-story apartment building across the street, old folks were sitting out on their patios, chatting and sipping tea. Nir wondered how they ever got used to the smell. It wasn't that it was foul; it was just very, very pungent.

"Your silence is deafening," Nicole said, her hand slipping from his.

To buy a little more time, Nir said, "Wait here a moment."

Just past the fish market stood a kosher bakery. Nir stepped in, and the change in aroma was like night and day. The scents of pastry and chocolate and melting butter filled the air. Leaning down to peer into a refrigerated case, he picked out four chocolate-covered eclairs with shaved almonds on either end. He paid and thanked the woman who had helped him, then walked back out.

Nicole had crossed the street and was looking in the show window of a hat shop. Stepping up behind her, he said, "Ready?"

Without saying anything, she began walking. Nir fell in step next to her.

Finally, he said, "Listen, Nicole, I can't tell you that it will be easy. But what I'm realizing is that this is not a you thing. It's a me thing. It's not that I don't trust you to take care of yourself. It's that I don't trust you to not have me take care of you."

"That made absolutely no sense."

She was right. He wasn't even sure what he had just said. "What I think I'm saying is that me feeling like I have to protect you is not because I don't believe you can take care of yourself. You can. You've proved that over and over. My struggle is that in certain areas, I can tend to be a control freak."

"Oh really?"

Out of his peripheral vision, he could see that she was grinning. A wave of relief flooded through him. So far, it seemed he hadn't said anything too stupid. "Hey, it's just in certain things. Things I really care about. And you just happen to be one of those things."

"Good to know that I just happen to be one of those things."

This time he saw her side-glancing him. There was a playful glint in her eye.

"You're not going to make this easy, are you?"

"Nope."

He took her hand, and she gripped his tightly. They turned to the right around the entrance to the fashionable Mercure hotel, which overlooked the upper corner of the triangular city park.

"The answer is yes. Yes, I will be able to control my overprotectiveness and trust you to do your job. It's yes because I need you there. It's yes because I trust that you can accomplish the mission. It's yes because there is no other person on the face of this earth that I would want there by my side other than you."

Nicole took his arm with her other hand and leaned tightly against him.

"Except maybe Dima."

She swatted his arm. "You are just mean."

"Although I saw Dima in a burka once. I don't know if modeling women's clothing is his calling."

The temperature suddenly dropped as low clouds moved in, blocking out the sun. They picked up their pace over the final two blocks. Nir held the door open for Nicole, and they made their way up to his office.

CHAPTER 24

15:10 (3:10 PM) CEST

When they reached the front door of Yael Diamonds, Nir pressed a button. A moment later, a buzzer sounded, and the door unlocked. Mila Wooters, Nir's executive assistant, was already on her feet and headed toward the door when they walked in.

"Nicole," she said, her arms open wide.

"Mila, it's so good to see you." The two wrapped up in a long embrace.

"Nir said you were coming in this morning. How was your flight?"

"Nothing exciting, which I guess is good when it comes to air travel."

"I brought you something," Nir said, holding up the bag and shaking it.

Mila's face took on a stern look. "Did you bring me more of those eclairs when I made you promise you wouldn't?" Turning to Nicole, she said, "I can't control myself with them. They're just so good." She took the bag from Nir and gave him a hug. But then she pulled back and turned to Nicole. "Wait. Does that mean he took you to that horrible Yiddish restaurant that's right by the bakery?"

"He did, and it wasn't so bad."

Mila put the bag on her desk and walked around to her chair. "Not so bad? Did you look at the menu? There's something on there called

Turkey Bone. Nothing else. No description. Just Turkey Bone." Turning to Nir, she said, "What is wrong with you? Take her someplace that has real food, not some place you go to just because they sometimes give you free food."

Nir put up his hands defensively. "What? I like it."

Mila shook her head. "Hopeless. Well, don't let me keep you. I'll bring in some coffee. I'd offer you one of my eclairs, Nicole, but he probably made you eat that awful noodle dessert, didn't he?"

"Thank you, Mila," interrupted Nir. "Coffee would be great."

When Nir closed his office door, Nicole said, "I love her. I want her to be my mom."

"Of course, you love her. She loves you."

"She loves you too. This place would fall apart without her, and you would too."

Nicole sat in an overstuffed chair, while Nir took the one opposite.

"Yeah, you're probably right. So, how are you feeling about the operation? You nervous?" Nir asked.

"Of course, but I'm not frightened. I've got faith that God is going to bring us through it. It's just too important."

Nir leaned back in the chair and drew in the smell of the leather. Nicole was always quick with her faith statements, but they had both been in situations that were extremely rough. Nir felt like "God is going to bring us through it" could too easily be a throwaway cliché.

"But what if He doesn't?" he challenged.

"Doesn't what?"

"What if God doesn't bring us through this? What if we fail, or get arrested, or one of us gets hurt or even killed?"

"Those are a lot of what ifs."

"But they're important ones. What if the worst-case scenario happens?"

Nir usually avoided thinking about the potential operational consequences, but ever since deciding a few days ago that Nicole should be part of this one, it seemed that he couldn't get all the downsides out of his mind. How could she be so calm when he was all nerves? Shouldn't it be the other way around?

A reassuring smile spread across Nicole's face, and Nir thought that he might never have seen her looking as beautiful as she did in that moment. "Nir, we've had this discussion before. I believe God will take care of me. But if He chooses not to, then that's okay too."

Usually, Nir balked when she began one of her God conversations, but he was genuinely curious this time. What was it that gave her so much faith that as long as she trusted God she'd be okay? Was it just blind faith? He didn't think so. She was too smart for that. She wouldn't be someone who just turned her brain off and said, "Yes, God. Yes, God. Yes, God." She was a reasoning person, so it seemed she must have a reasonable answer.

"So, that's what I really don't get. How is it okay if God lets you down like that—if He lets you get killed? Isn't that like saying, 'I believe there is a God. But even if I discover that there isn't, I'm good because at least I believed in something'?"

Nicole laughed. "It's not at all like that. Do you remember the story of Shadrach, Meshach, and Abednego?"

"Taking me back to *yeshiva*. I always liked that one. The king says to worship me. The three friends say, 'Not going to happen.' The king throws them in a fiery furnace, and they come out not even smelling like smoke."

"You're a born storyteller."

There was a knock on the door, and Mila opened it. She was carrying a tray with two cups of cappuccino on it.

"Wow, fancy," said Nicole when she took the cup from Mila.

"I finally taught her how to make Israeli coffee," Nir said, taking his own.

Mila snorted. "Don't let him fool you with his fancy Israeli coffee. I just finally convinced him to buy a Nespresso machine for the office."

"Giving away all my secrets," said Nir as Nicole laughed.

"You both good? Need anything else?"

"We're good. Thanks, Mila," Nir said. Nicole echoed his words.

When the door closed, Nicole said, "Back to the three friends. When they were speaking to the king, there was something they said that has stayed with me. King Nebuchadnezzar told them, 'When you hear the music, you better worship me or you'll be thrown into the fire. And what god can save you from that?' But the guys didn't freak out or panic. They said, 'If you throw us in the fire, our God can still save us from that. But even if He doesn't, we're still not going to worship you.'"

"Sounds like they were lacking faith that their God would come through."

Nicole reached over and put her hand on Nir's knee. "It's exactly the opposite. Their faith was so strong that they knew even if they died, it would be okay because God had a better plan."

Nir took a sip from his cup. "Seems God's better plan would kind of suck for them."

That smile appeared on her face again. "But would it really? I've told you before about the apostle Paul's words, 'For me to live is Christ and to die is gain.' That's what faith is. It's saying I am going to serve God best I can for the time I have on this earth. But when the time comes for me to go, I'll be dancing the Watusi because I know that I'll be with God in heaven."

"The Watusi?"

"Yeah, you know…" Nicole stood up and started moving her arms back and forth. Then she jumped, turning 45 degrees to her left and repeated her arm movements, all the while singing, "Waaaaaah, wah Watusi."

Nir clapped. "Bravo."

Nicole motioned for him to join her. He laughed. "Yeah, that's not going to happen."

"Really? Stick in the mud." Nicole dropped into the chair and crossed her arms. "You never take me out dancing anymore."

"I've never taken you out dancing. Now, wait here, my little ballerina. I have something I want to give to you."

Her face brightened. "Is it a pony?"

"You've been hanging around CARL too much," he said as he walked to his desk and opened a drawer. "They're rubbing off on you."

"Good. We can all use a little more CARL in our lives."

Her expression changed completely when she spotted what was in his hand as he walked back.

"What is that?" she asked, pointing to a ring box.

"This, my dear, is something very, very special." As he sat down, he opened the box. Inside was a ring with an enormous diamond surrounded by at least a dozen smaller, but no less dazzling, diamonds.

"Pretty amazing, isn't it?" said Nir.

Nicole said nothing.

He took it out of the box. "Here, let me see your hand."

Nicole jumped up, putting the chair between herself and him. "Nir, no. I can't believe you're doing this. We've talked about this."

"Talked about what?"

"What do you mean, 'Talked about what?' Talked about this."

Suddenly, Nir realized what was happening.

Tavor, you are the biggest idiot on the planet. Seriously, idiot number one!

"Nicole, please sit. It's not what you think. I'm so sorry. I'm not...I mean, this isn't that kind of ring."

"What do you mean it's not that kind of ring?" Nicole was already flushed red. But as her own realization set in, Nir could see her shock and anger morphing into embarrassment. "You mean, you're not...Oh, I'm such an idiot."

There were tears in her eyes as Nir jumped up and led her back to her seat. He felt like the biggest heel ever since the advent of boots. "No, I'm the idiot. I never thought that...I'm so sorry."

Nicole used her sleeve to dab at her eyes, then she looked up at Nir and gave a strained laugh.

"May I have your hand now?"

"You may," she answered, reaching forward. Nir slipped the ring onto her middle finger. "This is amazing. The diamond is so bright."

"It's a three-point-five carat natural marquise diamond. It's colorless, so it reflects absolutely everything. Don't get too used to it, though. It's just a loaner."

"A loaner? From whom?"

"I used to own it. Or at least, the stones all belonged to Yael Diamonds. But I convinced the higher-ups back in Tel Aviv to buy them. And at a hefty markup to put toward my 'Replace the Mercedes' fund. I sold them the stones, but they created the setting."

"Seriously? What would the Mossad want with a diamond ring?"

"Press down on the center diamond."

Nicole put her finger on the gem, but then pulled back. "I'm not going to blow up a car or shoot a poison dart, am I?"

Nir laughed. "No, just press it."

She did, and felt a faint click.

"Well, that was underwhelming."

"That is our panic button. If the operation starts falling apart, you press that, and a signal hits a satellite, which then triggers an alarm for the kids in CARL."

Nicole's eyes grew big. "Really? That's pretty cool. But how does that help us? It's not like they can send an exfil team to helicopter us out of Moscow."

"No, but there are other things they can do from their little hidey-hole in Tel Aviv."

They talked about the operation for another few hours before Mila sent them away, demanding that Nir get her a better meal than turkey bones. But it had been a long day for Nicole. So Nir had their Uber take her to her hotel, where she could order up some room service and turn in early. As the Uber was driving him to his place, he couldn't help but stew on how ridiculous it was that he had to have someone else drive him home.

CHAPTER 25

The chill hit as Nir and Nicole exited the doors of Sheremetyevo International Airport in Moscow. A fog hung in the air, and the moisture caused the cold to permeate their clothing directly onto their skin. Nicole pulled the top of her jacket tighter around her neck.

The flight from Brussels had been rough. So many of the major air carriers were not flying into Moscow because of the conflict with Ukraine. As a result, they had been forced to travel using Pegasus, a discount Turkish airline that had routed them through Istanbul. What the aircraft lacked in cleanliness, the staff more than made up for in apathetic service. Both Nir and Nicole were anxious for a comfortable hotel, some decent room service, and a good night's sleep.

A taxi driver who had been smoking against a concrete bollard straightened up and moved toward them. "Is it the Four Seasons for you then?" he asked in accented English.

"No, friend. I make money. I'm not made of money," Nir replied, using the predetermined response.

"Follow me," the man said, taking their two bags.

Nicole looked up into Nir's eyes and took his arm. He nodded, and they allowed the driver to lead them to a taxi. When he opened the rear door, Nicole ducked in, then slid over. Nir followed.

"He said the right thing," Nicole said.

"Yeah, he's our guy." Nir listened as the bags thumped into the trunk. The taxi had the faint cigarette smell of someone who cracked their window when they smoked, thinking that all the stink was somehow escaping the interior. The license mounted on the dash said the driver's name was Eduard Zurabov, but Nir figured that his name was Zurabov as much as Nir's was Naor Shapira, his alias for the mission. It was also likely that the Mossad had created as extensive and believable a background for this man as they had for himself.

The trunk lid was slammed shut and the driver got in. When he started the car, the heater began blowing on high, much to the delight of the passengers in the back.

"How long of a drive?" asked Nir.

"If all goes perfectly, it is about ninety minutes. But with Moscow traffic, nothing ever goes perfectly."

"Understood. What do I need to know?"

The man held up a hand. "Wait until we are away from the airport. Then I will tell you. After that, we will ride in silence."

Nicole's hand squeezed Nir's arm, and he suppressed a smile. When it came to international intelligence, you don't make friends. Instead, you make allies. They are men and women who would give their lives for you, and you would do the same in return. Yet there always remains a personal distance. You may sit down with them over a few beers and swap war stories. But even then, you know that half the tales are probably made up, just like the name of the person you are drinking with. This is not because intelligence agents are inherently liars, although that quality can be beneficial. It's a precautionary measure. The less you know about other agents, the less information can be squeezed out of you should you be in a situation where the bad guys are particularly effective in their squeezing techniques.

Once the airport was well behind them, the driver reached to the passenger seat and lifted a black canvas bag. He passed it back to Nir.

The driver spoke. "Inside, you will find a device to sweep your room for bugs. They are not as common as they used to be, but it is still a good precaution. Even if your room comes up clean, however, you must still be cautious in what you say. You have an audio jammer?"

"We do," answered Nir.

"Good. No device is foolproof, and new technology is always developing. I was told that you wanted no firearms. That's smart. If you're a foreigner caught in Moscow with a gun, it is a certain trip to Lubyanka and a date with the FSB. Even if you find yourself in a situation where, due to circumstances, you end up in possession of a firearm, dispose of it as soon as you can safely do so. I have included two tactical knives for you. Carry them at your discretion. I am now going to tell you a number two times. Memorize it, but don't write it down. Are you ready?"

Nir and Nicole confirmed they were, and the man said a ten-digit number twice.

Then he said, "Now I am going to give you a six-digit number. Memorize it also."

He did so, saying it two times.

"The first is a phone number. Use it only if you are in a desperate situation. Dial the number. When the line is connected, say the six-digit number. Then hang up. You will receive a callback within five minutes. You will be able to describe your situation and what you need at that time. Do you understand what I have told you?"

"We do," said Nir.

"Good. Remove all the items and place them in the woman's bag, then pass my bag back up to me."

After they returned the bag to the driver, he placed it on the passenger seat. "That is all the information I have for you. We will now ride in silence."

That was fine with Nir. He closed his eyes and began using a mental device to familiarize himself with the two numbers the driver had given them so that they would be easily recalled in a high-energy situation when their adrenaline was pumping. He awoke to Nicole squeezing his arm.

"We're just about to pull up," she said.

He felt the car turning to the right as he shook the cobwebs from his head. Looking out the window, he saw they were on a one-way street. To his right, yellow-painted bricks gave way to the large brown columns of the Ararat Park Hotel. Until recently, it was part of the Hyatt chain, but five months ago, the company severed ties with the hotel due to sanctions over the war with Ukraine.

The cab pulled to the curb and Nir's door opened. He began to slide out, but the driver stopped him. "Are you not going to pay me?"

Nir had seen the meter running, but for some reason had thought that it was just for show. After all, weren't they playing on the same team? But apparently in Moscow, nobody rides for free. He peeled some ruble notes from a large stack and made sure to include a hefty tip.

"Thanks for the ride," he said, and slid out.

Nicole echoed her appreciation and followed him.

As with most five-star hotels, the check-in process was smooth, and the two travelers soon found themselves with a bellman in a glass elevator with the floor of the atrium lobby falling away below them. Once they arrived in the Winter Garden Suite, Nir begged off the tour of the room and got rid of the man as quickly as possible.

"You've got to come here," Nicole called from the living room.

He followed her voice and found her standing under a domed ceiling that covered the full length of the room.

"It's beautiful," she said.

"Isn't it? When I saw it online, I knew this was the place. They have rooms with full terraces too. But I figured with the weather, we wouldn't be spending too much time outside."

"No, this is perfect." She gave Nir a hug, then went to look out the window. "Is that the Bolshoi?"

"It is. Then to the left just beyond our view is Red Square."

There was a knock at the door. "That's our bags. Would you mind getting it? I've got to make a call."

He pulled out a cell phone and punched in a number. After three rings, a voice answered, "Yes?"

"We're here."

Anatoly Kvashnin replied, "We have a problem."

"I don't want to hear 'We have a problem.' I want to hear 'Welcome to Russia, comrade. Everything is progressing splendidly.'"

"Welcome to Russia, comrade. We have a problem."

When Nir didn't respond, the oligarch continued. "Moshev has said he cannot come. He doesn't feel that it is appropriate."

Nir cursed. "Listen, we had a deal. My part of the bargain is paid up. It's time for you to make good on yours."

"What can I do? I tried to convince him. He said no. That is it. The event is off."

"No!" Nir growled, trying to put as much menace in his voice as possible. "That was not the deal. We have traveled all the way to Russia in wartime for a charity fashion show, and we are going to have a charity fashion show. You keep doing what you need to do to organize it. Let me figure out what to do about our problem."

"Very well. It is up to you." The phone went dead.

Nir dropped back onto a couch. All his hopes of a casual evening with good food, good company, and good sleep were gone.

What am I going to do about Moshev? Without him, this trip is a bust and the operation is dead in the water. Hey, God, if You're listening, mind letting something go smoothly just once?

He heard Nicole thank the porter, then close the door.

No use sulking. You've got work to do, and it's not going to get done by whining.

When Nicole walked into the room, he waved to her, then acted like he was passing something over the lamp next to him. She nodded and went to her purse. Moments later, she handed him the tool for detecting surveillance devices. Switching it on, he got to work.

CHAPTER 26

Nir sat at a table looking down at a cup of coffee. The color of the liquid was almost black, and the smell was rich and bold.

This would be perfect if I was an American. But I am Israeli. I need some milk with my coffee.

As he watched, a thick mocha-colored foam spread through the cup. A line began to trace through the bubbles, then another, then another. Soon, he saw a white Star of David etched into the brown surface.

Nice trick, Nir thought. He lifted the cup for a sip, then heard a voice say, "I'm afraid I can't let you drink that."

Looking up, he saw seated across the table a man in a doctor's smock. Nir recognized the man and knew that he wasn't a traditional doctor. He began to tremble. Memories of pain and blood, helplessness and hopelessness, and the question repeated over and over, "What do you know, Mr. Tavor? What do you know?" And through all the horror, this pseudo-physician had never stopped smiling. He was a man who truly loved his work.

The man's sick smile now opened, exposing black, rotted teeth. He lifted a serrated blade from the table and admired it in the light. "This isn't a time for coffee, Mr. Tavor. We still have business to attend to."

When Nir looked back into his cup, the coffee was gone, replaced by blood. The smell made him gag. He dropped the cup, and it shattered on the table.

Crying out, he sat up on the bed. The unfamiliar room was disorienting, and he worked to control his breathing. As he inhaled through his nose, he caught a scent that began to calm him. It was coffee, real coffee, the smell wafting in from outside of his room.

He climbed out of bed and crossed the room to the closet. From inside, he lifted out a soft white robe with *Ararat Park Hotel* sewn onto it in blue thread. After slipping it on, he walked into the living room. Over in the kitchen, Nicole stood wearing the same white robe. Seeing her there was exactly what he needed to begin to push the dream and the memories of his recent past from his mind.

She turned when she heard him, and her face lit up. "Oh good, I was hoping your bedroom had one of these too," she said, lifting the lapel of the robe. "Aren't they amazing?"

Nir just smiled as he crossed the room, still a little shaken. As he approached, she poured coffee from a carafe into two ceramic mugs. She held one out to him.

"I'm afraid all they have is the nasty creamer that comes in those little cups. But I ordered cappuccinos for us both with our breakfast."

Nir took the mug but couldn't bring himself to look down at its contents.

"You already ordered breakfast? How'd you know I'd be up in time?"

"I set an alarm for you."

"An alarm? I didn't hear anything."

Half bouncing and half walking, Nicole moved to the dinette table. "It's not an alarm you hear. It's one you smell."

Nir thought for a moment, then it dawned on him. He was holding her alarm clock in his hand. Walking over to where she now sat, he kissed her on the forehead before taking the chair next to her. "You know me too well."

"Yes, I do. So, what time did you go to bed last night?"

Once the two of them had finally come up with a plan to get Moshev to change his mind about the charity event, Nicole had turned in. Nir had stayed up for another hour or so clearing the work-around with Efraim and giving some tasks to the gang at CARL. By that time, he was so tired from the travel and from the last few weeks' activities that even now he had a hard time recalling anything from when he closed his bedroom door to the moment he woke up.

Except for the dream. You've had that one enough times that it's almost become part of your subconscious's reality.

"I crashed not long after you did," he said, answering her question. "Thumbs up on next steps. CARL is busy at work."

Nicole's face turned serious. "I heard you when you woke up. Another dream?"

"Yeah."

"Want to talk about it?"

"Not really."

A knock sounded at the door, and Nir decided immediately that he was going to give double the tip to whoever had just saved him from their conversation.

"Breakfast," Nicole said, jumping up. She let in a kitchen staff member who laid out their food on the table. Nir signed the bill, making good on the tip, and the young man let himself out. As usual, Nicole ate light. Nir did not.

Once they were done and the staff member had left after returning to clear the dishes, Nicole opened her laptop while Nir retrieved a device from his room. Setting the small black box on the table, he switched it on. White noise emitted from its speaker. Despite the fact that his sweep of the hotel room had indicated there were no microphones, as the cabbie had reminded them, one could never be too careful.

Nir had been skeptical when Lahav Tabib had first shown him one of these obnoxious-sounding little audio jammers, telling him that even if he spoke at normal volume, all a microphone would pick up was the hiss of the white noise. But then Lahav had demonstrated the jammer, using the microphone on his cell phone. Sure enough, despite Lahav reciting the entire "I am your father" scene from *The Empire Strikes Back*, complete with light saber action, when he played it back, all that was picked up was white noise.

Unsure that it wasn't just an iPhone glitch, Nir had led Lahav down to the Mossad's surveillance center. There, he had them test it out on three of their most sensitive microphones, limiting Lahav's vocal input to "Testing one, two, three." Again, nothing but hiss. He was sold.

Nicole plugged two ear bone microphones into the computer and handed one to Nir. The bone conduction microphone built into the earpiece would pick up the vibrations from their speech and convert them into sound. If they had tried to talk to CARL using the computer microphone, all the analysts in Tel Aviv would have heard was the hiss of the jammer. But because their speech was transmitting internally, it would not be affected.

I am so glad I've got a bunch of eggheaded geeks working with me, he thought as he slipped the earpiece in.

Nicole began typing. When she hit the return key, a link traveled from Moscow to an orbiting satellite to Berlin to West Covina, California, to Mityana, Uganda, to Añatuya, Argentina, to Panaji, India, to Tel Aviv, all with less than one second of delay. The screen switched from lines of code to CARL's conference table, surrounded by the four analysts.

"Nicole," they all called out.

Nir rolled his eyes. At least they were consistent in their slights.

"Hi everyone," Nicole answered with an emphatic wave. She pulled Nir over. "You do know that this guy is here with me, too, right?"

"Oh, hey, Nir," they said with much less enthusiasm.

"Hey, if I want to be insulted, I can go back to my sergeant in basic training."

It was evident by everyone's affirmation that insulting sergeants were epidemic in the Israeli Defense Forces.

The diminutive Liora said, "My sergeant called me Frodo through my entire basic training."

"That's just wrong," said Yossi. "Your feet aren't near hairy enough for you to be a hobbit."

Lahav spoke up. "Wait, your argument may be a non sequitur. It is still up in the air as to whether girl hobbits have hairy feet. I was reading in a discussion group—"

Nir interrupted. "Hold on a second. There is a discussion group that talks about whether girl hobbits have hairy feet? And you and others spend time in actual conversations debating the point?" Turning to Nicole, he asked, "Is this the world we're trying to save?"

"I'd read it," said Liora.

"Me, too," chimed in Dafna.

"Been there, read that," added Yossi.

"Unbelievable." He looked to Nicole for support, but she just shrugged at him.

"I'm in the non-hairy feet camp," she said.

"You're absolutely no help." Turning back to the screen, he said, "Well, amid all your hobbit research, were you able to figure out where the good General Moshev will be tonight? And please don't tell me he's dining at home."

"We have happy news on that front," said Dafna. "It appears that Mrs. Moshev has been staying with friends in Estonia since soon after shots were fired at Ukraine. The general must not be much of a home cook, because he eats most of his dinners out. His personal secretary makes the reservations for him, and then uploads the information into Moshev's personal calendar."

Nicole clapped her hands. "See? Isn't it easy to get into their calendars?"

"It is now that you showed us how," said Liora, giving a thumbs up.

"So, where will he be tonight?" Nir asked.

"Don't know," answered Dafna. "The secretary hasn't loaded it in yet. I'll let you know when he does."

"Good work. Item two, has the media department sent you the evidence yet?"

"We've got it," said Yossi. "It's good. Let me stream it, then I'll send you a copy after we're done."

The screen went black, except for a white speaker icon in the center. Voices began speaking in Russian. At the bottom of the screen, closed-captioning appeared in English.

Nemtsov: He is a peasant who has risen to a position beyond his abilities.

Moshev: Agreed. The president is poised to do more damage to this country than Yeltsin ever did. We cannot allow
another term.

Nemtsov: If my people have anything to say about it, he
won't.

Moshev: But how? The people are still behind him.

Nemtsov: There are other ways to remove a president from
office. Some of those ways also ensure that he will never
again be a problem.

There was a long pause.

Moshev: I love my country. What must be done, must be
done. Whatever you decide, Boris Yefimovich, I am with you.

Nir was amazed at how smooth and natural the conversation
sounded. "And they just pieced this together from speeches and
interviews?"

The black screen was replaced by the conference table with Yossi
speaking. "They did. But they didn't just pick out words and edit them
together. Then it would have been the audio version of a kidnapper's
ransom note made up of words cut from a magazine. They brought it
down to syllables and sounds. They described it as being like putting
together a 500,000-piece jigsaw puzzle."

"Incredible. What about the videos?"

"They only had time for two, but they are the same quality. Hang
on."

The screen went black again. Then a low-angle shot of two men sitting at a restaurant table popped up with a white "play" arrow in the
middle. One of the men appeared to be General Moshev.

"Who's the other guy?"

Yossi answered off screen, "Ravil Maganov, former chairman of
Lukoil, the Russian multinational energy company. He was an open
critic of Putin and the war against Ukraine. Fell from a sixth-story

window at a Moscow hospital last month. Official word is that he jumped."

Lahav's voice sang in the background, "I can fly with a little help from my friends."

Nir laughed and said, "Play the clip."

The video came to life. Again, Nir was amazed at the skill level of the techs back at headquarters. Here, not only did they have to piece together the words, but they had to CGI the video so that it looked like Moshev was talking when he had never actually been in the restaurant—at least, not that night. It was truly incredible work.

The first video lasted 130 seconds and was incriminating. The second, taken with another dead Putin critic, was three-and-a-half minutes long and was equally convicting.

"Upload them to me and thank the guys in the lab. Amazing."

"Will do," said Yossi. "Anything else you need?"

"No, just let us know the restaurant when you find out."

They signed off with CARL.

"I'm going to start getting ready," Nicole said, rising up and moving toward her room.

Nir settled back into the couch. "Take your time. Enjoy the room. Rest up. Once tonight comes, it'll be showtime."

CHAPTER 27

MATRYOSHKA RESTAURANT, MOSCOW, RUSSIA— OCTOBER 28, 2022—19:50 (7:50 PM) MSK

Several kilometers away from the Ararat Park Hotel, just across the Moskva River, Nir and Nicole followed a host through the Matryoshka Restaurant. Nir waited to allow her to precede him as they began to ascend a wood and iron stairway that led to a loft that ran the full perimeter of the interior. The tables were filled with the Friday night crowd, and there had been a lengthy waiting list. However, four 5,000-ruble notes slipped to the maître d' ensured that when the table Nir had his eye on opened up, he and Nicole were shown to it directly.

The atmosphere was noisy with an old-school Russian charm. The woods were dark, and the chairs were large and upholstered with leather or floral prints. The nesting dolls that gave the restaurant its name were thoughtfully scattered throughout the establishment. At the top of the stairs, their host led them to the left. They had passed two tables when he tilted out a quilted leather bench for Nicole. Before she sat, she turned her back toward Nir, and he helped her remove her overcoat. Underneath, she wore a black print Oscar de La Renta dégradé tulip poplin midi dress. The dress fit her perfectly, and her dark hair set off the bright floral print.

As she spun back toward Nir, the dress flared slightly, and he thought the moment could have been part of a spread in a fashion magazine. Undoubtedly, the lonely man sitting at the table behind him had taken notice. But there was one problem. This scene could never have made the pages of *Elle* or *Marie Claire* because Nicole's eyes were filled with tears. Nir removed his jacket, revealing a sport coat, light sweater, and dress slacks. He handed both Nicole's overcoat and his jacket to the server, along with three folded 1,000-ruble notes, then sat in his dark leather Queen Anne chair.

Moments after sitting, a server appeared, giving them menus. When asked for their drink orders, Nir requested a red wine for Nicole and a Baltika for himself. As soon as he walked away, Nicole spoke. She elevated her voice so that she could be heard above the din that was rising from the crowd on the main floor below.

"I just don't understand. How can it be off?"

"It just is," Nir answered, knowing that because of the way he was facing, his words didn't really matter. Still, he wanted to make sure Nicole's side of the conversation sounded natural. "Apparently, Anatoly doesn't feel that enough big-money people would come if the general didn't attend."

"So, that's just it. Just because some horrid general doesn't want to participate, the whole event is canceled, and we came all the way to Moscow for nothing."

"At least we got to experience the Moscow traffic and the bitterly wet cold."

"That's not funny," Nicole scolded. "Will Anatoly not reconsider? Maybe the event will not be as big, but it can still help. Seems any amount raised for the families of dead soldiers would be helpful. I've already waived my fee, but I'd also be willing to put 5,000 euros more toward the fund."

"I'd be willing to match that. But that's just a drop in the bucket compared to what some of these other businessmen would be able to donate. At least if their bank accounts are anything like Anatoly's."

Nicole opened her purse and pulled out a tissue. As she dabbed her eyes, she said, "But it doesn't matter what either of us are willing to do. It doesn't matter who could be helped. It doesn't matter the sacrifices we've made just to get here. One horrid general says, 'No,' and it's all over."

Nir reached across the table and took her hand. "I'm sorry, sweetheart. According to Anatoly, that is just the way it is in Russia. It is all about position and status. If there is no one from a high-enough level attending, then no one else will attend. The general was of that status. Without him, we are dead in the water."

As he said that last sentence, Nir watched Nicole's eyes move up and to the right. Inside, he smiled. *That was quick. The hook is set. Time to reel the fish in.*

From over his left shoulder, Nir heard, "Pardon me. I could not help overhearing your conversation. Are you speaking of the fashion fundraiser that Anatoly Kvashnin is putting on?"

Nir turned and saw the lonely man from the table behind them.

"Was putting on," said Nicole. "And yes."

"I thought I recognized you. You are the model. Nicole…" The man stretched out her first name, apparently looking for some help.

Nicole obliged. "Le Roux. I am. And you are?"

The man smiled widely. "Why, I am the horrid general."

Nicole gasped and Nir stood. Holding out his hand, Nir said, "General, sir, I am so sorry. We didn't mean to insult you. We don't even know you."

General Moshev shook Nir's hand. "Nonsense. Come, join me at my table. I think we may have a few things to discuss."

He held his hand out to Nicole. She looked at Nir, who nodded. Taking the general's hand, she stood and allowed him to lead her to the bench at his table. Looking to Nir, he said, "Please," indicating the place next to Nicole.

"Thank you, sir," Nir said as he sat.

Once the general had resumed his chair, Nir spoke. "Again, I am so sorry. We had no idea that you were right behind us."

Moshev held up his hand. "Stop. I don't mind a little subterfuge. In fact, it can be quite amusing. But please don't lie to me."

Shocked and chastened, Nir said, "Wait, you knew that we knew you were right there?"

Nicole lightly slapped his arm. "I told you and Anatoly that he'd see right through it."

The general laughed. "She is both beautiful and smart."

"Yes, she is," said Nicole, gripping Nir's arm.

"Now I do find myself at a disadvantage. You obviously know me. And I have discovered who you are, Miss le Roux. But I still don't know your name," Moshev said, looking at Nir.

"My apologies, general. My name is Naor Shapira. I'm from Antwerp. I am Nicole's fiancé."

Moshev's face lit up. "Fiancé? Congratulations."

"Thank you," Nicole said, lifting her left hand toward the general and waggling her fingers.

The general took her by the fingertips. "That is a beautiful ring. The stone is quite striking."

"Naor is a jeweler. He had it designed just for me."

"Of course! A Jew from Antwerp. Undoubtedly, you are in the diamond business."

Nir let the slight roll off him. "And you are Deputy in the Ministry of Defense General of the Army Leonid Anatolyevich Moshev."

"At your service," said the general with a slight bow.

The server arrived with Nicole's wine and Nir's beer, placing them on the table. He then refilled the general's wine glass. From what Nir could see of the bottle's label, it appeared to be a German Riesling. On a plate in front of the general was a long white fish filet with three brightly colored purees, each of which had been already dipped into. "Please don't let us keep you from your meal," said Nir.

Again, the general bowed. "Thank you. Their sablefish is a specialty. You must order it."

"It looks delicious," said Nicole. Then, with a wink, she added, "But I think you've already realized that you are the fish that we came here to catch."

The general laughed, showing his mouthful of food, and looked to Nir. "She's marvelous. You are a lucky man. Now, you must tell me— did Anatoly put you up to this? Be honest."

"His idea, but I agreed immediately," Nir lied. The ruse was purely Nir's idea. He had only informed Kvashnin of the plan by text. The oligarch had pushed back briefly, but had given in. He recognized the harmlessness of the plan. It was just a sloppy stunt that had no chance of not being discovered, but which Nir believed would accomplish his purpose perfectly.

"But you said no," Moshev said, pointing at Nicole.

"That I did," she answered, giving Nir a push.

The general took another bite of his fish. "Listen, I don't know if Anatoly told you why I turned him down. We are in a time of conflict. For many, it is quite unseemly for a public official to be seen attending something as frivolous as a fashion show." Turning to Nicole, he added, "No offense intended."

"None taken. And we understand your concern. We had the same qualms about agreeing to participate. But when we heard the cause—helping to alleviate the suffering of those who have lost loved ones in battle—well, let's just say that it hit close to home."

"How so?" The general appeared to be intrigued as he put down his eating utensils.

Nicole sighed, and tears formed in her eyes. "There is a girl, Viktoria, another model. I don't know her well, but I do know her some. We've been in a few shows together. We were in Seoul last March. It's always so crazy backstage before a show. Sometimes I step away just to get a moment of calm. As I was looking for a quiet place, I heard crying. I followed the sound and saw Viktoria sitting on the floor sobbing. When I asked her what was wrong, she said that she had just received word from home that her brother was dead. I couldn't believe it. She was a twin like I am, and I can't imagine losing my brother. I asked her what had happened. She looked at me for a moment without saying anything. It seemed like she was trying to figure out if she could trust me."

Nicole paused for a moment. She retrieved another tissue from her purse and dabbed at her eyes before continuing. "She waved me down and I sat next to her. Then she whispered to me, 'My brother was in the army fighting near Kyiv. The Ukrainians launched a counteroffensive. He was killed in the fighting.'"

"I remember that time. Our offensive had stalled, and our men were forced to dig in," the general quietly recalled.

"My heart broke for her. We just cried there together on that floor until someone found us and told us that we were both wanted by the stylists."

Nir put his arm around Nicole and pulled her close. She rested her head on his shoulder. This whole encounter had been a ruse, but the story was true. The tears that trailed down Nicole's cheeks were real. Nir spoke up. "That is what moved Nicole—both of us, actually—to say yes to the show here."

"I felt so helpless. There was nothing I could do for Viktoria. But maybe by walking down some stupid fashion runway, I thought I might be able to help someone else who has lost their brother or their son or their father or their husband," Nicole said, putting her hand on Nir's chest.

Moshev was silent. Nir noticed that he had not touched his food through the whole story. Finally, the general said, "I had thought it suspicious that two Westerners would come to Moscow for a charity event for the Russian army. Your story sets my mind at ease."

Removing his arm from behind Nicole, Nir leaned forward. "Anatoly told us about your work in the Ministry of Emergency Situations. I can't imagine the things you have seen, the suffering you have witnessed. And even though you helped so many millions of people, I'm sure there were times when you wished you had the ability to do more. But I also have no doubt you saw the impact that one small act of compassion can have on someone who has lost so much. It's a reminder to them that they are not in this alone. There still are people around them who care."

"Sometimes people just need a little light in their lives. The money raised at the charity event can provide that small spark of light," Nicole added.

Moshev continued in his silence. Then a smile spread across his face. He picked up his knife and fork and said, "You two are good." He cut off a piece of his sablefish, dipped it in each of the three purees, and put it into his mouth. "No wonder Anatoly sent you. I would have no problem saying no to him. He is a bloated billionaire with a hag for a wife and a whore for a girlfriend. But you two…" He took another bite. "You tell Anatoly Mikhailovich that I will be at his fashion show, but that I will be there because of her," he pointed his knife at Nicole, "not because of him. But that doesn't change the fact that he still owes me a big favor."

Nicole's face brightened. "Wait, you'll do it? Oh, thank you…thank you!"

"Tell him also that I want it all over the media outlets and social media that this is a fundraising event for the families of fallen soldiers. I want people to know that I am there for the troops, not because I want to see a bunch of sluts parade around in skimpy clothes."

Nicole squeezed Nir's arm, and he cringed on the inside for her. He said, "One hundred percent. I'll make sure of it. We are so grateful to you, General Moshev. And we're so honored to have someone of your stature at the event."

Moshev waved him off. "I've said yes. You can cut the crap. Save it for the fertilizer billionaire. You two can pay me back by staying and having dessert with me. They have a pavlova that will knock you off your feet."

A lonely man inviting two new friends to share dessert. It was the least they could do. "As long as we aren't intruding, we would love to."

"Intruding? Nonsense. Now, you can start by telling me how it is that the diamond trade has turned into such a Jew thing."

Nir's heart sank. It was going to be a long night. But at least the mission had been a success. He could deal with a little antisemitism and misogyny, especially when he knew what tomorrow night held for this man.

Settling back on the bench seat, Nir began, "It all started back in the Middle Ages, when Jews were prohibited from owning land or growing crops…"

CHAPTER 28

Nir walked from shelf to shelf, running his finger along the spines. He was surprised to learn that the hundreds of books in the spacious study were all real and not just decorative displays. The vertical Cyrillic writing made it impossible for him to know what most of the titles were, but he did find two wide shelves with French books and one whole bookcase of works written in English.

Reading the names in the English case, he recognized hardcover copies of numerous big-name thriller writers. Two of the shelves contained business philosophy du jour bestsellers of the past several decades, telling him the speed at which he should think, how big he needed to be to never fail, and what seven habits would make him most effective. There was also a shelf dedicated to biographies of businessmen like Carnegie, Rockefeller, and Jobs, and most of the US presidents since the 1980s.

He slid one book off the shelf that promised to tell him his emotional intelligence. But as he flipped through its pages, he got a mental picture of the gang at CARL watching him on some unknown hidden camera.

Yeah, I would never live that down, he thought as he quickly reshelved the volume. *I wonder how it's going for Nicole. She's definitely taking one for the team. I wouldn't wish Kvashnin's wife on anyone.*

Immediately after Nir and Nicole had been shown in the front door just after 3:00, a frantic woman rushed up to them. She introduced herself as Polina Viktorovna, grabbed Nicole's hand, and yanked her away, saying, "Where have you been? *Tolya* said you'd be here to help me prepare, not that you'd come sauntering in like some diva just hours before the event."

Nicole had turned back to Nir, who couldn't do anything except shrug and wave. He hadn't seen her since. Judging by the brief moment he had seen Polina and the warnings Anatoly had given about his wife, he knew that Nicole must be miserable.

What was that old proverb about living on the corner of a roof rather than living with a nagging wife? I think Mykonos and a girlfriend must be the billionaire oligarch version of a roof corner.

Kvashnin left Nir waiting in the entryway for ten minutes. When he did finally show, he was all business. He mechanically guided his guest on a room-by-room tour, but it was obvious that his agitation was increasing by the minute. Nir, for his part, couldn't help being awed by the estate. Located in the elite, mega-wealthy village of Zakharovo, a two-and-a-half-hour drive west of Moscow's city center, Kvashnin's mansion was 2,300 square meters on a 200-acre plot of land sandwiched between a golf course and a long, meandering lake.

As one door after another was opened, Nir recognized that the exquisitely decorated house was designed for appearance and not for comfort. This was not a family home. It was a spread in *Architectural Digest.* On the lower walkout level, Nir watched the steam rise as he listened to the dimensions of the pool being described as well as the sophistication of its heating system. Kvashnin opened the doors to an eight-lane bowling alley, a 30-seat theater, and a sauna that could comfortably fit a squad of burly Russian troops.

By the time he stomped into his study with his charge, Kvashnin seemed to have reached his boiling point. He curtly told Nir to remain in this room until he came to get him, then stormed off, firmly closing the door behind him, and turning the lock. That had been four hours ago. The only signs of life he had seen since was some butler or assistant who had brought Nir a sandwich, some caviar with toast, and a bottle of sparkling water. The man had also been kind enough to unlock, at Nir's request, a door that led to an adjoining bathroom.

The whump of a helicopter's rotors sounded overhead. Nir walked back to a rear window to watch as another aircraft landed on the helipad. They had begun to arrive about 30 minutes ago. As soon as it touched, a fully enclosed luxury cart rolled up. Two men exited the front of the vehicle, opened the chopper's door, and helped the passengers transfer from the copter. The men then drove the guests to the house while the helicopter ascended to make room for the next.

How much of this enormous wealth was made off the suffering of the nation's millions of impoverished citizens? How many hundreds of thousands of Russians are still living two to three families per apartment, barely getting by? All so the elite can fly their helicopters in to watch a fashion show while they pretend to care about the thousands upon thousands of young men they are sending off to be mowed down by the defenders of Ukraine.

Turning, Nir noticed a portrait hanging on the wall. He recognized the man with his bushy gray hair, full dark mustache, and beard so abundant that it would make a hipster jealous. Nir smiled. *I better be careful, Karl, or I'm going to start sounding like you.*

The lock turned and the door opened. A red-faced Kvashnin stepped in and slammed the door behind him.

"You," he said, pointing his finger at Nir. "You are going to get me killed."

"That's quite possible, Anatoly, but not tonight." Nir sat down calmly in a soft leather chair that gave off a wonderful aroma that Dima liked to call "new cow smell."

"This is not the time for joking. The general will be here in five minutes. I am prepared to tell him all about this stunt."

Nir knew he had to talk this man down. The Russian could be irrational, but he was smart. Coolness and logic were what he needed. "But that's not part of our deal, *Tolya.*"

"I don't care about our deal. And only my friends call me *Tolya.*"

"Calm down. You're going to have kittens. Sit." Nir gestured with his hands for the man to ease up.

Anatoly stood defiantly. Then he visibly deflated and sat on a couch alongside Nir.

"There you go, Anatoly. Now take a deep breath." When the oligarch had complied, Nir continued, "You are not going to tell the general about our little ploy."

"Why not?" It was obvious that the man was still in major internal turmoil.

"Because if you do, I'll have to kill you. And neither of us wants that." Immediately, Nir knew that was the wrong thing to say. But what's the point in threatening someone if you can't have fun doing it?

Kvashnin jumped up. "See, it's that. If I go through with this, the general will have me killed. If I don't, you're going to kill me. Either way, I am a dead man."

"I know, I know. It's the age-old Russian conundrum. Who's going to kill me first? But I will tell you the one path you have to surviving all this. You go through with the plan. I won't touch you. And neither will Moshev because he'll know that if he does, Putin will hear that he's plotting against him and will send him off to the Republic of Tuva, where he'll likely get stampeded by a raging herd of yaks."

The Russian glared at Nir, but then a smile spread across his face. "A raging herd of yaks. That I would like to see."

"Everything is in place, my friend. As long as no one gets cold feet, it will go off just as we planned."

"And you will tell him that you forced me into this? That you threatened my life?"

Nir stood. "I will tell him. He's ready to believe anything negative about the Jews. Besides, if I tell him I threatened your life, I wouldn't be lying, would I?"

In a moment, all the oligarch's calm fell away. "Why must you keep bringing up killing me? I get the point." He moved toward the door, but turned before opening it. "Continue to wait here. Someone will come and get you just before the show begins. There is a place for you to stand in the back. Once it is over, you will be led to a room near this one. When the general arrives here, I will have you brought in."

"Thank you, *Tolya*," Nir said, sitting back down. "And don't worry. For a man who sells crap for a living, you're going to come out of this smelling like a rose."

CHAPTER 29

20:45 (8:45 PM) MSK

Nicole strutted down the runway wearing a green silk chiffon midi dress. The V-neckline was cut by a built-in corset that matched the floral pattern. Calf-high leather boots completed the ensemble.

Nir wasn't sure if this was a Polina dress or not, but it was beautiful. With Nicole's hair pulled back tightly and her thousand-yard model stare, Nir once again wondered what a woman like this was doing with a guy like him.

This was her third outfit. If nothing had changed since they had talked during the ride out, she would have only one more—the finale of the evening. But he couldn't know for sure whether that was still the plan because he hadn't had an opportunity to speak with Nicole since they had first arrived. He hoped that he would get a few minutes alone with her before all the action began later tonight, but he was beginning to doubt he'd even get that.

But even if I can't see her, she knows what she's doing. She's ready.

The more Nir thought about it, the more he realized that seeing her before it all went down was more for himself than for her. She looked perfectly calm and in her element as she stopped at the end of the runway. She spun a 180, then turned back again. When she did, she caught Nir's eye and winked. Then she spun again and walked off. The audience cheered this moment of humanity, and quite a few turned his way to see who the lucky recipient of her notice was. They were disappointed. Nir had quickly slipped behind one of the dozen ornate columns that decorated the perimeter of the long dining hall.

When the next model hit the runway, attention turned away from his direction and Nir slipped back out. His nerves were at a peak. So much was riding on this evening. If Moshev refused to give him the information he needed, it could mean the deaths of thousands of his people, possibly tens of thousands. He had no idea for sure how big that number was because they were still in the dark about almost everything surrounding this Russian plot against Israel.

So many lives, and it's all about money. Well, money and religion.

Just recently, Nir had read about Putin making a demand for ownership of three religious sites on the Mount of Olives and one near the Church of the Holy Sepulchre. The news had started rumbling about six months earlier, but only now was it starting to heat up. It was obvious to everyone outside of Russia that Putin was making a play for popularity among the Russian masses. It was also apparent that if Jerusalem's government decided to block Russian state ownership of the churches, Putin could use that as a pretext for an attack on Israel.

As crazy as it sounded, Nir knew that it wouldn't be the first time a Christian site in the Holy Land was at least partly responsible for starting a war. A couple months ago, he had been on the balcony of Efraim Cohen's Tel Aviv apartment. His friend had grilled two beautiful steaks, and they were basking in the culinary afterglow while nursing bottles of Goldstar. The two were talking about Russia, and Efraim said, "Do you know the Star of Bethlehem started the Crimean War?"

"No, but if you hum a few bars, I'll try to jump in," Nir said, adding a rim shot.

"Idiot. I'm serious. How much do you know about the Church of the Nativity in Bethlehem?"

"It's where Jesus was supposedly born."

"Brilliant, Einstein. I mean the politics of it. It's always been a place of contention. It's one of the sites Constantine's mother picked out for a holy shrine. They built a church on it. It burned down. So, they built another one in the sixth century. When the Persians invaded the next century and started burning churches, they let this one stand. They saw some mosaic in it of the magi and said, 'Hey, those guys look like us. Let's skip this one.'"

Nir laughed. "Now their Iranian descendants want to nuke the place. Go figure."

"True, true. Anyway, you know how it is with the Christians. None of them get along and they all want their piece of the pie. So, part of the Church of the Nativity belongs to the Greek Orthodox, part to the Armenian Apostolics, and part to the Catholics. In fact, if you go down into the grotto, you'll see 15 silver lamps. Greeks get six, Armenians get five, and the Catholics get four."

"Pope's got to step up his game," Nir said, reaching for another two bottles from an ice chest. He popped the tops off each and gave one to Efraim.

"So, sometime in the 1700s, a silver star was affixed to the marble slab in the grotto that marks the spot where Jesus was born. On it were written Latin words that mean 'Here Jesus Christ was born to the Virgin Mary.'"

"Yeah, I've seen it." When Efraim raised his eyebrows at him, Nir added, "In pictures."

"Well, the Greeks were pretty ticked off about it. They were like, 'Hey, this is our part of the church, but someone put this star here that has Latin writing on it.'"

"Totally understand the outrage," Nir said, rolling his eyes.

"No kidding. But then, sometime before the Crimean War started, somebody stole the star. Everyone blamed the Greeks."

"Of course. You just can't trust those Greeks. Especially when they come bearing gifts."

"You going to let me tell this or what?"

"Yes. Just get to the point. This story is longer than a Netflix docuseries."

"So, the French were already ticked off at the Russians—"

Nir waved his hands around. "Wait, the French? When did they come into the story?"

"This is the eighteenth century. The French are in every story. Now shut up and listen. The French were already mad at the Russians and were looking for an excuse to enter the Crimean War. Catholic France said, 'Those Orthodox star-stealing Russians need to be taught a lesson or two.' So, they joined the war. Then Britain did the same after them, and Russia ended up losing."

Nir waited for the rest, but Efraim sat quietly drinking his beer. "That's the story? Seriously? I have so many questions. Like, wasn't it the Greek Orthodox who supposedly took the star, not the Russian Orthodox?"

"Doesn't matter."

"Did Russia have anything at all to do with the theft?"

"Doesn't matter."

"Did they prove that Russia had possession of the star?"

"No one had possession of the star. Seems someone made a replica of it in 1853 before the Crimean War started. They were going to replace the missing one, but before they could install the replica, the original was returned."

Nir was on his feet now. "No, no, no. You're saying that the star that was the reason for France getting into the war had already been returned before the war even started?"

"You got it."

Nir sat back down dumbfounded. "That is the stupidest story that I've ever heard in my life, and you've told me some pretty stupid ones. By the way, your little teaser that the star started the war was totally inaccurate. At most, it helped get France into it."

Efraim shrugged. "Maybe. But you've got to admit that while a headline of 'Did you ever hear how the Star of Bethlehem may have been a contributing factor to France's entrance into the already-raging Crimean War' might be slightly more accurate, it would have been far less compelling."

Nir smiled now as he recalled that night. But then his amusement was quickly tempered by the thought that Putin could be doing the same thing now that France had done then. When you want to fight a war, you'll look for any excuse to do so, and historically, religion seemed to be one of the more frequent excuses. This was one of the reasons that he pushed back so hard against Nicole's Christianity. Religion had done little over the centuries except give enormous amounts of power to a lot of bad people.

Nicole broke through the curtain in what Nir hoped was her finale outfit. This was a bright red chiffon dress with long sleeves and a heart-shaped cutout neckline. Even though it didn't make for a "wow" moment, it was a perfect ending to the show. The dress was Russian through and through, Nir thought. And the way Nicole wore it, one would think she was a *devushka* from Saint Petersburg instead of a surfer girl from Cape Town.

She was in full swagger mode as she reached the end of the runway. Once again, she did her turns, then walked back and through the curtain. Moments later, the models returned in a line. At the end, Polina walked out holding hands with Nicole. She waved as the guests stood to their feet and applauded her. After a couple minutes of glorying in the adulation, she walked back, followed by her entourage of models.

As soon as they were gone, a podium was quickly brought out. When it was set and the microphone loudly tapped and tested, Kvashnin walked out onto the stage. Standing at the podium, he went through his own tapping and blowing to ensure the microphone was working. Then he began speaking in Russian. Nir couldn't understand a word he said, but by the reaction of the audience, he seemed to be a dynamic speaker. They laughed. They cheered. When he pointed to Polina, who had found her way to a seat in the front, they all stood and applauded again.

Then Nir recognized the name Leonid Anatolyevich Moshev. The room erupted in applause once again as everyone jumped to their feet. The full-uniformed general didn't even look to the crowd as he walked up the steps to the runway. After shaking Kvashnin's hand, he stood behind the podium. The applause slowly tapered off as people found their seats again.

Moshev cleared his throat, then tapped the microphone and blew into it to make sure it was on. Nir shook his head. Then the general began speaking. The energy and excitement that had been so strong was immediately sucked from the room. There was no evidence of the man's personality from the night before at the restaurant. No affability. No enthusiasm. He was like a different person.

The man spoke for 30 mind-emptying, foot-cramping minutes. Nir wasn't sure if it would have been better if he could have understood the man. But as he scanned the vacant faces of the listeners, he realized that it was probably better the way he had it.

When Moshev finally finished, the people once again stood and applauded—this time, with far less enthusiasm.

Even in former Soviet Russia, this guy is a boring speaker. That's saying something.

Kvashnin, however, was as full of excitement as ever. He bounded up the steps to shake Moshev's hand once again. After saying a few more words, people began to rise to their feet. From the schedule that the Russian had given him ahead of time, the audience would now be heading to the indoor patio for cocktails. Nir, the oligarch had made clear, was not invited.

After the crowd had gone, he remained in the back as the staff quickly began remaking the room. Rather than set up tables for dinner, white tablecloths were spread across the runway. The place settings came next, then the chairs. Nir had to hand it to Kvashnin or Polina or whoever came up with the idea. It was ingenious, matching convenience with the whole fashion show theme. He could picture people talking about it to their friends later—"Then we ate right there on the runway. It was delightful."

A hand tapped him on the shoulder. He turned and saw one of the staff, who beckoned him to follow. Nir did, and he was led into a bedroom. The staff member motioned that he should sit in a chair, then said, "I get you in time."

Nir thanked him as he sat. The man nodded, closed the door as he exited, then locked it.

Nir sighed. *New location, same wait. Although I would rather be here than where Nicole is. Way too many people, all speaking a language she can't understand. Poor girl. She's got to be miserable.*

Suddenly, the lock turned and the door swung open. It was the same young man who had just shown him into the room.

"The general is preparing to leave. Mr. Kvashnin says you must come now."

A sudden dump of adrenaline released into Nir's system. He jumped up and followed the man.

CHAPTER 30

The door opened, and Nir heard Moshev's voice saying, "…to your fiancé."

Walking in, Nir saw the general leaning over Nicole's hand. All eyes turned his way when he entered. Nicole had a wide-eyed look of helplessness. Moshev looked disappointed, as if he knew Nir's arrival would cost him even more time. Moshev's two bodyguards were expressionless. And Kvashnin's scowl said that he was looking for an excuse to kill Nir and throw him in the lake behind the house.

Nir turned on the charm. "General, I am so glad that I caught you. I wanted to thank you once again, from the bottom of my heart, for sacrificing your time for this amazing cause."

Moshev released Nicole and took Nir's outstretched hand. "It was my pleasure. And may I once again thank you for the company of yourself and your future bride last night."

"It was our pleasure, wasn't it, dear?"

"Absolutely," Nicole said.

Kvashnin's phone chirped. He looked at it, then stepped forward and took his friend's hand away from Nir, shaking it himself. "*Lyonya*, thank you so much for coming. I would love to see you out, but Polina says there is an emergency in the kitchen and is requesting I meet her there."

"Requesting?" Moshev asked with his eyebrows raised.

Kvashnin let out a bitter laugh. "You know my plight too well, my friend. I will be in contact."

The general turned to the two remaining guests. "I'm afraid I must follow him out. My helicopter is due soon."

Nir took hold of his hand once again, preventing him from leaving. "If I may impose on you for just a moment, sir. I have something I want to show you that I think you'll find most interesting. I promise I will not be long."

"I'm sorry. I really must go." The man looked down with the beginning of concern as Nir tightened his grip.

"Please, General," said Nicole. She moved to the couch. "Come sit next to me. It will only take a moment of your time."

After a pause, Moshev smiled nervously. "I never could say no to a pretty girl."

Nicole laughed. When the general sat down, she followed, taking the cushion right next to him.

After they were seated, Nir went to the bookshelves and pulled something from the English fiction section. He walked back and placed it on the general's lap. It was an iPad.

"Sir, if I may. You might want to send your men out of the room."

Moshev's uncertainty grew. "No, they remain with me."

"Suit yourself." Reaching into his pocket, he pulled out a pair of Air Pods. Placing the case into the general's hand, he said, "Then, may I suggest you use these?"

The general watched Nir suspiciously as he removed the earbuds and slipped them in. Nir reached in front of the Russian and hit *play* on the iPad. Ten seconds later, the general pulled out the earbuds and pointed to his bodyguards.

"You! Wait for me outside!" When they hesitated, he added, "Now!"

When the door closed behind them, the general wheeled on Nir. "What is this?" he demanded.

"It's you committing treason, General."

"But…but this isn't me. I never said these things."

Nir looked down at the iPad. "It sure looks like you."

"And it sounds like you, too" added Nicole. "I have to admit, *Lyonya*, I didn't think you were the type."

"I don't know what little game you are playing, but this will never stand up. Everyone will know this is not me."

"But will they?" Nir asked. "You've seen only the first ten seconds. We've got almost ten minutes." The Mossad tech department had finished a third video file that morning, and CARL had forwarded it just before Nir and Nicole left the hotel.

"There are recorded phone calls on there too, General. It's all quite disturbing. You should watch," said Nicole.

Moshev's face was red, and he was visibly sweating. He put the Air Pods back into his ears and once again hit *play*. For the next ten minutes, the general cycled between anger, fear, frustration, and helplessness.

When he reached the end of the second phone recording, he hurled the iPad across the room. The earbuds followed. Nir nodded to Nicole, and she stood and moved to a nearby chair.

Nir squatted down in front of Moshev. "What do you think?"

"It will never hold up. People will see right through it."

"Sounds like you're trying to convince yourself, not me. This is primo quality, Leonid. Best there is. No one will be able to see through it because no one will want to see through it. Not in this political climate. People are out looking for traitors and scapegoats. And, even if somehow they do recognize them as fakes, the suspicion will remain."

The Russian silently fumed as he thought. He looked to Nir, then to Nicole, then back to Nir. "What is it you want from me?"

"That's a good question, General. It shows you are still thinking clearly. All we want is a little information."

Moshev shook his head. "No. I will not reveal classified information to you. I refuse to be part of some plot to kill the president or to help you carry out some sort of terrorist action."

Nir stood back up. "Wow! How interesting that your mind went right to presidential assassination. It's almost as if you were already conspiring against him. Don't you think, darling?"

"It appears we may have just saved Vladmir Vladimirovich's life," said Nicole, leaning back in the deep chair with her legs crossed. "Maybe we'll get a medal or something."

Moshev glared at her. "You may find this amusing, Nicole le Roux, famous model. But once I tell people about this attempt at blackmail, your career and your freedom will be over."

Nir squatted back down and put his hand on the general's arm. "You forget one thing, comrade. We have all the power. As soon as this hits social media, it will be a very short time before it reaches the news media and the president's desk. You know how quickly juicy bad news travels. And then, talk about losing your freedom—you'll be lucky if you get out of this with your life. Maganov, Rapoport, Nemtsov, Berezovsky, Litvinenko, Politkovskaya—you'll just be another name on the list of Putin's enemies who ended up dead."

"It is truly a remarkable Russian skill to be able to commit suicide by shooting oneself in the back of the head," Nicole said. Nir almost started laughing. It was evident to him now that she was fully equipped and prepared to handle any situation they might find themselves in.

"What is stopping me from having my men come back in and shoot you down like the dogs you are?"

"You are a very smart man, Leonid Anatolyevich. You know the answer as well as I do. We are just messengers. If we don't report in within the next thirty minutes, these recordings will be released. Oh, yes, and there's also the address Karusambla tee 60, Viimsi, Estonia."

Moshev lunged at Nir, grabbing him by his neck.

CHAPTER 31

22:10 (10:10 PM) MSK

You are threatening my family?"

The man was stronger than he looked. Nir's krav maga training would have had him yanking the man's hands downward as he kicked him in the groin. But he had placed himself in a bad defensive position by squatting down. So, instead, he pistoned himself up with his hands in a praying position. The force separated Moshev's arms, sending him falling backwards. Nir immediately let his legs fold again, using his body weight to add inertia to a palm strike in the middle of the general's chest.

The man began gasping for air. "Go listen at the door," Nir said to Nicole. "Make sure his goons aren't coming in."

As Nicole moved, Nir positioned the general back onto the couch. "That was stupid," he said.

A minute passed as Moshev tried to get his breath. It was obvious he recognized the address of the rental home into which he had moved his wife, children, and grandchildren for safety during the Ukrainian conflict. The general also understood the ramifications of Nir having that information. Finally, he gasped, "Don't hurt my family."

"There is a strike team positioned outside that address. Your family will get hurt only if we get hurt. Understand?"

Moshev nodded. A few more moments passed before he asked, "What is the information you want?"

"That is the question I've been waiting for."

Still putting on an air of defiance, the general added, "I'm not saying that I will answer you. I just want to know."

"That's fair. You and your government are planning a strike on Israel. I want to know the details."

Moshev sighed deeply. "You're Mossad. Of course. I should have known."

"Yeah. Kind of a helpless, sinking feeling, isn't it? I get that reaction a lot."

"You think that you are funny. You are not."

Nir shrugged. "I don't know. Dear, what do you think?"

Over by the door, Nicole noncommittally teetered her hand from side to side.

"Ouch. So, Leonid Anatolyevich, we're running out of time, and I have zero information from you. Tell me about the attack on Israel and when it will be."

Moshev laughed. "Why do you think that I would know this? Attacks on Israel are not part of my purview."

"I wondered the same thing. But then I spoke with someone who was very insistent that you were in the know. Over the years, I've developed a good sense of when someone is lying to me and when they are not. That is how I know that you are lying to me, and he was not."

"Someone's coming," Nicole said, stepping back from the door. She pulled a phone out of her purse.

"Be very careful what you say," said Nir, sliding back into a chair.

There was a knock on the door. It opened, and one of Moshev's bodyguards stepped in. He said something in Russian, and the general replied. The man walked back out.

"What did you say?"

"He said that my helicopter is here. I told him I would be done soon."

Nir turned to Nicole, who was looking at a voice translator app on her phone. She nodded.

"Good," Nir said. "Now, tell me about the attack."

"If I tell you, how do I know that you will not use this forgery to blackmail me time and time again?"

"I give you my word."

Moshev scoffed at this. "The word of a man who manufacturers evidence and threatens my family."

"The word of a man who would do absolutely anything, including risking my life by coming to Moscow, to save the lives of my fellow Israelis."

The Russian eyed him, then sighed and leaned back into the couch. "The date is November 15, soon after the American elections. Originally, it was going to be in late October, but you Israelis destroyed the missile delivery system. But it turns out this actually works better because it won't tilt the elections in a direction we don't want them to go."

"And what is the attack?"

Moshev remained silent, staring at Nir defiantly.

"Really? Now you go mute? I'm getting tired of this game, General. Nicole, call Yossi."

Moshev's eyes widened as he turned her way. She speed-dialed a number, then said, "Yossi, initiate phase one social media release."

"No!" Moshev called out. His eyes were wide, and he was breathing hard.

"Put that on hold a second," Nicole said, then brought the phone down from her ear.

This time it was Nir's hand that went around Moshev's neck. "I'm tired of your delays, Leonid Anatolyevich. Tell me now!"

The general coughed, then gagged. "It's a chemical weapons attack," he finally managed to croak out as Nir cranked his head farther and farther back. "Fired from Syria. The new missiles arrived three days ago."

Nir couldn't believe his ears. Chemical weapons. The agony, the death, the devastation would be incredible. This was low, even for Russia. His grip tightened even more.

"You're lying to me, General. A Russian chemical attack on Israel would start World War Three. There aren't a lot of countries that like us, but this would cross a line even for the ones that hate us."

"Naor," Nicole cried out. Nir noticed the redness of the general's face. He loosened his grip slightly.

The general sucked in a deep breath. "That's why it won't be us doing it. Please. Let go and I'll explain."

Nir loosened his grip more but didn't pull his hand away. "Talk."

"We've arranged it, but there will be no Russian fingerprints on the attack. The new precision missiles are Iranian. The ones firing them will be one of the ayatollah's proxy militias."

"And the chemicals. Where are you getting those?"

"They will be from Assad's chemicals stored under the city of Damascus. Iran had the missiles, Syria has the chemicals, and the militias will fire them off. We just supply the technology and the impetus. Our hands are clean."

"Why would Iran do this for you? They know that we'll retaliate."

"In their minds, you'll be so caught up in your own recovery that it will give them time to enrich enough ninety percent uranium for a nuclear weapon. You thought your great airstrike last year was the *coup de grâce* for their nuclear program. But you only knocked them back, not out. With a little help from us, they're already back producing limited supplies of highly enriched uranium. This will open the door for them to finish the job. Once they have a nuclear bomb, you'll have to think twice about retaliation."

"And what does Russia gain?"

"A weak Israel. And a weak Israel means natural gas exports slow, Abraham Accords bog down, the president gets his religious sites, and all that adds up to a boost in popularity despite the struggles in the special military operation in Ukraine. It also means a sure reelection in 2024."

"And all it will cost is thousands of lives."

"Thousands of Jewish lives. In many Russian minds, there is a difference. You must also understand that a weaker Israel also opens the door for a possible appropriation of your gas fields. You are becoming our biggest natural gas competitor. The voices calling for the president to do something about you are getting louder."

Nir fell back into his chair. "Stop this."

"I can't."

"We'll tell the media."

"No one would believe you. Besides, all it would do is delay. The only way to ensure the chemicals don't end up on your side of the border is to destroy them while they're still in Syria."

"Where are they in Damascus?"

"How would I know? I've never even been to Damascus. The only reason I was brought into this is because I understand mass casualty events more than any other general in the Russian army. And let me tell you, this will bring devastation like nothing you've ever seen."

Nir's mind was reeling. He'd seen pictures and videos from the gas attacks in Ghouta and Douma, both in Syria. To imagine that happening in Haifa or Tiberius or Tel Aviv was more than he could handle. "Nicole, have you forwarded this?"

"Done," she answered, just as she hit *send* on a text and returned her phone to her purse.

"Good," Nir said as he stood. "I'll be watching you, General. If anything happens to us on our way out, the information will be released, and your family will pay a heavy price. If you tell anyone about our conversation here, the information will be released, and your family will pay. Anatoly knew nothing about this. He was just paying a debt he owed me. If anything should happen to him, information will release, and your family will pay. Do you understand?"

Defeated, Moshev whispered, "I understand."

Suddenly, a side door swung open and Kvashnin strode in. He was followed by two men carrying pistols.

CHAPTER 32

Kvashnin's arms were open wide, and his demeanor was jovial. "You told him not to harm me, just as you promised. I didn't think you would. It is good to know, my Mossad friend, that you are a man of your word. I, however, am not. I got to where I am by exploiting opportunities, and it has been a very long time since I've been given this kind of opportunity."

Nir stood as the oligarch approached him. Kvashnin's speed surprised Nir as the man's fist connected with the side of his face. The power of the blow was also unexpected. As Nir stumbled back, his foot caught a chair leg and his body twisted. He careened off an end table, and landed on the ground.

"That was for threatening me," Kvashnin said, walking around the overturned chair. "This is for forcing me to spend time with my wife." He drove his foot into Nir's stomach. Nir curled into a ball.

From the ground, Nir heard a crash. Then he saw broken pieces of painted ceramic fall to the carpet around him. "Back off, toadface," Nicole said.

Nir looked around and saw Nicole with a porcelain owl cocked back in her hand.

"Toadface? Ouch. I pay a lot for this look. What are you going to do with that owl, little girl?" Kvashnin said from above him. The man's foot flew into Nir's chest. Pain flared through his body as he heard another crash. More shards fell around him. As he struggled to get some air, he heard Kvashnin say, "It's a good thing I don't like to hit women. Unfortunately for you, he doesn't have those same qualms."

Nir heard a slap and a thud. Looking over, he saw Nicole on the ground. Blood began trickling from her nose.

"Make sure they're clean, then put them on the couch."

Rough hands flipped Nir onto his stomach, then ran up and down his body looking for weapons. When none were found, he was hoisted up and manhandled over to the couch. Moments after he was pushed down, Nicole dropped next to him.

Moshev had moved and was now standing next to Kvashnin. It seemed that all the helpless energy that he had felt was now pouring out as he verbally tore into the oligarch. Kvashnin's smile, though, never left his face.

"English, please. For the sake of our guests," Kvashnin said with a wink toward Nir and Nicole.

"If you knew that this was a setup, why didn't you stop it before I told them about the attack?" the general demanded.

"It was a business decision."

"It was not a business decision. It is a military decision. It is a foreign affairs decision."

"Maybe for you, *Lyonya*, but I only care about military and foreign affairs as they relate to my bottom line. Of the fertilizer that Israel imports, fifty-five percent used to be from Russia. And of that fifty-five percent, forty percent was from me. Now with these sanctions brought on by your military decisions, my markets around the world are suffering. My exports to Israel are a fraction of what they were. But even that fraction accounts for millions of dollars. A major attack could totally wipe out my market in that country. That's bad business, my friend. Besides, I wanted to know why these two were so eager to meet with you. My curiosity simply got the best of me."

"Well, now you know. They are blackmailing me and threatening my family."

Turning toward Nir and Nicole, Kvashnin said, "Tsk, tsk, I am surprised at you. Such nasty business."

The two Mossad agents remained silent.

"But now you need not worry, *Lyonya*, because I've saved you from all that."

The general looked at Kvashnin skeptically. "How so?"

"You see, that's the problem with you military types. You don't think like criminals. Well, Prigozhin and his Wagner Group do, but that is because most of them are criminals."

"You're digressing," the general chastised.

"Right. You are concerned that the president and his people will not believe that these recordings are false, that they are actually Mossad creations."

"Exactly."

Kvashnin pointed at the two on the couch. "Now here is your evidence that what you are saying is true. Two bona fide agents of the Mossad captured in the act."

Recognition spread across Moshev's face. But then it darkened again. "But what about my family?"

"You needn't worry about your family. If any harm comes to them, these two would be charged not just with espionage but with capital murder. No, as soon as they let their people know that they have been captured, your family will be safe, and all of this will go away."

"And the attack?"

"It goes ahead, of course. This is such an egregious case of malicious spy craft that the president will be fully justified in attacking Israel. And he won't have to hide behind Syria to do it. All I would ask is that the government rewards my patriotism with the amount of money that I will lose on Israeli contracts."

Moshev seemed to understand now that his concerns were over. He clapped his oligarch friend on both arms. "*Tolya*, you are a good friend. I owe you a great debt."

"Yes, you do. And there will come a day when I call on you for a favor."

"Anything. You just ask." Then he turned toward Nir and Nicole. "And what do we do with these two?"

Kvashnin switched to Russian, and the two went back and forth for a minute.

Nir interrupted. "Hey, English please. It was good enough for you when you were gloating over your victory."

His eyes were locked on the oligarch's, showing all the bravado he could muster in an impossible situation.

The two Russians spoke their language again briefly. Then Kvashnin said, "We were talking about whether we should kill you."

From the corner of his eye, Nir could see Nicole turn toward him. She looked terrified. But he refused to look away from the billionaire.

"And what was the consensus?"

"We haven't yet decided. On the one hand, parading you in front of international media prior to a trial and execution would make for great theater. On the other, you are such a smug, obnoxious person that I would prefer to just kill you here. We could say you died in a shootout. Which would you choose?"

Nir pretended to think. "While I see the merits in both options, I would like to offer a third choice."

"Which is?"

"That I finally give that miserable wife of yours a moment of happiness by putting a bullet in your brain."

Kvashnin's appearance turned from excitement to malevolence. "You see? Smug and obnoxious. I'm going to enjoy watching you die." Turning toward his men, he said, "Lock them in the sauna until the guests are gone. We'll deal with them then." As the two guards motioned for Nir and Nicole to get up, he said to Moshev, "You should have your guards go with them. With that man, more is better than less."

Hands in the air, Nir, then Nicole, walked around the couch toward the side door. But Nicole's foot caught the sofa's leg and she stumbled. As she dropped, she pressed the center stone on her diamond ring. A second later, the lights went out.

CHAPTER 33

22:25 (10:25 PM) MSK

A few seconds of advantage, Nir thought as he jumped into motion. *That's all this darkness buys us.*

Like many modern homes, Anatoly Kvashnin's mansion was fully computerized. A central computer controlled the air conditioning, the heater, the kitchen appliances, the front gate, the entertainment system, and the lighting. Because of his wealth and position, the oligarch also had an incredibly robust firewall set up to ensure that nobody could tap into his house's "brain." Because of the complexity of his digital protection system, it had required a full minute and a half for Nicole to break into it earlier that morning using her laptop at the hotel.

Once she had control of the house, she was able to transfer that control to Dafna at CARL. When the ring's satellite signal hit the analyst's computer in Tel Aviv, her index finger, which had been hovering over the return key for the past two hours, extended, shrouding the house's interior in darkness.

Nir dropped into a crouch. As he fell, his hands reached under his belt and popped two small knives out of the leather. Everyone else in the room was momentarily stunned by the sudden darkness. But because he and Nicole were expecting it, they were able to move. One knife he threw in the direction he knew the guard to be whose gun had been trained on Nicole. The one in his left hand he held onto as he spun, then launched himself toward where he hoped the second guard would still be. Their two bodies collided, and Nir drove the knife into the man's wrist, causing him to loosen his grip on his gun.

Nir felt around for the man's pistol. A cry sounded just ahead of him, followed by a thump. Nir's first knife throw was meant to distract the other bodyguard enough for Nicole to throw her body at his knees. With any luck, the joints would fold, and he would drop.

This two-on-four matchup was one of eight different scenarios they had rehearsed in the back room of a gym in Belgium, each with a different number of guards positioned in various places around the room. Thankfully, this was one of the slightly less deadly of the potential situations.

Nir's hand wrapped around the grip of the gun. He began to move around the furniture, staying low to avoid potential gunfire. Earlier that day, he had used some of his wait time to count steps from one position to another and memorize where all the furniture was.

The moment the lights went out, Nir had started counting upward. He now reached seven. He stood and held out his gun. At eight, the room lit up once again.

Two steps in front of him was Moshev. To his left stood Kvashnin. The general's two bodyguards were just inside the room with their guns drawn. In the moment it took for everyone to get their bearings, Nir moved forward, wrapped his arm around the general's neck from behind, and put the gun to his head.

"Hands up in the air, everyone," he commanded.

Behind him, he heard a gun rack. Movement caught his eye to his right. It was Nicole stepping around with the other guard's gun pointed at the general's men.

"You heard him. Hands up and weapons down," she said.

Nir risked a quick look to the rear. In the fraction-of-a-second glance, he saw a man leaning over and holding his knee. A small knife was sticking out of his shoulder.

"Tell the man behind me to move to the front," he said to the general. The man obeyed.

Nir heard bumping and shuffling, then the man hobbled around toward Kvashnin. His partner was on the ground to Nir's left, holding his bleeding wrist and groaning. The two men with the guns still held their sights on the Israeli agents. Nir pressed the muzzle of his pistol into Moshev's temple hard enough to make him wince.

"Tell them to put their weapons down or I swear I will kill you and everyone else in this room."

The general said something in Russian. His bodyguards lowered their guns and placed them on the floor.

"Tell them to kick their guns into the corner. Then everyone needs to get down on the floor."

The general complied. The pistols flip-flopped over the carpet, and the three standing bodyguards dropped to their knees then stretched out flat. Nicole hustled over and tucked her gun into the back of Nir's waistband. She then went to the man with the blade imbedded in his wrist. Taking hold of the handle, she whispered, "Sorry," then yanked it out. The man cried out in pain. Moving back to Nir, she dropped down and began cutting the seams in his suit jacket.

"You, too, Anatoly," Nir said to the billionaire, motioning with the gun that he, too, needed to drop to the floor. The man mumbled something in Russian before lowering himself to his knees with two loud pops.

Once Nicole had made a few cuts, she began tearing, separating the lining of Nir's jacket from the outer layer of wool. Stainless-steel zip ties dropped to the ground. She gathered them up and went to the first of Moshev's bodyguards. Pulling his arms behind him, she began cinching him up.

"See if you need to use one of those to tourniquet that guy's arm," he said to Nicole.

"Will do."

"Your turn," he said to the general, using his arm to press down on the man's shoulders. The man went to his knees and then laid flat on his stomach.

As Nicole moved from person to person, Nir spoke. "Despite what my overly ambitious friend here said, General, nothing has changed. You belong to me. If you talk about tonight's events to anyone, I will release the footage of your betrayal. If you attempt to interfere with our escape, I will have your family killed and the footage will be released. I want twenty-four hours from you to leave your country. If my people see signs of your family attempting to flee their home in Estonia, they will stop them. If my people see evidence of a counterassault in Estonia, they will destroy the house with your family in it. After the twenty-four hours are up, my people will fade away into the night and you will never hear from me or them again. You have my word on that. You have a lovely family, General. Do not make me hurt them. Do you understand what I have said to you?"

"I understand."

"Good. The only part of our original deal that has changed is my request that you bring no harm to our friend *Tolya*. Due to recent unforeseen circumstances, my feelings toward him seem to have waned. He was part of this scheme from the beginning. So please feel free to do whatever you want to him. Have him arrested, have his bank accounts seized, send a Spetsnaz unit after him, anything you like. And if you need to know where he is, give me a call. We've always got eyes on him."

Nicole finished tying up Kvashnin. Nir pulled the gun from his waistband and gave it back to her. She trained it on the general, who was the only one left unbound.

Nir walked to Kvashnin and rolled him over with his foot.

The Russian was seething. "Do you think that I will just let you get away with this? You are a dead man. I have more resources at my disposal than you can possibly imagine."

Nir squatted down and rested the barrel of his gun on the man's forehead. He tapped it a few times and said, "So, what I hear you saying is, 'Please kill me now.'"

The man's eyes got big as they locked onto the black metal barrel that was right in front of his face. "No. Don't shoot me. I promise not to harm you or your friend."

"I don't need your promises, Anatoly Mikhailovich. I need your good business sense. I have found you before. I can find you again. If you attempt anything against me or her, you will die. And I'll make sure you are looking me in the eyes when I pull the trigger. Do you understand?"

The oligarch seemed to recognize that he was beaten. "I understand," he said.

"Good. Our ride should be arriving about now."

When Nicole had triggered the emergency signal, a deep-cover Russian Mossad agent was alerted to approach the estate in her car from a location ten kilometers to the east. A text from Nicole's phone now informed her to enter the long circular driveway.

Walking back to the general, Nir reached down his hand. When Moshev eyed him suspiciously, Nir nodded. The Russian took his hand, and he lifted the man to his feet.

"General, you are not bound because you are the only one here that I trust to think rationally. I know that you will act according to what is best for your family. You must understand that my actions here were for the same reason. It is my family who will be on the receiving end of this attack. I will do whatever it takes to protect my loved ones, as I know you will now. I am asking you to call your helicopter pilot and tell him that you are delayed for one hour. Then I want you to sit on this couch for that length of time. When the hour is up, please release everyone. Then say no more about tonight to anyone. I am not a monster. I wish more than anything for your family and my family to be safe. It is up to you to ensure that will happen. Do I have your word?"

Nir reached out his hand. Moshev looked at it but didn't take it. Instead, he stiffened, bowed slightly, and said, "You have my word."

"That's good enough for me." He tucked the handgun into his waistband and moved toward the door.

Nicole followed, but stopped before reaching the door. She quickly retreated to where Kvashnin was tied on the ground. Squatting down, she said, "Just so you know, while we were talking tonight, I had my people hack into several of your bank accounts. Congratulations on donating forty million euros to the Ukrainian Red Cross fund. Such a noble act, Anatoly. I'm so proud of you." She kissed her hand, touched his cheek, then followed Nir out the door.

The last sound they heard as they moved down the hall was the loud, mocking laughter of General Leonid Anatolyevich Moshev.

CHAPTER 34

22:35 (10:35 PM) MSK

N ir and Nicole came to a large staircase that curved down to the entryway. They quickly descended and made for the exit, hoping to escape without being noticed by anyone who was enjoying dinner beyond the open doors of the dining hall. Judging by the talking and the laughter, it seemed that the scare of the brief power outage had passed. They had almost made it clear of the room when a woman stepped out, almost colliding with Nicole.

"Polina," said Nicole, pulling up short.

The woman was obviously agitated. Nir got the feeling she was as unhappy to see them as they were to see her. "Oh, Nicole. Are you leaving without saying goodbye?"

"I'm so sorry. We must be going, and we didn't want to pull you away from your guests."

The woman eyed the two of them suspiciously, then said, "Okay. It's just as well. I'm in a rush to find my husband. The fool is ignoring his own event, and he isn't answering his phone. He's probably locked away in a closet with one of the serving girls." Then she added something in Russian that Nir hoped Nicole wouldn't try to run through her voice translator app.

Then a thought hit him. He couldn't let her find her husband. If she did, she would have the police swarming the place in minutes. But he also didn't want to zip tie her and throw her in a guest room. Well, maybe he did a little, but he knew it wouldn't be the best option. First, this woman would find a way to break free just based on meanness alone. But second, if both the host and the hostess disappeared from the dinner, people would notice, and they would talk.

To buy time until he came up with a better idea, Nir said, "Mrs. Kvashnin, I didn't get a chance to tell you this right after the show, but your designs were exquisite. They were a stunning combination of aesthetic beauty, femininity, and, may I say, a hint of sexuality. Even without being able to read the program, I still knew which creations were yours. Each one exuded luxury without losing their devotion to the land and culture of their creator."

The woman's face lit up, while out of her sight line, Nicole looked shocked. "Why, Mr. Shapira, that is the exact look that I was going for." She put out her hand, which Nir took gently in his own. "It sometimes feels like my country is filled with Neanderthals. I've always felt that my designs would be better understood in the West."

He lifted her hand to his lips. "I certainly hope you can show them soon. We in the West need a fresh perspective like the one that you bring."

The woman blushed as she removed her hand. "I agree completely. It was really so good of you both to come. You have brought a light to our humble house. Sadly, I must leave you now. I must find my lout of a husband."

Unfortunately, Nir's delay tactic had been unsuccessful. It was beginning to seem that hog-tying might be the best option.

"Please don't bother searching for Anatoly, Polina Viktorovna," Nicole said, taking the woman by the arm. "We have just come from him."

"Really? Tell me where he is. He must come and attend his guests."

"He will come, but he can't just yet. He is on a very important call."

The suspicion appeared once again on the woman's face. "What call could be more important than a roomful of very important persons?"

Nicole sighed. "I'm sorry, I don't know if I'll be much help there.

They were speaking Russian. But while General Moshev was talking to the man on the other end, Anatoly whispered that it was another general on the line. A General Shoonu or Shoogoo or…oh, drat. Darling, do you remember the general's name?"

"General Shoigu?" offered Polina, barely containing her excitement. "General Sergei Shoigu?"

"That's it," said Nicole. Now she lowered her voice and whispered conspiratorially. "Your husband said that he had heard about the charity event. He was calling to commend General Moshev and Anatoly."

"Anatoly is being commended by the minister of defense? I am not surprised. He is a good man, a respectable man. It is about time that someone in the government notices us and what we contribute to our nation."

Nir spoke. "I agree. Just look at tonight. Do you think that there is anywhere else in Russia tonight that tens of millions of rubles are being collected for the families of the brave men lost in battle? No, it is only here in your house, Polina Viktorovna."

Nicole added. "That is why he is not answering his phone. He was kind enough to step away to say goodbye to Naor and me, saying he could be on the phone for another hour or two. It sounded to me like General Shoigu isn't the only call they are expecting."

Polina stepped back. Her hands went to her face. "Do you think…? Could we possibly hear from the president himself?"

Nir answered, "I don't know. All I know is that I believe you should."

Completely flustered, Mrs. Kvashnin said, "I don't know what to do. What do you think I should do?"

Nicole took her arm and began to walk her back to the dining hall. "Attend to your guests. Don't say anything to anyone yet. But take time to rehearse in your mind how you will announce to those in attendance the honor that has been given to you. Then you will be ready for when *Tolya* comes down."

"Yes, yes. Bless you, Nicole. And bless you, Mr. Shapira."

As she hustled back into the hall, Nicole quickly returned to Nir, and they both exited through the front doors. In the driveway out front, a black SUV waited for them. Nir opened the door. Nicole climbed in and slid across the seat. Nir followed her. As soon as the door closed, the vehicle took off.

Once they were moving, Nicole turned to Nir. "Aesthetic beauty, femininity, and a hint of sexuality?"

"I had four hours by myself in a study with only Russian books and my phone to keep me entertained. Thought a little research on trending Moscow fashion might come in handy."

"Well, it was brilliant."

He put his arm around her. "No, what was brilliant was General Shoigu. How'd you come up with him?"

Nicole leaned against him and gave him a little punch. "You aren't the only one with Internet, mister."

Nir winced, and Nicole pulled back. "I'm sorry. I forgot what Anatoly did to you. Are you okay?"

"I'm fine. He hits like a girl." But Nir's ribs were sore, and he was hoping that nothing was broken.

Nir then noticed the driver was looking back at them. She had tucked her hair up under her hat, and the only evidence of her long brown hair were a few wisps that had managed to escape. They locked eyes for a moment, and he could see that she was a beautiful woman, not older than 30. She quickly looked away.

"How long of a drive?" he asked her.

In response, she only pointed ahead.

The two in the back seat fell into a tired silence. They were both anxious to debrief, but now was not the time. The woman in the front seat was known and trusted by her Mossad handlers, but she was unknown to Nir and Nicole. Because of that, they would bite their tongues and bide their time.

Four minutes later, the car slowed. The driver turned off the road and through a small opening in the line of trees that followed along the side of the road. The vehicle bumped and dipped, and everyone inside was jostled back and forth. A five-meter wall appeared to their left, and the driver angled in that direction. Carefully over the rough terrain, she drew alongside the wall and parked so close that the driver's side doors could only be opened mere centimeters.

"*Spasibo*," Nir said, thanking the driver. She said nothing in reply, but he noticed her watching them in the mirror as they slid out the passenger side.

Nir climbed on the hood of the SUV, then helped Nicole up. He felt his weight push indentations into the metal, but there was nothing he could do about that. Next, he went up onto the roof. Nicole followed.

The car was two meters tall. Nir was a bit less. That meant the top of the wall stretched a little more than another meter above his head, a distance easily surmounted. He pulled himself up, grunting at the pain in his side. Then he reached down for Nicole. Her dress was not the best outfit to be wearing for scaling walls, and when she made it to the top, even in the moonlight Nir could make out the red streaks on her knees.

He dropped down the other side of the wall, then held up his arms to help ease Nicole's fall.

"Now, you be a gentleman, Mr. Nir Tavor."

"I'll look the other way when you drop," he said with a grin.

"Well, that would be counterproductive." She dropped her legs over the wall and began to lower herself. As soon as she did, her dress caught and started riding up. "Oh, forget it," she said as she let go. Nir caught her by the waist and lowered her down.

"See, I had my eyes closed the whole time," he said, pointing to the evidence on his face.

She slapped his chest. "You're such a dork."

No one was supposed to be home on the sprawling property. Still, they kept low as they moved through the beautifully designed garden and across the lawn. They found a small grove of trees near the corner of the estate. It was a cold night, but at least the rain that had fallen earlier had cleared. Still, it was dark, and the leaves and grass were wet. The two huddled together to keep warm.

Nir heard it before he saw it. The whump-whump-whump told him that their ride was close. He stood and helped Nicole up. Lights appeared in the darkness and descended to the helipad. Driving to the airport in Moscow had been an option, but a two-and-a-half-hour trip not knowing whether at any time you were going to be stopped by the police or the FSB did not seem like a good plan. So, Liora had found this helipad-equipped estate, the owners of which would be in the Seychelles for the next three weeks.

As soon as the helicopter touched down, the two ran to it and climbed in. The interior of the 15-passenger AgustaWestland AW139 was warm and luxurious. They chose a couple seats in the middle, and the helicopter lifted off.

Once they were at elevation, the man in the right-hand seat in the cockpit slipped out and moved back to them.

"Good evening. We have approximately a twenty-minute flight to the private hangars of Sheremetyevo Airport. I'm sorry that I have no beverages to offer to warm you up. What I do have are changes of clothing for you both in the back of the aircraft. There is a Bombardier BD-700 waiting for you when we arrive, which will take you to Paris. That flight will be fully equipped, and I have no doubt you will enjoy its comfort."

Nir was used to men addressing Nicole only when the two of them were together, and this man was no exception. Still, he said, "Thank you for coming to get us on this wet night."

As if noticing him for the first time, the man responded, "Of course. It is our job."

With one more look at Nicole, he returned to his seat.

"Maybe I just need to cross my legs more when I sit," Nir said.

Nicole laughed and squeezed his face. "You're beautiful. In your own way."

"*Walla!* What does that mean?" He stood up and led the way to the back of the aircraft. Nicole slipped into the bathroom to change. Nir just swapped his clothes in the aisle.

Nicole returned to the seat next to him just as they were beginning their descent.

"You clean up nicely," he said.

"You're not so bad yourself."

Their time on the ground at Sheremetyevo was brief. An enclosed cart met them at the helicopter and shuttled them toward a hangar. Just outside its open door stood a 19-passenger corporate jet with its engines already revved up. The cart parked next to the plane's steps.

Less than ten minutes passed from the time the two climbed into the cabin to the moment the plane's wheels left the tarmac. Nir was still hopped up on adrenaline and was ready to finally hold their debrief. But Nicole fell asleep moments after giving the attendant her drink order, and she stayed asleep for the entire four-hour flight to Paris–Le Bourget Airport.

Their whirlwind return ended with them each rushing to catch trains home—Nir up to Antwerp, and Nicole down to Milan. As disappointed as he was to be saying goodbye to her, he knew that it wouldn't be long. They were both expected very soon in the *ramsad*'s office in Tel Aviv.

CHAPTER 35

FOUR DAYS LATER
MOSSAD HEADQUARTERS, TEL AVIV, ISRAEL—
NOVEMBER 2, 2022—08:55 (8:55 AM) IST

Seated at the conference table to Nir's left were four other Kidon team leaders. To his right was Nicole. The chairs across from them were empty.

Irin Ehrlich, considered the playboy of the group with his expertly faded hair and perfectly trimmed beard, said, "Hey, Nir, do we all get to bring our girlfriends to the meeting? I didn't get the memo."

"Wouldn't have mattered for you," said Nicole. "The building has a no pets policy." From the moment the other guys had begun to arrive to find both Nir and Nicole waiting at the table, the ribbing hadn't stopped. Until now, Nicole had been silently taking it. That appeared to be at an end.

Nir watched Ehrlich's face redden as the other guys laughed at him. "You started it, *achi*. Don't start whining because you lost."

Turning on Nir, he said, "What's she even doing here, Tavor? She's not an Israeli. She's just a South African Jew wannabe who was probably raised on her daddy's apartheid money."

Nir jumped up, sending his chair skittering backwards. Ehrlich did the same. The third man up was Zakai Abelman, Nir's closest friend amongst the team leads. He put his body between the other two.

These guys had no clue what Nicole had been through for this country, and Nir was sick of hearing her be disrespected. "Tell you what, *achi*, you can smack talk her next time you run an op in Moscow. Oh yeah, you've never been. How about in Tehran? Oops, haven't marked that one off your bingo card either, have you, Ehrlich?"

"Oh, so now she's some superagent? She wouldn't even be in this room if you weren't sleeping with her."

Nir stretched with all his might to get past Abelman. Lavie Bensoussan, a late-forties agent who had lost his right ear to a Palestinian terrorist, jumped up and put Ehrlich in a choke hold to try to calm him down. The only two still sitting now were 60-year-old Ravid Efrat, who was cleaning a thumbnail with a tactical blade, and Nicole, who wouldn't dignify the stupidity with even a glance.

A door across the table slammed open. Efraim Cohen stormed in, yelling, "What is wrong with you idiots? We're trying to talk in here, and you children are having a schoolyard brawl. Apparently, the only two with any common sense are the senior citizen and the fashion model. Now sit down and shut up before I have Nicole hack into the Ministry of Transport and cancel your driver's licenses."

Efrat's gravelly voice sounded for the first time. "Wouldn't matter to Tavor. You guys already took his car."

Nicole snorted a laugh. It spread, and soon, everyone joined in. Everyone except for Efrat, who had moved on to his index finger.

"Seriously, guys. Knock it off. It'll just be a couple minutes more," Efraim said, then closed the door.

Everyone sat back down. "Nicole is here because the *ramsad* asked her to be here," said Nir. "She's a big part of the reason we're in this meeting at all, because without her, we wouldn't have gotten the information from the Russian. So, show her some respect, *achi. Sababa?*"

Ehrlich looked over. "*Sababa*. So, le Roux, is it true you hacked the oligarch's banks and sent forty million euros to the Ukrainian Red Cross?"

Without turning his way, Nicole said, "I can neither confirm nor deny."

Laughter filled the room. "Have to admit, that was a nice touch," said Ehrlich.

They had to wait another five minutes before the door opened again. Efraim walked through first, followed by Assistant Deputy Director Karin Friedman, Deputy Director Asher Porush, and the *ramsad*, Ira Katz. After the Mossad head entered, two more men walked in.

The first was caretaker Prime Minister Daniel Ramon. The government of change, in which Ramon was a minister, had collapsed back in June. The citizens of Israel had finally understood how the previous prime minister's policies of social justice had led to national weakness and a growing belligerence from the country's neighbors. The ruling coalition fell apart, the prime minister resigned, and Ramon was installed as the interim governmental leader until new elections could be held.

Those elections had been held yesterday, and the results caused a sigh of relief within most of Israel's citizens, including Nir. The conservative party had won a surprisingly strong victory, and Nir was excited to see what Idan Snir, the man slated to step into the prime minister's role, would do with the country. A strong leader, he wasn't loved by all the world, but he was respected. When it came to international relations, Nir would take respect over love any day.

It was Snir who was the last one to walk into the meeting room. Nir had seen him numerous times but had never met the man. He found himself feeling a little starstruck.

The *ramsad* spoke. "Prime Minister Ramon, Mr. Snir, these are my Kidon team leaders." He went down the line, introducing them by name. He finished by saying, "These last two are the ones who just completed the Russian operation from which we gained our information—Nir Tavor and Nicole le Roux."

Snir smiled. "Ah, Israel's undercover Double O Seven."

Flushed, Nir said, "Well, I wouldn't quite put myself at a James Bond level."

"I was speaking to Miss le Roux."

As Nicole thanked the future prime minister for his compliment, Nir wondered if anyone would notice if he slipped out the door and disappeared forever into the rainforests of New Guinea. But judging by the smirks on the faces of the four men to his left, he knew that a quiet exit was not in the cards for him.

Mercifully, the *ramsad* began to speak again. "From start to finish, it was an excellent operation in conception and execution. One thing I am still unsure about, however. Why didn't Moshev or Kvashnin send someone after you? Seems that if they had killed you and presented dead Mossad agents to the world, the general would have been off the hook."

Nir had purposely left that part out of his report, knowing that there would likely be blowback. But now that he was confronted directly, he had no option but to confess. "We let the general know that we had a team ready to kill his wife and family, who were in a rented home in Estonia."

His answer ignited gasps and angry words on the other side of the table. Only the *ramsad* and Efraim remained calm.

Karin Friedman pointed her finger at him. "You're saying that you put together an unsanctioned hit squad to kill someone's family? That is so far beyond the pale. Something like that could end the *ramsad*'s career. It could bring down a whole government." Turning to Ira Katz, she said, "Sir, I am recommending that Agent Tavor be suspended until we are able to conduct an investigation into his outrageous conduct."

The *ramsad* dismissively waved his hand at her, then said to Nir, "Describe this hit squad to me."

"I have a jeweler colleague in Tallinn who has family in Ramat Gan. I called in a favor with him. I overnighted him a night vision camera, and I asked him to make the drive to Viimsi and spend the evening parked near the Moshev family rental. So, our assault team was a jeweler, his teenage son, and a camera."

"No weapons?"

"Can't say for sure. Maybe a pocketknife or two."

Prime Minister Ramon was not mollified by the explanation. "So, you lied to a Russian four-star general, telling him that you were going to slaughter his entire family if he didn't cooperate. And you think that's okay?"

Nir pretended to think for a moment, then said, "I see what you're saying. I should have just gone through with the slaughter. That way, I would at least have been telling the truth." Turning to Nicole, he said, "Note that for next time. Don't forget to slaughter the family."

Ramon's hand slammed the table. "I don't find you funny at all."

"And I don't take operational advice from an ex-prime minister," Nir shot back.

"Tavor, you're out of line," said the *ramsad*.

Judging by the faces across the table, Nir had taken a step too far. Only the incoming prime minister seemed amused.

"You're right, *Hamefaked*. I'm sorry. And Mr. Prime Minister, I apologize to you, also. My words were disrespectful and inappropriate."

Prime Minister Ramon mumbled something as he eased back into his chair.

The *ramsad* spoke. "While there are some who may question your methods, the reality is that you found a way to get the information that we needed. For that, you deserve recognition, despite your occasional impertinence. ADD Friedman?"

Friedman cleared her throat and said very matter-of-factly, "It was good work for the most part. You and your team will each receive commendations in your records for meritorious service. However, I do want to give a word of caution to you, Miss le Roux. Your manipulation of the oligarch's bank accounts was unnecessary and smacked of vigilantism. We would ask you to refrain from such acts in the future."

Someone on Nir's side of the table mumbled a sarcastic curse, causing Friedman to sharply glance to Nir's left. As she did that, the *ramsad*, with whom Nicole had forged a special relationship during a particularly harrowing operation last year, rolled his eyes and gave an almost imperceptible headshake. Nir suppressed a smile. Under the table, he used his foot to give Nicole a gentle tap.

The Mossad head continued, "We've been discussing what you discovered and, more importantly, what we can do about it. What to do about it is where you all come in. However, first, you need to understand a little more about the chemicals that we're up against. I've asked Deputy Director Porush to fill us in on their history."

CHAPTER 36

Asher Porush was a man whose expression rarely changed. Instead, it was his voice that made him compelling. To Nir, he was what David Attenborough would have sounded like if he had been born in the Jezreel Valley instead of Middlesex, England. Nir could listen to the man all day.

Porush began, "Up until now, Bashar al-Assad's government has been content to use his chemicals on his own people, so destroying his stockpile has not been a high priority to us. If Syrians want to kill Syrians, what is that to us? Maybe we can convince the Iranians to follow the same strategy. But now it seems that the target of Assad's chemical hoard has shifted from internal to external."

"What is it that they have? I know for sure there is chlorine," said Bensoussan.

Porush itemized a list. "There has been evidence of vesicating or blister agents like mustard gas that cause painful sores and respiratory issues. They won't normally kill you immediately. But the lasting effects can make your life miserable until the day they finally take your life. Still, we don't think that it's likely that a mustard gas attack would accomplish their goals. They want a more immediate effect, so it is more likely that they would use choking agents or lung toxicants, like chlorine, and nerve agents, such as sarin and VX."

"VX—venomous agent X," said Ehrlich in mock awe.

"Always thought it sounded like a Marvel villain," said Abelman. "Isn't VX what Kim Jong-un used to kill his half brother in the Kuala Lumpur Airport?"

"It is," answered the *ramsad*. "And while I appreciate any questions of clarification, let's remember the short time window of our guests. Mr. Porush?"

"They've got their chemicals over there, and they want to send them over here. So, let's talk delivery methods. We know they have artillery rockets, smaller ballistic missiles, and aerial bombs. But based on the information from the Russian general, it appears that the terrorists have been provided significantly more powerful missiles that can easily reach across our borders with much greater accuracy."

Nir spoke up. "Can we back up just a moment? You say they've got their chemicals, but do they really have enough to harm us? That's what threw me off when General Moshev was talking. Their original stash, I think, was supposed to have been from Saddam Hussein. But I can remember when they destroyed them all."

Porush opened a binder and flipped through the pages. "Okay, quick history lesson. Assad began using chemical weapons on his people in December of 2012. Seven people were killed in Homs when the government used Agent 15, also known as BZ."

"BZ?" asked Ehrlich.

"3-quinuclidinyl benzilate."

"Oh, that BZ." Ehrlich rolled his eyes.

"Don't ask a question if you don't want the answer. Now, that first attack opened a floodgate. March of 2013, there were chemicals used in Aleppo, Adra, and the suburbs of Damascus. April, again in Aleppo. In June, France said they discovered proof that the Syrian government was using sarin against its people. That truly escalated the equation. Just a drop of sarin on the skin can kill within minutes. And it's a horrible death. The nervous system quits working, bringing on tremors and seizures. The respiratory system shuts down and the victim dies of asphyxiation."

"But, again, weren't they all destroyed in like 2015 or something?" asked Nir.

"Destroyed? Yes. All? No. Mid-2013, the United Nations got involved. And, as we all know, once the UN is involved, everyone can rest easy."

A smattering of comments were made, none of which were complimentary of the august international body.

"The UN partnered with the Organization for the Prohibition of Chemical Weapons, better known by its acronym OPCW. The OPCW is out of The Hague, and they teamed up with the UN for inspections of Syria's chemical stash. Syria pushed back and made inspections difficult. But when a UN inspection team came under sniper fire in August 2013, it was the bump that tipped the kettle. The international pressure on Assad to get rid of his chemicals became too great, and he agreed to their destruction."

The interim prime minister spoke up. "This is when I was the permanent representative to the UN. I can remember that process."

Nir had forgotten that Daniel Ramon had been ambassador to the United Nations. It was one more reason not to like him.

Ramon continued, "First, all the chemical manufacturing sites were destroyed. The OPCW was able to inspect twenty-one of the twenty-three sites to ensure the destruction was thorough. The plan then was for the existing chemicals to be transported to the port in Latakia, where they would be loaded onto Danish and Norwegian ships. Then, under the protection of the Russians and the Chinese, they would be taken out to the US ship Cape Ray. Once there, the Americans would use a hot water and chemical process—"

"Hydrolysis," offered Porush.

"Hydrolysis to break down the weaponized chemicals."

"So, it was a global effort. I'm assuming it didn't go according to plan," said Bensoussan.

Porush took over. "This is the Middle East. Nothing ever goes according to plan. The Syrians dragged their feet. What should have been a simple process took months. Eventually, however, at one site or another, through one process or another, six hundred metric tons of chemicals were destroyed."

"Why am I sensing a 'but'?" asked Nicole, speaking up for the first time.

"But, despite Assad's assurances that all the chemicals were gone, they somehow ended up back in the Syrian army's arsenal. Chlorine was used in March 2015. Then, mustard gas in Marea in August 2015. There was a major sarin attack in Idlib in 2017 and multiple more deployments of chlorine in 2018. The international pressure once again grew enormous, and there have been no major attacks that we know of in the past four years. Assad says it's because there are no more chemicals."

Ehrlich colorfully voiced his response to Assad's assertion.

Porush continued, "That's what we said. His assertion is ridiculous because it's been proven to be false. You may remember that back in April of 2018, the US led a coalition strike on Syria's chemical weapons program. They destroyed a research center in Damascus and a couple weapons and chemical storage facilities near Homs. A couple years later, we got information from Unit 504 that Assad was once again developing the ingredients for sarin. So, in March 2020, we took out a villa outside of Homs that was the hub of their chemical manufacturing. We struck again in June of last year, hitting targets near Nasiriyah and Masyaf, killing one of their primary engineers in the process."

Abelman spoke up. "I'll be the first to admit that I'm no expert on chemical weapons, so this may be a dumb question. But is there a shelf life to these chemicals? I'm asking because of all of Saddam Hussein's weapons of mass destruction that everyone made such a big deal about. The rumor I've heard is that even though Assad destroyed a bunch of chemicals, he's still got some Iraqi-made stuff stashed away. If so, that would make them close to twenty years old. Is there an expiration date on that medicine bottle?"

Porush answered, "That's an excellent question, because for a long time, our thinking was informed by the Iraq WMD theory. According to that notion, in mid-March 2003, just before the Americans invaded Iraq, Saddam Hussein transported all his chemical weapons to Syria for safekeeping. There were reports of huge convoys of unmarked trucks traveling across the border to three different storage sites. One in tunnels under a town near Hama, one in a village by an airbase north of Salamija, and one on the border with Lebanon, south of Homs.

Then, as the civil war in Syria heated up, Assad had them transferred to storage facilities under the city of Damascus, where he was sure they wouldn't get into enemy hands."

"What never made sense to me about this theory was why Saddam would get rid of his most dangerous weapons right when he was about to be invaded," said Efraim.

Nir had wondered the same thing, and he was glad his friend had asked about it. If you have a huge army coming to wipe you out, the last thing you would want to do is weaken your arsenal in any way. That would be like limiting yourself to using a knife in a gunfight.

Porush answered, "That's a question that critics of the theory regularly bring up. I don't know the answer. Maybe Saddam thought that Bush the Younger was going to fight the war like his father and not finish the job. He could have been thinking that once the Americans left again, he'd be able to bring his WMDs back. Besides, he likely knew that if he used chemicals on US troops, George W. would bulldoze his country into the desert."

Idan Snir, the prime minister-designate, spoke up. "What I have learned about chemical weapons is that the sooner they are used, the more potent they are. Initially, they were thought to last just ten years. Later, they extended their viable shelf life to twenty. If these truly are Hussein's chemicals, then their usefulness to Syria or Russia or Iran is fast running out, which may be the reason they are wanting to use them immediately. However, I doubt that Iraq is the origin of our current concern. I think it is far more likely that they have been created in Syria, or possibly in Iran, and then shipped into Syria. Either way, the origin of these chemicals is not what is important, *ramsad*. I want to hear how they are going to be neutralized. Do you have a plan for that?"

"That, Mr. Prime Minister-Designate, is why we are here." The *ramsad* said the words to Snir, but he was looking at his Kidon leaders. "The prime minister, in conjunction with the incoming government, has decided that we must act to destroy once and for all Assad's chemical capability. It is indisputable that if he is willing to use them on his people, he will readily use them on us. We know of three primary facilities where chemicals are being manufactured and weaponized. In one week's time, we are going to render them permanently unusable with a major air-strike. However, we also know that under the city of Damascus, a number of sizable weapons caches exist, and within these storage facilities are either weaponized chemicals or chemicals that are waiting to be weaponized. It is the destruction of these chemical stashes that I am tasking you with. You will go back to your teams and, for the next twenty-four hours, you will discuss and brainstorm. Then at nine a.m. tomorrow, you will return here, each with a viable plan for the safe and thorough destruction of the chemical stores in Damascus. ADD, please pass out the information that we have learned from our intelligence and from Unit 504 about the locations and amounts of chemicals being stored."

Friedman stood and slid a thick brown envelope to each person. On top of each was a thumb drive, presumably with all the same information in digital form.

This was the fourth time that Ira Katz had pitted his teams against each other in what the gang at CARL had come to call the Kidon Olympics. Twice, previously, Nir's team didn't reach the podium. But, once, they took the gold medal, and that time, Nir had almost died. Still, he had to admit that he was more than a little excited about the competition and the opportunity to best the other team leaders.

"If there's nothing else, you are all dismissed. The rest of us have a few more items to discuss."

Once out in the hall, Bensoussan said, "As always, winner buys a round of beers."

Ehrlich put his arm around Nicole's shoulders. "For you, darling, we'll even make it a Carling."

Nicole stepped out from under him. As she walked away, she said over her shoulder, "Hard pass. The excess testosterone hovering around you boys is giving me a five o'clock shadow."

Nir grinned at the other team leaders and followed.

CHAPTER 37

Nir waited at the counter while Nicole claimed their usual table with a full view of the restaurant, the door, and the front windows. After the meeting, Nir had filled in the analysts at CARL with the information. Then he had given them a two-hour window to find as much useful information as possible about Syria's chemical weapons and how to destroy them.

Nicole was heading to her workstation when Nir called out to her. He knew that the best thing he could do for the analysts was to get out of their way. He also knew that he desperately needed coffee, but he didn't want to go alone.

The barista had begun their order as soon as she saw them walking into the shop. Now, she set two cappuccinos in ceramic mugs on the counter.

"Thanks, Eva," Nir said as he paid for the coffee.

When he reached the table, Nicole was thumbing a text into her phone. He put the mugs down, then sat and waited her out.

She finished and set her phone on the table. "Sorry, just my agent. She was booking me out for February of next year. It's a crazy month for fashion weeks. New York, then London, then Milan, then Paris."

Nir sipped his cappuccino. "I'll shoot a memo to Ayatollah Khamenei asking him to declare February 2023 a terrorism-free month."

"You're so sweet. Always looking out for me."

It wasn't just the view that made this their favorite spot in the café. Its location tucked back in the corner meant that they were often surrounded by empty tables, as was the case today. Still, Nir lowered his voice and leaned forward.

"You have any thoughts about what the old man tasked us with?"

Nicole slowly spun her cup in her hands. "It's hard to know without more information. All I care about is that whatever plan we come up with, it doesn't involve you ending up in a box again. I still can't get that visual out of my mind."

"Trust me, I'm all for that."

"How have the dreams been? That morning in Moscow, you kind of scared me with that."

Embarrassed, Nir said, "Sorry, I didn't know I was that loud. It's not every night anymore. Just now and then. But nothing to worry about. This isn't that kind of operation."

"The offer still stands to talk to my pastor. He's got a psychology degree and has a good way about him. No pressure. It's just a thought."

Nir knew that there were people in this world that he would want to talk to less than Nicole's Christian pastor. He just couldn't come up with any names off the top of his head. Time to shift gears. "Speaking of your pastor, Efraim and I had a discussion a little while back."

"Uh-oh, nothing good can come of that. Let's hear it," Nicole said. She drank down half her coffee, then leaned back in her chair.

Thankful that she didn't push back on his obvious deflection, he said, "We were talking about religion and war. So many wars have been fought over religion. And it doesn't matter what religion. Judaism, Islam, Christianity. In India, you've got Muslims fighting Hindus. In Sri Lanka, you've got those same two religions fighting with the Buddhists. Back during the Crusades, you had Christians trying to kill everybody. So many people are killing each other in the name of God. Which got two agnostics like Efraim and me wondering—what good is religion if all it's going to do is divide people and have them kill one another? How would your pastor answer that?"

Nicole was about to answer when Nir added, "And, just to be clear, I'm not trying to be combative. It's an honest question."

Nicole smiled, then swapped her half-filled cup with Nir's empty. It was a ritual they had carried out for as long as they had been coming to this coffee bar. "I know it is. And it's a good one. But like I've told you before, I can't answer for religion. True Christianity is not religion. It's about a relationship."

"I know that's what you say. But I don't know if I buy that. If you were to look up Christianity in an encyclopedia, the first words you'd read would be, 'Christianity is a religion that...' It seems that everyone else in the world understands what religion is. It's just your particular sect that wants to soften it up by changing the definition."

"Wow. You came fully loaded today," Nicole said with a laugh. "But it's good. Go get yourself another cappuccino so I can think about this a second."

"Another cappuccino," he repeated. "Two of my favorite words."

He quickly swallowed the remaining contents of her cup, then took the empties to the counter. He ordered another cappuccino for himself and a bottle of water for Nicole. When he sat back down, he could see in her eyes that she had come up with an answer and was ready to roll.

"Okay, mister, here goes. When God created everything, how was it? I mean, what was it all like?"

"The Torah says that it was all good."

"Exactly. It was all perfect. Now when you look around, would you still say that His creation is perfect?"

Nir snorted. "If it was, I'd be out of a job."

"So, what changed between God saying, 'It is good,' and you saying, 'If you don't tell me how you're going to attack my country, I'll kill your family'? What caused it all to go downhill?"

"Russia?"

Nicole laughed. "Seriously, what screwed up this perfect creation?"

"Us. People. Is that what you mean?"

"That's exactly what I mean. Whatever God creates is perfect. Then we get our grubby little hands on it and muck it all up. What started as an unspoiled relationship with God in the Garden of Eden has now become separation from God on a decaying planet where everyone wants to kill one another."

"*Oy vey.* Pessimist much?"

"It's reality, you goof. Besides, you know me. I'm the ultimate optimist. And I can be an optimist because I know that we can re-unspoil our relationship with God."

"Re-unspoil? Don't think you could get away with that in Scrabble."

The barista walked up and placed Nir's cappuccino on the table. Then she twisted the cap off a bottle of sparkling Pellegrino water and set it in front of Nicole.

"Thanks, Eva," said Nicole. Once the barista had walked away, she continued. "But even with that re-unspoiling—or, since you've suddenly joined the grammar police, we can call it reconciliation—even with that reconciliation with God, people got hold of it and tainted it like they do everything else."

"Okay, now you've lost me again. You keep telling me that once you're made right with God, you'll always be right with Him. Now you're saying that it can be tainted."

"I'm not talking about each person's relationship. I'm talking about the whole concept of Christianity. It used to be that *Christian* meant someone who followed Jesus Christ. When the term was first used, Christians were being persecuted in a lot of areas in the Roman Empire. You had to be fully committed if you wore that title because it could get you killed. But then people got hold of Christianity and watered it down. It became a concept instead of a relationship. It became ideology instead of action. It's gotten so bad now that being a Christian can just mean you were born in a supposedly Christian nation, or you simply go to church every now and then."

"And? I mean, I don't see the problem. If you go to a Christian church, then you're a Christian. If you go to a mosque, you're a Muslim. Synagogue? Jew. What am I missing?" It just wasn't connecting for him. She had just clearly stated what he and just about everyone else in the entire world believed religion was and said that it was all wrong.

"What you're missing is the reality of what being a Christian is. It's like that convertible GTO that Sharetsky had that you loved so much."

"The '69. Dream car."

"So, someone says, 'Nir, I have a green '69 convertible GTO for you.'"

"Verdugo green," he added.

"Verdugo green. Quit drooling and stay with me. They say that they have the GTO for you, but when you check out the car, you discover that it's just a hollow shell. There's no interior, no engine."

"No factory Hurst T-Handle shifter?"

Nicole let out an exasperated growl. "You're really making me regret this illustration. The car is an empty shell. How would you feel?"

"I'd feel ripped off. What would I do with an empty shell of a car?"

"Exactly. And that's what people have made of Christianity. It is an empty shell. It's worthless."

Nir began smiling. "Okay, I get it. You're saying that you have the interior and the engine. You're not Christianity in name only. You're the whole car."

"Factory shifter and all," said Nicole, leaning back with her arms wide. "We've got peace that will carry you through the worst times. We've got forgiveness for the nastiest sins. We've got hope for those who feel like their life is worth nothing. We have purpose for those who can't figure out why they're even on this earth. Most of all, we have a promise of eternal life so there is no more reason to fear anything in this life or beyond. All it takes is surrendering your life to Christ and following Him."

"Nooooo," Nir said, covering his face with his hands. "It was sounding so good. Then you ruined it with that terrible word."

"What word?"

He could see her replaying her statement in her mind.

Then she said, "Oh, never mind. *Surrender.*"

Nir moved his hands from his face to his ears. "Stop saying that horrible word."

When he saw that his antics had drawn the attention of people at a few other tables, he put his hands down and spoke more quietly. "You know me, Nicole. I'm a fighter and a bit of a control freak. The one thing I am not is a surrenderer."

Nicole laughed. "A bit of a control freak? Really? Anyway, I'm not talking about the kind of surrender you're thinking of."

"I can think of only one kind of surrender." He lifted his hands and said, "I give up. I am now your prisoner." Putting his hands back down, he said, "You know what happened last year when I put the control of my life into someone else's hands. It's not an experience I'm anxious to repeat."

She reached out her hand and took his. "I know, Nir. I wouldn't wish what you went through on anyone. But you're thinking of surrendering your will so that someone can force you to do what you don't want to do. I'm talking about surrendering your will so that you are free to do what you were made to do."

"Okay, you've lost me again. Can you explain it to me, but using a '67 Camaro this time?"

Leaning back, Nicole drank from her bottle, then squelched down a carbonation belch. "How about I use a dog instead. Have you ever seen a Rhodesian Ridgeback? The family of a friend of mine from school bred them. Very willful dogs. Hard to break. Always fighting and getting into trouble. But once they were finally broken and realized who alpha was, they were the best dogs around. They were bred specifically to hunt and to protect, but they do that best under the control of someone greater than themselves. Their joy came from living out what they were created to do, but in a controlled environment."

"Reminds me of the Belgian Shepherds in the Oketz Unit in the IDF. They're happiest when they're hunting down explosives and chomping on terrorists. But as soon as their handler says 'Stop,' they stop."

"Exactly, Nir. That's the kind of surrender I'm talking about. We were created to live under the leadership of our Creator. When we do, He'll give us the freedom and direction and opportunity to live out the life we were created for."

"So, you're saying that if I stop being such a willful dog and become beta to God's alpha, He's going to show me what I was made to do. But what if it's not the Mossad? What if He wants me to become an accountant or a hairdresser?"

Nicole laughed. "Do you really think God created you to be a hairstylist? There's a verse in the Psalms somewhere that says that if we delight ourselves in the Lord, He'll give us the desires of our hearts. What's cool about that is when we're following God, our desires will always line up with His. That's because He put those desires in there to begin with. I doubt that surrendering to Jesus would mean a career change for you. It certainly didn't for me. But even if it did, you would wake up one day surprised to realize that you loved what you were doing far more than anything you did with the Mossad. And that's because…" She indicated for Nir to pick up the line.

"Because I'd be doing what I was created to do. I get it. Are you sure that God wouldn't be willing to meet me halfway? I give Him some of what He wants. He gives me some of what I want. Both sides are happy."

"Tavor!" Nicole said, exasperated.

"Hey, you know me. I'm always looking for a bargain."

Nicole shook her head. "You're impossible."

"I'm just messing with you. I heard what you said. It all goes into the mental files," he said, tapping the side of his head. "*Surrender* is just such an ugly word to me. I've got to process that one for a while."

"Fair enough, you willful dog," Nicole said, winking at him.

"Want to skitch my belly?" Nir asked, moving his eyebrows up and down.

"Down, boy, or I'll have to get the spray bottle," she said, standing and lifting her purse from her chair. "On that note, we better get back."

Nir opened the door for her, and they walked into the beautiful sunshine of a fall day. He put his arm across her shoulders as they made their way up the street to where he had parked the small car he kept in Tel Aviv.

Surrender, he thought. *I hear what she's saying. But when we Jews have surrendered in the past, we've seen what it's gotten us. Nicole just doesn't understand that. There's got to be a better option.*

CHAPTER 38

CARL, MOSSAD HEADQUARTERS, TEL AVIV, ISRAEL—
NOVEMBER 2, 2022—12:15 (12:15 PM) IST

Nir stepped out of his office. The two hours were up, but everyone was still hard at work. Just to his left stood Chewbacca. Nir noticed that the Wookie mannequin was sporting new headwear. He read the words out loud: "'My other Corellian light freighter is a Tesla.' I don't even know what that means."

Lahav Tabib must have overheard him because he let out a snort followed by a frustrated sigh. Without looking away from his computer screen, he said, "The Millennium Falcon is a YT-1300 freighter manufactured in a Corellian Engineering Corporation shipyard and was originally designed to function as an intermodal tug pushing container in orbital freight yards. A Tesla is a car."

"We need to find you a girlfriend," Nir said. He walked over to the table. "Wrap it up. Two minutes, and I want everyone at the table." Nobody responded. Not even Nicole, whose fingers were rapidly transferring code onto one of her monitors.

He hoped that this gang of brilliant misfits had come up with something useful. After 30 minutes of mulling over their monumental task, he was still at a loss. There had to be a way to destroy Syria's chemicals before Russia had a chance to orchestrate their plot. But whatever that way was remained far beyond his grasp.

"Okay, bring it in."

Frustrated groans sounded through the room.

"Quit your whining. Hurry it up."

As they gathered around the table, Liora set down a yellow reusable grocery bag with the word *Shufersal* written in red Hebrew letters on the side. Before Nir had a chance to start the meeting, she poured the contents of the bag out onto the table. It was filled with packages of Pez refills.

"In honor of our earlier hairy-footed Hobbit discussion," she began. Then she reached to the bottom of the bag and pulled out a Lord of the Rings Pez Gift Set.

"*Mashu mashu,*" said Lahav. Everyone else, other than Nir, agreed with the awesomeness.

Opening the package, Liora passed out the dispensers. "I'll keep Frodo for obvious reasons. My best buddy gets Sam," she said, handing him to Dafna. "Yossi, on beard and hair alone, you get Aragorn. Lahav, you get Gimli the dwarf."

"Gandalf, the brilliant wizard and leader of the fellowship, goes to…" She turned toward Nir and held out the dispenser. But as he reached for it, Liora said, "Nicole."

She spun around and passed it off. Nicole smiled at Nir and opened and closed the head a few times toward him.

"And for our fearless boss, whom we all love and respect so much. Hold out your hand."

Nir did so, seriously regretting the philosophical leadership decision he had made long ago to humor these brilliant geeks in order to keep them happy, thereby increasing their productivity. He was now thinking that it might be more advantageous if he just swore at them more.

He felt Liora place a Pez dispenser in his hand. Looking down, he saw the bug eyes of Gollum staring up at him.

"It's perfect," he said. "But where did you find a Pez dispenser of my first girlfriend?"

Laughter and cheers sounded around the table. Liora surprised him by jumping up and hugging him around the neck. Looking at the other end of the table, he saw Nicole give him a thumbs up.

"Can we finally get to work?" he asked. They all quieted down and looked at him intently. But their smiles lingered.

Score one for the good guys, he thought.

"Okay, talk to me. What are the options for destroying the chemicals?"

Dafna began. "There are three primary ways that chemical weapons are destroyed. Each of us took one and spent our time determining its practicality. Meanwhile, Lahav, I don't know, he was off Lahaving something." The bespectacled analyst nodded, appearing to agree with her description of his contribution. She continued, "I investigated hydrolysis. This is where hot water and various solutions are used to essentially drown the bad stuff that's in the chemicals."

"Like what they did on the Cape Ray, that American ship where they processed a bunch of Assad's weapons back in 2014," Nir said.

"Exactly," said Dafna. She tilted Samwise Gamgee's head back and popped a Pez into her mouth, then continued. "The main problem with this method is obvious."

"Where would the teams get enough hot water?" said Nicole.

"Exactly. Unless you Kidon guys were able to travel with a five-thousand-gallon electric teakettle, hydrolysis is out."

"A five-thousand-gallon teakettle is enough to pour the entire population of Jaffa a cup of tea," said Lahav, smiling at the prospect. When he noticed no one else sharing in his enthusiasm, he added, "Okay, busted. I know what you're thinking. 'But, Lahav, there'd be about six thousand cups of tea leftover.' I just couldn't think of a city with 106,000 people."

"I can pretty much guarantee no one was thinking that," said Nir. "So, hydrolysis is out. Who's next?"

Liora spoke. "I looked into neutralization. In this method, the weapons are disassembled, and the chemicals are drained into a combination of hot water and some caustic compound like sodium hydroxide. And before you say anything, the answer is yes, hydrolysis and neutralization are essentially the same thing, just with a slightly different process and slightly different compounds. Unfortunately, Dafna and I didn't realize that until we were well into it."

"So, we'll take neutralization off the table for the same reason, correct?"

"Correct."

"Okay, Yossi, let's hear yours."

The long-haired analyst was in the middle of retying his man bun when he was called on. He quickly pulled a hair tie off his wrist and wrapped it around the hair ball on the top of his head. It was a process that made Nir uncomfortable every time he watched it.

"I researched incineration. This is the most common and most effective way of dealing with weaponized chemicals."

"That sounds promising," Nir said.

"It's not. When we're talking incineration, it can range from high-temperature burning to a plasma arc process to molten salt oxidation to hydrocracking process…"

"Okay, okay. Way too much information. Just tell me why it's not practical."

Yossi seemed a little frustrated at being cut off, but he continued. "They are all highly technical processes. It's not like you can just go in, pour a little gasoline on the chemicals, toss in a Zippo lighter, and do a Wolverine explosion walkaway. The burns must be done at a very high temperature and completely controlled. The smoke has to be captured and processed so that you aren't potentially pouring deadly by-products into the air. In other words, it is not a process that can be done by a bunch of amateurs in the basement of a primary school."

"And those are our three options? What about hauling the stuff away or blowing it up? Give me something."

Yossi responded, "The amounts are likely way beyond hauling away. And the locations are all in heavily populated areas."

"Nothing like a human shield," said Lahav sarcastically. "The weapons caches are what I was 'Lahaving,' which is actually really cool to say. I've always wanted to be a verb. 'We were in big trouble, but then we Lahaved our way out of it and saved the day.'"

"Get on with it before I kick your Lahav into next week," said Nir. Immediately, every voice around the table uttered a unique sentence of criticism, each containing the word *noun*.

Nir buried his head in his hands. He was right on the edge of lash-
ing out. Normally, he could roll fine with the joking, but whether it
was because he was tired or he was feeling the pressure of the competition, today, it was getting on his very last nerve.

In a quiet voice, Liora said, "Have a Pez. They're specially made to
make you happy."

Nir looked up. She had stood his Gollum dispenser on end so it was
looking at him with its bulging eyes. Despite his best efforts, a smile
cracked his face. He lifted the once-upon-a-time hobbit, pulled his
head a back, and flicked a candy into his mouth.

"Now, can I please hear about the chemical storage?"

"*Sababa*," said Lahav. "All you had to do was ask. There are four sites,
all in Damascus. Two are under primary schools. One is in an apartment basement in a residential neighborhood. The fourth is under a
business park in the heart of downtown. I've got them mapped out,
but I figure that much detail is irrelevant until we figure out first what
we're doing with the stuff."

"It is. Thanks. So, that brings us back to our original question. How
do we destroy this stuff?"

The analysts looked at one another, then Liora said, "We can't."

Nir wasn't expecting that answer. This brilliant gang of nerds had
never given up on any challenge. There was a solution to this problem,
and the ones best equipped to figure it out were sitting in this room.

"Sorry, that's not acceptable," he said. "This stuff needs to be dealt
with before it comes flying over our border."

Liora responded, "Listen to what I said. We can't destroy this stuff.
But that doesn't mean that it can't be destroyed."

Nir felt his temperature rising again. "Please stop playing games
with me. I know it can be destroyed. We've covered that already. But
now you're saying we can't destroy it. If not us, then who? Are we going
to ask Assad to do it?"

"Yes," said Dafna. "That's exactly what we should do."

Nir stood up and walked away from the table. He didn't know if
they were playing games with him, but he was completely fed up. It's
okay to goof around, but there were times when you had to put the

stupidity aside and get serious. Their answer to this chemical weapons problem was not serious.

He was halfway across the room when he spun back around. "My brilliant team of analysts. This is what you come up with. 'Excuse me, President Assad, would you mind destroying your store of chemical weapons before the Russians convince some proxy militia to lob them our way?' And I'm sure his response will be, 'Of course, my Israeli friends, anything to help out a neighbor.'"

Dafna continued, "I'm not saying he'd say yes—at least, not right away. He might need a little convincing."

"Nir, just hear them out," said Nicole.

Nir stood in the center of the room. All eyes were on him. He sighed and sat back down. He flipped back Gollum's head, but his dispenser was empty. Liora reached out, and he passed it to her. She began unwrapping a refill.

Nir said, "You're right. I'm sorry. Anything you have is better than what I've got, which is *bobkes*."

"So, again, we can't destroy the chemicals," said Dafna. "Instead, we force Assad to do it using a two-prong attack. First, we send four teams in, one to each site. Each team will document what they find there. It will be just like the Iran document heist back in 2018. We bring back video evidence and we figure out a way to bring samples."

Nir shook his head. "They'll still deny it. They'll say that all their chemicals were destroyed in the airstrikes and that we manufactured these stores."

Yossi took over. "No doubt they will. But this is where the second prong of our attack comes in. While the teams are documenting the evidence, they are also planting explosives. These are bombs that can be detonated remotely, and that will go off if tampered with or if someone attempts to move them."

The first little ray of light began to break through the dark clouds.

"What if someone discovers the explosives and messes with them?" he asks.

Yossi answered, "We'll make sure that they are clearly labeled, because these bombs must remain a bluff. The last thing we want is them going off. We'll let Assad know that we have proof about his under-the-city chemical weapons and his use of human shields. We'll also inform him that we are aware of the planned attack. When he denies it, we'll tell him about the bombs and let him know that he has two hours to evacuate the areas surrounding the sites because after that, we're blowing them up."

Liora took over. "And what will hopefully ensure his cooperation is that all our communication with him will be on the world stage. Assad denies he has chemical weapons under the city, so we call him out on the lie on the world news. We'll announce that we have evidence and that we have credible information about an upcoming chemical attack on our nation. We'll let the world know that a major power is behind the attack, then we back-channel Russia and let them know that we know it's them. We'll tell them that if any chemicals come our way, we'll inform the global media that they were behind it, and we'll back it up with our evidence. Everyone will be ready to believe it because the world already thinks Putin is the devil because of Ukraine. Once the eyes of the media are on Syria, we'll start the two-hour countdown and pray that Assad caves before we get to zero and turn a large part of Damascus into a chemically soiled wasteland."

"And you're prepared to have those bombs detonated?" Nir asked. "You can't bluff if you aren't prepared to go through with it."

Lahav spoke. "Decisions like that are for people other than us. But as for me, if it was either their families or our families, I'll choose ours every time."

It was quiet in the room, and the silence stretched for several minutes as each person contemplated the gravity of what they were recommending.

Finally, Nir said, "Yossi, keep working this plan. The rest of you, I want you to come up with at least three alternative options for me in the next six hours. I'm going to go run this by Efraim."

He stood, then said, "This was great out-of-the-box thinking. Now, try to come up with something else that doesn't involve blowing up chemical weapons stores and potentially killing tens of thousands of people." After snatching up his refilled Gollum from the table, he walked out the door.

CHAPTER 39

The cast master rechecked each man's equipment. When he got to Nir, he ensured his helmet strap was fastened, all pockets on his vest and pack were tightly shut, and, most importantly, that his flotation device was tightly secured to his body. Nir was the leader of the team, but for this helocast, the cast master was the one in charge. The man checked his watch and held up four fingers. Nir gave a thumbs up.

Turning, Nir tapped Yaron and held up four fingers. Yaron passed it on to the other three members of the team. They were in a Yanshuf helicopter flying low over the Mediterranean. Three nautical miles to their east lay the territorial waters of Lebanon. In front of them, to the north, flew three more helicopters, each carrying a five-man Kidon team. Secured with cargo straps underneath each Yanshuf was a Zodiac inflatable boat readied for a K-duck, or kangaroo duck, deployment.

When the time had come for the team leaders to return to the *ramsad*'s office, Nir went with mixed feelings. He was fairly confident that his analyst team in CARL was correct in its assessment that there was no way to cleanly and safely destroy the chemicals stored in

Damascus. But there was a part of him that was worried that the other four teams would each come to the meeting with some brilliant plan for their destruction. If that were true, then his "It can't be done" would look pretty lame, as would he.

But as each team reported their analysts' findings to Katz, Porush, Friedman, and Cohen, Nir was heartened to hear that only one Kidon team recommended destroying the chemicals where they sat. The leader for that team was the grizzled Ravid Efrat, who recommended an incineration method using "enough explosives to lower the city's elevation by ten meters." When Asher Porush asked him about the massive loss of civilian life, Efrat justified the action based on the old Talmudic philosophy of "If someone is coming to kill you, rise up and kill them first." Nir was relieved to hear the *ramsad* dismiss both Efrat's logic and his plan.

Bensoussan's team had created an elaborate scheme to start a shooting war between Syria and Lebanon. Ehrlich's analysts had recommended a plot to kidnap and hold President Assad as hostage. Abelman's team had come to much the same conclusions as the gang at CARL, particularly when it came to bringing in the global media. However, only Nir's plan included documenting the existence of the underground storage facilities and then wiring them up to explode. He couldn't help but feel pride for himself and his analysts when the Mossad leaders determined to go with their team's proposal.

The only question that was still hanging was whether Israel would actually explode the bombs if Syria called its bluff. That was not a decision the *ramsad* had the authority to make. And, even now, as Nir cruised at an elevation low enough to get saltwater spray in his face, he didn't know what, if anything yet, had been decided.

The cast master held one finger up to Nir. He turned to relay the one-minute message but saw his team already moving. Yaron, Doron, and Dima lined up at the open door on the opposite side of the helicopter. Imri shifted so that he was directly behind Nir. He clapped his hand on Nir's shoulder and gave it a squeeze.

Kneeling in the center of the floor, the cast master counted with his fingers from five. Nir watched him down to zero. The man pulled a release handle in the center of the floor, and the helicopter shuddered as the Zodiac dropped. But the moment it did, the turbulence from being so close to the water rocked the Yanshuf. The helicopter tilted heavily to the right and Nir felt himself tumbling out of the door.

He fell back-first into the water. A liquid burn rushed up his nose and into his mouth. Fighting the urge to thrash about, he stilled himself and let his flotation do its work. In seconds, he broke the surface. Immediately, he coughed out the seawater and sucked in a chest full of air. As he got his bearings, he saw a large form drop from the opposite side of the helicopter.

Dima. Last in line. That means everyone should be in the water.

As if to confirm his thought, Imri swam up to him.

"You okay?" he asked loudly over the sound of the helicopter.

"I'm good," Nir replied, watching the Yanshuf elevate, preparing to depart.

"Looks like we've got a problem." Imri swam toward the Zodiac. The boat was upside down. Nir figured it must have hit a skid when the helicopter rocked.

He followed Imri through the choppy water. When they reached the inflatable, Yaron and Doron were already there. The light from the full moon showed that Dima was just meters away and drawing close.

Yaron and Doron began untying the righting lines. As they worked, Nir heard the first engine start from one of the other Zodiacs. "Let's go, guys."

Once the lines were loose and draped across the boat, Nir, Imri, and Dima pulled themselves up. Taking hold of the ropes, they stood on the inverted watercraft.

"On one," said Nir. "Three, two, one." The men leaned back and let their body weight drag them down into the water. As they fell back, the ropes they were holding pulled the boat over so that it was right side up.

"Check the engine," Nir said to Imri.

The young operative took hold of the side of the inflatable and, with youthful dexterity, lifted himself into the boat. Even though the engine had been wrapped to protect it from this very eventuality, Nir was still concerned that some of the salt water could have leaked in and flooded the engine. The sound from all three of the other boats was already fading away. There was no way that they would, or even should, wait for his guys if they had to row 15 miles to shore.

Doron slipped over the other side into the boat, followed by Yaron. Nir went in next, and Dima brought up the rear.

Imri had freed the engine from its protection and attached it to the boat. Taking hold of the pull cord, he said, "*Otzma enoshit.*" He pulled, and the engine sprang to life. Twisting the throttle, he accelerated the boat in pursuit of the others.

"Human strength?" Nir asked over the whine of the engine.

"My dad was Battalion 931, Nahal Brigade. That was their motto. Growing up, every time I thought I couldn't do something or complained that some project or chore was too difficult, he'd say, '*Otzma enoshit.*' With human strength, there's nothing you can't do."

Nir gripped the man's arm, then turned to the front.

I wish I could believe that human strength would be enough for this operation. But to pull this off, I think we're going to need a little more. We're going to need assistance from above. God, here we are, going back into the jaws of the lion. You and I have worked out an arrangement—I help You, You help me. This would be a good time for You to keep Your end of the bargain and give us some supernatural support.

CHAPTER 40

Nir sat in the back of the boat with Imri as the other man controlled the outboard motor. The Mediterranean water that sprayed up was cool, but not cold. However, the 50-kilometer-per-hour wind blowing onto his wet clothing had him chilled to the bone.

As they neared their destination, they kept their orientation by following a light from the shore that flashed every 20 seconds. When they were close enough to see forms moving around in the moonlight, Nir braced himself for landing. They hit the beach and slid up the sand. Imri tilted up the engine so that it wouldn't dig in, and the boat skidded to a stop. Immediately, the team vaulted out onto the beach.

Two men ran up to them. Once he could make out their faces, he saw that it was *Alif* and *Ba* from their previous operation in Syria. *Alif* clapped a hand on Nir's shoulder and said, in Arabic, the language of all their inter-team communications on this operation, "Welcome back to the wrong side of the border. We were beginning to wonder if you guys had gone sightseeing."

Nir patted him on the back. "Boat got hung up on the helocast. I have to admit, I'm surprised to see you here. I figured after last time, you'd avoid me at all costs."

"Nah, I asked to team up with you. It's been a few weeks since I've been shot at. I'm getting a little bored."

The team already had the boat unloaded. Dima and Imri began pushing it back into the water. As they did, a young man who looked no older than 16 vaulted inside. When the water was deep enough, he lowered the engine, fired it up, and sped off to the south.

"Can we trust those guys?" Nir asked *Alif.* They had each grabbed gear, along with the rest of the team, and were jogging up the beach to where four large box trucks sat parked.

"As much as you can trust any smugglers. But these guys hate Hezbollah and all Iran's other proxies. The terrorists are nasty people who sometimes go raping and thieving in villages—villages that these smugglers call home."

"And they know that Hezbollah is not our target with this operation?"

"For them, they're all bad guys. There are the civilians, like them, just trying to get by and make a living. That's most of the population of Lebanon and Syria. Then there are the idiots who band together, blow things up, and drive their countries into the crapper."

They reached the trucks. A small group had congregated together. Nir recognized the three other Kidon team leaders—Bensoussan, Ehrlich, and Abelman. Efrat and his team had been excluded from the operation as unnecessary.

It's quite possible that the old man is still swearing at Efraim even now, Nir thought, pitying his friend.

As he walked up, Ehrlich said, "Here comes the diva, making his grand entrance."

"No grand entrance. I just enjoy making you wait."

He supposed that the other six men in the group were Unit 504, like *Alif* and *Ba.* The fact that there were no introductions confirmed his hunch. Each Kidon team was assigned two agents from the elite underground division—one Israeli leader and one Syrian operative.

"I know you guys wanted to come up directly into Syria, but the Israel-Syria border is just too hot right now after last month's operation," said *Alif* to the group. "Coming through Lebanon is a pain. However, there's a much better chance of not being detected. We're taking the smuggler's route through Joub Jannine. Then we'll cross into Syria just northeast of Mazraat Deir al-Ashayer. That border crossing is used mostly by local traffic and smugglers. If all goes well, the palms we've greased will get us across smoothly. If it doesn't, prepare to go loud. Because of the road quality, we've got about four hours ahead of us. That means we're hitting Damascus right at sunrise. So, when you get to your safe house, get in quickly and quietly. Activity begins tonight at midnight. Questions?"

Bensoussan spoke up. "I know the explosives are at the safe houses. Are they ready to go, or will we have to prep them in any way?"

One of the other Unit 504 men answered. "Our team has them all prepared, and I checked each one myself. All we need to do tonight is place and arm them."

"Any other questions?" *Alif* asked.

"Yeah, can we get going?" Ehrlich said. "I'm feeling a little exposed standing here on the beach."

The group broke up. Nir and his team followed *Alif* and *Ba* to a red box truck with *Auto Khaled* stenciled on the side, along with a couple phone numbers. The side door to the cargo area stood open. Nir's team climbed in. Just before Nir pulled himself up, *Alif* handed him something. Nir saw that it was a small disc perforated with tiny holes. The other man was holding a similarly sized disc.

"If we run into trouble, I'll press this. It will cause your coin to chirp." He demonstrated, and a sound like the arming of his car alarm beeped in Nir's hand. "If you hear that, come out hot."

"Let's hope it doesn't come to that."

"*Inshallah*," the other man said.

"*God willing*" *is right*, Nir thought. *If we can get through this without firing a shot, I'd call that a huge win.*

He pulled himself up into the truck and *Alif* shut the door behind him. As he did, an overhead light popped on, causing each of the men to groan as their eyes adjusted. To his right was a false wall made of plywood.

The truck started, then lurched forward, causing Nir's team to stagger. They had plenty of room for the five of them, and the Unit 504

guys had been kind enough to supply large pillows for them to sit on.
There were two coolers by the door. Nir opened them. The first held
fruit, pita bread, hummus, and a few other snacks. The second was
filled with bottles of water.

"Heads up," he said, and tossed a bottle to each man. He slid the
other cooler into the middle of the floor. "Got food in there, if any of
you guys want it."

As he expected, Dima was the first to open it up. The Russian began
to pull out items and toss them around. "Want anything, boss?"

"Fruit," said Nir, and Dima tossed him an orange. He bit the peel to
break the skin, then began pulling off strips. As he did, his mind drifted.

*God, seems I'm doing more of this talking to You lately. Who knows? It
might become a habit. Anyway, protect my men. I'm ready to sacrifice all
for my people and my team. Seriously, if it means my team coming home
and my country being protected from these chemicals, I'm ready to die. All
I ask is that if there is something after this life, that You don't forget me there.*

But that was the big question. Would God remember him? It was
that thought that plagued his mind. In his opinion, he had done more
than enough to earn the notice of a benevolent and merciful God. Sure,
there had been some not-great stuff in his life. Like most people, there
were plenty of things in his past that he knew he shouldn't have done
and that he now regretted. But in his mind, if you were to put what he'd
endured to protect the lives of the Israelis—the ones who were supposed to be God's chosen people—if you were to put all that stuff on
one side of a set of scales and the bad stuff he'd done on the other side,
he was pretty confident that the tilt would go his way.

*But Nicole said that isn't the way it works. You can't earn your way in.
Which kind of sucks because that's all I've got. It's like saving for your retire-
ment your whole life, then suddenly the government says, "Guess what—we're
changing our currency. Everything you've got in your accounts is worthless."*

As the truck bounced along, he tried to think of how Nicole would
answer that. The other guys got a card game going, and they invited
him in. He begged off. His compulsion to "devil's advocate" his own
argument was too great. Pulling another water bottle from the cooler,
he twisted the cap off and took a drink. Then it came to him.

Nicole would say something like, "Nir, it's like seeing an origami swan for the first time. You think it's amazing. Never seen anything so beautiful. So, you learn how to make origami swans because you figure that if you love them, so will everyone else. You spend all your time, day and night, manipulating and folding paper to make these swans. You fill your house with them. Then one day you decide you're going to make your fortune by selling all your swans. You put them up online, but nobody wants them. What you thought was so wonderful was absolutely worthless. You're the only one who had put any value to them."

For the first time, the concept made sense to him. The only reason he had for why works should matter for getting someone into heaven was because he thought they should. He had given them that value. So, when God said that works don't matter, he had gotten upset and said it's not fair. And why wasn't it fair? Because he was using his own standard and not God's.

Okay, God, I think I get it now about earning my way. Still, if I'm being totally honest, I've got to admit that subtracting good works from the salvation equation only leaves me more confused. How does putting my belief in another person do anything, even if people do say that person is Your Son? And that's another thing—the God of the universe having a kid makes absolutely no sense to me.

His mind started trying to process how the Creator of all things would go about making a family for Himself. Was Jesus the only Son? Were there any daughters? And, most importantly, who is Mom?

"Nope, not today," he said to himself, getting to his feet. "That one is way too complicated to figure out in the back of a box truck driving through Hezbollah territory." Walking over to the card game, he snatched a pillow, sat down, and said, "Deal me in."

CHAPTER 41

Nir's team finished loading up the military cargo truck with their gear. Each man wore mismatched equipment to simulate the typical hodgepodge of lower-level Syrian military units acquired through purchase, theft, or battleground scavenging. The fabric of Nir's uniform was printed with the TAP 47 or lizard pattern camouflage, which is great for the lush jungles of Africa but would do very little to conceal him in the concrete jungle of urban Damascus. He wore an SSh-68 Russian-made steel helmet on his head and Ratnik body armor, also from Syria's Eurasian benefactors to the north. On his thigh was holstered a suppressed Belgian Browning Hi-Power 9mm and strapped across his chest was a Soviet-era AKS-74 with a folding stock. Strapped to, tucked away, or hanging from his person, he also carried two RGD-5 grenades, two flash-bang grenades, two smoke grenades, a fixed blade tactical knife, flex-cuffs, a boatload of magazines filled with 5.45x39mm and 9mm ammunition, and Polish-made MU-3ADM passive night vision goggles.

It was this final piece of equipment that could turn out to be the most critical to the operation. That was why the Mossad brass felt it worth the risk to include them in each man's kit. If discovered, they were to say that the NVGs had been appropriated from UN peace-keepers in Lebanon, and, if the questioner was of high rank, they were to offer them as a gift. There were few officers who would say no to a present of that caliber.

Travel to the compound in Jdeidat Artouz, a town just to the south-west of Damascus, was blessedly uneventful. Other than losing 100 shekels to a Dima bluff in Texas Hold'em, it was a smooth trip. He wasn't sure at what point the trucks split up, but he figured it was when they were well across the border and nearing Syria's capital city.

The truck had entered the gates of the compound just after 7:00 a.m., and, once all their equipment was unloaded, they had settled in to get some rest in preparation for the night's activities. But Nir had been unable to sleep. He was too wound up. The safety of his team, the success of the operation, the whole feasibility of the plan were on his shoulders. It was very likely that people's lives would end tonight because of decisions he made. Whether friend or enemy, the existence of some, or possibly many, would cease. That was a heavy burden. He prayed that if anyone had to die, it would not be the good guys.

Now that night had come, he climbed up into the front passenger seat of the Russian-built GAZ-3308 Sadko, the exact model truck used during their earlier Syrian mission. Behind the wheel was *Alif.*

"Feeling a little déjà vu," Nir said in Arabic to the man who was wearing an American-made PASGT helmet and vest with the US Woodland camouflage pattern.

"Yeah, we've got to stop meeting like this. You ready?"

"As I'll ever be." He turned around and, through his coms, asked the guys on the other side of the glass, "Ready to roll?"

Yaron, who was responsible to make sure everything was packed and everyone was on board, said, "Let's do this."

Alif turned the ignition and the truck rumbled to life. He ground it into gear and rolled it to the fence. A boy of about nine, the son of the homeowner, slid the gate open, then stood at attention and saluted. Nir returned the salute, eliciting a wide grin from the child. After weav-ing through some neighborhood streets, *Alif* turned left onto Route 7, which would lead them northeast into the southern part of Damascus.

Somewhere around the city, he knew that the other three Kidon-Unit 504 teams were en route to their destinations. Bensoussan and Ehrlich were going to storage locations under primary schools. Abelman's team was heading downtown to a business park. Nir's team was on its way to Nahr Eshe, an extremely violent neighborhood tucked into the bottom part of a major junction in south Damascus. Enduring numerous battles and car bombings, many of the impoverished citizens of this war zone were beaten down and hopeless. When Liora had briefed his team on the plight of the residents, she had said that not long ago, a newborn baby girl was found along the side of the road wrapped in a pink blanket and laid in the weeds.

As soon as Nir heard about this neighborhood, he had known that this was his location. It was the most dangerous, but also the most in peril because of the number of residents. The schools would be empty at this time of night, as would the business park. But if something went wrong in Nahr Eshe, thousands of lives in the crowded community could be lost. It was impossible for Nir to leave that in the hands of any other team. Asserting his privilege as the originator of the operation, he laid claim to the neighborhood before any of the other team leaders had the opportunity.

Once they entered Damascus proper on Route 7, they exited onto Almotahalik Aljanobi Street. After six minutes, they took the M5 exit at the interchange heading south toward Amman, Jordan. Moments later, they veered onto a ramp that took them off the freeway and into Nahr Eshe. Halfway up the block stood a large, ornate mosque, out of place with the surrounding poverty. Even though the worship center was closed, a group of a dozen of what Nir would consider MAMs—or military-age males—stood smoking, talking, and warming themselves over a trash can fire. A few of them watched the truck as it passed, but military vehicles in this neighborhood were nothing new.

The danger Nir's team was facing was that this was not a government-friendly neighborhood, which was likely the reason Assad chose it for chemical storage. Should something accidentally leak out, the only ones affected would be a bunch of impoverished rebels. If this group in front of the mosque took umbrage at their truck entering their neighborhood, it would likely take only a few cell calls to gather enough people to cause Nir and his team a major problem.

"*Zay*, watch behind," Nir called out. Because this operation was back in Syria, he had decided to reassign each team member the same Arabic letter they had used for the previous op. Yaron was *Zay*; Doron was *Sin*; Dima, *Qaf*; and Imri, *Nun*.

A moment later, Doron replied, "Nothing suspicious. No one moved or reached for a phone."

That was good, but Nir knew that the men may have just been waiting until the cargo truck was out of eyeshot. "Everyone keep your eyes open. We're now officially on the neighborhood's radar."

Just past the mosque, they turned right. Old cars lined the streets, making them a narrow fit for the truck. Nir wondered how many of the beat-up vehicles still ran and how many were just oversized bits of debris brought on by warfare and a failed economy. Small shops were scattered here and there, but most of the structures were apartment buildings that rose three and four stories. Evidence of gun battles were chipped and pocked into the facades of many buildings, and more than once they passed a pile of rubble that had once been the homes of neighborhood residents.

A large lot appeared on his left. This was Nir's geographical marker to pay attention. Without turning his head, he focused his peripheral vision on the street that now opened on his right. The third building down was their target. Somewhere in there was a stairway that led to an underground chemical storage facility.

Nir expected there to be guards, and he was right. Two men with long guns stood outside in the moonlight. He swore to himself.

"Is the drone prepped?" he called back.

"It's ready," said Doron.

"Let it go."

"We've got visual," said Liora. Her voice surprised him, even though he knew that CARL had been monitoring them from the moment they left the compound.

"Check the roofs. Make sure there are no snipers or lookouts up top."

"Will do."

"What did you see?" he asked *Alif.*

"Two out front. Didn't have a good enough vantage to see if anyone else was around."

"Notice anything about their demeanor?" Nir wanted to know if *Alif* had made the same observation as he.

"Yeah, they were actually guarding. I mean, they weren't smoking. They weren't on their phones. They weren't telling stories. They were attentive, hands on their guns, locked into their surroundings."

That confirmed Nir's worry. "It's almost as if they've been warned we're coming. But I can't imagine that's true. We've got a very limited number of people who have been read into this."

Imri spoke up from the back of the truck. "If the attack is coming soon, it's possible that the activity level has increased as they're getting ready to move the stuff."

"Or, after losing their original delivery system to an EMP, they're being hypervigilant," added Yaron.

Liora spoke. "This is CARL. No sign of activity on the rooftops."

Another voice said, "Five minutes to launch." It was Nicole. Having her with the team in CARL gave him great peace of mind. All the analysts excelled at their jobs and Nir trusted them with his life. But Nicole had something extra. She had that spiritual side that made Nir feel like maybe God would be rooting for them.

The street they were on dead-ended into the M5 near the ramp they had used to exit the highway. *Alif* took a right, then another right, circling the block they had just been on. "Just about there," the Unit 504 man said.

"CARL, you ready to make it dark?"

"Ready, *Hamefaked.*" Nir gritted his teeth. He hated it when Nicole called him sir.

"This is it," *Alif* said as he slowed to a crawl. "See you around the corner."

Nir opened his door and leapt to the ground. A moment later, Yaron joined him, having jumped from the back of the truck. Nir had debated having Imri join him instead of the older veteran. He was young, fast, and had a wiry kind of strength. But Yaron had been putting bad guys down in every situation imaginable for a long time. That kind of experience was invaluable for an operation like this, in which everything had to go precisely according to plan. And, since no operation ever went precisely according to plan, you had to have the knowledge and capability to improvise.

Holding their AKS-74s at the ready, the two Kidon men cut between two buildings as the truck rumbled away. When they came to the street, they peeked to their right. Across the street and up two buildings stood the guards. Letting the rifles drop to their chests, Nir and Yaron each drew their suppressed pistols.

The sound of the Sadko turbo-diesel echoed down the street even before the truck made its turn. Once it rounded the corner at the far end of the block from where the two Kidon agents stood, it stopped. The guards turned. The engine revved, and the truck flashed its high beams. The two men stepped into the street.

The engine revved again. Nir and Yaron moved. With their pistols trained on the men, they walked smoothly across the street. The high beams flashed again, and the Kidon men fired. The weapons popped, and the two men dropped to the ground.

"Two down," said Liora. "Move in."

The truck rolled down the block as Nir and Yaron dragged one of the bodies from the middle of the street. They had just gone back for the other when the Russian transport braked in front of the house. The rear gate dropped open, and the remaining members of the team piled out.

"*Qaf, Nun*, let's clear the first floor," Nir said. "The rest of you, get this thing unloaded."

Nir was just about to the front door of the building when it flew open. A young, bearded man wearing jeans and an unbuttoned shirt ran out carrying an AK-47. He seemed as shocked to see Nir as Nir was to see him.

Then things got loud.

CHAPTER 42

NAHR ESHE, DAMASCUS, SYRIA— NOVEMBER 9, 2022—00:03 (12:03 AM) EEST

Nir's mind registered the muzzle flashes even before he heard the blast. The *thunk* of metal hitting metal sounded behind him, and he didn't know if it was the truck getting hit or one of the many old cars on the street. Nir levelled his pistol at the man, but before he fired, he saw Dima barrel into him. The two flew through the open door and crashed to the ground. Nir and Imri raced in after them.

The two agents each focused on a different half of the room, looking for movement.

"*Qaf*, you okay?" Nir asked.

"Better than him," Dima said. Nir stole a glance down and saw the Russian pushing up off the man. The Syrian's eyes were glassy, and his head was cocked at an unnatural angle.

"CARL," Nir said, "shut it all down."

"Shutting it down," Liora echoed to the team of analysts back in Tel Aviv.

This was Lahav's cue to complete the process of temporarily disabling the electrical grid for the city of Damascus. Last time he had done this was to a city in Israel, and it had earned him a healthy prison sentence. Tonight, it would hopefully get him a commendation. The lights in the apartment lobby went dark.

Nir flipped his night vision googles down over his eyes and powered them up. The room glowed in grayscale as the white phosphor NVGs bloomed to light. The other important element to the shutdown was Nicole crashing the systems of Syriatel and MTN Syria, the city's two cell service providers, while also disabling the landline system. It was essential that word not get around of what was taking place at any of the four chemical storage sites.

The three men continued to clear the first floor.

Nir heard Yaron's voice in the coms. "Lead, you better get out here. The natives are getting restless."

"Okay, come take my place." He kept moving forward until he felt a hand clamp down on his shoulder. Nir lowered his weapon and headed for the door, leaving Yaron to clear the rest of the area with Dima and Imri.

Looking around the lobby as he walked, he was encouraged to see the unloading process well under way.

He heard the shouting before he even made it to the door.

"You come here in the middle of the night and start shooting," cried out a woman's voice. "You woke up my baby."

A man's words then overpowered the woman's. "Who'd you shoot over there? Another kid? An old woman? Are you going to gas us next? We know what you people keep in that building."

When Nir rounded the truck, he saw across the street at least half of the apartment balconies occupied by very unhappy-looking people. Some were yelling. Most had cell phones in their hands, although a number of them were looking down at their devices apparently trying to figure out why the videos they had been taking were no longer streaming.

Ba was trying to calm the people while the rest of the team continued to unload the truck.

Behind him, someone said, "Oh great, there's another one. How many of you are there?"

Nir turned around and saw that two of the balconies on their own building had people looking down at them.

Beautiful. Not only are we surrounded, but they have the upper ground. If someone were to start shooting, we'd be fish in a barrel.

Ba was having little success trying to mollify the crowd. After listening for another minute, Nir made the determination that this wasn't the type of mob that was going to respond to apologies and kind words.

He walked over to *Ba* and whispered in his ear. "Be ready to back me up."

Turning toward the balconies across the street, he said in a commanding voice, "Everybody get back into your apartments and quit interfering with our work."

That got a very negative reaction from all. But there was one man Nir was watching—experience told him this guy was the bully on this block. He looked to be a gym-hound type who used his size to get his way. Sure enough, he rose to the bait.

"Who are you, soldier boy? This is our neighborhood. This is my balcony. You don't tell me when I can or can't stand on my own balcony."

Nir pointed at him. "Listen, you piece of gutter trash. I've got the authority of the armed services of the government of President Bashar al-Assad behind me, and I'm telling you to go back into your apartment before you and I are going to have a problem."

"Oh no, we're going to have a problem," the man said, feigning fear. He had an audience now and their laughter spurred him on. "Tell you what—I'll give you three minutes to pack up your truck and get out of here, or you and I really are going to have a problem." He pointed back at Nir as he spoke the last few words.

Nir leaned down to *Ba* and whispered. "I'm pretending to tell you something right now, so nod like I'm giving you an order. Then I want you to run inside like you're going to get backup. But I want you to tell everyone to wait in the building unless you hear a lot of gunfire."

Ba said, "Whatever you have in mind, it isn't a good play. I know Syrians. These are my people. You're going about this all wrong."

"Wouldn't be the first time. Now go do what I said."

Ba nodded enthusiastically, playing the part, then ran around the truck toward the building doors.

Nir looked back up at the ringleader. "This is your last warning. Go inside and shut your windows."

The man cursed at Nir. Then he said, "You just try and make me go in. I don't take orders from anyone, especially not some Jew-dog-sounding military criminal."

It wasn't the first time Nir's accent had given him away. There was a time when he was pretty good at imitating the local speech patterns. But then he had gotten some kind of mental block, and his skills had gone away. Now, no matter how much time he put in, no matter how well he knew the language, he still felt that he always ended up sounding like Yitzhak Rabin reading from a transliterated script.

Time to turn a liability into an asset, he thought, taking two steps forward.

"What did you just say about me?"

"I said you sound like you just drove in from Tel Aviv." Laughter sounded from the onlookers. "You better get your people back in the truck. You've got a long drive before Shabbat begins in a couple of days."

"Come down here and say that to my face, street trash." The crowd went silent.

"Right, so you can kill me. I know what Assad's people are like."

Nir lifted the strap to his AKS-74 over his head and laid the weapon on the ground. "If you're not a coward, come down here. But I doubt you will. You're just a small man with a big mouth."

That last statement wasn't exactly true. The man looked to be in his late thirties, as was Nir, but was at least two inches taller and had the kind of muscular build that made tight T-shirts scream for mercy. But Nir had put him on the spot, and now he had no choice but to rise to the occasion.

Jabbing his finger toward the street, he said, "Don't move."

Nir noticed two other men leave their balconies. From the strain on their T-shirts, they appeared to be the bully's junior workout buddies. As he waited, he scanned the faces of the rest of the crowd. They were hard to read. He figured at least some of them had been humiliated by this jerk in the past and just this once would be rooting for the army.

Yaron's voice sounded in his earpiece. "Lead, we're unloaded and ready to go. You need to wrap this up."

"Hang on. Should only need a second. I've got to shut down this mob before it turns into something."

The doors burst open, and the man strode out followed by his two friends. It seemed like his buddies had been pumping him up because he appeared ready for action.

As he moved closer, Nir asked, "You ready to apologize for calling me a Jew-dog?"

"I've got an apology for you," the man responded, balling up his fists.

Nir pulled his Browning 9mm and shot the man in the foot. He screamed and crumbled to the ground. Before his friends could react, Nir levelled the gun at their faces, moving back and forth from one to the other.

"Back up. Now!" The two men obeyed, retreating until they were pressed against the building.

Nir walked up to where the big man was writhing on the ground holding his foot.

"Quit your crying and listen to me."

The man noticed how close Nir was now. Then he looked to the gun in his opponent's hand. He whimpered.

"Roll onto your back." The man obeyed. Nir pointed the gun at the man's face and said, "Nobody calls me a Jew-dog."

He pulled the trigger and the suppressed pistol coughed out a round.

CHAPTER 43

00:10 (12:10 AM) EEST

Nir used the handgun to wave one of the friends over. Terrified, the man looked like he was debating whether to obey or to run. He seemed to conclude that a get-away was likely impossible, so he slowly started moving toward Nir.

"*Yalla!* Hurry up."

The man picked up his pace.

As he drew close, Nir said, "Take off your shirt."

Hesitantly, the man obeyed.

"Now, hold it tightly to the side of his head." The man looked down and seemed surprised to see his friend looking back up at him. There was a manic look in the eyes of the guy on the ground, like he wasn't quite sure whether he was alive or not. Between his wounded foot and the shot-away piece of his left ear, he had to be feeling a lot of pain. But the shock of what had just happened left him paralyzed.

The feel of the shirt pressing against his wounded ear seemed to wake the man from his stupor. Nir knew he had a very short window of time to finish dealing with this man.

Squatting down, he pressed the muzzle of his pistol against the man's muscular chest. "I could have killed you. I didn't. You belong to me now. Do you understand? Say it. You belong to me now."

"I belong to you now."

"Good. You don't know what's going on here. You'll probably never know. I just need you to remember that I am the man who didn't kill you. You are alive because of me. Do you understand?"

Still a bit dazed, he answered, "I understand."

"Good. I've got work to do here. I want you to make sure that no one bothers us. You're in charge. I don't want to see any of your friends. Not those guys who are hanging out down by the mosque. Nobody bothers us. Okay?"

He nodded.

"And why are you going to help me this way?"

"Because you're the man who didn't kill me."

Nir pulled a stack of Syrian pounds out of his pocket and handed them to the friend. "In the morning, get him to a hospital to get fixed. Understood?"

The friend nodded.

Nir stood up. The street was silent. Looking around, it seemed that most of the people had retreated inside their apartments. The ones who were still outside watched him blankly. No anger. No shock. No disgust. These people were obviously quite used to seeing violence.

Nir walked over and picked up his rifle, slinging it back on his body. With one last look at where the two men remained on the street, he rounded the truck and walked into the building. When he flipped down his NVGs and powered them up, he saw Yaron and *Alif* waiting for him.

Alif was shaking his head and laughing. "'You belong to me'? Did you really just say that?"

"Hey, I'm not expecting him to come live at my house and be my manservant. I'm just trying to buy us a little time. The neighbors were the biggest wildcard for this site."

"Well, hopefully, it will shut them down for a time," said *Alif.* He started moving toward a hallway at the back of the room.

Nir and Yaron followed. "Everyone at the stairway?"

"Just waiting on you." *Alif* started laughing again. "'I'm the man who didn't kill you.' It's as if John-Claude Van Damme attempted a *Dirty Harry* remake. The perfect blend of cringe and machismo."

Nir couldn't help but smile. Maybe he had gotten a little carried away. But when you're forced to improvise, sometimes you just go with the flow.

Ba and Doron were standing outside the last door to the right. Doron held his fingers to his lips. Next, he held up two fingers, then pointed to the floor. Then he indicated a dark light fixture on the ceiling and opened his hand.

Nir acknowledged the communication and entered the room, moving to where Imri and Dima were standing. He placed his hand on Imri's shoulder. Staying back in the shadows, he did a quick glance down the stairs.

Two guards at the bottom of the stairs, and the lights are on below. Must have a backup generator or something. I don't like this. That narrow stairway is a nasty choke point.

He nodded to his two men, then walked back out of the room. He continued past the rest of the team, tapping *Alif* on the back as he walked by. The Unit 504 man followed.

Once in the lobby, Nir said, "I don't like that choke point. And we have no idea what's waiting for us down there. Could be two. Could be twenty."

"And I don't like the idea of a lot of gunplay around those chemicals. Could a bullet puncture a tank? And, if it did, would we all be exposed? Too many unknowns."

"Way too many. So, here's my thought. Rather than sneak in, we go in like we belong there. If they protest, we tell them to call it in."

"Which they can't do."

"Exactly. The confusion should give us enough time to assess the situation and neutralize it. You take lead as the mouthpiece. Apparently, my accent makes me sound like a Jew. You good with it?"

Alif thought for a moment. "I've got nothing better. One question, though. If there are any guys down there I don't kill, can I keep them? You know, have them belong to me?"

Nir rolled his eyes as the other man grinned. Through his coms he heard a female at CARL snort with laughter. Unfortunately, he recognized that snort all too well.

As they walked, *Alif* said, "Seriously, it'll never get old."

When they got to the group at the end of the hall, Nir pointed to the coms unit in his ear. The others gave him a thumbs up. They had heard the plan. Next, he pointed to his NVGs, then powered them down and removed them from atop his helmet. They would be a dead giveaway that Nir and the guys were not Syrian military.

Walking to Imri and Dima, he went through the same routine with them. But before Dima removed his NVGs, Nir indicated that the big man should stay upstairs until either the room was cleared or shooting began. Because of his size and his distinctly European appearance, he would be out of place as part of a squad of Syrian army troops. They might be able to explain him away as a Wagner mercenary, but he wasn't uniformed as one and clarifying the situation would be more work than it was worth.

Once all were gathered over the stairs, Nir gave *Alif* a thumbs up.

"Hey, hey," the man called down the stairs. "Where are your guards? What kind of outfit are you running here?"

Immediately, both Syrian soldiers appeared silhouetted in the light below.

"Who are you? Identify yourself," one of them called up.

"Me identify myself? Why don't you identify the guards who are supposed to be up here watching the front doors? That way I can let General Suheil al-Hassan know who to put in front of the firing squad."

"You're saying you're from General al-Hassan? Why would the commander of the Tiger Forces be sending you to us?"

"Good question. Why don't you call him and ask him?"

There was a pause. "We can't call him. Our phones don't have service. You tell me."

"There are no guards. Your phones aren't working. Sounds like you all are operating a smooth-running machine here." *Alif* sighed as if he was being greatly put out, then said, "Very well. Since you are apparently ignorant of our coming here, I'll explain it to you. But I will not do it shouting down a stairway. We're coming down, and, if you value your career and your life, I highly recommend you don't shoot us."

Alif began walking down the steps. Nir followed, praying that the two guards remained calm and kept their fingers off their triggers. Stepping down to the floor, *Alif* turned to his left.

A blast sounded, and the Unit 504 man's lower face and neck disappeared in a spray of flesh, blood, and bone. As Nir was still trying to register what his eyes had just seen, a metallic sound clattered onto the steps. Instinct took over. He knew what that sound was, and that he had maybe three seconds left to live.

He scanned the steps and spotted a small orb. Snatching it up, he hurled it back around the corner from where it had come. Before it had time to hit the ground, it exploded. Nir leapt down the last two steps onto the floor, his rifle now in his hands. One man was on the ground, very much dead from the blast. The other was leaning back against two massive metal doors, trying to get his bearings. Nir put two shots into his chest, and he dropped.

The rest of the team poured down the stairs.

"Lead, are you good?" asked Doron.

Nir didn't say anything, turning and pushing past him toward *Alif.* *Ba* was already kneeling next to him.

Without looking up, he said, "He's gone."

"CARL, this is lead. It's gotten hot. We're one down. I'm at the bottom of the stairs. To my left are two large steel doors and to my right is a roll-up metal door. What am I looking at, and why didn't I know about this?"

Efraim's voice came on. "Lead, what happened? Who's down?"

"We tried a ruse to get to the guards. They obviously saw through it. *Alif* is out. Now, once again, what are these doors, and why didn't we know about them?"

"You know that our intel was limited. Hang on, let me—"

Lahav interrupted. "Don't bother. It's obvious what the steel doors are. They're the ones that get you into the storage area. The other door is just as obvious, and we're idiots for not having thought of it earlier. How do you think they got the chemicals into the storage area in the first place?"

"Lahav, I'm not in the mood for a Q and A. Just tell me."

"We were under the impression that there was some elevator system for loading and unloading the chemicals. Why? Because we're idiots. Our intel missed a much simpler explanation. They drove them in. I guarantee you that behind the roll-up door you'll find a truck-sized tunnel that will come out someplace on street level."

Turning back to the steel doors, Nir saw Doron and Imri examining them. "*Sin, Nun*, what do you see?"

Doron answered. "They're solid, but I don't think they are super thick." He tapped on the metal again. "There are no handles or locks. It doesn't look like they retract. I'm betting they open in."

"That would be the best option in this confined space," added Imri.

"Okay, *Sin* and *Ba*, find a safe place upstairs where you can put *Alif* until we can come back for him to take him home. *Qaf*, get that roll-up door open. I'm betting that behind those steel doors there's a welcoming committee waiting for us. We wanted to go in quiet. That's no longer an option. So, I think our only choice is to go in exceedingly loud."

CHAPTER 44

00:15 (12:15 AM) EEST

Nir's GPS showed that he and Dima had walked 100 meters south-east of the storage facility. They had retrieved their NVGs before setting out, but there had been little to see in the tunnel. The underground road had begun angling upward about 20 meters earlier, which told them they had to be nearing their destination.

"CARL, give me a sitrep on the other teams."

Efraim answered. "Teams one and two are in the intel-gathering phase. Little to challenge them."

That meant Bensoussan and Ehrlich were getting the job done at the primary schools. That was good news.

"And team three?"

Efraim's pause caused Nir to steel himself for bad news. "Team three met significant resistance. There are four out, including the team lead."

That hit like a punch to the gut. Zakai Abelman was Nir's age and had traveled a similar fast track to Kidon leadership. Just like that, he was gone, along with three members of his team.

"Fight now, mourn later," said Efraim. "Keep your head in the game."

"Head in the game," Nir repeated. He had already lost one on his team. He wasn't going to lose any more.

"Lead, door," said Dima, pointing ahead.

"*Zay*, got a door ahead. I'm pinging you the location." He pressed a button on his wrist GPS, which shot their location to everyone on the team and back to CARL.

Liora spoke, "Be aware. You are at the back portion of the shopping area directly across the street from the Ali bin Abi Talib Mosque."

The mosque. Why did it have to be by the mosque?

"Is our drone still active?" Nir asked as he watched Dima examine a roll-up door similar to the one through which they had entered the tunnel.

"It is. I've already sent it your way." A couple seconds later, she said, "Okay, check your device. I've got visual for you."

Nir already had the small screen in his hand. Sure enough, there was the mosque. And, whether it was the gunshots from a few blocks away or the blackout, the small group of men had grown to about fifty.

Just once, God, could You make things easy?

The men clearly seemed agitated. It appeared that a couple were trying to start chants. A shoving match was taking place in the center of the group.

Nir heard a metallic pop. Dima raised the door, revealing an empty service garage. On the other side of the floor stood a second roll-up door. The windows cut into it showed that it led outside.

"Okay, *Zay*, *Nun*, we're going to lay smoke out on the street. Your turn is right before the shopping area. We'll meet you on the corner and guide you in."

"*Root*," they both said, acknowledging his order.

"Let's go," he said to Dima.

They each undid a latch on either side of the second roll-up door and raised it up. After being in the tunnel, the open air felt good. But with it came the fetid smell that often accompanies impoverished areas where services were neglected by the government. The two men walked along the wall of the shopping center until they reached the street.

"We're ready to turn," said Imri.

Nir lifted his first smoke grenade from his vest. Nodding to Dima, he pulled the pin from the handle on top of the canister. Stepping around the front of the building, he hurled it toward the crowd.

Immediately, he pulled his second can and sent it sailing after the first. Dima did the same with his.

Smoke began hissing up into the crowd. Cries of surprise and anger rose into the air.

"Now," Nir said.

He heard the turbo-diesel rumbling up the street. But he kept his eyes forward and his rifle up and pointed toward the crowd.

Ten seconds later, he heard Imri say, "Here."

The smoke was thick, but some of the men had begun running out of the cloud.

Nir jumped up onto the step on the driver's side of the truck and said to Yaron, "Give me your smoke."

Yaron handed him a can, which Nir prepped and threw. Yaron tossed him a second canister, and he got ready to throw it. But then he saw a couple cans flying from the other side of the truck, where Dima was. Nir slipped the unused canister into his pocket and climbed back up onto the step. "Turn in here."

The truck lurched as it cut hard to the right. The road was incredibly narrow, no bigger than an alley. If Yaron swerved even slightly one way or the other, either Nir or Dima would be crushed against a wall. Halfway up the block, Nir pointed to the left. Yaron followed his lead, defying the physics and getting the truck through the garage door without a single three-point turn.

"Who planned that entryway?" asked Imri. "Can't imagine them getting anything bigger than this size truck through that door."

"Not without a lot of back-and-forth," said Dima.

"Go into the tunnel, then up sixty meters, and stop," Nir said. He knew that they had one shot at this, but that one shot was going to hurt. He just hoped that it would not put him out of commission. "Everyone still by the stairs, I want you to go up to the top and wait."

"*Root*," came the reply.

A minute later, the truck came to a halt.

Speaking through the open window, Nir said, "Yaron, I need you out. I want you guys to follow on foot behind the truck. Keep your eyes forward and your guns up. I'm sure they're waiting for us."

"Boss, you're not driving this," said Yaron.

"We don't have time to argue this. Get out of the truck."

"Listen, we all know that you would take the wheel if it were the smart play, but it's not. You're needed to lead right now, not to drive."

"He's right," said Imri. "Except that I should be driving. His sorry old body isn't built for this anymore."

"Lead, you know me, and you know what my sorry old body can handle. I've been fighting this battle since before junior here knew how to pee in a toilet. You need his speed and agility in the coming firefight. The man in here just needs to know how to drive straight."

Nir knew he was right. He grasped his friend around the back of the neck and looked at him eye to eye in the glow of the headlights. "Keep it between the lines, brother, and don't forget to duck."

Yaron nodded.

"*Qaf, Nun*, let's get behind."

"God protect him," a voice whispered in the coms. Nir repeated Nicole's prayer to himself.

"Everyone in position?"

A chorus of "*Root*" answered him.

"*Zay*, let's go."

The truck began to move, and the three men walked behind it. Soon they were jogging, then running. The big machine began to pull away from them. Up ahead, Nir could see the glow from the bottom of the stairs. When he was still 20 meters away, he heard an earsplitting crash. Metal impacting metal. He could see a new opening in the far wall and light pouring through.

They were in.

CHAPTER 45

The gunfire began immediately.

"Sitrep," he called.

A couple seconds later, Doron answered, "At least eight. No damage to the chemicals from impact."

That was a huge relief. Nir had figured there had to be a truck-loading area cleared behind the doors.

"Two rooms immediately left," said *Ba*. "At least two dirties firing from cover inside each. Another three or four are barricaded center floor. To the left of them is a series of small chemical tanks. To their right is a line of large ones. Explosive ordinance must not be employed on the center group. Control your fire; aim straight."

By the time the Unit 504 man finished his sitrep, Nir was at the room's entrance. The truck was fully through. The steel doors each hung by a top hinge and were heavily creased from the impact. The truck was laying on its side at an angle facing away from the two rooms on the left. Yaron was one of Kidon's most skilled drivers, and Nir had no doubt that he had purposely tipped the truck to give his team cover from the gunfire. Unfortunately, that meant the only protection available to anyone inside the cab was the thin metal of cab's roof.

The noise was deafening as gunshots echoed off the cement walls.

Most of the team was already engaging the enemy from around the backside of the truck. Imri was attempting to climb the exposed underside to a place where he could aim down on the shooters. Nir ran toward the front of the truck to see if he could find an angle from which to check on Yaron.

As he neared the front bumper, someone stepped around in a low crouch. Nir caught him in his sights. It was Yaron. His face was bloodied, and he was listing to his left side. Nir reached him as he stumbled forward. He caught Yaron and set him down against the back of the truck.

"Talk to me," Nir said.

"I'm fine. Might have banged up a couple ribs. Arm's not moving like it should. All in all, nothing major. Oh, and they may have shot me in my side. Not sure."

Nir looked down and saw a dark spot spreading just above the man's beltline. He lifted up his shirt to look, but Yaron slapped his hand away. "Go kill somebody. You can start getting all handsy with me when you're done."

"Did you…?" Nir indicated with his hand the truck tipping.

Yaron snorted, then grimaced with pain. "Yeah. Neat trick, huh?"

Nir grabbed the man's leg, then stood and moved toward the front of the truck. Most of the gunfire at the moment was coming from the bad guys, which told him that his team was lacking good firing angles.

From the front of the truck, he had a clear view of the playing field.

"*Nun*, give me some covering fire."

From the top of the truck, Imri laid a stream of full metal jacket bullets toward the targets. The steel casings clattered to the cement floor below. While the Syrians took cover, Nir sprinted around the far side of the row of large chemical tanks. By the time Imri had emptied his Bakelite mag, Nir had the soldiers behind the barrier flanked.

"Someone give them a target," Nir whispered. "And watch your crossfire." Moments later, all the bad guys began firing their guns at the same spot.

Nir crouched and slipped between two tanks. When he emerged from the other side, he spotted three men behind the barricade. He fired two rounds into the back of the first man. The other two began to spin toward him. He put two rounds into the second man, and he collapsed.

By the time he moved his rifle point to the third soldier, he was already in the man's crosshairs. The Syrian fired at him as Nir dropped to the floor. Bullets pinged off the metal frame holding one of the tanks. Nir fired back, but his angle was off, and he hit one of the two men who were already dead.

The third man ducked between the low tanks that ran in two rows along the far wall. Nir had him in his sights as he moved, but he held his fire. He had already dodged disaster when none of the Syrians' bullets had hit a tank. But if one of his own hit one of those smaller containers, who knew what would come leaking out?

A grenade blast sounded from the front of the room, followed by a second. Nir hoped it was his guys who had tossed them and that they were nowhere near the chemicals.

"First room cleared," he heard Dima say. Good news. One room to go.

The Syrian stood up across the room and fired at Nir. Bullet fragments deflected off the frame and peppered the side of his face. He felt the blood begin to ooze, then drip.

I've got to catch this guy in the open. But I can't do that without taking a bullet.

A plan formed in his mind. "This is Lead. Ignore everything you're about to hear from me," he said to his team. "Imri, get a bead on the small pots."

He stood and made as if he was going to attempt to cross the aisle to the shooter's side. Shots rang out and Nir dropped to the ground, feeling the pressure of the bullets passing just overhead. While the Syrian's ears were ringing from his own shots, Nir pulled the pin on the canister Yaron had given him by the mosque. He rolled it between the large tanks. Immediately, smoke rose into the air, accompanied by the sound of hissing.

Nir stood and cried out in Arabic, "He hit the tank! Get out of here! Go!"

He began to run up the aisle toward the exit. Then he heard a bang from atop the truck.

"Dirty is down," said Imri.

Gunfire erupted to Nir's right. Apparently, the two who were left in the second room decided that a possible death by bullet was better than a sure death by chemicals. They ran out with guns blazing, and Nir's team put them down.

"Clear the room," Nir said. "Make sure we don't have any other surprises. Do it quickly. We've got work to do." Then he added, "*Ba*, on me."

While the others paired up and walked the perimeter of the storage room, the Unit 504 man approached Nir.

"How're you doing?" Nir asked.

"I'm good," he replied. There was no emotion in his eyes. No anger, no sorrow, just a determination to get the job done.

Nir clapped him on the arm. "Good. It's what I'd expect from Unit 504. It's what *Alif* would expect."

"Ezer."

"What's that?"

"*Alif*. His name was Ezer."

Nir looked at the man. He received a hard stare back. "Thank you. Ezer was a good man. Now go clear the bodies of the dirties. See if there's anything we can learn from them."

"*Root*," the man replied, and trotted off to rummage the corpses.

CHAPTER 46

L ead, this is CARL."

Nir recognized Nicole's voice over his coms. "Go ahead, CARL," he responded as he watched his team at work. Doron was busy setting the six explosive devices. Each had enough power to blow apart several of the chemical tanks while bringing down the roof above. Imri was walking around with a video camera, documenting the contents of the underground bunker. *Ba* and Imri were testing surfaces and any possible in-flow areas. All they needed were a few traces, no matter how miniscule, to document the contents. Dima was guarding the top of the stairs. Yaron was still sitting, leaning against the truck, where Nir had banished the injured man.

Nicole continued, "We're alternating our monitoring between outside the house and over by the mosque. The situation is very active in both locations. Several people in the apartments in your building are yelling to people on the balconies across the street. I'm guessing they're giving them a running account of what they're hearing below them."

"Okay, keep an eye. What about the mosque?"

"That situation is much sketchier. They've got around a hundred military-age males milling about. They saw you turn into that dead-end street but haven't seen you come back out. They seem to be trying to—"

285

Yossi's voice cut in. "Lead, we just spotted the two friends of the foot-shot guy. They rounded the corner at the top of the street and are headed in the direction of the mosque."

"If they tell that mob where you're at…" Nicole said, leaving the rest of the sentence hanging.

She didn't have to finish her words because Nir knew exactly what she meant. At any moment, that mosque mob would find the truck tunnel. If part of the group went through the tunnel and the rest came to the house, they'd be boxed in.

We could make a break for it, but the guys are still working. If we don't finish our job, Alif—Ezer—*would have died for nothing.*

"*Nun*, on me. *Zay*, take over video. CARL, get the drone to the rear of this apartment and watch for us. I need your eyes."

"*Root*," said Yaron. Nir heard him grunt as he stood.

"Watching for you," said Liora.

Imri and Nir pounded up the stairs. Nir had seen a rear door at the end of the hallway, and they slammed out of it now.

"Got you," said Liora.

"Get us on an intercept path."

"*Root.* Go right, then quick left between buildings."

Nir and Imri followed her instructions. They crossed one street, weaved between another block of buildings, and crossed a second street.

"Okay, remember from the sat photos the large courtyard with all the trees? You're just about there. Go left."

Nir saw an earlier opening between buildings and turned toward it.

"No. Not those. You'll dead-end. Don't think, just listen." She led them through a few more turns before saying, "You're at your intercept point. Thirty seconds."

"All we're doing is stopping them, *Nun*. These guys aren't our enemies."

"*Root.*"

They flattened out against the side of a building and waited.

Liora counted down. "Fifteen seconds…Ten seconds…Five, four, three, two, one."

Nir and Imri grabbed the two men and pulled them in. Nir's guy was his same height but built like a rock. With his left hand Nir had covered his mouth, and he felt a warm blast of breath when he drove his right hand into the Syrian's kidney. But this man was solid, and, though he stumbled, he did not go down. He spun in Nir's grasp, bringing his elbow up. It connected hard against Nir's head. Thankfully, the Russian steel helmet he was wearing absorbed most of the blow. The man cried out and grabbed his arm while Nir stumbled back.

Before Nir could launch another attack, Imri and his guy fell into him. They were caught up in a tussle, both punching and trying to get the upper hand. Nir's guy saw his chance to escape. He turned to run.

Nir yelled, "Stop! I already shot your friend. Don't make me shoot you." The man stopped.

"Turn around and raise your hands."

The man complied. As he turned, Nir saw his eyes drop to the gun pointed at his chest.

Imri had finally gotten his guy in a side mount and had his forearm pressing hard into the man's neck.

"Let him up," Nir said. Imri complied.

"Go join your friend," Nir told the man.

Imri drew his weapon and stood next to Nir. There was blood dripping out of his nose and his cheek was beginning to swell. The other guy looked worse.

"I told you to stay put. You didn't. Tell me why I shouldn't shoot you."

"You're not Syrian army, are you? You are Jews or Americans or something, no?"

Nir said nothing.

"Listen, *habibi*, we hate the army. We hate Assad. We don't care who you are. We were just going to the mosque to buy some hashish."

"Don't lie to me," Nir growled. "Where were you going? You lie, and I'll shoot you like dogs in the street."

"Everyone already knows you're here. A group at the mosque believes you are Syrian army. They are already coming for you. We're not the ones you need to be worried about, *habibi*."

Why are there so many complications? I hate complications. I've already asked You, God, just give me one plan that goes the way it's laid out!

Liora broke into his thoughts. "Lead, the mob at the mosque has started to move. They're heading the direction of the garage. I'm guessing they've found the tunnel."

"Get on the ground. Face down," Nir commanded. The two men obeyed. "Cuff them up."

Imri kneeled next to them and flex-cuffed their wrists and ankles.

These two may very well have been telling the truth, but I can't take a chance.

"Stay there. If I see you again, there will be no talking. Only bullets."

Nir turned and ran back into the courtyard with Imri following. "CARL, get us back to the house."

In between Liora giving directions, Nir asked, "*Ba*, do we have enough samples?"

"I've got two positive tests for sarin and one for VX."

"That's enough. As soon as you can, go watch the tunnel. *Sin*, how are we on the charges?"

Doron answered, "Four out of six are set. Working on five."

"We need to be done now. Finish that one. We'll leave the other behind. *Ba*, at the tunnel, if the mob shows up, do everything you can to avoid a gun battle. We have superior weapons, they have numbers. Either way, we lose."

Liora had them take a detour to avoid some people who had come out onto the streets. "CARL, what is our exfil plan?"

Efraim's voice came on. "You know that truck you just demolished? That was your exfil plan."

"Noted. How about exfil Plan B?"

"Steal a car. Drive out."

"Very few of the cars around here look like they work."

"Find a car that works. Steal that one. Drive out."

Liora yelled for them to drop to the ground. They did. A Toyota hatchback that looked like it was from the '80s slowly drove up the street. As they lay with their faces in the dust, Efraim said, "See, some cars work."

"Yeah, and you saw the size of it. Unless it has hidden clown pockets, we're not fitting our team in one of those."

Liora released them, and they began running again. Efraim continued, "Okay, new plan. Find two cars that work. Steal them both. Drive them out. And, before you ask, there is no Plan C. Once you get out of the city, we can get you. In the city, you've got to be resourceful."

Efraim was right, and Nir had known that this eventuality would likely come to pass from the moment he had decided to crash the truck into the steel doors. He had just hoped that their escape wouldn't be in a mad rush with an angry mob on their tails.

They were almost to the rear of the apartment building when Nir found himself stumbling to the ground. Imri tripped over him and also went down. Nir tried to stand up again but found himself swaying. Small bits of plaster rained down around him. Looking up, Nir saw dust and grit falling from the building next to him. That's when he realized what was happening.

When he was a kid, he had spent a week at a summer camp. It was the middle of the night, and Nir and his friends were all asleep on their bunk beds. Suddenly, there was a loud clatter. The bed he was on began rocking back and forth and scooting across the floor. All the young boys were crying out, terrified at what was going on. Then, just like that, it stopped.

The counselor, who had remained calm throughout, explained what they had just experienced, using a single word.

Earthquake.

CHAPTER 47

00:55 (12:55 AM) EEST

Nir and Imri were back on their feet running. "*Zay*, Lead. Talk to me." When Yaron answered, Nir noticed an emotion he had never heard before from the old veteran—fear. "The tanks shifted, and a couple teetered. Seem stable now." Yaron sucked in a couple deep breaths. "Lead, we've got to wrap up and get out of here. I mean now."

"Do it. We'll be there in under a minute. *Ba*, tell me about the tunnel."

"I hear voices. They're getting closer."

"Shoot off some rounds. Scare them back out. This could just be a foreshock. I don't want those people in that tunnel if something bigger comes."

"*Root.*"

Something else Nir's camp counselor had told him and his friends was that most major earthquakes are preceded by a series of smaller quakes. These foreshocks might occur days and weeks ahead of time, and they will rarely register with anyone except those who monitor seismic equipment. But sometimes there are only hours or even minutes between a sizable foreshock and a significant event. Nir and his buddies had walked around camp paranoid for the entire next day.

What Damascus had just experienced very well may have been the mainshock. However, if it was a foreshock, then it was possible that the whole city was about to get rocked even more. Nir wasn't going to have his team holed up underground with thousands of gallons of liquid and gaseous toxic chemicals while they waited to find out.

As Nir followed Imri into the house, the sound of automatic gunfire rose from underground.

Come on, you idiots. Run away from the gunfire. Get out of the tunnel.

As Imri started down the stairs, the ground started shifting again. The young operative lost his footing and went tumbling down the long flight.

"CARL, talk to me," Nir called as he slammed into a wall.

Dafna's voice came on. "The quake was four point five. No indication of more."

"Check again! We're in one now!"

"Oh, crud! Hang on," Dafna said.

Nir squatted down and prayed his steel helmet would deflect anything that might drop from above.

The shaking stopped. He jumped to his feet and raced down to check on Imri.

"*Nun*, talk to me."

The young operative was groaning, and he rolled from his back into a sitting position. "Well, that sucked."

Nir kneeled next to him. "You good? Anything broken?"

Imri shook his head. "Thank God for Russian steel," he said, rapping on his helmet with his knuckles.

Nir helped the man up and they moved to the busted metal doors.

Dafna spoke. "Lead, CARL, that second one was five point two. But both have been shallow. I've seen estimates between three to five miles deep."

"Damage?"

Yossi joined in. "I've been monitoring social media, but nothing is being streamed out of Damascus."

"It's because we shut down the cell service, you *yutz*," said Liora. "Lead, you may want to consider undoing our shutdown. I'm sure there are a lot of scared and confused people across the city. They need information, especially if anything bigger happens."

It was a risk to open communication again, but she was right. Without the ability to learn what was happening, the risk of panic would significantly increase.

"Reinstate the cell service. Bring the power grid back online." As he spoke, Nir watched the team gather their equipment.

"Hold on!" said Efraim. "That's not your call. There will be plenty of time to go back online once we get you and the other three teams out. If we do it now, it will put all of you at serious risk. You've got nearly twenty other operatives in that city too."

"*Habibi*, if we don't go back online, it could put the whole population of Damascus at risk. And you don't have to remind me that there are other teams out there. I guarantee you those team leaders would agree with my call."

As Nir said that, he thought again of Zakai Abelman, and a pit formed in his stomach. There was no doubt which way that hero would have voted in this situation.

Nir was determined to not back down on this. "Listen, the proportionality is all wrong. Risking that many innocents goes against everything—"

Gunshots rang out behind him.

"Lead, I'm taking fire," said *Ba*.

"Just do it, *habibi*," Nir said to Efraim as he ran toward the tunnel. Then he added, "*Sin*, get your final charge and follow me."

"*Root*," said Doron.

More shots sounded. They had the distinct sound of old-school AK-47s.

Nir arrived next to *Ba*. "Fire high. I just want to get them quiet for a moment."

Ba complied, emptying a magazine in a direction that would hopefully keep ricochets from hitting anyone. It must have been enough to cause people to drop, because as the echoes faded, there was a momentary silence.

Into the quiet, Nir shouted, "Go back the way you came. I've got explosives. I will blow the entrance to this tunnel, and you will die. Leave now."

Voices filled the tunnel. But then one stood out above the others.

"You don't make the rules in this neighborhood—we do. Put down your weapons, and we'll decide what we're going to do with you."

Shouts and cheers sounded from up the tunnel.

Doron ran up. Nir told him, "Put the charge just past the entrance to the tunnel, but don't arm it yet. I'm hoping we won't have to use it."

"*Root*," he said.

Addressing the unseen mob once again, Nir said, "This is your last chance. Leave now or die."

"Your last chance has now passed," came the response. The report of AK-47s was deafening in the tunnel. When the gunfire stopped, the ringleader shouted, "Your opportunity for surrender has now been forfeited." Cheers sounded from the mob.

"*Sin, Ba*, ready flash-bangs. On my command," Nir said into his coms. Then, down the tunnel, he said, "You were warned."

He pulled the pins on his flash-bang. "Now," he said as he tossed the perforated can as far down the tunnel as he could. Then he ducked, opened his mouth, squeezed tight his eyes, and covered his ears.

Three blasts rang out in succession.

The sounds of panic echoed off the cement walls.

That should keep them back long enough for us to get out of here. After that, if they want to get caught down here with a bunch of deadly chemicals during an earthquake, that's their call.

"*Sin, Ba*, get upstairs." Nir ran back to the storage area. As he did, he said, "Efraim, I want the lights on and the cell service back up. You know that I'm right. And if we start shaking again, I want the dead man's switch punched for all the charges across the city. We don't want any of our explosives adding to any disaster. You can tell the *ramsad* I said that."

When his friend made an extremely derogatory comment in response, Nir knew that he had won the debate.

Liora's voice sounded in the coms. "Lead, CARL, I'm seeing people exiting the garage. A lot of them."

Finally, something went right. Now if we can just find a vehicle.

"Everybody, up to the lobby. CARL, see if you can spot a van or truck near us. Something big enough so that we won't have to split up."

"*Root*," said Liora.

Nir counted his team as they went up the stairs. *Ba*, Doron, then Imri with his arm around a limping Yaron. Dima was already upstairs. That was everyone. Nir followed them up.

CHAPTER 48

"Leave your NVGs behind," Nir said. "We need to look as Syrian as possible. CARL, tell me what's going on outside."

Dafna answered, "We've got the drone out looking for transportation. But your street has been getting crowded. Seems everyone wants to get out of their apartments."

Nir didn't blame them. In this neighborhood, he figured most certificates of occupancy were gained via thick envelopes filled with cash rather than rigorous inspection. But a full street created a difficulty for his team.

The naked hanging bulbs in the lobby popped on. A muffled cheer sounded from the street.

Thanks, Efraim. You made the right call.

"Okay, when we go out, we go out together. Stay close. This crowd is a tinderbox. If it goes up, I don't want us separated."

"What about *Alif*?" asked *Ba*.

"When we get our transport, we'll come back here and get him. Fair?"

"Fair."

Liora spoke. "Lead, I've found a van. From the outside it looks better than most. It's two blocks up by the large open lot. You're going to have to be careful, though. There are people around it."

"Any way to get to the van without an audience?"

"Negative."

Yaron said, "*Achi*, there's no good way out of here. So, we make the best of the worst."

"Agreed," said Nir. "Imri, take point. *Ba*, you're our mouthpiece. We go out hot. *Yalla*."

They went to the door, and Nir pulled it open. Imri walked out first with his rifle up. *Ba* and Doron followed him, while Nir and Yaron trailed. Dima brought up the rear.

Immediately, the crowd began yelling threats at them.

"Stay back," yelled *Ba*. "We are here on orders of President Assad. If you attempt to harm us, we are authorized to use lethal force."

But the people weren't listening. A full water bottle bounced off the side of Doron's head. Another one fell at Nir's feet. A rock pinged Imri's helmet. Two more flew in, hitting Doron on the wrist and upper thigh. It seemed he was in the unfortunate position of easiest target.

"Keep moving," encouraged Nir.

A fist-sized chunk of concrete hit Yaron in the face, knocking him down. A cheer went up through the crowd. Nir helped him up while Dima turned and scanned the growing mob through his rifle sights.

"Tell them we're prepared to fire on them," said Nir as he tore open a packet from his vest and handed Yaron some gauze to hold against the bleeding wound on his cheek. The situation had him worried and ready to lash out. He was hoping threats would be enough to back them down.

Ba called out, "You must desist. If you continue, we will be forced to protect ourselves."

Another chunk of concrete hit Doron's helmet, causing him to stagger.

Nir turned toward the crowd, aimed his rifle just above their heads, and fired five rounds. "One more rock, one more piece of concrete, and I will shoot someone. Do you understand me? We have full authorization to protect ourselves. You harm my men, I will kill you where you stand and still sleep well tonight."

Something slammed into Nir's chest, knocking him off his feet.

Just before his helmet hit the pavement, he heard the report of a gunshot. Vainly, he tried to draw air into his lungs. Yaron was down next to him. "Lead, talk to me."

"Don't shoot back," he eked out with what little air he could draw in. But he knew it was unnecessary. His team was too well trained to fire into a crowd. If they spotted the shooter, it'd be a different story.

Dima fired three shots. "Sniper down," he said.

Apparently, he spotted the shooter. Holy mother of Moses, that hurt.

There was frightened screaming mixed with angry yelling. Rocks began pelting them in greater numbers. Yaron tried to help Nir up, but the pain in his ribs was too much. He tapped *Ba*, who pulled Nir up.

Back on his feet, Nir said, "Let's move." Then he broke into a cough.

Imri, Doron, and *Ba* kept their weapons forward while the other three remained trained on the rowdy crowd that was following them. A rock hit Nir in the helmet and was quickly followed by another, which nailed him hard on his chest. His knees buckled briefly.

"How close are we?"

"Block and a half," answered Liora. "Are you okay? We need to know."

Nir knew who was behind that question. "Russian helmets, Russian armor. I'm a fan of both."

"Boss, we've got a problem."

It was Imri. Nir turned to the front and saw young men streaming around the corner one block ahead.

"CARL?"

Dafna swore. "We've had our eyes watching for weapons on your group—we didn't see them coming. We're getting elevation." After a brief pause, she said, "It's the mosque group."

"Give us an alternative," Nir said. "Come on. We need one right away."

The rocks kept coming. Both Doron and *Ba* were bleeding from their faces. Nir had grenades and a good amount of ammunition. They could fight their way out of this. But it would be a slaughter. Men, women, and children would all lose their lives.

"CARL, come on! We need something now!"

Nicole said, "You're boxed in. We're trying."

Dima fired three more rounds. "Third floor. Directly across. Man with a rifle. I think I missed him."

Nir scanned the building Dima indicated but couldn't make any-thing out in the moonlight. Suddenly, a muzzle flashed to the left of his aim, and he felt a bullet whiz past his head. He shifted and fired three rounds. Yaron and Dima did the same. The glass in the right half of the window burst into tiny shards, while in the open half a man doubled over and his rifle dropped to the ground below.

The shouting of the mosque group now joined the din from the crowd behind the Kidon team. A glass bottle hit Nir's helmet. It shat-tered, and he felt cuts open on his cheek. To his left he saw Yaron drop to one knee, holding his damaged ribs.

"CARL!"

"We're trying," Nicole answered frantically.

The ground began to lurch under Nir's feet, and he knew right away that this quake wasn't like the other two. It was like being in a fun house where the floor would drop out below you, then suddenly drive you back up. He took a knee, hoping the stability of a low center of gravity and one leg on the ground would keep him from stumbling around. The rest of his team followed suit. It didn't help, and they found them-selves with their hands on the ground trying to remain upright.

The sound was like what he'd heard in videos of troops under artil-lery attack. It was an almost unbearably loud rumble punctuated by boom after boom after boom. Behind him, a crunch broke through the din. He looked back and saw a long crack zigzagging up the brick-work of the building behind them.

"Go!" he shouted, knowing he likely wouldn't be heard. They all lurched to the center of the street. Half the building slid downward and tumbled into the next structure over. The side of the apartments caved in, causing the roof and most of the top two floors to collapse into bricks and dust. The images of arms and legs flailing within the falling rubble seared into his mind.

Dima hit his arm and pointed up. Above them, a weaver's loom of wires and cables swayed back and forth. A tank tipped off the roof of a building just in front of them. It landed on the wires, and a whole series of poles snapped in two as the tank took them to the ground.

Two more buildings across the street imploded into piles of rubble. Dust shot out from where they collapsed and joined a growing cloud. In fact, the dust became so thick that the opposite side of the street faded from view.

The crash of the buildings, the blare of car alarms, and the screams of the people in the streets and those still alive in the buildings made it so Nir could barely think. He began wondering if the world would ever again be still.

Someone was calling into his coms, but he couldn't make out the words or who it was.

The shaking stopped. It had gone on for less than 15 seconds, but it had seemed much longer. Nir tried to stand, but stumbled to the side. He felt like he had just gotten off a boat with his legs wobbling on solid ground.

"Cover your mouths!" Doron shouted.

Nir pulled a rag out of a pocket and tied it over his nose and mouth. The dust was so thick now that it blocked out the moonlight. Nir could see the shapes of the men around him, but that was all.

Standing on the street in the darkness felt surreal. Everything around them was quiet except for the car alarms. It was as if everyone was waiting to see if the shaking really was done.

Then a woman screamed, and all hell broke loose.

CHAPTER 49

01:15 (1:15 AM) EEST

Stay tight," Nir yelled, trying to be heard over the shouts and screams. "CARL, confirm you tripped the dead man's switch on the explosives."

"*Ramsad* shut them all down," answered Efraim. "Soon as the shaking started."

Nir exhaled hard in relief. "Can you give us a sitrep?"

The concern was strong in Nicole's voice as she answered. "Negative. We've lost you in the dust. We've gone to elevation to get a wider picture."

"And?"

"It's bad. It's so, so bad." The emotion in her voice was evident. A lump rose in Nir's throat. He didn't hate these people. Most of them were no different than he was. They just happened to be born in a country ruled by a despotic regime that had become a puppet of an even more despotic Russian regime. He didn't wish this kind of suffering on anyone.

"Tell us what you see," Nir said. He pulled out another rag and was wiping down his rifle. Enough dirt and grit could cause it to lock up. Judging by what little movement he could discern, the men around him were doing much the same thing.

"Buildings are down everywhere. I'd say maybe twenty-five to thirty percent. Everything the direction of downtown is dark. Can't tell you how it fared. I have to think it's better than where you are. I'm sorry, Lead, it's just too dark to see."

"No, you're good. Give me a second."

Nir slapped Dima on the butt, signaling "It's team-meeting time." Dima slapped whoever was next to him. Nir thought it was Yaron, but he couldn't tell for sure. The shadows drew in, and eventually he could discern faces. Everyone was there, which was a relief.

"Who has the satellite phones?"

Yaron and Doron both said, "Me."

Speaking loudly to be heard over the surrounding noise, Nir said, "Good. Keep them powered down. It's all about battery conservation now. I need everyone to make sure you've got your weapons clean and in working order. Consolidate your mags. Dump everything you don't need. I'm guessing we've got a lot of walking ahead of us. I want you to buddy up. You go nowhere without your buddy. If you go to wash, he's handing you the soap. If you've got to dump, he's holding the paper. Understood?"

"*Root*," sounded from all.

"Okay, get to work."

A young man came running into their group and straight into Dima. He bounced back as if he had just plowed into a wall. Nir grabbed him and spun him around. The man looked at him with frantic eyes.

"Go, *habibi*," Nir said, clapping him on the shoulder. He ran off.

Nicole was saying something, but Nir couldn't hear over all the din. He plugged his left ear and cupped his hand over the other, which held his coms unit.

"CARL, say again. You're hard to hear."

"I said that we're going to be without eyes on you for a while. We're up to two hundred meters and the dust cloud keeps rising."

"As long as it's dark and we've got the dust, the drone is worthless to us. Are you able to land it someplace and put it in some kind of battery-saving mode?"

Lahav spoke up. "I can find a place and put it in a passive mode without shutting the whole thing down. It'll extend the battery life significantly."

"Good, do it. It's all about movement and batteries now. I'm going to have us start making our way back to the safe house in Jdeidat Artouz. Find out if it is still okay for us to go there. I'm going to power down our coms to save the batteries. Every thirty minutes, I'll check in. We've got two sat phones and a cell. There's plenty of juice in those to keep us connected if we're careful. If I'm two hours late calling, then we're in trouble. If I'm three hours late, don't bother attempting an exfil."

Suddenly, loud shouts and screams sounded to Nir's left. He felt a concussive wave, even as he heard the deafening crash. His face and body were pelted with chunks and chips of brick, and a fresh wave of dust roiled over the small group of men. Nir squeezed his eyes tight in time to save them from a fresh coating of dirt and debris.

He swore loudly. "There are still buildings coming down around here. We've got to get moving." He wiped a layer of brown from his G-Shock watch, then said, "It's 01:20. I'll check in around 01:50."

"Be careful, Lead," said Nicole.

"I always am."

In his mind, he could see the worry on her face. But he also knew that mixed with the concern there would be peace. More than once, she had said that the source of her peace was prayer.

As Nir took out his pistol and began wiping it down, he prayed, *Hey, God, we keep hanging out, people are going to begin to talk. I can remember hearing in* yeshiva *about Solomon. You were playing genie and granting him a wish. He could have asked for money or power or anything else. Instead, he wished for wisdom, and You gave it to him.*

I don't know that I have any wishes coming to me, but I'm asking for the same thing. I'm asking for wisdom to get my men home safely. I'm asking that You let me know the right thing to do in any situation. Nicole says that You answer righteous prayers. This is about as righteous as a guy like me can get. I'm hoping that You'll answer this, so I'm going to trust that whatever comes into my mind that sounds kind of God-ish is coming from You.

He slapped Dima's butt again. Soon all gathered close.

"You heard what I said to CARL. Shut down your coms." He looked at the compass on his watch, then pointed right. "The end of the block is that way. That street will take us to the M5. From there we just reverse the route that got us here. We've got at least five hours until sunlight. If the path is clear, we can be on the outskirts of Damascus before people can start seeing us. We stop for nothing. Our number one priority is reaching that safe house. Got it?"

"*Root.*"

Nir pulled his coms unit from his ear and stuffed it down into a cargo pocket. The other men followed suit. He took off at a fast walk, knowing without looking back that the other men had fallen in with him.

A man's voice cried out through the dark. "My daughter! Somebody help me! Please!"

Nir kept moving forward.

"Help me! It's crushing her! Someone!"

Stop.

That word echoed in Nir's mind. It was his inner voice, but it didn't feel like it came from him.

He answered himself, *Can't stop. We've got to get out of the city before it's light. I've got my men to think about.*

He kept moving.

Stop.

Nir felt a slap on his backside. He turned. Yaron stood behind him.

"Stop," the veteran said. He moved his face close enough so that Nir could clearly see the man's eyes. "The man's daughter is dying."

"*Habibi*, we've got to make time."

Yaron stared hard at Nir. "Unless you directly order me not to help, I'm finding him and getting his daughter out. And even if you do order me, I'm still going over. But I'll do it having lost every ounce of respect that I've built up for you over the past decade."

Nir felt something in that moment that he couldn't remember ever experiencing before on an operation. He felt shame.

He's right. God, I'm such an idiot. I prayed for You to give me wisdom, and I immediately ignored You.

All the men had leaned in close now. Over the noise, Nir said, "You all know the risk and the potential ramifications? This one decision could very well cost you your lives. Is this man's daughter worth that?"

Each man answered affirmatively in his own way.

"Good. Don't forget your buddy. And remember, you're a Syrian soldier and these people hate you. Watch your backs. Got it?"

The men all nodded.

"Okay. Let's go find this girl."

CHAPTER 50

01:20 (1:20 AM) EEST

The dust continued to settle, allowing the moonlight to aid their adjusting eyes. Trying to keep his mind above the despair that surrounded him, Nir thanked God for a cloudless night.

Blessing number one. That's what's going to keep us sane amongst the insanity. Noticing the little blessings.

As a group, they moved across the street toward the sound of the father's cries. It was slow going because of the amount of rubble and debris scattered everywhere. There were so many voices and screams and moans that it was difficult to track to just one.

A hand hit Nir's shoulder. He saw Dima's long arm reach past him and point. Following his finger, Nir spotted a man just a few meters away standing on a pile of large bricks. He had his hands to his mouth, and was shouting, "Help me! She can't breathe!"

Kneeling next to him were two men trying to lift a chunk of cement. Nir and his team hurried up. "Where is she?" he asked.

But rather than get the grateful look he expected, the man stepped back. He held up his hands. "No, no, we don't want any trouble. Please, we're just trying to save my daughter."

One of the men had jumped up, and, in two strides, was directly in front of Nir.

Angrily, he said, "Get out of here. Can't you see what's around you? What's wrong with you people? Leave so we can dig out our dead!"

"We're here to—"

The man pushed Nir in the chest right where the bullet had hit his vest. "I said to get out of here."

Guns were raised. Dima shot his hand in and took the man by the shirt. He whipped him off his feet to the ground. But before the man could hit on the hard, rough rubble, Dima pulled up and gently set him down on his back.

Nir rubbed his chest and said to the father, "*Habibi*, we are not here to hurt anyone. You called for help. We're here. What is more important right now—the clothes I am wearing, or the girl's life?"

The man's visage shifted from fear to resolve. "Come," he said.

As they began to move, Nir saw Dima reaching his hand down to help the other man up.

We'll call Dima blessing number two. Keep them coming.

The third man was older and looked enough like the father for Nir to peg him as the grandfather.

"She is right here," the old man said. He indicated a small hole under what appeared to be tons of rubble.

Nir pulled out his Maglite and shined it into the gap. A little girl who couldn't have been more than six looked back. Her long, dark hair was matted in dust, and her big brown eyes looked terrified. She was shivering, and her breathing was shallow and rapid.

"Hello, *ya amar*, are you hurt anywhere?" Nir remembered that appellation from a book he had read as a child, in which the father had compared his daughter's beauty to that of the moon.

She didn't answer.

"You may answer, Derifa. He's a friend," said the father.

"Derifa? What a beautiful name. Are you hurt, Derifa?"

The girl looked to her dad. He said, "It's pressing on her so she can't take a deep breath. I believe it is crushing her."

"Are you able to move around at all?"

The girl thought a moment, then shook her head.

"Okay, *habibti*, I want you to hold as still as you can. Your father is very strong. We're here to help him get you out. Alright?"

She nodded.

His team had been examining the collapsed building while Nir was talking. Pointing to the debris pile spread above the girl, Yaron said, "We need to clear all that stuff off this cement beam. Once we expose it, I think we might be able to shift it enough to release her."

The nine men began clearing the rubble piece by piece. Most chunks could be thrown to the street by one person, although there were some that needed two, three, and even four of them to push and shift and send chunks tumbling.

As they worked, the father said to Nir, "I am Wael. The older man is my father, Yusuf, and the other is my brother, Muhammad. My wife and my mother we found over there," he said, pointing to what used to be the back side of the building. By the way he said "found," Nir knew that he didn't mean "found alive."

"*Allah yerhamha*," Nir said, wishing God's mercy on their souls.

"*Shukran*. Help me with this." Nir took one side of a slab with ceramic tiles still attached. It wasn't huge, but it was heavy. The two men heaved it up and let it clatter down the stack.

"You don't need to tell me who you are. But just answer me—are you the ones who were here from earlier tonight?"

Without looking at the man, Nir said, "*Habibi*, can we just focus on freeing your daughter?"

"That's what I thought. Can you tell me whether you are Americans or UN or someone else? You don't look Russian. Well, except for the one who threw Muhammad to the ground. But he can't be a Russian, because a Russian never would have stopped him from hitting his head on the bricks."

Instead of answering, Nir looked at his watch. He was fifteen minutes late for his call. He clapped Wael on the arm, then moved to Doron and made the "I'm going to make a call" motion with his hand next to his ear. Doron reached into his pocket and pulled out a sat phone.

Nir dialed, hoping it would be Nicole who answered.

CHAPTER 51

02:05 (2:05 AM) IST

The phone rang, and both Nicole and Efraim reached for it, knocking it over onto the desk of her workstation in CARL.

Efraim stepped back. "Answer it. Just put it on speaker."

Nicole lifted the handset and hit the green button. "This is CARL."

"Speaker, speaker," said Efraim. Nicole pressed the appropriate button.

"CARL, Lead. Sorry we're late." Hearing Nir's voice flooded her with relief. Her mind had been racing through every possible bad outcome even as she had been praying and trusting God. She was a confused mess.

But she couldn't let that show. He didn't need her to emote or to worry or to bring him down in any way. He needed to hear optimism and hope, so that's what she would give him.

"Oh, were you supposed to call? We were all binging Netflix."

Nir chuckled. "Sorry to interrupt. Just checking in. We're all okay. Yaron is still overdoing it, and I'm a little worried for his stamina."

Efraim spoke up. "Rest him when necessary, but it's imperative you keep moving forward. How much progress have you made?"

Nir was a master at dodging questions, and Nicole recognized that was exactly what he was doing when he said, "Hey, *achi*, fill me in on the other teams. What's happening with them?"

Efraim was quiet. He looked at Nicole, and she whispered, "You need to tell him."

He nodded. Taking a deep breath, he said, "It's not good. We haven't heard from Abelman's team since the quake first hit. Bensoussan was shouting something about VX gas, then he cut off. His whole team has been quiet since."

Nir was silent on the other end of the phone. Nicole knew that he was either fighting the urge to swear loudly or about to break down in tears. Two teams were gone. Fourteen men. It was incomprehensible.

"Ehrlich. Tell me about him."

Efraim answered, "You know Ehrlich. He's like a roach. He could have a nuke go off next to him and still come walking out unscathed."

There was another long pause. Nicole looked around the room. Everyone was still, straining to hear what was being said. She waved them over and they hurriedly complied. "Have you figured out how you're getting us home?"

"Not yet. Like you, Ehrlich is on his way to the safehouse. The *ramsad* was talking about possibly reaching out to the US and the Brits. They're always quick to respond to disasters."

Nicole added, "He's also going to talk to them about recovering bodies. The *ramsad* is committed to bringing home *Alif* and all the others."

"The US won't help, not with this administration. Maybe the Brits. I'm sure the *ramsad* is anxious to get us out before someone realizes we're here."

Efraim answered. "One hundred percent. Social media is already reporting some horrific scenes. The earthquake footage is bad enough. But they're also starting to show victims with the tell-tale signs on their faces and bodies of chemical poisoning. It seems that Assad's strategy of storing lethal liquids and gasses under his population areas is backfiring in a huge way."

"If we're found here, we'll be made convenient scapegoats for the chemical leaks."

Efraim nodded and sat down in Nicole's office chair. "True. Because the prime minister let the *ramsad* trigger the kill switches on the explosives, we don't have to worry about any charges going off. But if you're caught in the country, there will definitely be a major incident. However, the positive, if there can be a positive in this nightmare, is that your mission was a success. There is no way that Assad or Putin can use these weapons against us now that the world can see their effects on the Syrian people. The prime minister is going to let Moscow know that we are on to them, and we are letting American intelligence know of their plot. That should cause the Bear to retreat to his cave, at least for a time."

"Pardon me if I don't cheer. Hold on a second." In the pause, Nicole could hear more clearly the mayhem taking place on the other end of the line. It sounded like a nightmare, worse than any disaster movie she had ever seen. This was raw and it was real. When Nir came back on, he said, "Tell me something. When we forwarded you those chemical results, did any of them show signs of chlorine?"

Dafna spoke up. "There was chlorine, VX, and mustard gas."

That confirmed Nir's worries. "That's not good. I keep getting these flashbacks to when my brothers and I used to go swimming in the public pool. There's definitely a chlorine leak going on around here. On top of everything else, these people have to deal with that." This time, Nir did swear.

But he wasn't the only one. Nicole and Efraim had recognized the same thing in what Nir had just said. Nicole's response was internal, but Efraim's was very loudly external.

He was seething. "Lead, what do you mean by 'around here'? Where are you? And if you tell me anything less than four kilometers from the storage site, I'm going to order our air force to give you the Soleimani treatment."

Nir was silent. Nicole knew he was trying to figure out how to break the news to Efraim—news she had already figured out as soon as he said those two words. She hated the fact that he was still in the neighborhood, but she loved him for being the kind of man who couldn't leave.

She decided to help him out.

"Who is it?"

"Who is who?" he snapped.

"Who are you helping that's kept you in the neighborhood?"

Nir's voice softened. "She's a six-year-old girl. Her father could touch her but couldn't get to her. Her life is slowly being crushed out of her."

As soon as Nir started speaking, Efraim stood up, took hold of Nicole's chair, and sent it spinning across the room on its casters. He stomped off, following its path.

"What's her name?" asked Nicole.

"Derifa. Her mother and grandmother are dead under some rubble at the back of the apartment. She's all the dad has left. I couldn't leave her. We couldn't leave her."

Tears filled Nicole's eyes. "Of course, you couldn't. Are you close?"

"It's slow going. Once we get most of the rubble off, we've got a huge piece of cement we've got to move. I don't know how we're going to pull that off."

Efraim was back. "Listen, *achi*, I know you've got a big heart. You always have. Great. Fine. I get it. But you've got a team to protect and get home safely to their families."

"This wasn't just my decision, *habibi*."

"No, I'm sure it wasn't. But you're the team leader. You're their father. When the kids want to make bad decisions that can get them killed, it's time for dad to say no."

It was evident that the pressure had built up in Efraim so that he was at a boiling point. Nicole understood. He was trying to protect the Mossad's agents. And he was worried about his best friend.

Nir's silence blew Efraim's pressure valve, and he yelled into the phone. "Do you know what's happened in that city? Do you know the death toll? It's up in the thousands, and once the bodies start to be found, it's going to reach the tens of thousands. And you're there trying to add six more to the body count. I appreciate what you're trying to do, Nir. I really do. But that city is filled with trapped little girls. Face it, you can't save them all."

"No, but maybe we can save this one."

The call ended.

"Lead! Lead!" Efraim yelled at the phone.

"Talking louder doesn't help once the call disconnects, FYI," said Lahav.

Efraim spun around to see that all eyes were on him. The four young analysts looked like a small school of millennial piranhas with teeth made of razor-sharp sarcasm, and Nicole could tell they were about to go into a feeding frenzy. The only way to save the assistant deputy director was to throw some raw meat into the water, sending the fish elsewhere.

"Dafna, Liora, they are somewhere in that neighborhood. Trail back with the drone until you find them. I want a visual in five minutes. Yossi, see if you can track anything on social media coming from Nahr Eshe that mentions chemicals, specifically chlorine. Lahav, you're the smartest one here. Figure out something brilliant to do that will blow us all away."

As each person heard their assignments, they peeled off from the group around Nicole's workstation. Lahav, however, remained glaring at Efraim—until Nicole added, "Efraim said all that because he loves Nir, and he loves the ops team. Besides, you have much more important things to do than to bring any harm to the assistant deputy director. Understood?"

Lahav nodded, did the "I'm watching you" motion with his fingers, then walked away.

Nicole's chair came rolling across the room, courtesy of a very accurate push from Yossi. She caught it and told Efraim, "Sit."

He obeyed while she retrieved a second chair from the conference table. She sat facing him, their knees nearly touching.

"He's going to get them killed," Efraim said quietly. "Why can't he just be one of those guys who goes in, gets the job done, and comes out?"

"Maybe he is. Maybe instead of Nir changing, we just need to redefine the job."

"Are we about to have one of those Christian talks that Nir always tells me about?"

That comment took her off guard. Her first reaction was anger that

Nir was sharing their private conversations. But that was quickly super-seded by a warm happiness that he cared enough to discuss "those Christian talks" with his best friend. On top of that, it meant that the truth was getting to two people and not just one.

"No, Efraim, we're not. But I'm always up for one when you want it," she said with a wink. "What I'm saying is that maybe the mission is more than just the mission. Maybe it's showing the Syrians that there is a better way of doing things. Maybe it's demonstrating force with compassion. Maybe it's reminding the world that it's important to sep-arate innocent civilians from the despotic regimes. Maybe it's proving that righteousness and strength can go hand in hand."

"But how will that happen with one little girl in the middle of the 'I don't care' part of Damascus? Let's say she is rescued, but Nir and the team are killed. How will that make a difference?"

Nicole felt her eyes well up again. Frustrated over her emotion, she looked around for something to blot the tears before they streamed out. Efraim spotted a paper napkin on her desk and passed it to her.

As she dabbed, she said, "I don't know. It's something I can't even think about. What I do know is that righteousness never returns empty. From the least act to the greatest, God can and will use it. It's not our job to think about the end results. Our job is to just do the right thing in every situation and leave the rest up to Him."

Efraim reached over and took her hands in his, wet tissue and all. He looked her in the eyes, then let his head hang down. He stayed like that for a minute before standing up and saying, "I've got to go talk to Porush and the *ramsad*."

Nicole watched him walk out. Then she turned around to her screens.

CHAPTER 52

02:10 (2:10 AM) EEST

How's it coming?" Nir asked as he came up next to Yaron. The man was trying to lift a sizable piece of building, but his injuries were making it extremely difficult.

"I thought you went off to get us beers or something," Yaron answered. Nir took hold of the jagged piece of cement, and the two of them heaved it down to the ground.

"I'm not telling the others yet, but both Abelman's and Bensoussan's teams are out of communication and presumed dead. Only Ehrlich and us are left."

Yaron didn't say anything. It was impossible to see the man's expression under the rag tied over his face, but Nir knew the man was hurting just as he was. They were all part of the same violent, dysfunctional family. And they would readily give their lives for one another.

"Efraim ordered us out of here."

Without looking up, Yaron said, "What did you say?"

"Didn't get a chance to say anything. The call somehow disconnected."

Yaron nodded as he strained to lift another piece of debris. Nir reached to help, but the other man snapped, "I've got it."

Nir reached for a different chunk, and began lifting and tossing pieces of the apartment building.

Efraim is probably right. This might be a fool's errand that gets us all killed. But I can't walk away from this girl. And I'm not keeping any of my guys here against their will. We'll get little Derifa free, then I'll get my men to the safe house.

"Everyone, on me!"

It was Imri. Nir lifted his rifle to shooting position and moved toward the voice. When he finally saw him in the dark, the young operative wasn't holding his gun. Instead, he had his hands on the large piece of cement that was blocking access to the little girl.

As everyone congregated around him, he said, "It shifted. Come on. Everyone on it now." The father, his brother, and the grandfather put their hands on it, as did the rest of the Kidon team. They pushed. It moved a couple millimeters.

"Call your people over," Nir said to Wael, the father.

Wael cried out, and men began appearing from the darkness. Some took one look at the Syrian military uniforms and quickly faded back into the night. But others lined up next to them.

"You lead," Nir told the man.

Wael said, "Okay, ready, and push." This time, the cement beam shifted centimeters. "Push." More movement. A little at a time, the beam moved. Then, it tipped, fell, and broke into three pieces.

Wael ran to his daughter and lifted her out. He held her to himself, and she wrapped her arms tightly around his neck.

There was cheering all around. One moment of light during a very dark night. Wael's lips were moving, and it appeared that he was praying a blessing over his little girl. His eyes opened and he saw Nir.

"*Shokran,*" the man said as tears ran down his face. Nir couldn't help but get choked up as he thought of what this father faced. His wife and mother were dead. His home and belongings were in ruins. But from the look on his face, it was as if he realized that hope still existed. His child was safe and in his arms.

A piece of cement hit the side of Nir's helmet. He stumbled sideways, stepped on some loose debris, and went down. Immediately, Imri was hovering over top of him with his rifle ready. More rocks and bricks and chunks of cement began to fly at them.

"Get her out of here! *Yalla*," Yaron said to the father.

Nir felt a sharp pain in his left shoulder from his landing, but confirmed that he had all his movement. He got to his feet but kept low.

In the moonlight, he could see a dark mass of people. Shouted insults and threats were coming from them.

"You and Assad made this happen!"

"This is our neighborhood, not yours!"

"We're going to send you to hell, where you belong!"

The team had formed a tight circle. The projectiles appeared to be growing in size and quantity.

Suddenly, Yusuf, the grandfather, appeared next to Nir. "Go to the mosque. Quick, to the mosque. You must trust me." A stone hit the old man in the forehead, and he staggered sideways. "To the mosque. Go now." He ran off.

"I've got no better plan," Nir said to this team.

"Sounds like it's the mosque," said *Ba*.

"Going to the mosque means going through them," Nir said, pointing to the mob.

"Trust me, I'm ready for that," said Dima.

"I want to do this without a body count. These people are not our enemies. They just think we're theirs. Let's lay some cover fire, then bull rush through. Keep your buddy near you. If you're in trouble, drop a flash-bang so that the rest of us know. Let's go!"

Using their rifles, the team fired over the heads of the mob. There were screams, and the people dropped to the ground. The band of men bolted.

Somehow, they made it off the pile of rubble and onto the street without anyone falling and breaking a bone. As they drew closer to the throng of angry Syrians, they could see that their path was blocked by maybe three dozen men who were just beginning to raise their heads again from the ground.

"Fire again," Nir yelled. More shots rang out, and the heads dropped back into the dust.

They were in the midst of them now. Nir felt a hand hit his shin and he tripped forward, but managed to keep his balance. Ahead of him, Doron fell to the ground. A man jumped on top of him, bringing his hand down onto his chest. He lifted his hand to hit him again. Nir slammed the side of his rifle against the man's temple. As the man swayed, Nir brought the rear of the gun against the back of the man's head. The rifle stock was folded up, and it landed with an audible *thwack*. The man dropped.

"Hold," Nir yelled.

Nir reached down to help lift Doron up by his body armor. When he grabbed hold of him, the collar of his vest was wet. Nir understood immediately what had happened.

He wasn't punching him! He was stabbing him!

"Man down! Man down!"

The team formed around him. Two of the men fired their weapons again into the air. Nir had Doron up on his feet, but he couldn't stand by himself. Imri slipped under one arm, while Nir slipped under the other.

"Let's go! Anyone follows us, shoot them," Nir called.

They made it beyond the mob. Dima flung a flash-bang grenade into the group so the Kidon team could get some distance.

There was a *whump*, and the street lit up. In that moment, Nir could see the devastation of the neighborhood. It bore no resemblance to the place they had driven into just a few hours before. When the world went dark again, it was very dark. Nir swore at himself for not closing his eyes so that he wouldn't lose his night vision in the flash of light.

"Left here," he commanded. A little more than a hundred meters ahead was the mosque. Nir had no idea what they would find there, but it couldn't be worse than what they were facing now. His only hope was that the old grandfather somehow felt indebted to them and knew a way to help.

Doron wasn't moving his legs at all now. Nir and Imri had his full weight on their shoulders as they carried him. Most of the car alarms were silent now, and all Nir could hear was their footsteps, the rasp of Doron's breathing, and the occasional rumble of a collapsing building.

The street was crowded with people, but most were walking around dazed. Many were digging in piles of rubble or sitting on the sidewalk crying next to a dead loved one. It seemed that they had left most of the troublemakers behind.

Suddenly, in the darkness, the large white structure of the mosque appeared. One of the outer walls had collapsed, and much of its tall minaret lay in the street. But the dome on its roof was still intact.

A man ran toward them. Dima lined up his gunsights on him. The man stopped and raised his hand. "I am Abdul. I am Yusuf's oldest son. You must follow me."

He began running back toward the mosque, while the Kidon team remained standing where they were.

Abdul stopped and waved them forward. "You must come now. It will not be not long before they will be back looking for you."

"Heads on swivels," Nir said. He and his team followed the man into the mosque.

CHAPTER 53

02:25 (2:25 AM) EEST

The man led them past the main entrance into a narrow alley. The alley opened to a small courtyard. There were bricks and shards of decorative pottery strewn across the cobbled walkway, and Nir and Imri had to slow down so that they could safely step their way through with Doron draped over their shoulders.

At the end of the open area, the man opened a door into the mosque. Stepping back, he waved them through.

"Turn into the first room," he said.

Yaron and *Ba* led the way with their guns pointed forward. Nir and Imri were behind them, carrying Doron. Dima brought up the rear. The room appeared to be a sleeping quarters with three foldout cots, one against each wall. Nir and Imri laid Doron on the cot against the back wall.

Nir pulled open his friend's vest and then his shirt. But as soon as he did, Dima took hold of his shoulders and pulled him back. The Russian took Nir's place next to the wounded man, and Yaron stepped in beside him. Doron was the one on the team with the most medical skills, but Dima and Yaron also had significant training. All Nir could do was stand back and listen to his teammate's chest rattle as he struggled to breathe.

As he watched, he noticed a dark stain of blood on Doron's leg. Now he understood what had happened. The man must have lashed out with a knife as the team went by, catching Doron's leg and bringing him down. Then the Syrian had pounced on him and driven his knife into Doron's chest just above his protective vest.

Such a random assault. He's survived so many firefights, and to be taken out this way?

Dima and Yaron frantically worked on their friend. But Nir had been around enough dying people to recognize the sound in his lungs. Even if they could temporarily stabilize him somehow, what then? They were a group of Jews hiding out in a Syrian mosque in the middle of a natural disaster.

Nir grabbed Dima by the arm. Dima shook him off. Nir grabbed him again and squeezed. As he did, he looked Yaron in the eyes. Yaron stopped what he was doing, nodded, then stepped back. Dima didn't look at Nir. He just followed suit with the older man.

Taking Doron's hand, he leaned toward him.

"Thank you," Doron wheezed in Hebrew. "Afraid Dima might do permanent damage."

Nir smiled briefly. Chances were Doron didn't even realize the language he was speaking, but the last thing Nir would do to his dying friend was correct him. Instead, he replied in the same language. "I'm so sorry, *achi*. If we had just gone to the safe house."

Doron's brow furrowed. "No! Derifa's alive. My life for hers. Fair trade." He sucked in a deep, gurgling breath, then coughed hard. Blood and saliva flew from his mouth. "I've hurt people. My life for hers. Fair trade."

Yaron knelt next to the cot and laid his hand on Doron's head. He began reciting the Mourner's Kaddish in Aramaic. Typically, it was said as a prayer at a funeral, but it felt appropriate here. Even though they were deep inside enemy territory, the familiar words took them back home. Doron's agitation calmed. A peace came over him and his eyes closed as his respiration rate slowed.

Yitgadal v'yitkadash sh'mei raba b'alma di-v'ra chirutei, v'yamlich malchutei b'chayeichon uvyomeichon uvchayei d'chol beit yisrael, ba'agala uvizman kariv, v'im'ru: amen.

Y'hei sh'mei raba m'varach l'alam ul'almei almaya. Yitbarach v'yishtabach, v'yitpa'ar v'yitromam v'yitnaseh, v'yithadar v'yit'aleh v'yit'halal sh'mei d'kud'sha, b'rich hu, l'eila min-kol-birchata v'shirata, tushb'chata v'nechemata da'amiran b'alma, v'im'ru: amen.

Y'hei shlama raba min-sh'maya v'chayim aleinu v'al-kol-yisrael, v'im'ru: amen.

Oseh shalom bimromav, hu ya'aseh shalom aleinu v'al kol-yisrael, v'imru: amen.

In his mind and in his heart, Nir prayed along with him:

Glorified and sanctified be God's great name throughout the world, which He has created according to His will. May He establish His kingdom in your lifetime and during your days, and within the life of the entire house of Israel, speedily and soon; and say, Amen.

May His great name be blessed forever and to all eternity. Blessed and praised, glorified and exalted, extolled and honored, adored and lauded be the name of the Holy One, blessed be He, beyond all the blessings and hymns, praises and consolations that are ever spoken in the world; and say, Amen.

May there be abundant peace from heaven, and life, for us and for all Israel; and say, Amen.

He who creates peace in His celestial heights, may He create peace for us and for all Israel; and say, Amen.

Tears streamed down Nir's face. This wasn't supposed to happen. This team had been through gunfights and ambushes. They had survived the impossible and pulled off the incredible. And now for this hero to go at the hand of some street thug with a knife.

Why didn't I use the other end of the gun against him? One shot. Would have made the world a better place.

Nir's anger was building, but then he stopped himself. That wasn't what Doron needed right now. He held onto his friend's hand and watched him suck in a breath. Then he was still. Ten seconds passed. Doron pulled in another breath. Nearly thirty seconds more passed, and Nir was sure that he was gone. But then he drew in another breath. Then silence. They waited. Thirty seconds. A minute. Two minutes.

He was gone.

"Lead." It was *Ba*. Nir turned to find him holding the arm of the man who had led them in, Abdul. *Ba's* pistol was pressed against his temple. When he spoke, it was in Arabic. "He was standing here the whole time. He heard everything."

Abdul looked terrified. "You...you are Jews."

God, You just don't let up, do You? Any other surprises for us? Anyone else You want to kill?

"Lower your gun but close the door." *Ba* complied.

Abdul spoke. "When my father called, he said you might not be who you said you are. But I thought that meant you were probably Russians."

"Well, we're not," said Nir, standing and walking over to him. "We're not Russians. We're not Americans. We're not Iranians. We're not even Chinese. We're Israelis. And one of your friends just killed my man. So, what do we do about this predicament?"

Nir stood right in front of the man, who was at least four inches shorter and sixty pounds lighter. Abdul put his hands forward to keep space between them. He said, "I said that because I am surprised. And I am confused. Nothing more. You are just different than what I've been taught about Jews. I would have expected you to gleefully let little Derifa die, not risk your lives to save her. When you first arrived here in Nahr Eshe in your military truck, we supposed that you were government soldiers come to do something with the chemicals that devil Assad put in our neighborhood under the homes of our families and our children. Now I find it is the Jews who have come instead. Have you come to destroy the chemicals?"

"What we're doing here is none of your business," said Nir.

Abdul waved his hands around. "Okay, okay, it's none of my

business. That's fine. But you are not on Assad's business, and that is good. You have come to deal with the chemicals that are threatening our families and you saved the life of my niece. Those are also good. My friend, you have nothing to fear from me."

"And what assurances do I have that you will not betray us?"

"You have none. And I have no assurances that you will not shoot me as I walk out of this room. But still, I will go, and I believe you will not shoot. I'll return with food and water and with changes of clothing so that you can get out of those uniforms." Then He looked to Dima. "Although I think I will have difficulty finding clothing for that one."

He brushed past Nir and walked to Doron. Placing his hand on the dead man's head, he uttered a barely audible prayer. Then he walked out of the room.

"*Nun, Ba*, I want you to keep a watch on that door." Nir turned back toward Doron and saw that Yaron had removed a blanket from one of the cots and was covering their friend. Reaching his hand toward Dima, he said, "*Qaf*, give me the phone, then check on *Zay*. I think he may have a gunshot wound to his side."

Walking to a corner of the small room, Nir punched in a number.

Nicole answered. "This is CARL."

Nir knew it would take everything he had to keep himself together and remain professional. This wasn't a time for emotion. It was time for business.

"CARL, this is Lead. We've taken refuge in the Ali bin Abi Talib Mosque. A local is helping us with clothing and supplies."

"Do you think you can trust him?" asked Efraim.

"We have no choice. He is the uncle of the girl we saved, so hopefully that will mean something. From now on, I am changing protocols to checking in every two hours. We will remain here until either you or we figure out next steps."

"Every two hours," said Nicole. "*Root*."

Nir took a deep breath. "*Sin* is gone. He was taken out by the mob who had come from the mosque."

Sounds of shock and sorrow came through Nir's headset.

"How? What happened?" asked Nicole.

"We'll fill you in later. I'll check back in two. Lead, out."

Nir hung up and breathed in deep. He stood there for a couple minutes staring at the wall. A hand rested on his shoulder. It was Yaron. His shirt was off and he had gauze wrapped around his midsection.

"This is not on you," the veteran said. "It was a fluke. A random act of murder, not military action."

"If I hadn't kept us there…"

"You couldn't have made us leave. You heard what Doron said. He died a contented man because his death meant something. It meant that Derifa had life. Don't take that moment of glory from him by making this about yourself."

Nir looked at his friend. It was a harsh statement, but it was true. This was about Doron's success, not his own self-assessed failure. Nir clapped Yaron on the back and nodded.

Yaron walked over to let Dima continue working on him, but Nir didn't move. His friend may have given him a better perspective, but he hadn't changed the facts. They were in an earthquake-decimated city in enemy territory with no transportation and no way back across the border. It would take a miracle for their body count to remain at only two.

CHAPTER 54

13:30 (1:30 PM) EEST

The morning had passed slowly. Abdul had returned with bread, bottles of water, and five sets of clothing. Dima's almost fit him, but not quite. The Syrian told Nir that they could stay there through the daylight hours but asked that they leave at nightfall. The five men rotated watch on two-hour intervals. While the intention was to get some rest and replenish energy for later in the day, Nir hadn't noticed anyone actually sleeping. His check-ins with CARL were brief and perfunctory.

Efraim had let him know that Irin Ehrlich's team had reached the safe house, which, thankfully, was still intact. Ehrlich had wanted to go searching for Nir and his team, but because he had two members who needed medical attention as soon as possible, the *ramsad* had ordered him to evacuate. So, they were on their way back along the smuggler's route to Lebanon, where they would be picked up and taken home to Tel Aviv.

After the loss of the other two teams, Nir was relieved to hear that Ehrlich was making his escape. Already, this had to be one of the biggest losses of life in the Mossad's history. It would take some time to rebuild Kidon, and, with the deepening friendship between Russia and Iran, time was one thing that Israeli intelligence didn't have.

He was lying on the cot, staring up at the ceiling, trying not to think of his dead friend and teammate who was stretched out under a blanket just a meter away from him. His mind went to the missiles that were to be used in this attack. Russia wanted to get at Israel for economic and, possibly, religious reasons. So, they tasked Iran with shipping precision missiles to Syria to be used by their proxy militias. Even without the chemicals, these weapons were game changers. The Katyusha rockets the militias currently used were next to worthless. Half of them never made it across the border, and the rest were either destroyed by the Iron Dome defense system or fell harmlessly into open fields because their aiming system was crap.

But these precision missiles are different. They can fire a hundred at once, knowing that the Iron Dome will take out at least 70 percent. But the 30 missiles that make it through can cause major damage and loss of life. Now, multiply that out to the real numbers. What did Efraim say? Between Lebanon, Syria, and Gaza, there are 250,000 rockets aimed at Israel. If they began firing them all, the Iron Dome would run out of ammunition in the first few hours. All they would need to do is use the Katyushas to bleed out the Iron Dome, then they could switch to these precision missiles to devastate our cities and villages.

What was most frightening is that this wasn't just a hypothetical. Already, thousands of rockets had flown over the border from Syria. If they had these new weapons, why wouldn't they use them? The very reason that Nir was in Syria was because the militias had planned to use these precision missiles at the instigation of Russia.

Russia. They were at the center of so much that was wrong with the world.

"*Qaf*, come here," Nir said as he sat up on the cot. Dima came over and sat next to him. "I'm trying to make sense of Russia and what Putin is doing in Ukraine."

"*Habibi*, if you do, you'll be the first," the big Russian replied, shaking his head.

"You lived over half your life there. Help me understand. Is it all just paranoia? You know, like what we talked about in Hungary. But instead of it just being Putin's paranoia of internal threats, he's terrified of external attacks."

"*Paranoia* is the perfect word to describe Putin's mindset. Think about it. Over the past few hundred years, other countries have attempted to invade Russia more than fifty times. That will create some major generational trauma."

"And now he sees NATO, and thinks, 'Here they come again.'"

"Precisely. He's thinking, 'Hey, we got rid of the Warsaw Pact because there was no more need for it. But you guys are still hanging on to NATO for some reason. What could that reason be?' he wonders. And there is only one answer he can come up with. 'They want to invade us, like all those others did in generations past.'"

"So, when he hears that Ukraine might be joining NATO, which would bring the West right to his doorstep, he strikes preemptively."

"Yes," said Dima, slapping Nir on the knee. "But what he doesn't realize is that the very fact that he is the kind of leader who would preemptively invade a country based on his own paranoia is the very reason why NATO says, 'We better keep this thing going.'"

"It's a vicious cycle."

"A vicious cycle. Yes. Russia is the richest country in the world when it comes to natural resources. To the kleptocratic Russian mind, they can't understand why anyone would not want to take these resources from them. So, they must give themselves a buffer. They aren't worried about the East. You cannot understand just how vast and uninviting Siberia is. If China ever tried an invasion, they would run out of steam well before they even reached the Ural Mountains. Putin doesn't feel like they need to worry about anyone to the south. To the north is the Arctic. So, it's only what's to their west that they're afraid of. And, through NATO, they feel Europe and America creeping closer."

"Which is why they can't lose to Ukraine. And why Putin will resort to tactical nukes if he feels they are necessary for victory."

"And it's also why he likely won't stop with Ukraine. That need for a buffer will push him to take the rest of the Baltics, too, eventually."

Nir leaned back so that he was propped against the wall. "And the attack on Israel fits in how? It's all just gas, right?"

"Back to the paranoia. But with Israel, it's economic paranoia. Russia is full of natural resources, but the greatest is energy. Oil and gas.

Those are the moneymakers. The global sanctions hit them hard at first, but they've found ways around them. What they're looking at now is the possibility of losing their biggest customer base, Europe, to us, little old Israel."

Nir nodded. It took him back to Imri and his bowl of fruit illustration. "And in the past, Russia didn't really mess with Israel because we spoke softly and carried a big stick—that stick being the United States. But now, our stick is turning into a twig."

Dima smiled at the picture. "In the Tanakh, how did the Assyrians put it to King Hezekiah? 'You're trusting in Egypt, that splintered staff, which will pierce every hand that leans on it,' or something like that. America has turned into a piercing staff. Just ask the Afghans. Everyone in the world has seen it. That's why Iran has become so emboldened in their nuclear program. That's why the squatty dictator in North Korea is shooting off ballistic missiles like they're bottle rockets. And that's why Putin can say, 'I think it's about time we conduct a hostile takeover of our energy competitor.'"

"'Out of the far north.' Isn't that what one of the prophets wrote about Russia?"

"Ezekiel. Somewhere toward the end."

Nir slapped Dima's arm with the back of his hand. "Look at you. Bet you were number one in your class in *yeshiva*."

"Nah, my parents weren't much for religion. They were Soviet atheists. After a few years of Putin, they decided it was time to get in touch with their Jewish roots and made *aliyah*. All I know about the Tanakh is self-taught."

Nir wondered how he could be this close to his teammate and never have known this about him. Maybe he could give him a perspective on the whole religion thing he was working through.

He was about to ask when the ground started shaking again.

CHAPTER 55

13:43 (1:43 PM) EEST

There was a time when Nir believed there were two kinds of earthquakes. There was the shaking kind and there was the rolling kind. His life experiences had taught him that in the Middle East, the temblors fell into the latter of the two categories. Then, in an in-flight magazine on one of his many flights from Israel to Belgium, he had read that differentiating between the two types was a false dichotomy. The different feels were due to one's proximity to the epicenter. Near ground zero, one bounced around like kernels of corn in a hot-air popper. But the farther away one went, the more the movement felt like smooth ripples that flowed from the violence of a stone breaking the surface of water.

There was no rolling at all under the mosque.

Of course, shaking versus rolling was nowhere in Nir's mind at the present time as the roof above their heads cracked, then split.

"Go!" Nir yelled.

"But Doron," cried Imri.

"We'll come back if we can." But just then, the outside wall collapsed into the room, burying the cot that their friend's body was on.

The power of the shifting earth was like nothing Nir had ever experienced. They were all flung from wall to wall in the hallway outside their room. Dima reached the outside door first. He flung it open but didn't go out.

"It's blocked! Turn around! Turn around!"

The hall was filling with men who had exited other rooms. They were running toward the Kidon team.

"Turn around. It's blocked," Nir yelled.

They moved the other direction, looking like they were in the mosh pit at a punk rock concert. Bodies flew into each other, then bounced back into the walls. Nir saw two men lurch to the ground, only to be pulled up by those behind them. Nir followed them knowing that they could find a way out better than he could. Plaster was falling from the ceiling, and Nir shielded his eyes. The hall emptied into the main prayer room, a large, open space. Already it was littered with debris from the ceiling. The doors ahead were open.

The team sprinted across the open space.

Reaching the exit, Nir waited to make sure his team got out. Imri, then Yaron, then Dima ran past him. Where was *Ba*?

Nir saw him staggering across the floor, his hand pressed against his left hip. Dust and debris were falling all around him. Nir ran toward him, but made it only a few steps before a jolt flung him to the ground. A deafening crack echoed through the chamber. Nir looked up to see the high dome split into three pieces, then drop.

"No!" he yelled as *Ba* dropped to his knees, covered his head, and was buried by untold tons of rubble. Cement and bricks continued to fall from overhead. Dima appeared and grabbed Nir by the arm, spun him around, and dragged him through the door.

The walls of the mosque fell in behind them, and the force of the collapse lifted them off the ground and threw them into the street. Once again, dust filled the air. Nir sucked in a lungful of it and began coughing.

"Link arms," ordered Yaron. Nir felt the man's arm hook around his, and he reached out to hook in Imri. Nir could barely make out Yaron's face, even though he was right next to him. The white dust from the mosque left an eerie sensation of standing in bright light while not being able to see anything. "If we get separated, we'll never find each other," Yaron yelled at the top of his lungs, trying to be heard over the deafening tumult.

They kneeled in a tight circle in the middle of the street, hoping for a little stability as the ground around them bucked and kicked. At one point, all four of them found themselves in the air, bounced upward like they were on a trampoline. They landed hard on their knees, but managed to stay linked together. Another rush of air littered with cement projectiles flew into their little group. A large piece hit Imri in the chest. He would have doubled over, but Nir's and Dima's arms kept him upright.

Abruptly, the shaking stopped. Nir and his teammates slammed into each other, their bodies still trying to compensate for the violent shakes. There were far fewer car horns than last time, and there was far less screaming. The four men remained where they were, kneeling on bloody knees in the middle of the street, waiting for the dust to settle.

Minutes rolled by. Nir noticed that he didn't hear the occasional cracking and crashing of buildings like he did after the first quake. While normally that would be a good sign, in this case, Nir thought it was just the opposite. What it told him was that this time, there was likely not much left to collapse.

His suspicions were confirmed as shadowy figures turned into shapes, and shapes turned into what his mind branded as a postapocalyptic moonscape despite their disparate contexts. The neighborhood that had been filled with three- and four-story apartment buildings was now essentially the same single level of rubble. Here and there, corners and pieces of buildings still stood, but for as far as he could see, there was no complete, standing structure.

Off in the distance, Nir saw pillars standing with what looked like walls leaning against them—fallen bridge spans. Yaron saw him looking. "That's the junction with the M5 freeway," the veteran said. He looked like a cartoon version of a ghost with his hair, face, and clothing completely white from the dust of the fallen mosque. Dima and Imri looked the same, as he supposed he did also. It would have been comical if it wasn't so tragic.

Imri was carrying Doron's satellite phone. He handed it to Nir. "Let them know we're still alive. I mean, that most of us are still alive."

Nir turned to where the mosque once stood. Under the rubble were two of his men. It pained him to realize that it was not only the place of their deaths, but also where they would remain buried.

He took the phone and dialed.

"Nir? Is that you?" Nicole was frantic.

Nir found that he couldn't say anything. The moment was overwhelming, and he just held the phone.

"Nir? Nir? Are you there?"

"I'm here," he croaked.

"Oh, thank God. Thank You, God. Are you all okay?"

"We lost…we lost *Ba*. And Doron's body is buried in the rubble. We tried…we couldn't get to them. No one can get to them."

"Oh, Nir, I'm so sorry. Yaron, Dima, Imri, are they okay? Are they with you?"

"We're all together. It's like something from a movie, Nicole. It doesn't seem real. Damascus is gone. I mean, it's just gone. Nothing left but a pile of rubble."

"Nir, I want you to listen to me." It was Efraim. "The *ramsad* is working directly with the head of MI6 to get you out of there. Multiple countries are already flying relief supplies into Syria. They can't fly directly to Damascus because the airport runways were so heavily damaged by the first quake. I don't know where they're going to go now. But we're working on getting an aid vehicle brought somewhere near the city that you'll be able to drive south to the border. I wish we could bring you one ourselves, but, quake or no quake, there's no way they're letting us across the border from our side."

"If we make it to Israel, how do we get across the border? That was the whole reason we went through Lebanon."

"Assad's regime was on the verge of collapse after the first quake. I figure this second will put it over the edge. That may give you the opportunity to get through the border. But realize it's going to be anarchy there very soon. You need to keep your eyes open."

"There won't be any anarchy here, *habibi*," Nir said bitterly as he looked around at the remains of the neighborhood. "I don't see enough people left alive for there to be chaos. It's like a world of zombies. Everyone is in shock."

"I understand. It's not the survivors in Damascus I'm worried about. It's all the militias and scavengers who will come to pick the bones of the city."

Nir hadn't thought of that. He still had his pistol tucked in the small of his back. He hated carrying it there, because despite what the movies showed, it was impossible to quickly draw from that location. But he didn't have any other option. He also carried three extra magazines with him and a tactical knife. The other three men were outfitted similarly.

That won't be enough if we come up against a militia unit driving a technical with a DShK heavy machine gun mounted in the bed. We need to keep a low profile. That's the only way we make it.

"When will you know about the vehicle?" asked Nir.

"I don't know, *achi*," said Efraim. "This new quake changes everything. Check back in two hours. But I'll make this commitment to you. Even if I have to drive there myself, I'll have you home within three days."

"Only if you're driving my Mercedes, brother."

There was emotion in Efraim's voice. "You bet, *achi*. You bet."

Nir shut down the phone. The guys had found water running out from under a pile of bricks. They were splashing it on their heads to wash away the dust and using rags to clean their faces. Nir squatted down next to them. He dipped his hand in the water and examined it. It was muddy, but it didn't smell of sewage. Taking out his rag, he began to clean himself.

As he did, he filled in his teammates on the phone call.

"The airports are north and east from here. The border is south. What are you thinking?" asked Imri.

"South. I think we'll have a better chance finding a vehicle or taking one from some roaming band of schmucks than we will getting one from the Brits. Not that they won't want to help. It's just a logistical thing. I have no idea where they're going to land relief planes. Yaron?"

"South."

"Dima?"

"South."

"Imri."

"South it is. Let's keep our eyes open on the way. As much as we can find in way of water and food, we need to grab it. Once we're out of the city, if we don't have a vehicle yet, then we're in for a long, thirsty trip."

Nir finished cleaning himself, then looked around. While everything had been frantic after the first earthquake, all was eerily calm and silent now.

God, it hasn't gone too well with my prayers so far, but I'm going to try one more time. Let me get these last three guys home. Please. And if there are any more Derifas on the way, make sure You let us know.

CHAPTER 56

Nir could smell the city of Al-Kiswah before he could see it in the moonlight. For the final two kilometers approaching the town's limits, the air was thick with smoke, sewage, and death. Once the remains of the city began coming into view, he could see that here, 15 kilometers south of where they had begun their trek, the devastation was the same. Nearly all the buildings were down. The electricity was out. People were wandering around aimlessly like they were the walking dead.

Entering the city, it was obvious to the Kidon men that not everyone had given up. There were pockets of activity where people were desperately digging, trying to save a loved one or a neighbor. Despite the pull Nir and the others felt to jump in and help, they walked on.

They had joined in on three rescue efforts before leaving the heap of rubble that once was Damascus. Each one had turned up only dead bodies, and all the Kidon team had to show for their labors was a noticeable limp by Yaron and Imri's heavily bandaged hand. They had put in their attempts. They had expended all their energy. They had saved one girl but lost two of their own team. Each of them, including those who had died, would say that the sacrifice was worth it. But they were done. It was time to go home. Professionals were on their way from all over the world. It was their turn to take over.

Because they couldn't be sure what to expect on the roads, they had waited until nightfall to head south. They walked along the M5 freeway, sometimes having to wander off into the scrub to get around areas where the asphalt was so separated or broken up that it was impassable.

They weren't alone on the thoroughfare. There was a flow of people leaving the city, hoping to find aid and shelter down the road. Other than subdued conversations and occasional sobs, the crowd shuffled along in a stunned silence. Nir was thankful for their change of clothes, which allowed them to blend in. Dima did get the infrequent once-over with his big body and too-short pants, but it never went beyond that. There were many more important issues for people to worry about.

Now that their four-hour hike had brought them to Al-Kiswah, Nir had two things on his mind: water and their next destination. At some point along the way, a man had offered Yaron two bottles of water. The ops agent had tried to pay the man, but he refused any money. The four men eagerly shared the provision. But now they were desperately thirsty again. If they were going to keep moving, they had to hydrate.

"It looks like people are congregating over there," said Imri, pointing with his good hand. All around, groups were gathering and starting small fires to keep themselves warm. But through the dim light, Nir could see a restless crowd standing together like gazelles at a watering hole.

"See what you and Dima can do about getting us some water. I'm going to check in with CARL."

"I'll go with them," Yaron said, obviously miffed at being left out.

"Forget it, old man. You stay and rest."

"I'm not an invalid. You don't have to coddle me."

"Isn't this around the time you're supposed to tell us to leave you behind? 'I'm only slowing you down. Leave me and save yourselves.'"

"What would you say if I did?" Yaron asked, grinning now.

"I'm still weighing my options," Nir said with a wink. "Rest up, *achi*. You're going to be needed soon enough. If all goes well, you're going to have some driving to do."

Yaron eased himself down against a low remainder of a brick wall. Nir could see that the man was far more hurt from the truck crash and bullet wound than he was letting on.

You can't worry about it. Let a man be a man. He doesn't need you looking over his shoulder.

Nir pulled out the satellite phone that had once been carried by Doron and dialed CARL.

Nicole answered. "Lead, this is CARL. Is all okay?"

Because of the large number of people nearby, Nir answered in Arabic, and he would keep his side of the conversation vague. "We've arrived in Al-Kiswah. Very similar damage to Damascus." He could hear Efraim giving a real-time translation in the background.

"How's everyone holding up?"

"The old man keeps whining about his leg." He glanced at Yaron, who gestured his disapproval of Nir's statement. "Otherwise, we're good. The other two are off looking for water. Maybe a little food, but I doubt it. Any thoughts about where we're going?"

Earlier, the *ramsad* had worked out a deal with the UK. Nir and his men were to head northeast of the city toward Aleppo. After two or three days, depending on when the Brits could get their aid to the country, the Kidon men would rendezvous with an English relief vehicle. That vehicle would take them back to the staging area, and when the next British plane rotated out, Nir and his men would be on it, heading to jolly old England.

By Nir's math, that meant they might not get home for another week or more. That sounded far from ideal. At the time they had heard about the plan, they were already ten kilometers south of Damascus and in some fresh air. The guys had voted, and the *ramsad* lost. There was no way they were going to backtrack through the city. Efraim reminded him of the level of the *ramsad*'s anger if he were to be disobeyed, but Nir figured he'd get over it. If he wanted to always be obeyed, then he shouldn't have intentionally put together a team of operators and analysts who had a track record of insubordination.

Yossi spoke into the phone. "Nine kilometers southwest of you is Zakiyah. It's known to be a hotbed for the Lebanese pro-Iranian

Hezbollah militia. The IAF fired some missiles there a couple years ago, and temporarily, the militia scattered like roaches, but now they're back."

"Sounds like our kind of people. Any chance of getting eyes on it?"

"In process. I've got a drone on its way there now. Should get there about an hour ahead of you guys."

"Excellent. *Shukran, habibi*. I'll call when I'm close."

Nir ended the call, then sat down next to Yaron with a groan.

"You sound as old as me," his friend said.

Nir tilted his head back against the wall and closed his eyes. "You going to be able to walk another nine kilometers?"

"I'll walk as far as you need me to go. Despite your subtle hints, you're not leaving me behind."

"Wouldn't dream of it. Can't afford to lose another man." The two were silent after that, both wrapped up in thoughts of Doron. A few minutes later, Yaron elbowed Nir. When he opened his eyes, the veteran pointed forward. Against the light of a trash can fire, a tall silhouette and a very tall silhouette moved rapidly toward them.

Imri said, "Up you go, guys. We've got to get moving." As Nir got to his feet, the young operative handed him a plastic Coke bottle. It was open and filled with clear-ish liquid. Nir turned on his flashlight underneath the bottle. The water inside was a very light brown, and the swirling sediment was gradually finding its way to the bottom.

Nir flicked his flashlight back off. "I wish I hadn't done that."

Dima had Yaron on his feet. "Really, we must go now. There was a big line, and we didn't have time to wait."

Out of the darkness, two older women appeared. They were moving as rapidly as their age allowed and were making it clear what they thought about the two agents' manners and ancestry.

"Yaron, if there were any time that we could leave you behind to take one for the team, this is it," said Imri.

"Not a chance," he replied as he hobbled away. The other three hustled to catch up to him.

CHAPTER 57

His face bloodied, Nir limped toward the gate. His shoulder was under Yaron and his arm around his waist as he dragged the stumbling man forward. Yaron's head tilted to one side. Nir tripped and lurched forward, but managed to keep on his feet. He wrapped his other arm around the front of the older man to keep him from dropping to the ground.

"Get out of here!" a guard yelled. A second man walked up next to him.

"Please, help," Nir called out. "We fled Damascus. There were bandits outside of Al-Kiswah."

"We have nothing for you here. You must leave now, or I will shoot you."

Nir kept shuffling forward. The guards had their flashlights on them now. "Please, I beg you. My father, badly hurt. He's old and feeble. Please help!"

"Quiet! You'll wake the camp. You must leave now."

"Please," Nir cried out. He dropped to his knees two meters from the guards, laying Yaron on the ground. Putting his hands together in supplication, he begged, "We already lost our family in the earthquake.

We're trying to reach relations in Al-Qleiaah. Please, sir. Please, you must help."

Yaron started groaning loudly.

"Please, my father is dying! Help us! Will someone in there help us?" Nir called toward the camp beyond the gate.

"This is ridiculous," said the second guard. Stepping forward, he drove the stock of his rifle into Nir's shoulder. "Get out of here now or I will kill you and the old man."

Nir folded over from the pain. "Please. Please help my father."

"That's it, I'm done with…"

The guard stopped abruptly. Nir peeked up. With one hand, Imri was taking away the rifle from the guard who had struck him. His other was holding a pistol to the back of the man's head. Behind them, Dima was doing the same with the first guard.

Next to Nir, Yaron sat up. "I'll show you old and feeble," he said, pushing Nir so that he toppled from his kneeling position.

"I just call them as I see them," Nir said, standing up.

The guard who had struck him now had his hands clasped in front of him, begging, "Please don't kill me. I have a family. I am sorry I hit you."

Nir tapped him lightly on the face with an open hand. "The old 'attacked by bandits' ploy. I can't believe you terrorist folk still fall for it. Listen, *habibi*, we've seen way too much death lately. If you do what we ask, you'll survive this. If you don't? I guess we'll see a little more." As he spoke, he prayed that his accented Arabic wouldn't give him away. His hope was that these Lebanese terrorists would simply conclude he had some obscure Syrian way of speaking.

Imri pulled a rolled-up rag across the guard's mouth and tied it tight. Dima did the same with the other guard, then brought him over.

"Ground rules," said Nir. "You make noise. I kill you. Try to run. I kill you. Disobey an order. I kill you. Look at me the wrong way. I kill you."

Nir knew that he was being overly dramatic in his bravado, but he was so tired that he defaulted to tough-guy mode. He took a couple breaths and calmed himself down. Because of the state their bodies were in, it was their minds that would give them this needed victory. Given the choice, he never would have run an operation in their seriously fatigued state. But they didn't have a choice. According to their last report from CARL, Bashar al-Assad had fled the country, and coalitions were now forming around various generals who were putting themselves forward as the new face of Syrian leadership. Instead of the anarchy that Efraim had predicted, Syria was slipping toward a multisided civil war.

During a call soon after they had left Al-Kiswah, Efraim had told Nir to get his team out of the country as soon as possible by whatever means necessary. The situation was deteriorating quickly and their window for escape would soon be closing. Relief planes that were ready to be sent from countries all over the world remained on their home runways as their governments debated whether it was safe enough to send them. Nir had to get his men on the other side of the border, and he had to do it fast.

That's why they were at this camp sneaking up on these clowns. Undoubtedly, they weren't Hezbollah's A team. If they were, they wouldn't have been sent from Lebanon to populate a training camp in South Goat Turd, Syria. But they had guns and probably at least a bit of training, which made them dangerous.

Nir eyed the guard who had hit him. He couldn't have been more than 21 years old.

With this type, mixing a little friendliness with intimidation can go a long way.

"Is anybody else in the camp awake right now?" Nir asked. "Any cooks or mechanics or anything?"

The man shook his head.

"Good. I need you to take us to your commander. And don't worry, we aren't planning on killing him. Unless we have to. And whether we have to will be up to you. Understood?"

The guard nodded.

Nir pulled the man's gag forward. "Tell me your name."

"Baqil."

Nir replaced the gag. "Okay, Baqil, don't let me down."

They walked into the camp. Nir was already familiar with its layout from the drone that was hovering high overhead. He also knew which building appeared to be the primary barracks, and which was likely the quarters of the commander. If Baqil led them the wrong direction, Nir would know, and it wouldn't go well for the young Lebanese.

They angled to the left, the direction of the commander.

"You're doing well. Almost there."

They arrived outside the door. "Does he stay alone?"

Baqil nodded.

Nir looked to Imri. "Come."

The door opened to an office, across which stood another door. The two men crossed the floor and cautiously stepped into the next room. Using the red function on his flashlight, Nir saw a dresser, a few chairs, an end table, and an occupied bed.

CHAPTER 58

02:58 (2:58 AM) EEST

Nir looked down at the sleeping man. His salt-and-pepper beard and the beginnings of crow's feet around his eyes pegged him at mid-fifties.

Nir counted down from three on his fingers. Imri clamped his hand over the commander's mouth with enough force to push his head down into the pillow. The man opened his eyes to see the black hole of Nir's gun muzzle pointed between his eyes.

"Hey, *almughafil*! Idiot! Wake up," Nir said.

The man was thrashing and grabbing at Imri's arm. Nir clocked him in the forehead with the butt of his pistol just hard enough to get the man's attention. Still, he twisted and clawed. Nir fired his suppressed pistol into the wall right behind the man's head, hoping that the pop wouldn't wake anyone in the barracks across the camp. The man stopped moving.

Nir switched his flashlight from red light to white light and shone it on the commander's face.

"If you listen to me, commander, you and your men will survive the night. If you do not, I will kill everyone here, starting with you. Do you understand me?"

The man nodded.

"Let him go," Nir said to Imri.

"Who are you?" the man demanded as soon as his mouth was freed.

"As for who we are, that is not your concern. How many we are—that's what you need to be worried about. There is me and my friend here. There are two more that I've brought into your lovely compound. Then I've got ten more just outside the fence with nightscopes pointed into your camp. If anything happens to me, those men will snipe your entire squad. Then, they'll come in and kill you slowly. Might be a little extreme, but my men love and respect me. So they're a bit protective. Do your men love and respect you, commander?"

"Yes."

"Good. Let's hope so. Because we're going to put that to the test." Grabbing hold of his shirt, Nir lifted the man up out of his bed. "Get up. Put on some pants and a uniform shirt. Can't have you leading your men in just your boxers. Oh, and if you try anything, my friend here is going to shoot you in the spine."

Once the commander was dressed, Nir and Imri walked him out to an open area in the middle of the camp.

"Baqil, come here," Nir called.

Yaron let the man out of his grasp. He trotted up.

"Commander, tell your man here to go to the barracks and bring everyone out. Have him tell them that they will be searched. If I find so much as a knife on any of them, I'll shoot him. Then, I'll shoot you in your...some place. I'm not sure where yet. It's been a long day and I'm having a hard time coming up with creative locations that sound especially painful."

As the commander repeated the order, Nir caught Imri grinning at him. Nir shrugged. He just wanted this part to be over with so they could get on the road. Baqil saluted the commander, then began walking toward the barracks.

"*Yalla!*" Nir called after him, and the man broke into a run.

As they waited, the commander inquired, "You are Jews?"

Nir shook his head in frustration. "Seriously? Was it the accent?"

"That, and no one else would dare harass a Hezbollah camp. Were you in Damascus?"

Nir didn't answer.

"Is it as bad as they say?" the commander asked.

"Worse than you can ever imagine."

The commander shook his head. "My family is in Beirut. The quake knocked pictures off the walls. Broke dishes. That's over a hundred kilometers away. The shaking was enough to terrify me down here. It had to be a nightmare up in the city."

"I couldn't even describe it to you. Going through something like that, it changes you."

They were both silent for a minute.

"Those changes, is that why you haven't just killed us?"

The conversation was getting too personal for Nir's tastes. The man seemed so decent, like the kind of guy he'd want to have a beer with and swap stories. Nir had to remind himself that he was a terrorist whose primary goal in life was to destroy Israel. Hatred came much easier at a distance and without a face.

"Here's how it's going to work, commander. When your men come out, I am going to leave you in the care of my colleagues. Baqil is going to lead me and one of my men into your garage. I am going to take a technical and a troop transport from your motor pool. Then we are going to leave you alone. I have considered tying you up. I have considered destroying all your communications equipment. I have considered just shooting you all. But doing that would be time-consuming and unnecessary. Instead, what I will ask is that you give me your word of honor that you will not follow us, nor will you send out any communications about us for the next hour. That is time enough for me to get to where I need to go."

"To the border," said the commander.

Nir didn't acknowledge his statement. Instead, he said, "If you make that commitment to me, once we pass through those gates, you can head back to bed and have a pleasant night's sleep. If you break your word to me, then I swear by all things holy that a squadron of Israeli jets will rain terror down on your little camp here before the sun comes up in the morning. Do you give me your word?"

"You have my word."

The commander held out his hand. Nir looked at it, then turned away.

The barracks doors opened, and a line of men came out with their hands on their heads.

"Nice touch," said Nir. "Baqil is an overachiever."

Once the men were seated on the ground, Nir had the commander explain the situation to them. Then he directed him to join his men.

Leaving Dima and Imri to guard the dozen or so Hezbollah terrorists, Nir had Baqil lead him and Yaron to a large building. Inside were two pickups, four technicals, one of which had a heavy machine gun mounted in its bed, and one large transport truck. At Nir's instruction, the Lebanese man pulled keys for the transport and the technical with the gun from a box on the wall. Nir took the technical's key for himself.

The truck key Nir gave to Yaron. "Take the big truck and Baqil, and go wait for me by the others."

Yaron nodded. Soon, he and Baqil were rumbling through the large doors.

When they had first walked in, Nir noticed that the building also functioned as the camp's arsenal. He had seen a few items that he thought might come in handy, so he did a little shopping and loaded them into the modified pickup's bed. Then he went to the wall box and took the remaining vehicle keys.

The commander is charming, but he also happens to be a terrorist. Better safe than sorry.

CHAPTER 59

03:10 (3:10 AM) EEST

Nir slid into the front seat of the Toyota and started it up. By the time he rolled up next to the transport, Baqil was seated with the Hezbollah members and Dima was in the cab of the big truck. Imri climbed up into the bed of the technical, keeping the AK-47 that he had taken from the first guard pointed at the group.

"Don't let me down," Nir said to the commander. He honked the horn, and the transport started moving.

Once they were half a kilometer outside the fence, they stopped to prolong the ruse that there were more than just the four of them. Who knows whether the Lebanese bought it, but once you created a story, it was best to carry it on to the end. After keeping the brake lights lit long enough for their imaginary squad mates to load up, they began rolling down the road again.

Two more kilometers passed, and they pulled over a second time. Yaron and Dima dropped out of the cab of the transport and walked back to the Toyota. While Dima jumped in the back with Imri, Nir slid over, allowing Yaron to get behind the wheel.

"You sure you're good to drive?" Nir asked, enjoying the opportunity to speak in Hebrew again.

"On my worst day I'm a better driver than your best day."

Nir laughed. "After seeing what you did with that truck in Damascus, I won't argue with you." Thoughts of Damascus eventually quieted them both, and their conversation for the rest of the trip was minimal. Meanwhile, in the back of the truck, Imri and Dima were having a great time trying to see who could throw vehicle keys the farthest.

Although the drive was just an hour, it felt like forever. When the lights of the border crossing near Quneitra finally came into view, Nir's adrenaline kicked in. Finally, they were just about home.

Dousing the lights, they pulled over. Dima and Imri jumped out of the back and stood by the side windows to listen. Nir laid out his plan, and they all agreed that it had a better than 50-percent chance of working. Considering his average lately, those were pretty good odds. Imri and Dima mounted back up and they slowly drove forward.

When they had just entered the glow of the border station's lights, still about 30 meters from the main building, they stopped the truck. Yaron and Nir stepped out. Yaron walked to the back, while Nir moved to the front. He could see the guards watching him closely. He counted ten of them, but there could be more.

One of the items he had permanently borrowed from the Hezbollah camp was a megaphone, probably used during training drills. Nir brought it up to his mouth. "Gentlemen, I am asking your permission to drive through this border crossing into Israel. Your president has fled the country and your military will soon be at war with itself. Meanwhile, you all likely have family in Damascus and the surrounding areas who need you. My recommendation is that you all lay down your rifles and return home. Otherwise, you may find yourselves on the wrong side of some faction's weapons or the wrong side of mine."

As he said this, Yaron and Imri stepped out to either side of the technical holding rocket-propelled grenades. They kneeled and aimed the RPGs at the guard stations. Meanwhile, Dima stood tall in the back of the pickup. He pulled back the charging handle of the mounted DShK heavy machine gun.

On the other side of the DMZ that separated the two border fences, a Shayetet 13 special forces commando unit was ready to deploy if things went sideways. But Nir had asked Efraim to make sure they stayed quiet unless they were needed. Rumblings from the Israeli side of the border would only escalate the situation.

"So, what's it going to be? Let one vehicle through, or risk dying here at the border when your families need you most?"

A man wearing an officer's uniform stepped forward. He stared at Nir for a full thirty seconds before turning and calling to his men, "Weapons down."

The Syrians all quickly complied.

Nir raised the megaphone back to his mouth. "Please step forward, then move to your right at least twenty meters from your weapons. Two of you, remove the barrier from the gateway."

Once that was done, the Kidon team returned to the truck. Dima remained behind the machine gun with it trained on the gathered guards. Slowly, the modified Toyota pickup rolled out of Syria and into the DMZ. Dima kept the group in his sights until the truck was fully inside Israeli territory.

The young Israeli border guards watched the technical roll by. They didn't know who was inside, but they knew what they were. Stories always circulate, and undoubtedly the legends of what had happened with the Kidon teams caught in the Damascus earthquake had already begun to be told.

Yaron angled the truck into a roadside pull-out. Efraim stood in front of a van waiting for them. He was smiling, but the smile was somber. Seeing his friend's face brought the weight of the last few days down on Nir's shoulders. The loss of *Alif* and *Ba*. The earthquakes. The successful rescue of Derifa and the failure of the other attempts. And losing Doron. How could he face everyone back at headquarters when he had left Doron behind?

Yaron stopped the truck.

"You ready, *achi*?" he asked.

"No," Nir answered as he reached for the door handle.

As soon as Nir stepped out, Efraim wrapped him in a hug. When he finally stepped back, he said, "Nicole wanted to come, but the *ramsad* refused to allow anyone else here. He said it was for safety. I think it was because he didn't know what shape you all would be in." He looked Nir up and down. "I think he made the right call."

"It was a nightmare, *habibi*. Unimaginable."

"I can't...I just..." Efraim's voice faded, and the two stood looking down at the ground.

Then Efraim said, "Come here. I have something to show you." He led Nir around to the other side of the van. There, polished and shining in the lights of the border crossing, was Nir's Mercedes.

"I make a promise. I deliver."

Nir smiled. "That you do, my brother."

Efraim held out a key fob to Nir, but Nir put up his hand. "Thanks, I appreciate it. I really do. But I've already got a ride."

Nir walked around the van and got into the back. Dima, Imri, and Yaron were already inside waiting for him. Dima leaned out and pulled the door shut, and the van rolled off to Tel Aviv.

CHAPTER 60

The video looked like a scene from a high-budget Hollywood disaster film. As the drone traveled across what once was the Damascus skyline, Nir strained to see any signs of life. But other than pockets of rescue workers here and there, the city was empty.

Efraim had called this morning. During their conversation, Nir had asked about the source of the quakes. Efraim said the culprit was the Serghaya fault, which runs to the west of Damascus. From the time Nir was in school, he had learned about the Dead Sea fault system, but he had never heard of this eastern branch. Seismologists had downplayed concern about the power of the Serghaya, but now it had risen up and proved them wrong.

Nicole's chin rested on her hands, and her hands rested on Nir's shoulder as she watched the scenes displayed on his iPad. In front of the bench on which they sat, the waters of the Mediterranean gently washed the sands of Sironit Beach in Netanya. Nir had begged off Asher Porush's request for a meeting by claiming that after being gone so long from Yael Diamonds he had some urgent business to attend to at the Netanya Diamond Center. That business had taken him less than 45 minutes to complete. Now he had the rest of the day to spend with Nicole, who had jumped at the opportunity to join him for a little "business" trip.

"Go back to the video list," she said. When Nir did, she pointed to a thumbnail and said, "That one."

Nir pressed it, and more drone images filled the screen.

"Recognize it?" Nicole asked. Again, she pointed. "That's the M5 interchange." She wrapped her arms around Nir's arm and now rested her chin directly on his shoulder.

"Wait, is this Nahr Eshe?" Nir couldn't believe what he saw. It was as different from the pre-op satellite photos as the Arabian Desert was from the Amazon rainforests. Where once there was bustling life, now everything was still. A white dust covered every surface, making the whole scene ghostly.

Nicole's light-blue painted fingernail tapped the screen. "Right there. That's the mosque."

The main building was flattened, of course. Nir had been there when that happened. But there were still seven or eight meters of the minaret standing.

Somewhere under there are Doron and Ba. *I let them down, and now they're buried forever in a mosque, of all places. What kind of twisted irony is that?*

Nir set down the iPad on the bench. He had seen bits and pieces of the earthquakes' aftermath, but for the most part, his last day and a half had been spent asleep in his apartment. This was the first that he had looked at Damascus in depth. There had been a blissful ignorance, almost an innocence, when his perspective was limited by the moonlight. But now that the sun was out, the truth shone in all its ignominy. It felt unreal that he had been there.

"Sorry, it's just too much to look at right now," he said.

"I don't doubt it. They're estimating more than 150,000 dead and nearly that same number missing. It's unbelievable. But, in a way, it's also not. Not long ago, I heard a preacher online saying that this very thing would happen to Damascus."

Nir looked skeptical. "He said the city would be leveled by an earthquake? That's pretty amazing."

Nicole brought up her legs and crossed them on the bench so that she was facing Nir. "He didn't mention an earthquake. He just said that Damascus would be destroyed. It's from Isaiah 17:1. I looked it up after the first quake." She looked upward as she tried to quote the verse. "It goes something like, 'A message came about Damascus: "Look, the city of Damascus will disappear! It will become a heap of ruins."' Pretty eerie, isn't it?"

"That's crazy. Did the preacher say why it would happen?"

"He just talked about it being one of the things that has to happen before the rapture of the church and the tribulation."

Nir put up his hands. "Slow down. I didn't realize this was going to get us into the whole 'I'll fly away' thing, then the seven years of really bad luck. I wouldn't have asked."

Nicole rolled her eyes. "I know you think it's weird. But it makes sense to me. Especially when you combine it with the whole thing with Russia too. They're furious that the PM called them out on their plot. But at least it forced them to stand down for a while. But they'll be back. And the whole alliance thing with Iran and Turkey. This guy I watched read right where that all came from in Ezekiel. So, don't go saying that's just my Christian New Testament church stuff. Remember, Ezekiel is Old Testament. That's your Bible, not mine."

Nir raised an eyebrow at her.

Nicole slapped his arm. "You know what I mean, mister."

"I do," Nir said, nodding as he watched the water rolling onto the sand. Turning to her again, he asked, "And you really believe all that?"

"Again, it makes sense to me when I read the Bible."

"But—and don't take this wrong—there are a hundred, a thousand different ways to interpret the Bible. I don't get why you say there has to be only one right way to read it."

"Because that's who God is. I think of it like this: God took one shot at communicating everything He wanted humanity to know. That one shot was the Bible. Does it make sense to you that He would spend all that time having it written by all those different writers only to make it totally ambiguous? Do you think He'd be like, 'Eh, as long as they get something out of this, that's good by Me'?"

Nir laughed. "Probably not."

"Definitely not. God is all about truth. With Him, there is no 'my truth' or 'your truth.' There's just truth. Something either is or it isn't. Once, when Jesus was praying to the Father, He said, 'Sanctify them by Your truth. Your word is truth.' So, if the Bible is truth, then there is only one correct way to look at it."

"And you've got the right one?"

"I do. I know it because it all comes together perfectly up here," she said pointing to her head. Then she lowered her hand to her chest. "And in here."

"I get it. I know you wouldn't join up with something if you hadn't studied it. It's just…I don't know, Nicole." He was feeling that awkward blend of conviction and confusion that he often got when she was talking about her beliefs. The best remedy was typically a subject change. "Hey, you'll be happy to know that God and I did a lot of talking while I was in Damascus."

Nicole raised her eyebrows, waiting for more.

"I've got to admit, though. I'm not sure we're on speaking terms right now. I'm not overly thrilled with the way He handled things in Syria. We had problem after problem through the whole operation. Then we lost Doron." Nir paused before continuing, "I mean, what good is it having a God if He's not even going to save a life that most definitely deserved saving?"

"You mean like Derifa's?"

The name jolted Nir. He hadn't thought much about her other than to have her put in a cameo appearance at some point in his dreams yesterday.

"What do you mean?" he asked. He felt a little defensive, but he wasn't sure why.

"Was Derifa's life worth saving?"

"Of course, it was. But what does that have to do with what we're talking about? Are you saying we should all be worshipping Allah since she was saved and Doron wasn't?"

"Stop. Breathe. Think about what you're saying, and let's try again," Nicole said. Although her words were a correction, her smile was sweet and her eyes were filled with compassion.

"Last night, I visited Eva and the kids," he said. "She's trying to show her strength, but losing Doron…I don't know how she's going to get through it."

Nicole took Nir's hand. "I already know you were there. Eva called me after you left. Said she's worried about you."

Nir opened his mouth, but he had no words, so he just leaned forward with his elbows on his knees. They sat in silence for a few minutes while Nicole watched the gulls and Nir watched the ants.

Finally, he said, "It was supposed to be me, Nicole. That was the deal I made with God. If anyone was going to not come home, it was supposed to be me. But here I am sitting on the beach while Doron is in Syria buried under fifty tons of rubble. It was a simple deal, and I don't know how God could have gotten it so wrong."

Nicole put her arm on Nir's back and slowly brushed her hand back and forth. "I understand, Nir. You loved Doron like a brother, just like you do everyone on your team. But just because God did it differently from what you wanted, does that mean He got it wrong? I mean, who's more likely to be right, you or Him?"

"Okay, maybe *wrong* is the wrong word. I just don't understand how it was loving."

"Again, maybe you're just working off different definitions. In your mind, *loving* means everyone coming home. Maybe in God's mind, *loving* meant someone sacrificing themselves so little Derifa could live."

Nir sat up straight. "That someone was supposed to be me."

"Maybe in your mind. But in God's plan, He gave that blessed honor to someone else. Doron willingly joined in the rescue of Derifa knowing it could cost him his life. Don't take that away from him. All of you were ready to sacrifice your lives for her. Why? Because it was the right thing to do, the loving thing to do. So, you didn't hesitate. Now think of that in terms of God. You tell me all the time how it doesn't make sense that Jesus would die for you. Think of yourself in that moment of decision to save Derifa. Now do you understand why Jesus died for you?"

Nir's thoughts wrestled inside his head. *What she says makes so much sense. So why am I trying so hard to muddy up the waters in my mind? It's like I want to hold on to my confusion.* Then he realized the flaw in her thinking.

"Where your logic breaks down is that God doesn't need us. He would be perfectly fine without us being around, right? Why would He give His Son's life for a bunch of people when all they're going to do is rebel against Him and make His life miserable? It's a bad deal for Him and it makes no sense."

Nicole's mouth spread again in that sweet smile. "Did you need Derifa in your world? She's a Syrian girl, the child of your enemies. If that little girl had died in that rubble, it would not have affected you in the least. Yet you were ready to die so that she had a chance at life. If that's the kind of love and decency that's in your heart, Nir, then what do you think *is* in the heart of the God who is the author of love? There's a verse in Romans 5 that says that the way God demonstrated His amazing love for us was that when we were still sinners, Christ died for us. Think about that. While we were His enemies, He gave His life."

He had never thought of it that way before. For so long, he hadn't been able to get over his need for a transactional salvation. You give to me; I give to You. That's how the world worked. But that little Syrian girl had nothing to offer him. She couldn't earn her rescue. There was no bargain to be made. It was just Nir and his team—men who would be killed in a heartbeat by the crowd if their true identities were discovered.

It was just us sacrificing out of love, expecting nothing in return. Nicole's point is that this was the same way Jesus sacrificed Himself out of love, knowing that there was nothing I had to offer that was worth the price He paid.

"That makes sense, Nicole. For the first time, I get it."

Nicole took his hands in hers. "So, does that mean you're ready, Nir? Salvation is just a commitment away. It's just a prayer saying that you're ready to accept Jesus as your Savior and your Lord."

"Right here on the beach? No fancy ceremony in a church somewhere? Don't I need some water to get dunked in?"

"Nope. Just you, me, God, and the seagulls."

Nir nodded. "Tell you what—you know that I won't even buy a

toaster without sleeping on it first. I'm still exhausted from the op. Tomorrow morning, let's try Benedict again. Maybe we can both get a real breakfast this time. If this is still making sense then, we can talk next steps. Deal?"

He lifted her hand to his lips and kissed her knuckles.

Nicole sighed. "Deal."

She turned so that she was facing the Mediterranean again. Nir put his arm around her, and she laid her head on his shoulder. They sat like that for another hour, enjoying the sounds of the waves and watching the birds as they rode the wind currents that blew in from distant shores. Nir nodded off a couple times, and Nicole suggested they head home. They held hands as they walked to his little hatchback. Then they made their way back to Tel Aviv.

AUTHORS' NOTE

Out of the Far North is a bit of a departure from our previous two novels. In *Operation Joktan* and *By Way of Deception*, we included real Mossad operations in our overall fictional narrative. From targeted killings to the stealing of nuclear information, we were able to place our characters in actual situations to reveal to our readers some of how the elite Israeli intelligence service works. The reason we could do so was because our focus in the first book was Iran's proxy militias, and in the second it was Iran itself. With those targets, there was a plethora of operational lore to choose from.

But now we've moved on to Russia. In doing so, we are essentially refocusing from the past to the future, and, with that, shifting from historical operations to speculative actions. Tensions are already high between Jerusalem and Moscow. As this book clearly shows, the time will soon come when Russia, for political, economic, and religious reasons, will attack Israel. When it does, it will be in direct fulfillment of biblical prophecy.

This book was written to bring to light the increasing force pressing on the dam that is holding back Russia from Israel. Already, through the broken nation of Syria, they are just a border crossing away from invasion. Also in Syria is Iran and its many proxy militias with tens of thousands of rockets pointed to the south. Never before have we been closer to the devastating war predicted in Ezekiel 38.

Without giving too much away, we also want to explain the reason for the latter portion of the novel. Through the prophet Isaiah, God has said to us, "The burden against Damascus. 'Behold, Damascus will cease from being a city, and it will be a ruinous heap'" (Isaiah 17:1). This level of destruction has never taken place in the history of the city. Therefore, it is a prophecy that is yet to happen. Speculation has always been that warfare of some type will cause this event to happen. We have offered an alternative option.

As always, our ultimate purpose in these books, beyond the entertainment and teaching, is to clearly present the journey of a secular Jew as he is confronted with the reality of Jesus Christ. Our prayer is that if, like Nir, you do not have a personal relationship with Jesus, you will find in these pages both the reasons and the motivation to begin one.

Awaiting His return,
Amir Tsarfati
Steve Yohn

OPERATION JOKTAN

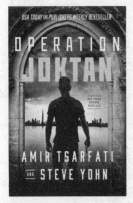

Nir Tavor is an Israeli secret service operative turned talented Mossad agent. Nicole le Roux is a model with a hidden skill. A terrorist attack brings them together, and then work forces them apart—until they're unexpectedly called back into each other's lives.

But there's no time for romance. As violent radicals threaten chaos across the Middle East, the two must work together to stop these extremists. Each heart-racing step of their operation gets them closer to the truth—and closer to danger.

For believers in God's life-changing promises, *Operation Joktan* is a suspense-filled page-turner that illuminates the blessing Israel is to the world.

BY WAY OF DECEPTION

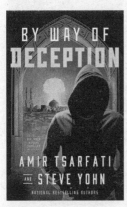

The Mossad has uncovered Iran's plans to smuggle untraceable weapons of mass destruction into Israel. The clock is ticking, and agents Nir Tavor and Nicole le Roux can't act quickly enough.

Nir and Nicole find themselves caught in a whirlwind plot of assassinations, espionage, and undercover recon, fighting against the clock to stop this threat against the Middle East. As they draw closer to danger—and closer to each other—they find themselves ensnared in a lethal web of secrets. Will they have to sacrifice their own lives to protect the lives of millions?

This Nir Tavor thriller reveals breathtaking true insights into the lives and duties of Mossad agents—and delivers a story that will have you on the edge of your seat.